HURRY

John Wain was born in 1925 … attended St John's College, Oxford, earning a BA in 1946 and an MA in 1950. A prolific author and man of letters, Wain wrote poetry, novels, criticism, and biographies during a writing career that spanned more than forty years.

Wain started out teaching at the University of Reading, but in 1953 left to pursue writing full time. His first novel, *Hurry on Down* (1953; published in the United States as *Born in Captivity*), was a bestseller and launched Wain's career as a novelist. The book ran into several hardcover printings and was often reprinted as a Penguin paperback; it became a defining book of what the media called the 'Angry Young Men' movement and paved the way for later British classics of the 1950s, including Kingsley Amis's *Lucky Jim* (1954) and John Braine's *Room at the Top* (1957). Wain would go on to publish over a dozen more novels and story collections, but though many of them were well received by critics, none of them matched the popular success of *Hurry on Down*.

In 1973, Wain was appointed the first Professor of Poetry at Oxford University, and the following year his biography of Samuel Johnson won the James Tait Black Memorial Prize. In 1982 he won the prestigious Whitbread Award for his novel *Young Shoulders*, and his services to literature were recognized in 1984 when he was awarded a CBE. In the late 1980s, he began his 'Oxford Trilogy' with *Where the Rivers Meet* (1988), and the final volume, *Hungry Generations*, was published shortly after his death in 1994. Though his obituary in the *Times* suggested his most enduring contribution might lie in his literary criticism and biographical studies, Wain's novels deserve rediscovery; several of the best, including *Strike the Father Dead* (1962), *The Smaller Sky* (1967), and *A Winter in the Hills* (1970) have been republished by Valancourt Books.

John Andrew Fredrick has published four comic novels and a book on the early films of Wes Anderson. He is the principal singer and songwriter for the black watch, an indie rock band that has released eighteen LPs to considerable underground acclaim. He was born in Richmond, Virginia and lives in Los Angeles and spends as much time as he possibly can in N.W. London.

Living in the Present (1955)
A Word Carved on a Sill (1956)
Preliminary Essays (1957)
The Contenders (1958)
A Travelling Woman (1959)
Nuncle, and Other Stories (1960)
Weep Before God: Poems (1961)
Strike the Father Dead (1962)*
Sprightly Running: Part of an Autobiography (1962)
The Young Visitors (1965)
Death of the Hind Legs, and Other Stories (1966)
The Smaller Sky (1967)*
A Winter in the Hills (1970)*
The Life Guard: Stories (1971)
Johnson as Critic (1972)
Samuel Johnson (1974)
Professing Poetry (1977)
The Pardoner's Tale (1978)
Lizzie's Floating Shop (1981)
Young Shoulders (1982)
Dear Shadows: Portraits from Memory (1986)
Where the Rivers Meet (1988)
Comedies (1990)
Hungry Generations (1994)

JOHN WAIN

HURRY ON DOWN

A Novel

With a new introduction by
JOHN ANDREW FREDRICK

VALANCOURT BOOKS

Hurry on Down by John Wain
(Original U.S. title: *Born in Captivity*)
First published London: Secker & Warburg, 1953
First Valancourt Books edition 2013
Reprinted with a new introduction 2020

Published by Valancourt Books, Richmond, Virginia
http://www.valancourtbooks.com

ISBN 978-1-948405-71-3 (*trade paperback*)
Also available as an ebook and an audiobook.

Set in Dante MT

INTRODUCTION

I LOVE THE FACT THAT, in this his first and arguably funniest novel, John Wain employs as one of his epigraphs a line from good old doughty old Wordsworth that goes: 'A Moralist perchance appears'; for I have always thought that comedy—and by extension all good satire—is *the* most moral genre. Here the pretentious get their comeuppance. The censorious and sanctimonious their just deserts, served well-chilled. The ridiculous the ridicule they warrant, the neurotic the antidote to psychological malaise (if they can bear to recognize themselves). And the arrogant, snobbish, and prideful the humiliations that, perchance, bestow humility.

Hurry on Down is tremendously-uproariously hysterically funny—and it at once 'instructs and delights', as every great critic from Aristotle to Shelley to Matthew Arnold has insisted that high art must do. Allow me to spoil just a bit of Wain's prodigious humor for you (for every explanation of *why* something is hilarious, as we all know, ostensibly cripples if not throttles the joke). But first let me show you, by way of a little autobiographical story, *how* John Wain's singular style occasions such great good chuckleworthiness.

Not so very long ago, a dear old friend called in a favor. Might I meet and entertain two acquaintances of hers, two people who (in the parlance of Wain's time) were 'going round together' and who'd just moved to Los Angeles and who knew absolutely nobody in my fair city. 'They've just finished an MFA program they did together and they're keen on meeting fellow writer types like you,' my friend said, adding, 'I think one of them's even read your book on Wes Anderson! She's a screenwriter; and I think he's writing a novel or something.' This sort of *ménage* not sounding much fun of any kind (for me), I decided I'd do best to invite them over for tea. Much easier, after tea and cakes and ices, to usher them precipitately out of my apartment (saying

I'd work to do and regrettably must throw them out, and how nice to meet them, ta for coming, good luck, etc.), than to visit them and risk being unmannerly by having to concoct some rum excuse to skedaddle. The world's not just divided, as Jung suggested, into Extraverts and Introverts; it's also split up into such categories as Hosts and Guests. And I greatly prefer being the former to the latter.

Arrangements made, they turned up, shook hands, and came through as I heartily said 'Come through, come through!'; and they were as pinched-looking and awkward and impossible as I suspected they might be. Which of course made me—who fancies himself the best of Hosts (in even the worst of circumstances)—do my level best to give them heaps of sympathy with their tea, and thus make the best of a bad sitch. I'm pretty sure all they really wanted were some hints on how to a) get published; and/or b) sell a screenplay—both of which I'd managed to do. During one of the (innumerable) inevitable lulls in the (dull) conversation, I clocked the gent staring at the top shelf of one of my bookcases where all of Kingsley and Martin Amis are—there is no other word for it—enshrined. I asked if he'd, uh, ever read, say, um, *Lucky Jim*? (Oh how we love to find that others like the stuff we like, no matter whether we like the others we're asking about their likes!)

'Oh no,' said he, 'I can't stand Kingsley Amis.'

Never having heard anybody, with or without a Master's degree, say such a thing, I asked, pray, what it was that he objected to in Amis' stuff?

'Oh, I've never read any of his stuff,' the fellow said. 'I hate all comic fiction.'

As I sat there reeling, or goggling, or choking on my gulp of Earl Grey, or whatever I was doing, his partner (in the parlance of our time) explained: 'He doesn't want to be manipulated, you see. That's what comedy-writing does to you. It manipulates.'

'That's what all twits and incorrigible manipulators *always* say, you jejune and tedious and insufferably *pretentious* dilettantes,' I said—or wanted to say, but didn't.

Hello, dear presumably much-less-supercilious and narrow-minded reader. What I've just pulled here, this little rhetorical trick, is of course very John Wain: the surprise truth of what one's really thinking that abracadabras one's deepest, most fractious and frangible urges, desires. The 'if only' phantasm-fantasy of getting (at last—after yonks of repression, hours on hours of appallingly painful *politesse*) to say what you want to and to mean it, and to mean it and have it sting or singe. Or at least jolt, prod, expose. What sort of a jabberwocky of a poseur wrote off categorically the undeniable delights of *all* comic fiction?

Consider the novel's novel and enchanting opening (and how it ushers us straight into Charles Lumley's at once internal and external worlds):

> 'Can't you tell me, Mr. Lumley, just what it is that you don't like about the rooms?'
>
> There was no mistaking the injured truculence in the landlady's voice, nor her expression of superhuman patience about to snap at last. Charles very nearly groaned aloud. Must he explain, point by point, why he hated living there? Her husband's cough in the morning, the way the dog barked every time he went in or out, the greasy mats in the hall? Obviously it was impossible. Why could she not have the grace to accept the polite lie he had told her? In any case he was bound to stick to it. He looked into her beady, accusing eyes and said as pleasantly as he could, 'Really, Mrs. Smythe, I don't know what's given you the idea that I don't like the rooms. I've always said how comfortable they were. But I told you the other day, I really need something a little nearer my work.'
>
> 'And where do you work? I've asked you that two or three times, Mr. Lumley, but you've never given me any answer.'
>
> 'What the hell has it got to do with you where I work?' he would have liked to say.

Note how the landlady (a perennial, stock enemy, as any renter will tell you) strikes an immediate note of offensive incredulity (that the narrator more finely defines as 'injured truculence'). And how the only recourse the prototypical British person has to countering such temerity is restraint (he 'very nearly' groans aloud) times that altogether *English* knack for masking rage and derision with seething niceness ('and said as pleasantly as he could'). Here

Wain turns the Anglo-characteristic ideal of 'making an effort' on its aching side; for his main character is striving fiercely in this passage not to snap in the wake of Mrs. Smythe's putative pettiness, pushiness, and lack of empathy. Note also how her didactic tone can seemingly only (if only in fantasy) be answered by like-sententiousness: that wonderful touch of 'point by point'—plus the way in which the author one-ups the landlady's use of the word 'dislike' to the non-euphemistic 'why he *hated* living there' [emphasis mine]. The insinuation here is that the bourgeois type is forever graceless; and the fact that she doesn't accept 'the polite lie' points up how society itself is ostensibly based on mendacity and crushing convention. Strong, bold (and very funny), stuff indeed. How, the also-inference is, the infamous 'stiff upper lip' begins to quiver-quaver in post-war Britain. How, now the war's over (but never really over), is one supposed to behave in society—especially as one's got to wonder what was it all for?

John Barrington Wain was the furthest thing from a dabbler or dilettante imaginable. He published poems, plays, novels, short stories, and biographies (his one on Dr. Johnson rivals that from the great W. Jackson Bate for psychological insight and writerly sympathy); he was a reviewer and a radio personality and friend of such other greats as Philip Larkin and Larkin's particular chum, the aforementioned Kingsley Amis. Early on, Wain was associated with two artistic groups, The Angry Young Men (novelists John Braine, John Osborne, Alan Sillitoe, and Keith Waterhouse) and The Movement (poets Donald Davie, D.J. Enright, Elizabeth Jenning, Thom Gunn, and Robert Conquest). Though I suspect that each of these writers might agree with Amis' statement in one of his letters that touched upon his relationship to Larkin: 'Though we agree a lot I don't think we're very alike.'

And the main thing I think the writers above would agree upon was that the starchy, as Wain puts it, 'tradition of [one's] class and type' must go. How to make one's way in a world where one 'did not fit into their world or speak their language'. How oppressing, this constant awareness of one's relation to others solely in terms of class and upbringing and achievement, not to mention class-indicative accents. In 1950s Britain, one opened one's mouth to speak—and instantly (for the conventional masses / classes, high, middle, and low) prejudices or at least preconceived notions flew right in.

Early on in *Hurry*, Charles is quite the not just Angry but Frustrated Young Man as he interacts with two smug, banal, conventional types with whom he's scraped acquaintance:

> It was no use, of course. Speech would never work with these people. Indeed, it was inconceivable that anything could be got across to them by means of language, unless one overpowered them and left them gagged and bound in the presence of a gramophone record endlessly repeating a short, concise statement. It would have given him pleasure to begin the composition, there and then, of such a statement; to have outlined in a few simple sentences the nature of the crime against humanity that they and their kind were committing by the mere fact of their existence.

People in the novel are, by turns, 'furry-faced gawks', 'old fools', 'twitching buffoons', 'identical marionettes', 'scarecrows', a 'particular type of slut', 'these down-and-outs', 'pumpkin faces', a 'knobbly slattern', 'the [literary] Society's bore' and all sorts of other amusing epithets. Yet the inclusion of the word 'composition' in the passage above hints at a very important concept here: Lumley's story, his (mis)adventures as he, a University graduate, rejects adopting a conventional lifestyle and takes a series of odd jobs (window-washer, driver for a drug mob, hospital orderly, chauffeur, nightclub bouncer and then on to the ultimate and quite nice job he's most suited to and for which he's most handsomely remunerated) isn't merely picaresque—it's a sort of training ground for the 'situation' (in the parlance of Wain's time) I'll let you find out about.

What fun, by the by, Wain has with the reversals in this novel. (For plot might be defined as 'a system of reversals'.) Having found an initial sort of contentment in what his friend the foolish novelist Froulish terms 'a too-narrow routine' (window-washing, a packet of fags, a watery pint with his Dickensian partner Ern), Charles has a spanner thrown into the works of his life in the form of that time-honored wrench / plot device: a pretty, mysterious, and dangerous girl, the romantically-monikered Veronica Roderick:

> A girl came in [to the hotel, significantly, rather than customary pub where Charles sits drinking alone]. She was small and dark, miraculously neat, with tiny fragile bones and an oval face. Her clothes were expensive and simple, with the kind of simplicity that carries within itself a hint of the extravagant. Huge dark eyes smiled up at the smooth man [who accompanies her]. Charles knew that he would never get that smile out of his mind again . . .

Of course his drink is now spoiled: 'It tasted like urine.' Of course he throws it 'savagely into the fireplace'. Of course he 'felt sick'. What are fetching girls (who are 'with' some other bloke) for, if not to make cynics sick and expose them for what they truly are: true romantics-at-heart. For every cynic hopes against hope that some dark lovely will float into his ken, then his life, and throw him for the loop he knows, deep down, he needs to navigate; preclude him from going, socially speaking, from pillar to post. 'For,' Wain tells us later on, 'like all the immature, he had looked down on romanticism for its immaturity.'

Brilliant.

Hurry on Down precedes by about a year the novel I asked the dilettante about, the novel that is much better (and undeservedly) known. There are many such oddities and injustices in the history of English literature, and I can only account for this particular one by quoting good old doughty old David Bowie who infamously said: 'It's not who does it first, it's who does it second.'

The novel you now hold in your hand did it first, more's *not* the pity—for, no matter the history, you're about to keep it alive redux by, I hope, I hope, reveling in its incomparable joys of language and sentiment and characterization and vim. You're in for a proper treat, you lucky thing.

JOHN ANDREW FREDRICK
June 2020

Hurry on down to my place, baby,
Nobody home but me.

Old Song

A Moralist perchance appears;
Led, Heaven knows how! to this poor sod.

WORDSWORTH, *A Poet's Epitaph*

NAN'S, ARNOLD'S

1925–1953

I

'Can't you tell me, Mr. Lumley, just what it is that you don't like about the rooms?'

There was no mistaking the injured truculence in the landlady's voice, nor her expression of superhuman patience about to snap at last. Charles very nearly groaned aloud. Must he explain, point by point, why he hated living there? Her husband's cough in the morning, the way the dog barked every time he went in or out, the greasy mats in the hall? Obviously it was impossible. Why could she not have the grace to accept the polite lie he had told her? In any case he was bound to stick to it. He looked into her beady, accusing eyes and said as pleasantly as he could, 'Really, Mrs. Smythe, I don't know what's given you the idea that I don't like the rooms. I've always said how comfortable they were. But I told you the other day, I really need something a little nearer my work.'

'And where do you work? I've asked you that two or three times, Mr. Lumley, but you've never given me any answer.'

'What the hell has it got to do with you where I work?' he would have liked to say. But after all he supposed it was, to some extent, a question she had the right to ask. He had puzzled her from the beginning, he knew that; neither in speech nor dress resembling the dapper young clerks and elementary-school teachers to whom she was accustomed to let rooms. And yet it had been out of the question to say, bluntly: 'I have just come down from the University with a mediocre degree in History, I have no job and no prospects, and I am living on fifty pounds I happen to have left in the bank, while I consider my next move.' No! he shuddered, as he had often shuddered, at the thought of the demoniac eagerness with which she would have seized on him and his problems; the advertisements of 'Situations Vacant' she would have found for him in the paper, the enquiries she would have 'felt obliged' to make into the state of his finances. 'I shall have to ask you to pay in advance, Mr. Lumley. Your money won't last for ever, you know.' He could hear her saying it, her reedy voice full of suspicion.

'I don't understand it. You seem to have some objection to telling me what you do for a living. It's not as if I was an inquisitive person, not at all.'

He had been a damned fool not to think up something in readiness for this situation. What could he be? A teacher? But what blasted schools were there in Stotwell? He ought to have made a note of one, somewhere about five miles away so as to support his original untruth. Well, what did he know about Stotwell? There was a greyhound racing track. Could he be employed there? Working the totalisator perhaps. He realized with a start that he had never even seen a totalisator. Besides, he had been at home in the evenings too often. Articled to a solicitor? But she would ask him what solicitor, and where his office was; and it would be useless to invent one, for her suspicions were violently aroused and she would check his story with passionate thoroughness. He must speak. He forced his tongue into action, trusting that it would say something of its own accord, without any help from him.

'Well, it's like this, Mrs. Smythe. You've heard of—of Jehovah's Witnesses?'

Her head swivelled round. She was trying to keep her startled eyes on his.

'You don't mean to say you're one of them?'

'Well, not exactly one of *them*. I mean, not *one* of them.'

'Mr. Lumley. *What do you do?*'

'I'm a private detective.'

The words jumped out of their own accord. This was it.

'Private detective? Jehovah's Witnesses? Just whatever do you mean? And you'd better tell me, young man, you'd better tell me. I've never had any lodger here but what I've known he was respectable, yes, and in a steady job too, and here you come and won't tell me what it is you do and now you come out with all this, a detective, a man that has to mix with criminals, and bringing them to my house before long I shouldn't wonder, that is *IF* it's true what you're saying.'

Charles dragged out a packet of cheap cigarettes. 'Just a minute,' he mumbled. 'Left matches in bedroom.' 'Never mind matches now,' she shrilled, but he dashed out, slamming the door behind him, and pounded up the stairs to his bedroom. On reaching it his first impulse was to hide under the bed, but he knew it was useless. He must steel himself. Lighting his cigarette, he took a gulp of the acrid smoke and turned to face the landlady as she ran into the room. Then, suddenly, his mind cleared. She had asked for an explanation, and he would give her one. Before she could speak he had launched into a long and circumstantial narrative: how he was employed by the Central Office of the Jehovah's Witnesses to keep his eye on one of the four regional treasurers, a Blackwall man, who was accused of bringing discredit on the movement in various ways which—his voice dropped to a confidential undertone—she would forgive him if he did not specify. He invented a name for the agency in which he was a junior partner. Did she remember the Evans case, the one that got so much space in the *News of the World*? But then, she did not read the *News of the World*, of course, she would not have seen it: anyway, he, Charles, had been responsible for bringing that man to justice. He talked on and on, thoroughly bored but surprisingly calm. And now, to come back to his original point, the suspected man had moved into a small hotel in the town (as she opened her mouth to ask 'What hotel?' he forestalled her by asking, gently, if she would mind not forcing him to reveal its name) and he felt it to be his duty to move into the same hotel.

'And so, you see, Mrs. Smythe, when I said that I needed to move so as to be nearer my work, it was,' he smiled gravely, 'very literally true.' And for the first time in fifty-six years Mrs. Smythe was speechless. She had taken in perhaps a third of his involved narrative, and her mind was a swirling chaos. If she had one desire in the world, it was to see the last of Charles Lumley. His point was gained.

Suitcase in hand, Charles stumbled next morning over the greasy hall mat for the last time, and lurched out into the July sunshine. Lying awake in the night, he had dwelt lovingly on the kick he would plant, scientifically and deliberately, in the dog's mouth as it yelped at him; but to-day, for the first time since he had entered the house, the animal was somewhere else, and his exit was silent.

He was aware of Mrs. Smythe's gaze, half suspicious and half impressed, from behind the yellowed lace curtains of the front room, and tried to assume a swagger as he moved away down the street. Yet it was clear to him that his three weeks at Stotwell had been so much wasted time; twenty-one aimless mornings, stupefied afternoons, and desperate evenings, during which his thoughts had obstinately refused to be clarified. How often, in the tumultuous muddle of his last year at the University, he had congratulated himself on having found a way out of the familiar *impasse*; when the insistent question of where, after the few fleeting months were over, he was to find a living wage had intruded itself, he had shrugged it aside, promising himself that he would deal with that and all his other problems in a few weeks of quiet and solitude. 'Sorry,' he would say in answer to questions about his future, 'but I'm not making major decisions just now. One thing at a time, you know. At the moment I'm working for an examination—and,' he would add pompously, 'trying to live like a normal human being at the same time. When all this comes to an end, I'll turn my attention to the problem of earning a living, without trying to isolate it from all the other big problems.' It had all been very comforting. He had even held a modest ceremony at his lodgings, at which, in the presence of a few friends, he had decided on the town to which he should retire for his all-important spell of concentration. Asking them to write down the names of a dozen or so towns on a sheet of paper, avoiding the big cities where lodgings might be more expensive, he had then, with a fine air of casualness, stuck a pin into the list at random. 'I'm quite indifferent,' he had said, loftily; 'a country village or an industrial town—my gaze will be directed inwards.' By a ludicrous coincidence his first jab with the pin had landed on the name of the one town in England that was useless for his purpose, the town where he was born and bred and where his parents lived; it had been written down in all innocence by one of his guests. The second jab had landed on the extreme edge of the paper, and was voted inconclusive, but the third had unequivocally indicated Stotwell. Full of hope, he had scurried across country to this dingy huddle of streets and factories, only to spend his precious weeks in nail-biting indecision. Nothing had been settled, not even the obvious and simple question of a trade, certainly not the deeper and more personal problems which he had shelved for years on the promise of this tranquil interlude.

Why was this? Why had he failed? he asked himself as he dragged the heavy suitcase down the main street towards the station. The answer, like everything else, was fragmentary: partly because the University had, by its three years' random and shapeless cramming, unfitted his mind for serious thinking; partly because of the continued nagging of his circumstances ('Go out this morning or she'll *know* you haven't a job—come to a decision to-day before you waste any more time—look at the papers to see what sort of jobs are offered'), and partly for the blunt, simple reason that his problems did not really admit of any solution. At least, he comforted himself, he had remained stationary; if he had been surrounded by the well-meant fatuity of those who had always sought to 'guide' him, there was no telling what disastrous steps might already have been taken. As it was, his position was precisely the same as it had been before his attempt to face the problems that hemmed him about; he had not yet realized, what circumstances were soon to teach him, that his predicament was not one that could be improved by thinking.

It was inevitable, then, that a sense of defeat should bow Charles's shoulders and line his forehead as he paid out his last pound note for a ticket to the town where his parents, relatives, and acquaintances were waiting to ask where he had been. If it were not for Sheila, he thought grimly as he waited for the few shillings' change that now represented his total resources, he'd hold out somehow, sleeping on park benches, selling newspapers for a living. But he had to see her, even though he had nothing to bring her that would make sense of his silence, nothing that would bring their marriage nearer or make it more attractive. What a mess it all was! Charles sighed as he stuffed the ticket into his waistcoat pocket and gathered up the change.

The train drew in, and he clambered indifferently into the compartment that was facing him as it stopped, heaved his suitcase on to the rack and slumped into a corner seat. With the exaggerated reserve implanted in him by his upbringing he studiously averted his eyes from the other two occupants of the compartment, seeing them only as blurred forms, a middle-aged couple without distinctive features. It was only when the train had left the station and the broad fields of a Midland landscape were streaming past the windows that he became aware that they were studying him, timidly, but with an intense interest that was obviously on the point of forcing them to break their silence. He looked up and met their gaze. Yes! Where had he seen them before?

'It's Mr. Lumley, isn't it?' said the man at last.

'That's my name,' Charles assented cautiously, mumbling on a rapid undertone, 'not sure where had the pleasure remember face of course, let me see.'

The woman, who clearly did not share in the embarrassment, leaned forward with an encouraging smile.

'We're George Hutchins's mother and dad,' she volunteered kindly. 'We met you when we came up to see him at the College.'

At once Charles remembered a scene which he would gladly have forgotten. George Hutchins, an unpleasantly dogged and humourless young man, had lived on the same staircase and had indulged a taste for lecturing Charles on the virtues of hard work. 'No system,' he would say contemptuously, looking round at Charles's bookcase, 'just a random collection of texts, no real system. You're just playing at it. Now I can't afford to play at it. I go over each little plot of the subject carefully. Preliminary survey, then a closer reading, and then, three months later, revision. And the whole thing's tied up. That's how these men like Lockwood have got where they are, and I'm going after them.' Lockwood was a dreary whey-faced tutor of the college for whom Hutchins had a deep and sincere admiration, and who encouraged him along the road to complacent prigdom. After one of these lectures, Charles would sit staring into the fire, inert and crumpled; the half-fantastic, half-shrewd gleams and pin-points of intuition which served him as a substitute for intellectual method damped and fizzling out in the clammy atmosphere of Hutchins's brutal efficiency.

'I s'pose you've heard all about George's success,' said Mr. Hutchins; his voice was bright and confident, but with a curious undertone of bewilderment and pathos. 'He's got a Fellowship,' he added, using the strange word in inverted commas, grafting it like some strange twig on to the stunted trunk of his artisan's vocabulary.

For the next few minutes the conversation arranged itself on purely mechanical lines; a steady flow of 'deserve congratulation worked hard for it now got it' *clichés* from Charles, and an answering dribble of 'Well it's what he's always wanted not that it hasn't been a struggle' from the withered couple opposite. Behind the mask Charles was genuinely sorry for them; it was so obvious that they were even more bewildered than on the day, two years ago, when he had walked into Hutchins's room with a request for the loan of a toasting-fork, and found the three sitting dumbly and stiffly together. Hutchins had been so abjectly and obviously ashamed of his parents' working-class appearance and manner that he had tried to avoid introducing them, evidently in the hope that Charles would not realize the relationship. But the family likeness had proclaimed itself, and Charles had lingered, chatting for a few minutes, partly out of a malicious pleasure at Hutchins's discomfiture, and partly out of a genuine desire to comfort these decent and kindly people, to show them that if their son was an ungainly snob there were others who were not, and to try to give them a few pleasant minutes in what was so clearly a disastrous visit. They had never appeared again, and Hutchins had never mentioned them. Charles, with no other intention than to be pleasant, had once asked him if his parents were keeping well, but the scowl he had received in answer had made it clear that Hutchins had regarded the question as a simple insult. The raw cult of success by which he lived could allow of no tolerance of the couple who had spawned him; they were neither prosperous nor celebrated, their Birmingham speech exposed in an instant the unreality of his own diction (an unbelievably exact reproduction of Lockwood's donnish snivelling), and, in short, his resentment of them could go no farther. Amid all the problems that beset him, Charles found time to rejoice that he was not as Hutchins was, that his soul, stretched as it was on the rack of his ludicrous predicament, was alive. He was not given to quoting, but a favourite fragment swam into his head, and he muttered, 'I am one of those who have created, even if it be but a world of agony.' 'Beg pardon?' said Mr. Hutchins, surprised, leaning forward. 'Just nothing, just nothing,' Charles replied; he wished to sound airy and nonchalant, but the words rang out brassily and the effect was one of impertinence. In despair he stood up, dragged his case down from the rack, gabbled 'Must get ready getting out next station,' and fled down the corridor in search of a fresh compartment. The only one that appeared to have a vacant seat was occupied by four blue-chinned men banging down cards on a suitcase, who looked up at him with such hostility that he retreated again, and, fearing to stand in the corridor lest Mr. or Mrs. Hutchins should come out and see him, spent the forty minutes that remained of his journey cowering in the lavatory.

Despite this discouraging start to the day, by half-past four that afternoon Charles had negotiated a surprising number of obstacles. Arriving at his destination, he had left his suitcase at the station cloak-room, and, determined to put off his official home-coming until it was forced on him, walked rapidly the hundred yards from the station to the long-distance 'bus depôt, to wait for a coach to the village five miles away where Sheila and her parents lived. The need to see her, which he had fiercely repressed for months, flared up in his body and brain as the 'bus crawled through the leaf-green lanes; it was so much what he needed—a return, a recognition, a point of rest, which yet involved no recriminations and no immediate practical decision. But this peace was still to be won, and the violence of his inner tension caught and shook him fiercely as he walked up the garden path.

But the situation, once again, was due to collapse into anti-climax. In answer to his unnecessarily firm and prolonged ring at the bell, the front door was opened by a plump, grave man of about thirty-five. It was Robert Tharkles, the husband of Sheila's elder sister Edith. His expression of gravity deepened into positive melancholy, tinged with irritation, at the sight of Charles. This fool again! And the fool had still not smartened himself up! When was he going to smarten himself up?

'Sheila isn't here,' he said without waiting for Charles to say anything, and without any greeting.

'Mind if I come in all the same? Come some distance,' muttered Charles.

'There's only Edith and me here,' said Robert, as if warning Charles that by coming in he was exposing himself to an unpleasant ordeal; which was true.

Without answering, Charles levered himself past Robert and went into the hall. Edith came out of the kitchen and confronted him. 'Sheila isn't here,' she said. 'Know,' said Charles, speaking too quickly to be fully intelligible. 'Robert told me. Mind if come in perhaps cup of tea? Or when Sheila be back wanted to see her if I could.'

Under their patronising and hostile stares he pulled himself together, walked into the kitchen, and sat down on a chair.

This was typical of all the interviews Charles had ever had with Robert and Edith. It was not because he was unsuccessful that they objected to him; lack of success, in their eyes, was not a punishable offence; one simply left such people alone. What annoyed them was that he did not even seem to be trying. Though they could not have put it into words, their objection to him was that he did not wear a uniform. If he had worn the uniform of a prosperous middle-class tradesman, like Robert, they would have approved of him. If, on the other hand, he had seriously adopted the chic disorder of the Chelsea Bohemian, they would at least have understood what he was at. In their world, it was everyone's first duty to wear a uniform that announced his status, his calling and his ambitions: from the navvy's thick boots and shirtsleeves to the professor's tweeds, the conventions of clothing saw to it that everyone wore his identity card where it could be seen. But Charles seemed not to realize the sacred duty of dressing the part. Even as an undergraduate he had not worn corduroys or coloured shirts. He had not even smoked a pipe. He had appeared instead in non-committal lounge suits which were still not the lounge suits of a business man, and heavy shoes which were still not the sophisticated heavy shoes of the fashionable outdoor man. Moreover, all his tentative efforts to ingratiate himself with them had been ill-judged. He had suggested to Robert, the first time they met, that they might slip out for a drink before lunch. Robert never slipped out for drinks, preferring to open half-pint bottles of gassy beer which he took solemnly from a mahogany cabinet. When he had helped Edith with the washing up on the maid's day out, she had so fiercely concentrated on the probability of his breaking something that in the end he had dropped and smashed an irreplaceable gravy-boat. When Robert, playing up to his position as the steady, responsible husband of the elder sister, had asked this candidate for the hand of the younger sister, what he intended to Do, and what his prospects were, Charles had responded in the fashion of the university with evasive and facetious answers. He did not fit into their world or speak their language, and after a perfunctory attempt to fit him into their prim, grey jigsaw puzzle they had disliked and rejected him; without, however, leaving him alone. As they stood and looked at him Charles realized that he would have to accept, as the price of his cup of tea, another lump of advice; as hard to swallow, and as useless to the system, as the cotton wool it so much resembled.

It was Edith who began the offensive, fixing her absurdly small eyes on him as she stood squarely beside the sink, a Woman on her Own Ground, in her hideous dress and splashed apron.

'I suppose you wanted to speak to Father,' (thank Heaven at least she did not refer to the yellowed scarecrow as 'Daddy') 'now that you've taken your degree you'll be wanting to put everything into a bit better order, I suppose.' (An oblique, but not too oblique, reference to his haphazard approach to life.) 'He's been wondering when you'd show up.' (Implying that he had been skulking out of the way of his responsibilities).

Charles foolishly let himself be hooked. 'I don't know that I wanted to see your father exactly,' he said. 'I mean, there's nothing immediately—er—'

He realized that he had been trapped. His last half-dozen words would take so little twisting into a weapon against him (he had 'even gone so far as to say', 'seemed unaware of', etc.).

Edith's mouth had opened to yelp out the prepared condemnation, when Robert unexpectedly cut in.

'I met your parents the other day. We had a few minutes' chat about things in general. I must say'—his tone became firm and brisk, the executive with a grasp of essentials—'I think you ought to realize there's a pretty widespread dissatisfaction with the way you're going on. For one thing the way you just disappeared after taking your finals. Your father told me you hadn't even given them your address. They had absolutely no means of getting in touch with you. I must say I think that's pretty shabby.'

Charles had indeed made use of the obvious and only method of keeping his parents from surging into his life, shaking it up, wrenching it to pieces, and obscuring with a fog of emotion everything that he was trying to study under his laboriously constructed microscope of detachment. But of course there was no answer to this booby's conviction that a refusal to wallow, at every crisis, in the emotional midden that his parents had spent twenty-two years in digging, was 'shabby'. A suffocating sense of utter inability to communicate, as in those nightmares in which the dreamer sees himself put away for lunacy, had already begun to drench his mind.

The voices of Robert and Edith splashed on and on. Charles tried to be oblivious of them, but the smug phrases, the pert half-truths, the bland brutalities, ripped down his defences. It was finally a remark of Edith's that brought him to his feet in a sudden rush of anger.

'You never seem to want to repay any of the people who've tried to help you.'

In a swirl of resentment Charles saw the faces of those who had 'tried to help him': and behind the faces flickered a radiance, the colour of dawn on snow-capped hills, that might (he suddenly knew) have been in his life if he had been left alone to make it without 'guidance': if all the people who had cloaked their possessive fumbling under the words 'trying to help you' had been, by a miracle, persuaded to leave him in peace. And now she spoke, once again, of repayment!

On his feet, gripping the back of his chair, Charles sought for a quick, devastating reply: a few words so swift and bitter that they would scorch themselves into Edith's mind and live with her, waking and sleeping, till she died.

It was no use, of course. Speech would never work with these people. Indeed, it was inconceivable that anything could be got across to them by means of language, unless one overpowered them and left them gagged and bound in the presence of a gramophone record endlessly repeating a short, concise statement. It would have given him pleasure to begin the composition, there and then, of such a statement; to have outlined in a few simple sentences the nature of the crime against humanity that they and their kind were committing by the mere fact of their existence.

'Your shaft seems to have gone home, Edith,' said her husband. 'Our friend doesn't quite know how to answer you. It's reduced him to silence.'

Charles focused with sudden clarity on Robert. All at once it seemed to him that the stiff brown moustache which he wore to give dignity to his face was curiously non-human. It looked as if it had been clipped from the face of an Airedale.

'I wasn't really thinking about what Edith had said,' he replied half apologetically. 'I was just wondering why no one's ever found it worth while to cut off that silly moustache of yours and use it for one of those brushes you see hanging out of windows next to the waste pipe.'

He spoke quietly and courteously; nevertheless they realized, after a short pause in which their minds groped for the meaning of his words, that he was being definitely insulting. Edith's face seemed to swell up to twice its size, her eyes bulged and she began a loud and unsteady tirade, quavering with hysteria but heavy with menace. Robert, on the other hand, had no difficulty in selecting the basic attitude proper for him to adopt. His mouth tightened, he squared his shoulders, and he moved forward, lightly and yet decisively, like Ronald Colman. When his crisp and well-timed 'That's enough of that sort of talk' had failed to penetrate to Charles's consciousness, and Edith's cackle had begun to take on a distinct flavour of tears, Ronald Colman disappeared, and in his place stood Stewart Granger, dangerous, alert, powerful. He grasped Charles by the lapel of his jacket.

For an instant surprise gripped Charles and held him motionless. How quickly, how fatally, the situation had developed! So now, finally, he had put himself in the wrong. 'Quite abusive. In fact Robert had to put him out. Impossible to have him in the house again.'

Robert's pouchy, inane face was thrust aggressively into his. Hell! They could have it if they wanted it. With a sudden twist he broke free, lunged across to the sink and snatched up the washing-up bowl. Edith had just finished washing up when he arrived, and for some reason she had not thrown the water away. Half of the scummy grey flood poured over Charles himself as he dragged the bowl wildly out of the sink, but the other half cascaded gloriously as, with a tremendous sense of release, he swung it round. Almost simultaneously three sounds filled the kitchen—the water's gulping splash, Edith's loud squealing, and the clatter of the empty bowl landing in a corner. It had hardly landed before Charles clawed open the back door and rushed out. A backward glance showed him Edith's face framed in wisps of wet hair, and Robert trying to blink the soap from his eyes.

As the gate clicked shut behind him, and he stumbled forward into the road, Charles suddenly realized the truth about what had happened. It was not Robert and Edith he had quarrelled with: it was Sheila. He had loved her with a passive persistence ever since the burning, spinning evening, when he was seventeen, that had taught him what love was, and she had entered his character and become its core. After a reasonable period of vacillation, she had agreed to marry him when this should be possible, and the prospect had been the foundation of his life in thought and action. Now, in the dusky street, his own footsteps beat into his head the knowledge that it could not happen. Her face rose before his eyes: that air of positive calm, of confident and sweet repose, smashed into his mind—always before it had reassuringly entered as an expected guest—and he saw behind her eyes the eyes of her mother, solemn, spectacled, judging him; in the bones of her chin he saw the chin of her father, jutting and scraped clean of its greying stubble below a tight, fussy, mouth. No! He had never been scared of the fact that she would grow older, losing the confident hardness of her limbs in dumpiness or scragginess; but now he saw her not merely growing old, but growing daily more and more of a piece with the prim, hedged gravel from which she flowered. With Robert's complacent whine, with Edith's angry squawk, still in his ears, he knew that he could never face it. It was over. No more Sheila.

At the thought of finality his mind was flooded with images: the ivory bald patches behind her ears, the quivering of her pointed chin as she had raised her face to be kissed for the first time, her delicate wrists ... his heart lurched over and over in his breast like a cricket ball lobbed along a dry, bumpy pitch; a shudder seized him, so violent that he was flung off his balance and lurched against the stone wall of a prosperous man's garden. The rough solidity of the stone flicked his mind empty again, and a new set of images crowded in: he saw Sheila's face, pale, luminous, resolute, and behind her the meanly precise face of her father, the tame and lumpy face of her mother, Edith's spiteful plucked eyebrows, and presiding over the scene, Robert, with his detestable calf's head and waving plump hands.

'I can't marry Robert!' he said loudly in his agony. A middle-aged woman and a small boy, standing at a 'bus stop, spun round and stared into his face with insane curiosity as he passed. Charles broke into a gallop. He only wanted to get round the next corner and hide his back from their eyes, but as he ran he knew that he was running away from everything that, up to that moment, had been his life.

It was over. 'No more Sheila' and 'SNUG' were written across each other on a yellow-lit pane. Half dead, he clutched at a brass door knob and swung himself over the threshold of the bar parlour.

'Well, all I know,' said the landlord, 'is that he was no good when he worked for me.'

He spoke with truculence, as if contesting an unfair judgment. But the red-faced man answered, calmly and with emphasis:

'He could buy you up to-day. Every brick and blade of grass in the place, if he wanted.'

The landlord was rapidly becoming downright angry. He glared venomously at the glass which Charles passed up to be refilled, and scowled so that his forehead, already unusually low, disappeared altogether.

'I'm not going to say, mark you, that you couldn't trust him,' he said with the air of one striving, with unheard-of generosity, to find some redeeming trait in a worthless character. 'I don't say as I ever had reason to think that he pinched anything, either money out of the till, or drink out of the stock, or glasses or ash-trays or anything—not like some of 'em. But what I DO know,' he said menacingly, leaning forward, 'is that he didn't know which was his right hand and which was his left. And if he could write his own name it was just about all he *could* write. Sometimes, when we was busy and I used to have him behind the bar, I used to think he couldn't read the labels on the bottles. They'd come in and ask for Double Diamond, and they'd be lucky not to get a Guinness.'

Charles, who had been standing patiently at the bar, trying to concentrate on nothing but the three pints already inside him and the fourth he was trying to buy, was suddenly jerked into attention by the word 'Guinness'. 'No thanks,' he said hastily, 'I'll just have the same again.' The landlord, ignoring him, leaned over the bar to sneer at the red-faced man with indescribable malice. He imagined himself to be reasoning calmly.

'His fingers was all thumbs,' he said to clinch the argument.

The red-faced man patiently repeated, 'If he was to come in here and like the look of the place he could afford to buy it.'

The landlord, livid with fury, clutched convulsively at the handle of the beer engine and released a swirling flood of the cloudy liquid into Charles's glass.

'I know two fellers as work for him,' said the red-faced man, following up his advantage. 'Six pound ten a week they get, double time Saturday afternoons if they want it.'

Moodily the landlord pushed the full glass towards Charles, and swept his shilling into the till.

'Contracts, that's how he does it,' said the red-faced man. 'Does it all by contracts. Goes to some big place, a block of office buildings or a hoe-tel, and gets a contract to clean their windows regular. Then he just sends the bill in to 'em every three months.'

'Bill!' the landlord burst out passionately. 'When he was working for me you couldn't trust him to pick up sixpence for half a pint of mild. When they heard it was one of our busy nights and he was behind the bar, we'd get all the riff-raff of the place in here, just because they knew he couldn't add up. They'd order five drinks and pay him for three. But now he's working for *himself*,' he emphasized the word in tones of agonized loathing, 'he knows enough to send in a regular bill. And with no mistakes in it neither.'

'I didn't say that,' said the red-faced man. 'I expect he overcharges 'em most of the time.' He laughed delightedly at his own polished repartee.

Charles set down his empty glass and made for the urinal. When he got back the topic had been changed; it was evident that the landlord had been no more than mildly interested in the incompetent who had grown rich. What seemed like apoplectic bad temper was merely the conversational style that made him a 'character': no doubt it was worth a thousand a year to the brewery that employed him. 'Same again?' he shouted angrily as Charles walked up to the bar. 'No, a whisky, please,' Charles replied, for he wanted more than anything in the world to get drunk, and he had now only six shillings left. Perhaps if he mixed his drinks sufficiently it might be enough. After the whisky he could have a gin, and then, if he had any money left, a glass of stout ought to finish him off.

Hitherto the three of them had been alone in the snug, but now the place began to fill up. Half a dozen robust middle-aged women, obviously regulars, entered within ten minutes and began their evening ritual of Guinness and conversation. Quite by chance Charles had seated himself in the exact centre of the half circle of chairs which were sacred to their use, and they began by a barrage of meaning glances and loud asides to try to move him. But the mixture of whisky and beer, coming as it did on an empty stomach, was beginning to take effect, and he sat with half-closed eyes, oblivious of their angry gestures and comments. The landlord, a rapidly blurring figure, moved a cloth over the surface of the bar, and from the centre of his alcoholic mist Charles saw himself with a cloth in his hand, passing it, not over a bar, but a window. *Gets a contract to clean their windows regular. Sends the bill every three months.*

The women were frankly talking over, round, and through his head; snatches of their speech mingled with the phrases that insistently barked inside his brain.

'So I said, if you want to know why he's not at school, I said, just you come round to the back,'

He could buy you up.

'and look at the word he's written on the coal-house door, I said.'

Two fellers who work for him. Double time if they want it.

'Well, where else would he hear a word like that? I said. A nasty dirty word. If that's what they teach them, I said,'

His fingers was all thumbs. He was no good when he worked for me.

'I hope for your sake, I said, that you're not suggesting that he hears language like that AT HOME, I said.'

I expect he overcharges them. Every blade of grass.

'School attendance officer or no school attendance officer, I said.'

In Charles's breast pocket was a paper packet containing his last cigarette. He took it out carefully, but it had somehow been bent, and the paper was broken in the middle. He began to smoke it, holding it so that one finger exactly covered the torn spot, inhaling deeply. The hot storm-centre of alcohol in his stomach rose to meet the smouldering pool of nicotine in his lungs, and, the burden of guilt and fatigue slipping from his shoulders, he breathed a silent prayer of gratitude to the twin deities of his world.

Then, as his mind cleared momentarily, he became aware of the stout-laden east wind of hostility that blew around him. Embarrassed and scared, he jumped up from his seat and went over to join the dense crowd round the bar. The landlord and his two daughters were working hard filling glasses and taking money, but he never seemed to get any nearer to being served. Several times he edged his way to the bar, waiting until all those before him had been attended to, but always he was curtly thrust aside just as he opened his mouth to give his order. After twenty minutes all the ebullience he had derived from the whisky and the cigarette had been drained away, and all he felt was the fatigue of standing for so long after a day without proper food. Determinedly he held his glass out and rapped it on the counter. 'Gin, please,' he shrilled. 'Four bitters, a Guinness, three rolls, and Martha says have you got 'ny Weights?' rapped out a stocky man at his side. Charles turned on him fiercely. 'Just a minute,' he snapped, 'I was here long before you.' The man looked at him coldly for an instant, but before he could reply, his order, complete with a packet of cigarettes, was handed to him on a tray, and he rapidly counted out the required money and departed. Charles sank to the bottom of an Atlantic of frustration. It was obvious, even to a mind dulled, like his, by exhaustion and disappointment, why he was getting nowhere. This establishment, or at any rate this particular room of it, was predominantly working class in atmosphere; consequently it was peopled by raw, angular personalities who had been encouraged by life to develop their sharp edges. His sharp edges, on the other hand, had been systematically blunted by his upbringing and education. From the nursery onwards, he had been taught to modulate the natural loudness of his voice, to efface himself in every possible way, to defer to others. And this was the result! He had been equipped with an upbringing devised to meet the needs of a more fortunate age, and then thrust into the jungle of the nineteen-fifties. The hive was full of wasps, all workers and all identical; but he, who differed from the others in nothing else, had been deprived of his sting.

'Now then, move away from the bar when you've been served,' shouted the landlord, leaning across the bar in his bullying way. 'I haven't been served! I want a gin and a glass of stout!' Charles shrieked with sudden violence. A silence fell, and everyone turned to look at him for an instant; then, indifferent, they turned back to their own conversations. In this way they succeeded in conveying, once more, the all-important fact—that he was imprisoned in his class, not one of them, condemned to solitary confinement if once he strayed from his own kind. And yet he hated his own kind: Robert Tharkles, George Hutchins, Lockwood. He gulped down the gin and immediately raised the stout to his lips. His long wait at the bar had sobered him up, and it was important to mix his drinks quickly if he wanted release.

It was not long in coming. As the long, slow gulps of stout followed the quick dash of gin into his stomach, his previous drinks seemed to wake from their dormancy. One by one, the familiar signs of approaching intoxication began to assert themselves. His tongue felt slightly numb; pressed against his lower front teeth, it seemed to be covered with a sheath of flannel. The bar, as he stared down its shiny length, began to rise and fall gently. High in the ceiling, the three electric lights which glared down through the clouds of smoke began to circle one another in a solemn dance.

'Got a light, mate?' came a croak from beside him. Before answering Charles raised his glass and, without hurry, poured the last third of the stout down his throat. As it foamed and splashed into the dancing ocean that awaited it, his sense of liberation became complete. When sober he would have spun round, anxious to be of service, to ingratiate himself; he would have dived for his matches, probably spilling his drink as he did so. Now, he was calm, insolent, able to live on the same level as the majority of his fellows.

'Got a light?' the voice husked again, but without resentment; thirty seconds' wait is no inconvenience. Charles carefully turned and did his best to focus on the man's expanding and contracting face. Without a word he took out his matchbox, and, with extreme care, drew out the inner compartment. As it was upside down, the matches cascaded to the floor. Immediately Charles stooped to gather them up, violently thrusting against the legs of someone standing at the bar. The man staggered, protesting vehemently, but with no thought of apologizing Charles concentrated doggedly on his task of collecting the matches. Whether they were in fact swimming in a puddle of spilt beer, or merely appeared to be swirling and writhing to his disordered vision, he could not tell; but it was some minutes before he had picked up the last one, and replaced them in the box with their heads all pointing the same way. Erect once more, he turned to the man who had asked for the light, and whose face was no longer expanding and contracting but alternately coming close and receding to an immense distance. Again he opened the box, and selecting a match from its circling nest, struck it and held it out. But at that instant the face, which had been unbearably close to his, rushed back into the distance. With a muttered exclamation of annoyance, Charles thrust the burning match out to the full extent of his arm.

Immediately the face ceased to be a face, and became a purple sphere of fury with two vast coloured eyes. As the match sank sizzling into his limp moustache, and the flame flickered for an instant up his nostrils, the man started back with a hoarse cry of pain and anger. Charles, too, lurched backwards, unnerved by the sudden noise. Since the bar was by now too full to allow of any sudden movement, elbows were violently jogged, jets of beer shot out in several directions, and a loud volley of oaths rose above the general rumble of conversation.

In his normal condition, nothing could have exceeded Charles's terror and shame in such a situation. He had been the cause of a disturbance! He had broken the sacred law of self-effacing, mute compliance—he had made, the phrase ran, an *exhibition of himself!* Normally, he would not have waited, except to stammer out his apologies; the burnt man's injured shout of 'It's 'is fault! Throw the clumsy bastard out! Had too much he has!' would have found him half-way to the door. But now the healing mist of alcohol, half gentle detachment and half fierce arrogance, protected him even against the menacing approach of the landlord. Instead of quailing before the hailstorm of abuse that swept at him from behind the bar, he merely blinked benignly for a moment at the landlord's whirling face—now dominated by the out-thrust nose, now grotesquely receding under the overhanging eyebrows—and then, turning coolly on his heel, calmly opened the door and went out, to be greeted by the warm silence of the summer night, and the village street opening and closing like a huge oyster shell.

Leaning against a wall, he waited for it to make up its mind, and soon it had settled down to a gentle heaving over which it was possible to walk. He had nowhere to go, no money and no plans, but the night was warm to the point of oppressiveness, the moon shone powerfully, casting deep shadows, and he had enough drink inside him to protect him from his anxiety. Unsteadily, but happily, he began to wander down a side turning between the gardens of cottages. And as he walked his mind gathered speed, until it was racing at the frantic speed which he had learnt to associate with drunkenness.

Charles had, indeed, often amused himself by pouring scorn on the conventional representations of this state in fiction, as a lazy and lethargic state of semi-paralysis. On the contrary, in his case the state of his reasoning faculties was precisely that of a motor engine accelerated to the maximum point with the clutch held out. Freed from its usual responsibilities—not only the responsibilities of fear and guilt and the crushing load of his ingrained conventionality, but even the basic duties of physical balance and direction—his mind raced and was capable of reaching major decisions in a few minutes, decisions which he seldom felt the need to reverse when his 'normal' incapacity was restored. Now, as he sank down on a grassy bank where crickets chirped and leapt dizzily in the moonlight, the experiences of the last few days merged with the lessons of his lifetime, and amid the circling, surging landscape the new adjustment began.

But not coolly, not analytically; for here, where analysis of his situation would have been deceptively easy, and would probably have led to a weary, half-cynical recapitulation, a decision to go back, to adapt himself, to take up the broken threads of his cocoon and glue them together again, his new clarity came to him as a series of cleanly etched visions and a rapid re-living of all the major emotions of his life in a series of sharp bursts. It was very simple: he saw himself bowed over books, listening to instruction, submitting to correction, being endlessly moulded and shaped; edging his way for years between the delicate areas of other people's sensibilities. One step too far in any direction and some one or other of them will be 'hurt', offended, disappointed. His schoolmasters shaking their heads, his father perplexed and angry, his mother wheedling or sulking, down to Mrs. Smythe's leading questions and Edith's yapping reproach—how they had all trampled over him! His mind accelerated still more; he rolled over on his back, so that he could see the moon-silvered spire of the village church waving like a reed in the quiet sky, and the images crowded in faster and faster. Sheila leaned towards him, her eyes tenderly seeking his, but her hairline suddenly slumped down to within half an inch of her eyebrows and her face became that of the landlord, coarse and domineering. A line from a modern poem he had recently read fell like a pebble into his mind;

And I a twister love what I abhor.

George Hutchins appeared, kicking savagely at a football: it sailed away towards the goal, where Lockwood stood wearing a green jersey and cap; as it revolved Charles suddenly saw that it was no ordinary football, but the head of Mr. Hutchins, senior. 'Don't mind me, Mr. Lumley,' it said deprecatingly in a Black Country accent, 'our George has worked so hard for his success.' The line of verse boomed out again, but this time in an altered form: it was, with him, one of the usual features of intoxication.

And I a lover twist what I abhor.

Charles jerked himself upright, and forced himself to walk on. It was easier to think when one was covering ground. Think of what? There was only one question: how to use the first twenty-two years of his life as a foundation for the next fifty. If, indeed, there was to be a next fifty; and the mushroom-shaped cloud that lived perpetually in a cave at the back of his mind moved forward for a moment to blot out everything else.

And twister I, abhorring what I love.

Still, one must behave as if there was going to be. Any other assumption led only to suicide.

The ditch by the roadside ran out and seized him by the ankle, and he fell forward into a dry bed of leaves, which began to sway back and forth determinedly. Charles knew that he would soon be sick; but his mind remained clear and unimpeded. The bed of leaves rolled completely over him, yet in the midst of his physical wretchedness he felt a new elation, a new freedom. He had inside him a few pints of liquid, and possibly a few undigested scraps of his last meal, eaten many hours earlier. In a minute or two he would get rid of them.

And I a whore, abtwisting what I love.

Could he not, just as easily, cast up and be rid of his class, his *milieu*, his insufferable load of presuppositions and reflexes? He climbed to his feet again, and stood for a moment staring up into the spinning centre of the sky that gyrated above him.

Love eye and twist her and what I abhor.

Why should it not end here, and he be reborn, entering the world anew, to no other music than the chirping of the crickets and his own retching?

II

The wash-leather made a pleasant noise, half slosh and half squelch, as Charles dipped it in the pail of water and then wrung it out. The feel of it in his hand varied greatly with its condition: slippery when it was wet, and tenacious, almost corky, when it was dry. He went over the panes once more, this time with the dry wash-leather. Then he dropped the wash-leather into the pail, and left it there while he took a dry duster out of the pocket of his overalls, and gave the panes a final polish. The hot sun, beating directly on to the glass, dried up the last traces of moisture and showed how clear and transparent it had become. The windows were really clean.

That was the lot. The last window of the last house he was going to do that morning. And as it was Saturday, that meant that work was over for the week. He had worked, he had earned his living for a whole week! His heart gave a great leap of joy as he climbed backwards down the ladder, holding the pail expertly in his left hand. He seemed to have been doing it all his life: perhaps, in all but a literal sense, that was true. His life had only really begun a week ago. Until then he had merely been an offshoot, an appendage, a post-script, to the lives of several other people. This new life was really his own.

Not, perhaps, entirely his own, he reflected with a sudden flicker of hard canniness, until he had paid back the five pounds. But he would very soon be able to do that. He had borrowed it from an uncle who was a solicitor; ironically, he had found it very easy to get the loan, by pretending that he needed it to settle some gambling debts left over from his student days. If he had told the old fool what he really needed the money for—this pail, ladder and handcart, these rags and overalls—he would never have unbuttoned his pockets in a thousand years. But 'a few pounds lost to his friends at the cards!' That was a different matter. His uncle always said 'the cards', instead of simply 'cards', thus showing that he approved of the pastime; he had even used the expression 'Debts of honour'! Charles had hardly been able to repress a sneer as he took the five pounds. Already his new job, though he had not yet earned a farthing at it, gave him the feeling of being miles above the world of small snobberies and appearances, as represented by his uncle. Still, the old ass had behaved decently, according to his standards, and he should have his money back. Charles went to the back door of the house and was handed his money: seven and sixpence. It had taken him about half-an-hour to earn it. Left to himself, he would never have asked for so much, but he had taken the precaution of finding out the usual rates of pay.

Even there, the directness characteristic of his new situation had made itself felt. In the 'old days'—up to a week ago, in fact—to what evasions, what roundabout routes would he not have been driven, in his efforts to get this piece of information! How he would have circled and hinted, asking half his question here, the other half there, driven into wilder and wilder lying, until the situation became finally impossible! But now, he had merely gone straight to the Warden of the Y.M.C.A. hostel where he was staying, and asked him directly what he usually had to pay to have the windows of the place cleaned. And equally directly the old man had replied, 'It works out at about sixpence a window.' Very well! Sixpence a window it should be.

Everything had cleared itself up, fallen into perspective,

assumed a new and saner proportion, ever since the chill summer dawn when he had risen from his bed of leaves with the knowledge that his old life was over. With one bound he had leapt clear of the tradition of his class and type, which was to see molehills as mountains and mountains themselves as a mere menacing blur on the horizon: and now, even the mountains had come closer and revealed that easy and well-trodden paths led to their heights; even, it seemed, to their glittering snow-crowned summits. Decisions had to be taken at once, because he had no reserve of money and therefore none of time. So he took them quickly. Five minutes' reflection had led him to the choice of a relative from whom he should borrow the money, and to the resolve to make it the smallest sum he could possibly manage with. As it was, he had found that a good ladder was too expensive, and was managing with an old one with several rungs missing, whose journey to the scrap-heap or the bonfire he had halted until, in a week or two, he could afford a new one. It was the same with his 'hand-cart'; the five pounds would never have run to a good one, and he had found a rag-and-bone man willing to sell him the ruins of an old pram—it had no coachwork, just the frame and wheels—for five shillings. Only his pail and his various cloths were of the finest quality that money could buy. He may have shed all other middle-class attributes, but the ideal of fine quality, of a good job well done (always a bourgeois rather than working-class ideal) had accompanied him into the new world.

Again, the choice of a town to live in had been an easy one. It must be a place where he had no relatives; it must not be too small, or there would not be enough business; nor too large, for he disliked the city atmosphere; and perhaps it would be as well to choose a place where he might start with some advantage, or possibility of advantage. Where did he know of any large institution which might see fit to give him a *contract*? (That was his magic word, for the remarks of the red-faced man in the pub constituted his whole professional training.) At first he toyed with the idea of going back to his university town, and trying to get a contract from his college; but he immediately reflected, not only that they would be unlikely to give him one, but also that he could never, now he came to think of it, remember having seen a professional window-cleaner at work in a college. Probably the authorities preferred, with characteristic narrowness, to include window-cleaning among the duties of the college servants. Where else?

Well, he could always go back to Stotwell; and besides, as he suddenly remembered, not ten miles away his old school stood among its village. A contract! Now was the school's chance to live up to some of the pious platitudes about *esprit de corps.* He remembered how powerful and how genuine had been the emotions that ran through him on his last morning at school, when he had stood with the other furry-faced gawks in the Sixth Form, droning out for the last time the termly intercession for 'those who here shall meet no more':

> May their seed-time past be yielding
> Year by year a richer store.

The store referred to was, of course, an inexpensive one of associations and loyalties, taken out of the drawer with the House tie for the annual Old Boys' shower-bath of nostalgia and falsity; but here at least was the school's chance to provide one granary with something substantial. A contract! The holy word echoed through his mind as he clambered out of the 'bus in the market square and walked up the hill to the school.

Complete and joyous as his rejection of the past had been, he still could not walk into this ivy-clad red building—a fake Rugby like so many minor schools of its period—with the sang-froid of one who had never been there before. Although the eight years he had spent here were part of a former life, that former life had the power, at least, to cause him discomfort enough to pierce his new-found calm. To be recognized by the janitor; to be conducted, in the afternoon drowsiness, down the corridor past that row of dingy form-rooms where the pitiful farce of his childhood had been played out act after endless act, and where the dragons, gods, and wizards who had peopled that fantastic region sat now, even this minute, building their endless crumbling structure in the minds of a fresh generation. It was uncomfortable; but the discomfort dropped away when he was left alone in the headmaster's waiting-room, for with solitude returned the consciousness that he had cut away the tentacles that bound him to the kind of life that this place represented. So soon after his seed-time, he was here to ask for a limited and definite harvest. A contract!

At last he was ushered in to the headmaster's study: that room which, with its careful arrangement of the 'traditional' props of leather armchairs, classical busts, glass-fronted book-cases, had been the scene of the utmost disasters and triumphs of his boyhood, though he had been too average a boy to enter it more than four or five times during his eight years. And there was the familiar sardonic face wryly hovering behind its thick lenses.

'Well now, Lumley; and what can I,' here he paused for an instant, and spoke the next three words with unnecessary distinctness, as if to parody them, 'do for you?'

'You could look straight at me, to start with,' Charles almost replied, for Scrodd was up to his usual game of peering ironically in his direction, vaguely taking in with his short-sighted glance the general area within which his interlocutor might be found, like one who has seen a tiny insect on the wallpaper, lost it again, and is half-interestedly looking for it. But annoyed as he felt at this habitual, perfunctory insolence, he refrained from any sign of impatience, for, in the three years during which he and Scrodd had not met, he had become familiar with the peculiar psychological burden under which the schoolmaster was sinking. Fresh from the world of Hutchins and Lockwood, he could read the bland imbecile like a newspaper: the early ambitions, the resolve to apply half his energies to his ordinary duties and half to the studies that were to lead him to the limelight, and finally the fading of his dreams, leaving him rigidly set in a travesty of his original position, with half his attention focused on whatever he was doing or whomever he was talking to, and the other half feebly glinting out from the paralysed area of his mind, focused, with terrible obstinacy, on nothing.

'I thought you might be so kind as to help me professionally, sir,' Charles said briskly.

Scrodd gave a slight twitch that brought his wandering gaze to within three inches of Charles's shoulder. A sneer appeared on his face.

'I could have saved you trouble, Lumley, if you had mentioned in your letter what it was you wanted to see me about: I could have told you that this school is fully staffed, and that I have no influence elsewhere.'

Charles leaned forward in incredulous pity. The scarecrow actually thought that he, a free human being, wished to enrol in his shambling regiment of pedagogues.

'My intention is not to enter the teaching profession, Mr. Scrodd. My vocational requirements are,' he hesitated, 'simpler and easier to fulfil.'

For a moment as he faced the enormity of the task in hand, Charles felt a renewal of his old confusion, guilt, and blankness. His tongue stiffened so as to choke all utterance, and he became the same ludicrously insecure figure he had been during all his previous visits to that study. Then, immediately, the mists cleared, and the sanity he had so dearly bought swept him forward on its powerful current until his feet were once more on solid ground.

'And in what way,' demanded Scrodd insolently, looking ironically past him, 'are they easy for *me* to fulfil?'

Charles leaned back in his chair, and fixed his eyes on the thick lenses opposite.

'This school has windows. Someone must have to clean them from time to time; either someone from outside, or one of the school servants who could be better employed about his ordinary duties. Now this, as you yourself once remarked to me, is the age of the specialist.'

Scrodd seemed to have fallen into a trance: his eyes were groping in Charles's direction as if searching for an invisible opponent.

'So why not give the job regularly to one of your old boys? I could make a journey over here, without any reminding, say at the beginning or end of each term, and make a couple of days' job of it, and of course my charges would—'

Scrodd was on his feet, and the miracle had happened. He was looking directly at Charles.

'I am still hoping,' he articulated distinctly, 'that this will turn out to be some foolish joke on your part.'

'—be less than whatever it is you're having to pay now.'

'Perhaps a touch of the sun. It has been hot lately.'

'Look at it this way. Suppose you don't get anyone in from outside, who is there who can do it decently? No one. Smith's too fat and rheumatic to get to the top of a ladder, and as for Bert, you must know that he can't be spared from the coke-shovelling—'

'Lumley! Spare me the trouble of ringing for the janitor and having you taken out of here by force!'

'—except during the summer, and then he has to act as groundsman. I could take the whole thing off their hands, and make the windows a credit to the school.'

Scrodd's hand jerked to the bell, and pressed the button, holding it feverishly down. Charles stood up. He had about one minute, the time it would take Smith to plod back down the corridor, in which to say his last words to Scrodd. It was inconceivable that they should ever meet again. And yet he had not the slightest urge to say anything, either cutting, furious, or conciliatory. The time for summaries was over. He had no breath to spare for his past life and its débris.

Oddly, it was Scrodd who felt the need to elaborate.

'I can only conclude, Lumley, that you felt some kind of grudge against me that impelled you to come back and waste my time with this foolish joke. Window cleaning! I suppose the implication is that your education has unfitted you for anything worth doing, and you seek to drive the point home by coming here with this foolish talk about having turned artisan. You need not have spoken in parable.'

Charles turned away as Smith opened the door. He felt no wish to comment on Scrodd's reading of the case. He merely said, over his shoulder, 'Why not in parable? I spent eight years here being taught to think metaphorically.'

And as Smith held the door for him to go out, he broke suddenly into the drowsy quiet of the corridor with a rendering, as musical as he could make it, of his obsessive fragment:

'May their seed-time past be yielding
Year by year a richer store!'

Smith, scandalized, hustled him down the service stairs and out into the sunshine.

Real leisure is a blessing granted only to those who have definite working hours, and when Sunday morning dawned calm and bright, Charles awoke with the blissful taste of idleness on his tongue for what seemed the first time in his life. He had spent the entire week in unremitting work, for he felt justified in counting the afternoon's visit to Scrodd as work, and even Saturday afternoon had seen him effecting some overdue repairs to his 'cart'; reflecting as he did so that if he could only trace the present whereabouts of the first baby to be wheeled in that pram, he would present it to him for the use of his grandchildren.

So there he was, out among the idlers in the town's one main street at half-past nine, with the day his own except for the six o'clock gathering for hymns and prayers which the Y.M.C.A. exacted, and quite rightly, as a form of spiritual rent. In other days the prospect of so many hours without formal employment would have filled him with a desire for companionship: but he now recognized this for what it was, the subterfuge of a mind unable to face the prospect of doing *nothing*: talking was a fake occupation to soothe the confused brain in its dread of vacancy.

He thought, as he leaned on the parapet of the town's bridge and watched the tiny brown river drifting beneath it, of all the expensive young men of the Thirties who had made, or wished to make, or talked of making, a gesture somewhat similar to his own, turning their backs on the setting that had pampered them; and how they had all failed from the start because their rejection was moved by the desire to enter, and be at one with, a vaguely conceived People, whose minds and lives they could not even begin to imagine, and who would in any case, had they ever arrived, have made their lives hell. At least, Charles thought with a sense of self-congratulation, he had always been right about *them*, right to despise them for their idiotic attempt to look through two telescopes at the same time: one fashioned of German psychology and pointed at themselves, the other of Russian economics and directed at the English working class. A fundamental sense of what life really consisted of had saved him at any rate from such fatuities.

Meanwhile there was the problem of avoiding contact. He must form no roots in his new stratum of society, but remain independent of class, forming roots only with impersonal things such as places and seasons, or, in the other end of the scale, genuinely personal attachments that could be gently prised loose from all considerations involving more than two people. The first thing to do was to get out of the Y.M.C.A. hostel, for it involved him in a certain degree of corporate life, and he had already drifted dangerously close to the dreaded state of becoming a member of his community. He had been spending his evenings following up hints about accommodation, usually from scrawled post cards exhibited ('6d per week') in wire-netting cases outside small general shops. But most of these had been entirely useless for his purpose, for they had involved becoming 'one of the family'; others had been merely squalid, and Charles shared the general human attitude towards squalor—he enjoyed his own but disliked other people's.

By eleven o'clock he had had to move on three times from his lounging-point, because of attempts to start conversation on the part of his fellow idlers. It was difficult to have to avoid this so persistently, and Charles was reminded of the various accounts he had read of the adventures of those escaping from prison camps in war-time: the nights spent in marching, the days in hiding, always in terror of being addressed because, as officers and gentlemen, the fugitives could not speak any other language than their own. A close parallel, he mused, for his accent would have given him away even if he had made a serious attempt to pass for a 'typical' window-cleaner; and ultimately, conversation would have led to arrest and a closer detention in the prison camp. The way to stay outside the barbed wire was to keep his mouth shut.

As his thoughts wandered over these and similar topics, he was strolling between chestnut trees in the town's park, beyond which only a brewery blocked the advance of the unspoilt countryside. The sun was hot by now, and the park presented its usual summer appearance: families sprawled on the grass, children ran swiftly up and down imitating aeroplanes, chattering as they neared one another to represent machine-gun fire; hundredweights of waste paper lay in heaps, waiting for a breeze to start them on their long pilgrimage; broken bottles glinted in the sun, and every few yards lay a young couple in what appeared to the averted gaze to be the last throes of sexual enjoyment.

It was therefore a long way from Charles's mind that anyone might interrupt his reverie, still less that they should abruptly thrust themselves into his notice. He almost staggered with surprise when an ungainly, unkempt figure, registered by his eye a moment before as a heap of old clothes at the foot of a tree, sprang suddenly to its feet with a hoarse cry of 'Lumley, I dreamt about you last night!'

Spinning round to peer into the bloodshot eyes that glowed behind the lank hair, Charles recognized a College acquaintance, Edwin Froulish.

Without knowing Froulish particularly well during their undergraduate years, Charles had known a good deal about him; inevitably, for Froulish had exploited his natural gift for self-advertisement with tremendous perseverance and zeal. From early adolescence he had seen himself as the boy who, though as yet undistinguished in the eyes of the world, would reveal himself in due season as a great novelist. His whole life was lived in the pages of that monumental biography which was to be written, after his death, by some short-sighted silver-haired professor: every incident in his profoundly ordinary existence was already translated, in his mind, into the professor's stately academic prose. He saw the running titles at the head of each page: 'A Hampshire Boyhood', 'Passion for Butterflies', 'Early Unconventionality', 'A Tyrant Defied' (the last heading would refer to his refusal, at the age of thirteen, to do an imposition unjustly set by the Physics master: it was the one courageous action he had to his credit, and he had been caned and the imposition doubled as a result). Long before leaving school he had sought out and read attentively any accounts of the boyhood of great writers. Most of them had shown an uncanny skill in the business of providing material for quotable anecdotes. Pope had been expelled from his first school for writing a satire on the master, Southey for declaring himself opposed to corporal punishment; Tennyson lived in thousands of hearts as the wild-eyed boy crouching in a deserted quarry and staring, long and incredulously, at the stone on which he had scratched the words 'Byron is dead'. Film! Pure film! Try as he would, Froulish never succeeded in rivalling the Hollywood-sense of his idols. And even if he had descended to actual plagiarism it would, he knew, have been useless. Whose name could he scratch on a stone? The only famous author to die at a suitable time for such a demonstration was Rudyard Kipling, and he was sure it would be quite out of keeping for him to be found staring, wild with misery, at the words 'Kipling is dead'. His friends would simply have laughed at him, the contemptuous and barely tolerant laugh that Tennyson probably never heard in all his life.

And so the very earliest pages of the professor's biography seemed likely to be rather bare of anecdotes: though there was no reason, Froulish often reminded himself, why he should not invent a few in later life. But at the University everything had been easier. The machinery of self-display was so much more accessible; within three weeks of his arrival he had managed to get himself talked about, and by his second term he was a recognized eccentric. And all done so easily! merely by a few random pantomime tricks, such as carrying a grey parrot in a cage wherever he went, wearing a bowler hat indoors, standing motionless for hours on end in the exact centre of the quadrangle, and so forth. His contemporaries, being typical undergraduates and therefore inhabitants of a hinterland of indecision, had scoffed readily enough, but had soon formed the habit of accepting him at his face-value, listening almost respectfully when he read papers to literary societies on such topics as 'The Alleged Inversion of Surrealist Psychology'. In short, he had become a figure. Looking now at Froulish's fat, dough-coloured face and his twitching hands, Charles realized for the first time the extent to which he, too, had been hoodwinked. Without ever pausing to think it out, he had accepted the legend of Froulish's genius for years, and now it was too late to change. Out of the abandoned tangle of his earlier life, he could at least pluck a ready-made attitude to this fellow-creature, which was less artificial than the attempt to see him as if for the first time.

And so he relapsed, mechanically, into the tone of half-jocular admiration which throughout the years he had reserved for his conversations with Edwin Froulish, as he said:

'Why, hello. I didn't expect to see you in this place. Looking for local colour, I suppose?'

'We can't talk here,' Froulish muttered furtively, ignoring the question. 'Let's—' his face contorted and he clutched at his right ear—'go and have a drink somewhere. Preferably somewhere quiet.'

Once in the bar, Froulish made straight for the darkest corner and slumped down, leaving Charles to get the drinks. Betraying no surprise at this—and, indeed, feeling none—Charles carried over two watery pints and set them down. The interview was free to begin.

'You asked me what I was doing here,' muttered Froulish in the intervals of gulping at his beer with a characteristic mixture of avidity and distaste. 'Of course I'm not looking for local colour—I'm not that kind of novelist, I don't go in for reactionary photographic stuff.'

'All right, spare me the catchwords—you'll be calling yourself non-representational and all the rest of it in a minute,' said Charles with a sneer. He was a window-cleaner and above all this sordid intellectual chatter. 'And tell me, unless you've decided to keep it a secret, what you *are* doing in these parts.'

'Well, the fact is,' said Froulish, twitching and jerking his stubby fingers, 'Betty found a place for us here, and as far as I'm concerned I don't care where I go while I'm writing The Novel. It's quiet enough here.'

'Betty?' said Charles, groping amid the miscellaneous memories that were stacked in the back of his mind waiting their turn to be thrown out.

'Surely you remember Betty. She used to go to Alan's parties.'

Charles had only been once to a party given by the unsavoury young man referred to, and had on that occasion withdrawn before the amatory stage was reached, but something stirred amid the heaps of débris in his memory, and he had a mental glimpse of the principal ornament of that party—tall and stringy in slacks and flowing hair down to the shoulders.

'I didn't know you had,' he searched vaguely for the word, 'linked up with her.'

Froulish guffawed, swaying his thick-set body backwards and forwards. 'Linked up! We were living together all through my third year.'

'I suppose that helps to account for your going down without taking a degree?' As the words passed his lips Charles marvelled at himself—how direct, how splendidly coarse and uninhibited he had become. How, in the old days, he would have suffered any fate rather than say anything so crudely personal and challenging, even to one as self-centred and egotistic as Froulish; who, of course, was not embarrassed.

'Oh, degree!' he groaned thickly, blinking rapidly through the strands of hair. 'What's the use of a thing like that to me! I'm a Novelist. All I need is a table and chair, pen and paper, a woman, food and—' here he eyed his empty glass—'drink.'

The old Charles would have jumped up and scurried to the bar at once on a hint as broad as this: the new Charles sat calmly lighting a Woodbine.

'You can wait till I've finished mine. And where is this place where you and Betty live? Is it a house?'

'Well, no,' Froulish admitted, 'one can't have everything, of course. Actually it's a sort of shed that used to be used as part of a builder's yard. The bottom part consists of just one big room, without any partitions—that's where the timber used to be kept. The upper floor—you go up to it by a ladder—was divided into small rooms as offices. Betty's managed to rent the upper part for us. Look here, if you've got any money, why don't you buy me a drink, you mean bastard?'

Charles crushed out his Woodbine and went over to the bar. This might be what he was looking for; it would be ideal for storing his equipment, and no doubt for cheapness. But there was something else more important: an escape that seemed to be offering itself from the problem of environment, of the clash of outlook and status. He, who had rejected and been rejected by both the class of his origin and the life of the 'worker', might find the classless setting of his dreams in sharing a roof with a neurotic sham artist and a trousered tart.

When Froulish had been pacified with a fresh pint and a Woodbine, he leaned forward and continued his confidences.

'It seems the place hasn't been used as a builder's yard for a good many years. The concern moved to a bigger place, but kept this one going to store odds and ends in. Finally the old man who ran it died, and the widow sold the other place, the real headquarters of the business, but couldn't sell this. The purchaser wouldn't look at it because they hadn't kept it in repair. So she had no way of making anything out of it except letting it for human beings to live in—the old bitch.'

'Sounds a nice old party. What does she charge you for it?'

Froulish groaned, and a look of intense misery appeared on his face.

'A guinea a week! I ask you: twenty-one bloody shillings for every seven days in that hell! Of course, it's about the least you could possibly pay anywhere for a lodging for two people, and the old cow would like to charge more, much more, except that it's illegal to have anyone living there at all—it has to be strictly on the q.t. or else the sanitary authorities would probably send the lot of us to prison.'

'What exactly is the sanitary position? Any running water?'

'No, but there's a well quite close by, with water that hasn't been declared unfit to drink, as far as we know. And a kind of rough-and-ready jakes down in the yard, surviving from the days when there were men working there.'

The place was filling up. A labouring man walked over from the bar with his pint, and sat down on the bench next to Froulish. Taking out a plug of twist, he began to cut shavings off it with a knife and collect them in the palm of his hand.

'Now look here,' said Charles in mounting excitement. 'Who pays this guinea a week? Surely you—I mean—'

Among the nameless crimes he had seen hinted at in newspaper reports, or half-heard as a child in whispered conversations among scandalized elders, was one known as Living on Women. The phrase evidently embraced the whole range of possibilities from the full-scale organization of prostitution to the regular accepting of valuable presents from rich old ladies. Where did Froulish fit in? he wondered as he looked across at the twitching mask of dough with its pink deep-set eyes. At what point along the scale should he be placed? For surely, he was Living On A Woman.

'Oh, yes, I dare say it shocks your bourgeois feelings,' sneered Froulish bitterly. 'I know what you're thinking. Yes, Betty pays the guinea a week. And the two pounds odd it costs us for food and fuel every week. And it's not nearly enough. We need more now and God knows what we shall need in the winter. But she pays it. And I suppose you, with your blasted conventionality—'

His tirade was drowned in an attack of choking, for the labourer next to him, after arranging the shavings of twist in a clay pipe, had actually gone to the length of lighting them. Dense blue smoke gathered around Froulish and forced its way into his eyes, nose, throat, and lungs. Charles started back before he, too, should be overwhelmed. Getting up, he took his drink and stood about six feet away from the evil-smelling volcano.

'You say to yourself,' came Froulish's voice in a strangled shout, '"What a spineless swine he must be to let a woman keep him! Why doesn't he work for a blasted living like me?"' Again he collapsed into helpless coughing. The labourer puffed serenely on. 'But you and your damned smug kind don't care, oh blast this smoke, whether Art lives or dies. I've only got to finish this novel and I'll be famous; then I'll give her it all back with interest. And anyway, oh, God, I feel sick! Are you still there? Anyway, never mind the material aspect of it. Betty's glad to help Art! She really cares, I'm going to faint any minute, whether the Novel—whether Literature lives or not! Damn this filthy smoke! Lumley! Where are you? I can't see anything!'

Froulish dragged himself to his feet; his figure could be dimly made out through the fog. 'This way!' shouted Charles. They had become characters in a film trying to escape from a jungle fire, or convicts breaking away in a Dartmoor fog. Clawing the air in front of him, his face green and soaked in perspiration, Froulish emerged; and Charles, swiftly catching his swaying figure, seized him by the arm and dragged him out into the clear air.

It seemed natural, though Froulish uttered no word of invitation, for Charles to accompany him to his dwelling; once he had recovered from the fumes, the novelist slouched rapidly away down a side street with the air of one who expected to be accompanied. Neither spoke as they moved through the tangle of little streets at the edge of the town, where amid the drabness of backyards and terrace houses the countryside made small incursions, thrusting a green tendril here and there, a bank of nettles, a hedge, a tall tree. Presently they drew near a long wooden shed with an empty yard in front of it. As Froulish led the way across this yard, they heard the sound of female voices raised in angry dispute. There were two of them talking at once, so that it was difficult to gather what they were saying, but after a moment it became clearer that the shriller of the two was repeating over and over again, 'Not another hour! Not another hour!'

'Hell fire!' exclaimed Froulish, stopping dead. 'It's her! We'd better not go in.'

Evidently the burdens which Betty had shouldered on behalf of Literature included facing the enraged landlady single-handed; for Charles felt no doubt that it *was* the landlady; the passion in that voice told him plainly that the subject under discussion was money. Froulish had turned away and was beginning to scurry back across the yard, when a window flew open above their heads and a seamed malicious face, the face of a witch, surmounted by thin grey hair drawn back into a bun, was thrust out.

'Mr. Froulish!' screamed the widow. 'Don't you think you can get away! I've seen yer—come up here!'

Twitching hideously, the man of letters hesitated. Flight seemed so easy, surrender so repellent.

'It's yer only chance,' shouted the harridan in triumph. 'Either yer do business with me or there won't be anywhere for yer to come back to—you and yer WIFE,' she scoffed, packing a world of incredulity, hatred, and envy into the last word.

At that, another head appeared at the window, several inches above the widow's vibrating bun. It was a long, haggard face, with high cheekbones, a scarlet mouth, and one eye just visible through cascading hair. It spoke with a voice as far below the other's as its position in space was higher.

'You'll have to come up, Ed,' it croaked. 'She's got us where she wants us. Who's that you've got with you?'

Without a word Froulish shambled into the building and began to climb the ladder which led to the upper floor. Charles, tense with excitement, followed. Before he was half-way up the ladder he had occasion to wish that he had been cautious and allowed Froulish to get right up before beginning to climb, for the storm of abuse that broke round the latter's head as soon as he poked it up above floor level was so intense that for a dizzy instant it seemed likely that he would release the ladder and slide down helplessly. However, after a short and perilous pause, he dragged himself up the remaining rungs and stood safely within the room. Charles would have followed, but the sight that greeted him when his head cleared the floorboards was such as to freeze him to the ladder.

The room was large, occupying about half the length of the shed. Three windows illuminated one wall, and, since they lacked several panes, ventilated it also. In one corner was a large old-fashioned bed, evidently picked up in a junk shop; it was heaped with clothes and, for some reason, piles of newspaper. In another corner was a stove, and beside it a rough shelf holding saucepans, a few plates and cups, and some tins of food. Between the two biggest windows, in what was evidently the place of honour, stood the only solid piece of furniture in the room—a substantial oak table, with two drawers underneath it. On it was a typewriter half concealed by a mass of papers. The litter that cluttered the rest of the room was pushed carefully away from this shrine. Charles felt a surge almost of awe. This was the dwelling of a dedicated man.

At the moment the dedicated man was shrinking back against his table feebly trying to fend off the old vixen who owned this palace. She had grasped him by both lapels, and, with her wizened face almost touching his fat, damp one, was squalling her refrain.

'Not another hour! *Not—another*—HOUR do you stay in this'—she could hardly say 'house'—'do you stay 'ere without paying my rent. Two weeks overdue! You may have yer 'ead full of fine ideas, you may be able to live on air and big talk, but the rest of us 'ave to pay our way—and pay it with MONEY!'

She was drawing breath for the next instalment when she felt a sharp tap on the shoulder. Charles was standing beside her with his wallet in readiness. All the fear he might once have felt when confronted by this toothless virago had utterly vanished from his ken. He no longer came of the class that treated women with deference; he was her superior in physical strength, and he had the means to pay her what she was owed.

'Two weeks overdue,' he said curtly. 'And you're charging a guinea a week, is that right?'

'What's it to you if I am? These—' the widow was beginning, but he put his wallet back in his pocket and turned away in so loutish a manner that she realized that she was dealing with one of her own stamp and would have to talk sense. So she said simply, 'Yes.'

Charles, still with his back to her, opened his wallet and got out three pound notes. To these he added a half-crown and a sixpence from his pocket, and turning, handed them to her.

'There's three. One week in advance. Now leave us in peace.'

She glared at him, and seemed inclined, now that she had her money safe, to give herself the luxury of a little more scolding. So he turned on her with a bullying gesture, and snarled, 'You can go down the same way as you came up.'

In silence, the widow departed. Peace returned, seeping in with the summer air through the broken windows, radiating from the silent typewriter on Froulish's table.

The August evening sunshine slanted on to Froulish's matted locks as he sat pounding on his machine, while Betty stood like some gaunt bird, brooding over the saucepan that spluttered on top of the stove. Charles leaned back in utter contentment, a glass of beer at his elbow, and watched them. Inwardly he felt, as he had felt so often in the past month, a surge of delight that formed itself, silently, into the words:

'It's working! It's working better than I ever thought it would!'

Nothing showed so clearly the wisdom of his new policy of taking life as it came, as this miraculous stumbling upon a ready-made *ménage*. It answered perfectly to his simple needs; while neither comfortable nor clean, it served as a place to store his few possessions, to take his meals, and to sleep in at night. The notion that Home was an idea to be respected, an object to be slaved for, did not trouble him; he had cast it aside with the other relics of his upbringing.

'Supper's ready, if you wouldn't mind laying the table, Charles,' came Betty's deep croak. As he obediently rose to spread clean newspapers on the upturned packing-case, and put out three plates and an assortment of cutlery, Charles realized that these were the first words any of them had spoken since he came in an hour ago. They seemed from the first to have dispensed with speech; for different reasons, none of the three felt the need of conversation. Froulish was preoccupied, moodily silent except when one of his dormant grievances happened to be aroused, when he became vehement and oratorical. Betty was too stupid to wish for conversation, and too much wedded to her *femme fatale* manner to keep up the normal chatter of the silly young woman. Charles was physically tired and contented when he returned after his day's work, and was in any case full of thoughts which neither of his companions would have understood or wished to share.

They drew up their chairs, Froulish merely swivelling his round from the writing-table, and Betty brought over the saucepan from the stove. Her cookery was of the simplest; it consisted merely of mixing together in her one saucepan every kind of food available, and subjecting the mixture to the uncertain heat of the paraffin flame. It seemed to work, and, if there were occasional failures, Froulish never noticed what he was eating and Charles was always hungry.

Even as they sat so close together, almost touching, the three seemed remarkably oblivious of one another's presence. Charles realized for the first time how odd it was. Betty sat opposite him, hunched on a soap-box in her baggy slacks and a dirty flowered smock, peering abstractedly through her cascading hair at the newspaper under her plate; she was trying to read it upside down. Froulish, slumped in the only comfortable chair, scowled abstractedly into his plate, twitching and dropping food into his lap and on to the floor. The two seemed to have absolutely no contact; she never asked him about his work, and he would talk of nothing else. Yet he knew that they were happy together; it could not be said of either of them that they were capable of being in love, as most human beings know it; their natures did not permit it, his being too self-centred and hers too bovine. Yet to both the idea of a life which did not revolve round some kind of *liaison* would have seemed fantastic, and the suggestion insulting. The traditions of the 'Bohemian' artistic life, as lived in the Latin quarters of English industrial cities, were too strong to be questioned. One felt that they had not singled each other out, but merely come together by chance, and stuck.

At first Charles had anticipated a good deal of embarrassment in the situation of a *ménage à trois*. He had arranged for his bedroom to be at the other end of the loft, and had fixed a second ladder from the yard so that if he returned late at night he might be able to get to it without entering their main living-quarters, where Froulish and Betty slept. He had also felt rather nervous in Betty's presence for the first few days; he had little experience of the particular type of slut she represented, and was afraid that if given any encouragement she might offer him a share in her favours—the last thing he wanted either in the present or in any foreseeable future.

He need not have worried. Betty seemed wholly wrapped up in Froulish. While taking no apparent notice of him for days on end, she gave so little attention to anything else that Charles was finally convinced that this was the case. She had no recreations, and, except for half-an-hour's shopping each morning, never even went out, except on the one day a week when she absented herself on a visit to some vaguely-defined relative in the neighbourhood. As for the elaborate pains he took to safeguard their privacy, they were repaid with an attitude of mingled amusement and indifference. Froulish even unbent so far as to inform him that his trouble was unnecessary and that if he did chance to come in at night he would find them peacefully sleeping, since most of what he chose to describe as 'the funny stuff' took place in the afternoon when Charles was out. All in all, it was obvious that the item he had often placed at the head of his undergraduate list of topics to be thought over and got straight—'Sex'—was still capable of being coolly thought over; he was not going to be rushed into any decisions. And for the moment, emotionally satisfied and physically tired by his work, he felt no need of action in that sphere.

On the whole, money was his biggest worry. After his triumphant beginning, when to earn a few shillings had seemed miraculous, he had soon discovered that the town was already quite well provided with window-cleaners, who had cornered the really profitable markets—the big stores, hotels, and so forth—leaving only the residential quarters. And even here it was noticeable that most householders seemed to have decided to do without professional care for their windows. How often he crunched his way up the gravel drive to some prosperous-looking house, with two cars in the garage, only to have the door-bell answered by the lady of the house—evidently there were no servants—and to be told that they 'already had a regular window-cleaner'! He knew who that regular window-cleaner was: it was Daddy on his afternoon off from managing the bank.

Even worse than the shortage of work was his constant feeling of being an outlaw, on the run from an unseen but powerful organization that sought to crush him. He knew nothing about his fellow window-cleaners; he had never had the opportunity to learn a reliable fact about any kind of manual worker; but he had always gathered that they belonged to sinister societies known as Unions, and that anyone who tried to earn a living with his hands without the blessing of the Union was in a very dangerous position. Whenever he saw in the distance another figure wheeling a cart with a ladder and buckets, he fled in panic down the nearest turning, taking it for granted that any other window-cleaner could feel nothing for him but hatred and resentment. In spite of this it never entered his head to make any move towards joining the Union or regularizing his position; that would have meant official enrolment as a member of the working class, and his aim was to be outside the class structure altogether.

Nevertheless, there were lean weeks when he was very glad of Betty's 'allowance'. This was £2 10s. a week, and it seemed never to dry up. It was, he gathered, given to her by an elderly maiden aunt, living about twelve miles away. The old lady must have been decidedly eccentric, for, while the supply never dried up, she always insisted on Betty's calling to see her once a week, when she handed the money over in cash. On the day this happened, Charles and Froulish usually took any money that remained from the week's budget and spent it on a drinking bout, so that she returned, at midnight or later, to a penniless household. Her 'allowance', though too small to leave a margin and thus unable to prevent difficult situations such as the one Charles had originally found them in, was sufficient to keep them going in the bleak spells when Charles's weekly earnings came to less than a pound. It was curious to reflect that, but for his meeting with these down-and-outs, he would never have been able to continue in his new life.

And he wanted to continue in it, for he passionately prized it, and honestly thought that no humiliation could overtake him now that he earned his bread at an honest, useful craft that he had taught himself without being helped, and minded his own business, and looked the world in the eyes.

Wherever could he have got hold of such an idea?

III

Froulish did not often leave the loft; a week or more might see him go no further than the impromptu wash-house in the yard below. But sometimes he went out for long solitary walks, and on this Saturday afternoon Charles, settling down in the warmest corner for an after-lunch nap, was not surprised to see the novelist struggling into his tattered overcoat.

'I suppose you go out for these walks of yours to get ideas,' he said.

'Ideas, nothing,' sneered Froulish. 'All you people ever think about is ideas. I suppose it never struck you that in a work that has a certain chromatic range—that is, chromatic, somatic, vatic, any of the catch-words you prefer—different physical states are necessary in the artist at different times.'

'You mean there are some passages you can only write when you're tired, or hungry, or have a cold in the head?'

'More or less, yes,' said Froulish seriously. 'I have to write six pages expressive of intense weariness just now. So I'm going out to get physically tired. Not nervously, because the passage is supposed to have a certain repose: muscular fatigue is what I need. I shall walk at least ten miles and then write this evening.'

Betty said, 'And when you've made yourself ill I suppose I'll have to look after you.' She looked at him morosely. 'You big ape, Ed, you silly big bastard,' she said in a voice that Charles had not heard before. It was hoarsely caressing: her mating call. With a start he realized that some kind of genuine emotion must be forming in the breast of this knobbly slattern.

'Why don't you come out and clean windows with me? I'll make you tired,' he said to Froulish.

'If that's meant as a joke it's pretty corny,' was the writer's only rejoinder as he clambered painfully down the ladder. His overcoat reached to his ankles. He must have taken it from a big scarecrow.

When he had gone, Charles dozed, smoked, and sprawled. Betty sat dully and quietly opposite him, engaged in some incomprehensible work with a needle. She seemed to be sewing lengths of old sacking together. Perhaps Froulish needed a scarf. At four o'clock she put the kettle on the paraffin stove, and Charles sat forward, happy and lazy, anticipating a cup of tea. This was peace, this was comfort.

Footsteps clacked across the courtyard; not Froulish's shuffle, but a brisker tread. A man's voice mumbled. A woman's voice sounded clear and bell-like.

'No, I think this is the place. Probably up in that loft. Anyway, let's go up.'

Charles looked in alarm at Betty. A change had come over her. She was sitting upright, quivering and tense, like a gun dog pointing. But instead of happy eagerness she was registering hatred and anxiety.

'What's up, baby?' he asked, surprised into an unwonted familiarity by his concern for her.

'The bitch,' she said slowly.

The head and shoulders of a young woman appeared at the top of the ladder. Fair, short hair in a fringe; a square, determined face with large steady eyes.

'Does Mr. Froulish live here?' the head enunciated clearly.

Something in the calm impudence of the voice penetrated inside Charles and shook him.

Betty did not answer. After a pause Charles said, 'Yes, but he's not in at the moment. Won't you come in and leave a message?'

The young woman climbed up the remaining rungs of the ladder and stood facing them.

'Oh, yes, of course,' she said, looking at Betty as if she were a gall stone on an X-ray plate. 'We've met, haven't we?'

'Once,' said Betty laconically. 'Pity it had to happen twice.'

A young man climbed up the ladder and stood in a curious attitude, half arrogant and half obsequious, by the girl's side. It was George Hutchins.

Charles looked at him sympathetically. He was obviously rather ill at ease. None of the lessons he had learnt in the normal context of his life were of any use in this situation; least of all his canny orderliness and slick social climbing. Charles felt like an ex-convict who goes back to the prison on visiting day and sees the others still there and hates himself for getting pleasure from the comparison between his freedom and their imprisonment. He stared at Hutchins through a grille: you'll never come out, yours is a life sentence. How are they all at home? Nevermind about that. This is your home now.

'Hello, George,' he said. 'Won't you do some introducing? The ladies don't seem to know one another's names.'

'I know her name all right,' said Betty. 'I just don't use bad language, that's all.'

Hutchins swayed slightly on his feet. He was broadshouldered and plump, so that the effect was of a sack of meal on a shifting floor. His red face glistened.

'This is Charles Lumley, June,' he said to the young woman. Charles waited for him to complete the introduction by telling him her name, but some kind of inhibitory tension prevented him. He did not seem able to speak her name. Perhaps he was in love with her.

'I'm June Veeber,' said the girl to Charles. She looked at him gravely and impudently. He had been feeling calm, but suddenly his knee-joints turned to water and he felt glad he was sitting down. Being a window-cleaner, he did not need to stand when introduced to a lady. He was not attractive to women, but nevertheless it had happened to him now and again to receive sultry looks and the rest of the pre-bedroom signals from them. No doubt they had been doing it to keep in practice. No doubt that was what Miss Veeber was doing it for, though in her case he divined that it was probably automatic and involuntary.

He clutched the tattered arms of his chair with damp palms. 'How do you do?' he muttered. She ran her eyes over him. His spine felt like a row of cotton reels strung on a wire. Then the wire became red hot and melted and the cotton reels clattered to the ground.

Betty spat out, 'You don't mean to say you didn't know her already?'

'No,' he said limply, shifting his eyes to her flushed, angry face. She had gone a dull brick red, so that for once the texture of her skin was in harmony with its colour.

'I can't believe it. What did you do with your spare time when you were at the University?'

'I played indoor games,' he muttered idiotically.

'Well, there must have been one you didn't play, or you'd have played it with her. They all did.'

Hutchins stirred restlessly. June Veeber said, frosting the air, 'I came here on business.'

'I never knew you go anywhere for anything else,' said Betty. 'You've been on overtime ever since I knew you.'

'I shall have to ask you to be more courteous,' George Hutchins said to her. His tone implied that it was a good thing June Veeber had a man to look after her. Charles nearly laughed out loud.

'And I shall have to ask you to take a running jump at yourself,' Betty told him. 'If you've come on business, why don't you spill it and go back to the cage?'

'Perhaps I'd better leave a note,' said June Veeber distinctly. 'I hardly feel you could be trusted to hand a message on.'

'Not if it's your usual kind of message. I don't know enough dirty words.'

Charles stood up. 'Look,' he said, 'I'm getting tired of this. I can't offer you a cup of tea or anything, Miss Veeber, because this isn't my home. I'm only the lodger. But if you'll give me your message for Edwin Froulish I'll see he gets it. And stop looking at me like that,' he nearly added.

'I've come on behalf of the Stotwell Literary Society,' she said.

'Of which she is President,' put in Hutchins portentously, feeling himself back on more familiar ground.

'I knew Mr. Froulish slightly at the University,' she went on. 'It was well known that he was working on a remarkable novel. When I heard that he was living here, in'—she glanced at Betty—'in retirement, and getting on with completing it, I thought it would be interesting if he would come and read some passages to us one evening. The next meeting is in five days, next Thursday evening. It isn't much notice, but would you tell him we'll assume he can come unless he telephones me?' She gave him her number. 'We meet at the Girls' High School at eight o'clock.'

Before Charles could answer, Betty croaked, 'All right. That's your message. Now let's see the back of you and your boy-friend as well. Poor fish,' she added venomously, glaring at Hutchins.

'I think she wants you to go,' said Charles apologetically. Hutchins turned and went down the ladder. June Veeber stood for a moment looking from one to the other. Then she said to Betty, 'You really mustn't worry, my dear. I shan't make a pass at him.'

'Why not?' Betty asked. 'He wears trousers, doesn't he?'

They faced each other. The contrast between them was an unforgettable sight: one gaunt, unkempt, trousered, ready to scratch or bite at the drop of a hat, the other sleek, feminine, a purring dynamo with any number of lethal jolts in reserve. Charles felt sorry for Hutchins, sorry for Froulish, and—somehow, obscurely—sorry for himself. Was he really safe? Could he go on standing where they had fallen?

June Veeber got her feet on the ladder and began to climb down it. When she was hidden from the waist down, her breasts seemed unusually pronounced as they jutted above the floor level. Betty bent down so that their faces were close together.

'I've kept my hands off you this time,' she said. 'But don't come back here bringing trouble. I wouldn't know where to store it.'

Without answering the visitor left them.

It was October. The first high wind had filled the gutters with yellow leaves, and it was dusk as Charles pushed his cart homewards that afternoon. His mind still full of Betty's outburst, he wondered whether it would have blown over or whether the atmosphere in the loft would still be tense when he got there; and, being tired, decided to fortify himself with a cup of tea.

'Harry's Snacks' was open. He parked the handcart in the pool of light outside the front window, and went in. Collecting his chipped mug of dark brown swill from the counter, he sat down at the nearest table, heavily, loosely, tired and indifferent to his surroundings. The place was nearly empty.

'Wud that be yoor cart outside?'

The flat Lancashire voice startled him. A thick-set, short man in a cap and muffler, his fallen cheeks indicating near-toothlessness, sat in the corner nearest him.

'Yes, that's my cart,' he said levelly, sustaining his character as the self-sufficient man, giving nothing away, asking for nothing. But the mere fact that he answered was enough to impart a new familiarity to the man's tone when he spoke again.

'Work all on your own, eh?'

'Yes.'

'Like it best that way?'

'Much the best.'

'Find it pays better, eh?'

Charles stood up, on his way to the door. 'I said I liked it best, let's leave it at that.'

But the stocky man was on his feet, too, with a note of urgency in his flat confidential voice.

'Nay, nay, don't get in a 'uff. A've got a perfectly sensible reason for me questions. Sit down. 'Ave another cup.'

'I don't want another cup.'

'It's on me,' said the stocky man with the air of explaining a difficult point and making all plain; the implication being that no one in his right mind will refuse a cup of tea if it is free, even if he has already had enough.

So Charles was chained to the table by another scalding half-pint. In his old life he would have felt obliged to sip it slowly, and give the donor another fifteen minutes of his company out of politeness, as a way of paying for the tea. Now he saw no shame in draining it immediately and starting for the door. But it was too hot. And even his new code would not allow him to walk out and leave it untouched. He was trussed.

'A'll come straight to t'point,' began the stocky man, silently accepting a Woodbine from the tin Charles held out. 'A've seen you going up and down with your cart and things. And A've said to meself, "That feller's working a one-man business. And very nicely he's doing. But," A've said to meself, "he'll never get no farther." '

'What if I don't want to get any farther?'

The other smiled toothlessly at this pleasantry. It needed no answer. It was just a joke.

'So do you know what else A said to meself?'

'How could I? I wasn't there at the time.'

'A said,' and he nodded his head deliberately in time to the words, ' "What that feller needs is a partner. A partner as could help to put it on a bigger futting." '

Charles sat back and stared at him sourly. He did not reply, for several reasons. For one thing, while his soul recoiled from the idea of admitting any other person inside the stockade of his independence, it was also true that the idea had begun, lately, to cross his mind more and more frequently. His clientèle was still rather small; new work was slow in presenting itself, and the coveted 'contracts' simply had not materialized. A partner who could tap fresh sources of work, and help him to carry it out, certainly had seemed the best solution.

'A bigger futting,' the toothless man repeated with grave self-satisfaction. Woodbine smoke poured out of his mouth and nose. Charles still did not speak.

'Now look at it this way,' said his adviser, leaning forward. 'You're yung. You've not 'ad a lot of ecksperience. When it come to running a business, you're all right while it's just a matter o' taking the cart round and doing a winder here and a winder there. But you can't stay like that for ever.'

For ever! But the whole idea of doing anything *for ever*, of thinking in terms of *for ever*, was something that belonged to his old life, not his new. This Manchester voice was speaking the wrong language.

'Now, Ah could do a lot to 'elp. A'm not a local man'; there was no need to state this, but, like most men with strong regional accents, he was oblivious of it; 'but A know a good many Stotwell folks. A've been 'ere a yeer or two.'

'To put it in a nutshell,' said Charles slowly, 'You're willing to come in with me because you think my business could be built up.'

'That's it. That's just it. Now, what d'ye think of the idea?'

'It beats me, that's what I think about it.' Something, perhaps the unstilled protests of his inward soul, caused Charles to speak defiantly.

'Beats yer? What beats yer?'

'I can't make it out, that's why. Here you are, at a loose end for some reason, and you decide to take up window-cleaning, and then instead of starting off on your own, you decide to join up with me. But why? I've got nothing to offer you—no money, next to no equipment, not much trade. What do you stand to gain?'

'It's not what Ah stand to gain. It's what we both stand to gain,' said the stocky man with sudden energy, crushing out his Woodbine. 'Ah'm a business man at 'eart. We all are, up in Mannchester. And the essence o' business,' he repeated the phrase with great emphasis, 'the essence of business is to com-*bine*. Suppose Ah 'ad started on me own? There'd just a been two of us cutting each other's throats, and neither of us able to expand at all. Besides, you've got it all wrong. A didn't sit down and think to meself, "A'll go in for winder-cleaning," and then look around for an opening. A did it t'other way round. A was at a loose end, as you call it, and A looked round for somebody as could use my organizing ability and initiative.'

The last few words were so obviously the result of brooding over the 'Let Me Be Your Father' type of success advertisement, that Charles felt an acute twinge of distrust. The man was a curious mixture, and besides, Charles had little or no experience of the type he represented. A Lancashire accent, to him, was something associated with music-hall humour. And yet it was always some special kind of humour, he suddenly realized; always the flat, puncturing kind that relished an attack on the pretentious or the far-fetched. The humour of practical men. And of Philistines.

Well, what of it? He needed help, and here it was offered. A young man running a window-cleaning business single-handed couldn't have all the world to choose from when it came to finding a partner.

'It's a deal,' he said seriously.

The stocky man's face creased into what was, after all, a very attractive grin, in spite of the yellow stumps it revealed. (Why did the canines resist decay longer than the molars or incisors? Charles had often wondered before.)

The stocky man held out a square hand. The finger nails were ragged and black.

'Ern Ollershaw,' he said.

Charles took the hand and gravely pronounced his own name. They were partners.

They were to go back to Ern's lodgings to begin detailed arrangements. Ern moved off to the back of the café, either to go out to the lavatory or to have a word with Harry or some member of his family, and Charles, rather than wait any longer in the greasy atmosphere, stepped outside. His cart was waiting by the kerb, and he moved over towards it. Suddenly a violent shove carried him almost off his feet. Staggering, he crashed into a dark doorway next to the entrance to Harry's. A huge hand gripped the front of his jacket. A heavy body leaned against him, making it hard to breathe. A bald head gleamed in the lamplight.

'Just a minute, son. Feel like getting yer bloody neck broke?'

Silence.

'Answer. D'yer feel like getting yer bloody neck broke?'

Why didn't Ern come? 'No.'

'Then keep yer bloody mouth shut. That's your cart, ain't it?'

The second time he had been asked that question! But this time he couldn't please himself whether to answer or not.

'Yes, it's mine.'

'It's yours. And yer run a nice little winder-cleaning business, all on yer own. Well, listen to me. See this?'

The hand that was not gripping him was bunched. Something gleamed palely on the fist. It so happened that Charles had never seen a knuckle-duster before, but he recognized it. The bald-headed man considerately turned it this way and that, so that he could get a good look at it. The brass studs reflected dim rays of light from the yellow street-lamp. It made him think of murder.

'Just keep on takin' the bread out of other folk's mouths. The first time I catch up with yer, yer'll get this. The second time, yer'll get yer bloody neck broke.'

Footsteps. Someone was coming along the pavement.

'Keep still.'

The knuckle-duster pressed against Charles's windpipe. It was dark in the doorway. The man who happened to walk past saw nothing. Either nothing, or just two drunks affectionately leaning in a doorway together.

Where was Ern?

Charles did not think of himself as a coward. Since reaching adult life he had not actually been involved in a fight, but he had always imagined that if it ever came he would give a good account of himself. But then he had imagined it differently. His mental picture had been of a clear space, two men facing each other, fists whirling and plenty of light to see by. Not of a dark doorway with his arms crushed against his sides, a vile breath forcing its way up his nostrils, and a knuckle-duster held against his throat.

'Go back where yer bloody came from,' advised the bald-headed man earnestly. 'Yer won't last a week from now if yer don't.'

The door of Harry's opened.

'Keep still,' and the knuckle-duster in the throat again.

It was Ern. Glancing neither to right nor left, he stood for a moment outside Harry's, then began to walk with an even pace, towards and past them. Charles's heart stopped beating, from sheer disappointment and fear. Then, when Ern was exactly in the right spot, he slid his arm, still without looking, round the bald man's face, forcing his head back viciously. The bald man could either let go of Charles's coat and let himself be dragged backwards, or have his neck broken. He let go. Ern still did not look at him.

The bald man suddenly spun round in a violent twist, flailing his fist through the air. He wanted to smash the knuckle-duster into the back of Ern's head. In the same instant Ern crouched and drove his shoulder into the bald man's stomach. Their combined weight and impetus sank the shoulder sickeningly far in, and the bald man hung tottering, winded. His stomach muscles were contracted with the agony into a mass of iron; he could not even retch. Ern's fist smashed into his face. He fell down.

Charles moved out of the doorway, shivering. He wanted to go, to be somewhere where they could sit down and be quiet. Ern was nearly ready to move off, but he had not quite finished with the bald man yet. Stepping over to where the knuckle-duster gleamed palely on the outstretched right fist, he stamped on it with his heavy boot.

As they walked away, Ern said calmly, 'He'd better get that dooster off quick if he wants it off in the next week or so. Before that 'and swells up good and proper.'

Charles did not say anything.

'And so, for our first meeting of the winter session,' said June Veeber's bell-like voice, making the words sound like an invitation to some kind of orgy, 'we welcome Mr. Froulish, who will read extracts from his Work in Progress.'

She sat down. George Hutchins jammed his chair against hers and surreptitiously took her hand under cover of a newspaper.

Froulish leaned forward, his face a blind, twitching mask. He jerked his arm and knocked over his glass in a gesture so unnatural it must surely have been intentional—yet for that very reason Charles put it down to genuine nervousness.

Everyone waited for him to speak. He stared at them, fingering the top sheet of his pile of typescript, jerking his left leg spasmodically. A man cleared his throat with a noise like a cavalry carbine being fired in a railway tunnel. It was the society's bore: Mr. Gunning-Forbes, senior English master at the local grammar school. Charles had once cleaned his windows.

'Ladies and gentlemen,' Froulish whispered hoarsely. Smoke

began to curl upwards from where he had dropped his cigarette on to the hearthrug. Hutchins moved forward officiously and stamped on the smouldering patch.

'I'll start without any preamble by reading the opening paragraphs of the work.'

'What's the title of your book?' demanded Gunning-Forbes suspiciously, resting his hands on the stained knees of his flannels.

'No title,' said Froulish impatiently. 'Just a dark blue binding. No lettering, no title-page.'

'What's the idea of that?' growled the schoolmaster, with increased hostility. 'Thought becomes impossible if things haven't got names. Thought, in fact, *consists*—'

'I should have thought it was obvious,' cried Froulish passionately. 'I should have thought it was axiomatic. No title—impossible to give in a few words any idea of what it's about. About things that *can't* be put in a nutshell. About human life. Just a book—you want to know what it says, you read it and find out. Resisting the idea that things of any importance can be labelled and fitted into categories.'

Gunning-Forbes was on his feet, but June Veeber leaned across and put her hand on his sleeve. He turned and stared at her, then slowly sat down, his steel-rimmed spectacles flashing grimly.

'First few paragraphs,' said Froulish, taking off his collar and tie and throwing them into the fire—surely a contrived effect, but impossible to be certain. 'Nothing to do with the actual *action* of the book. Just a melodic and oblique stroke or semantic preparation.'

'Say that again,' rapped out Gunning-Forbes.

'I said,' Froulish repeated, 'a melodic and oblique stroke or semantic preparation.' There was a silence.

'A king ringed with slings,' began Froulish without more ado, 'a thing without wings but brings strings and sings. Ho, the slow foe! Show me the crow toe I know, a beech root on the beach, fruit of a rich bitch, loot in a ditch, shoot a witch, which foot?'

Hutchins stirred uneasily in his seat.

'Clout bell, shout well, pell-mell about a tout, get the hell out. About nowt. Court log wart hog bought a dog.'

Gunning-Forbes's glasses sparkled with fury. The school-teachers and bank clerks stared in bewilderment. Hutchins caught June Veeber's eye and smiled lasciviously. Charles took deep breaths of cigarette smoke. Froulish droned on.

'Deep in the grass, a cheap farce, glass weeps for Tom Thumb, a bum's dumb chum. That's the end of that part,' Froulish concluded. His audience returned to life. Drooping heads came upright.

'Well, if that's the preamble, what about the story? Why don't you outline the plot?' demanded Gunning-Forbes.

'Outline the what?' sneered Froulish. He seemed itching for a quarrel with the old man.

'The plot. Outline the plot and then read us a few extracts to show how your characters are developed.'

'Don't make me laugh, I've got a split lip,' said Froulish contemptuously. Opposition had braced his fibres: thanks to its tonic effect he was alert, happy, even gay. Gone was the usual neurotic unrest and gloom; he was a living proof that every man is biologically equipped with marvellous reserves of power to be called on when defending what he really believes in. Charles, from his corner, saw the transformation and was humbled, thinking of Betty's ferocious defence of her mate. So much, so much that he had never guessed at!

'Nevertheless, Mr. Froulish,' June Veeber cut in frostily, before the brawl could develop any further, 'do read us some more. Couldn't you pick some passage that illustrates a central theme or tendency of the book?'

'Now you're talking,' replied the novelist, who was quite docile so long as the word 'plot' was not uttered. 'I'll just explain the central situation. Six people are trapped in a lift between two floors of a skyscraper—a musician, a surgeon, a charwoman, a conjurer and his female assistant, and a hunchback carrying a small suitcase.'

'Containing some sandwiches, I hope,' chuckled the local curate. 'They're bound to get hungry before long.'

'You can fill in the details for yourself,' said Froulish, not realizing that the man imagined himself to be joking. 'Where was I? Yes, these six are in the lift. Part of the book consists of a series of flashbacks, every one twice the length of the average novel, over the previous life of each of them. Not their physical lives, just the psychic currents that flowed through them. It's expressed chiefly through patterns of imagery.'

'God help us,' said Gunning-Forbes loudly.

'Meanwhile,' Froulish went on, 'they're trying to send a message to the chief electrician, who lives in the basement, to do something about getting the lift going. At least, there's a door marked "Chief Electrician", but no one's ever seen it open or seen anyone go in or out. Messages have to be written in a ritual code and slipped under the door.'

Gunning-Forbes had begun to take an interest. 'Not a bad touch that,' he commented. 'Illustrate the way the working classes have got above themselves since the war, eh?'

Fortunately Froulish ignored him.

'They don't seem to be able to get a message through. At first they pass the time trying to keep cheerful. The conjurer draws billiard-balls out of the musician's ears, the surgeon diagnoses everyone's physical condition and says what operations he recommends, the charwoman sings Edwardian music-hall songs. The hunchback is the only one who doesn't do anything. He doesn't speak either.'

'Doesn't seem much point in having him there,' from Gunning-Forbes.

'A couple of days pass, and gradually they're being driven mad with hunger and thirst. Finally, when they're in the last stages of exhaustion and despair, the hunchback offers to put them out of their misery. He takes a hand-grenade out of his suitcase. Exploding in that confined space it's quite enough to kill them all. Then they have a long debate as to who shall pull the pin out to make the thing go off. There's a theological point there, among others. The one who does it will be guilty of both suicide and murder.'

He paused. His audience looked at him apathetically. Betty's eyes never wavered from June Veeber's face.

'Finally the conjurer comes to their aid. He *conjures* it out. Makes it jump out without seeming to touch it. Before he could be shown to be guilty of suicide, it would be necessary to *prove* that he'd touched the pin, and that's not possible.'

'Oh, come,' cried the curate from the back row. Froulish, in his stride, ignored him.

'Anyway, now they're all dead. The blast frees the lift, and it drops down to the ground floor. So the corpses are taken out. Naturally, in laying them out, any papers they have about them are removed and studied to help in identification. That's how they find out,' he paused dramatically, 'that the hunchback was the Chief Electrician.'

There was a silence.

'Well, go on,' said Gunning-Forbes encouragingly.

'That's the end,' scowled Froulish.

There was a scraping of chairs.

'So that's your plot, is it?' said Gunning-Forbes judicially. 'D'you want to know what I think of it?'

'No, but you evidently want to tell me.'

'I think it's got the makings of a fairly good yarn, provided of course that you cut out this verbal tomfoolery and make it clean-cut. Except for one bad flaw.'

He waited for Froulish to ask what that was, but the novelist was rolling himself a cigarette and showed no sign of hearing, so he went on.

'That man wouldn't have had a hand-grenade in his suitcase. People don't. It's just not true to life.'

'Couldn't he have been a traveller for a firm that made hand-grenades?' asked the curate. Charles wondered whether he was mad or just drunk.

'Not possible,' Gunning-Forbes shook his head. 'He was supposed to be the Chief Electrician. He couldn't have combined the two jobs. No good novelist would bring in anything as farfetched as that. A course of Thackeray, that's my prescription—soon weed out these little faults. Then you might make some real headway.'

He sat back benevolently. Froulish flushed scarlet. He began to sway backwards and forwards in his chair, feverishly flicking his short fingers: the usual sign that he was violently agitated. Charles held his breath for the outburst. But it was forestalled.

Hutchins had hitherto been mercifully silent, dividing his energies between fawning on the thick-set siren beside him and looking superciliously round the room; but now he decided, evidently, that the time had come for him to put on his act and dazzle the company. He took out a pipe and filled it. Charles could see from the light colour and stringy texture of the tobacco that it was some kind of very mild mixture; he was not surprised, for Hutchins, though needing a pipe for the successful acting of his part, was handicapped by a weak stomach. Even now he did not light the pipe, but stuck it in his mouth, pulled it out again, twiddled it in his fingers, and finally jammed it between his front teeth and spoke in an exaggeratedly precise, high-pitched voice.

'I suppose, Froulish, that what you're doing there is something that might be described by an ordinary chap like me—' he smiled boyishly, to show that they were not to believe him—'as a return to allegory. Would you place yourself in a direct line of descent from Kafka?'

He waited for Froulish's reply with the calm, condescending air of a man who is accustomed to examining ideas and putting them in order, but is nevertheless prepared to have patience with those who habitually leave a mass of tangled loose ends. The young scholar doing a little intellectual slumming.

'No,' replied Froulish shortly. 'My masters are Dante, Spinoza, Rimbaud, Boehme and Grieg.'

Hutchins champed agitatedly on his pipe-stem. His face lost a little of its buoyant expression; he was not sure whether his leg was being pulled, and it was important for him, having entered the lists under the eye of his lady, to come off best.

'Grieg, now that's a very interesting point,' he said. He pointed at Froulish with his pipe. 'What made you put a musician into a list composed otherwise of writers? You may think it's only a small point' ('Not a point at all,' from Gunning-Forbes) 'but what we're all interested in here, is how the minds of chaps like you work. Our own minds,' he smiled again to indicate that they need not think he meant all their minds were as good as his, 'work by the ordinary methods, travel by, I think I could say, the ordinary routes. But chaps like you seem to have discovered, er,' he did not want to say short cuts, it sounded too trite, so ended, 'short-circuits.' Hell, that was wrong. Short-circuits was wrong.

Froulish told Charles afterwards that he been on the point of replying, 'I refer, of course, to Aloysius Grieg, the seventeenth-century Abbot of Helsingfors, author of the *Tractatus Virorum et Angelorum*, and particularly to the spurious third book,' but in fact, he contented himself with saying stiffly, 'Of course, I didn't expect everyone to pick that point up, though I expect most people would see it all right. I mean, of course, Grieg's tone colours, and particularly his handling of the wood-wind. I regard the vowels "e" and "u" as the wood-winds of the verbal orchestra, and an accurate count would reveal, as you doubtless noticed, that they predominate over the rest in what I might call the slow movements of my work.'

Hutchins summoned all his dwindling reserves. June Veeber was looking at him in a way that did not help much.

'Well, no, I can't say I did notice,' he said, jolly and aggressive, the manner of the don when he tells you he does not understand something so as to convey that he thinks you a fool for pretending you do, 'you chaps do tend to give the rest of us credit for perceptions about your work that we don't, I think, always have.' He looked round the room for support, but they stared at him stonily; the discussion had gone on too long. 'Was that, for instance, the bit you read us just now—was that a slow movement?'

'No,' said Froulish calmly. 'It was a cadenza.'

Meeting Hutchins's bewildered gaze, he stared at him triumphantly, at the same time taking out a pocket comb and running it through his hair. A shower of dandruff was plainly visible under the electric light.

June Veeber rose. She was determined, evidently, to end the proceedings before the society should be permanently crippled. Besides, she wanted to get George Hutchins by himself and give him a few remarks on making a fool of himself in public. June's young men were kept up to the mark.

'Coffee will be served in a few minutes—Miss Wotherspoon, would you be frightfully kind and do your usual? Thank you so much.' Miss Wotherspoon's 'usual' was to trudge down to the school kitchen, make the coffee, and carry it up. 'And meanwhile I'm sure we all thank Mr. Froulish very much for a most stimulating evening, and we look forward with great interest to the time when his book will be published.'

'You look forward a damn long time, then,' returned Froulish curtly. 'This is only the first draft. The thing probably won't be finished for fifteen years. My name isn't—Trollope.'

He pronounced the last word with so much deliberation, and looked so fixedly at June Veeber, that Charles could have sworn the insult was intentional. His feeling seemed to be shared; startled by a sudden low neighing sound, he looked round. Betty was laughing.

IV

Winter had come, and with it the pace of life had slowed down. Wheeling his cart out every morning, Charles felt solid, respectable and habit-ridden. Of course, working with Ern had a lot to do with it, for Ern had introduced method and regularity into the business. Everything was organized. Part of the time they worked separately, but for 'big jobs'—shops, hotels, or tall buildings that required complicated ladder-work—they combined. And at the end of each day, whether they had been together or not, they met for a formal sharing-out of the money they had earned, and a close investigation into whether it was the full amount they had reckoned on when planning the work in advance.

'Isn't it rather a fag seeking each other out every evening?' said Charles once, tentatively, after a two-mile trudge back to Harry's from an outlying job. But Ern had been firm.

'Not on yoor life. It's the first principle of runnin' a business like this. Quick turn-over, quick share-out. Level it up while there's nobbat a few bob in it.'

'But surely we can trust each other?'

'Why shudd we?' Ern had returned with something like a sudden vehemence. 'What do you want to go trustin' *me* for? You don't 'ardly know me from Adam.'

This was unanswerable. Not only did Charles know nothing about his partner, he seemed never to get any closer to him as the months went by. Ern was not taciturn; he talked freely, commenting on all that went on around them, elaborating new ideas for the running of 'the business' (for so, under his guidance, Charles came to think of it), and, as they sat over their sandwiches and tea in Harry's, reading out passages from the newspaper with comments.

'Spindle Operatives to Go Slow,' he would announce; 'never knew 'em do anything else. Earl Leaves Estate to Actress—"My Dear Friend." Well, I expect she 'ad to work 'ard enuff for it. 'Ere's a good wun. Swans Served in Restaurant. Chef Denies Knowledge. T'menu must a been in French.' And so he would ramble on. But the talk was never personal. This suited Charles. He had always resisted the idea of collaboration, for he had not dared to hope for a partner who would be without the simple, heavy curiosity of the provincial working class; he had imagined himself being pumped, and dreaded having his dead past raked up as a spy in an enemy country dreads interrogation. For the rest of his life he was to travel without a passport, and it was important not to be held for questioning.

Ern, however, was perfect. Not once, in the months during which they worked harmoniously together, did he ask how Charles came to be earning his living by cleaning windows. Nor did he volunteer any reason why he himself came to be out of a job, or say what had brought about his decision that evening in Harry's. He seemed to regard it as the most natural thing in the world that they should do this work and do it together. And since the episode of the bald-headed man, Charles was in no mood to disturb what seemed to him an excellent arrangement. Nothing like that had happened since; a cautious investigation had indicated that the bald man was neither a window-cleaner himself nor likely to have been incited to his action by one. He was just a rough, well-known locally, who had never had a job for long and seldom stayed out of gaol for twelve months together. His attack on Charles had probably been either inspired by a fit of semi-insane jealousy or part of some roundabout scheme for extorting money out of him. He did not represent a permanent menace, particularly as for the next four months he could be seen every Tuesday and Friday attending the Out-Patients' Department of the local hospital with a dirty bandage over his right hand.

And so, while admitting to himself that Ern was a mystery, Charles valued the bond of non-inquisitiveness between them.

And it comforted him, too, to know that if Ern should ever start asking questions, he could ask a few embarrassing ones in his turn. What was a capable, confident artisan in early middle life doing in a back-water like Stotwell, scratching a living at window-cleaning? And why, after each day's work, did he go straight back to his dingy lodgings, never (after the first time) inviting Charles there, and never emerging till it was time to work again? Was it for pure love of the life of a robot?

Christmas came and went. The days lengthened microscopically, and became colder and wetter. Apart from this, nothing altered. Charles began to wonder what had happened to his life. Regularity seemed to have claimed it.

'What you need is a change,' said Froulish one evening, sitting back and looking at him attentively for the first time for weeks. 'Your life's too narrow, that's your trouble.'

He himself had not been out of the loft for more than a couple of hours at a time since he first moved into it, and neither given, nor received, hospitality. But then he was a dedicated man. He did not need a change.

'Too narrow,' he repeated, dragging his fingers through his matted hair.

Charles was impressed. If the self-absorbed monomaniac had noticed a difference in him, and been moved to comment and advice, it must be serious indeed. He determined to irrigate his life a little. The dismal winter months must be made to pass more cheerfully.

So the next evening he set himself the task of stretching the resources of his limited wardrobe as far as they would go in the direction of everyday respectability. The dark suit he had been wearing when he first entered his new life was, fortunately, not too worn; he had soon given up wearing it for work. And he had a shirt and tie that were scarcely worn at all. His shoes were old and cracked, but they would pass muster, and he had nothing else except the Wellingtons he wore on his daily round. Dressed once more in the uniform of the class he had renounced, he surveyed himself critically in Betty's looking-glass. Apart from the fact that his frame had broadened, giving him something of the characteristic heavy-shouldered carriage of the manual worker, he still looked much the same. A cheap haircut had left him with an ugly matchstick-length crop, but that was the only class badge he was wearing, and it was not a conspicuous one.

Thus equipped for a raid into enemy territory, he pushed through the swing doors of the town's Grand Hotel at dinner-time, determined to live at the rate of a thousand a year for the next few hours. Although he had, on occasion, cleaned the hotel's windows, no one recognized him; nor did he feel any fear that they would; and in any case they could not turn him out. Settling himself near the imitation log fire in the Oak Lounge, he sipped at a glass of good sherry and broke into a packet of expensive cigarettes. This was enjoyment.

The door of the Oak Lounge swung softly open on its easy spring, and a smooth, fleshy man padded in. He was plump, but not yet running to seed; aged about forty-five to fifty. His well-cut dark suit, neat bow tie and horn-rimmed glasses marked him as a prosperous business man of some kind. A few years earlier he had had luxurious fair hair, and he still had most of it now. He held the door open with a soft, gentle hand.

A girl came in. She was small and dark, miraculously neat, with tiny fragile bones and an oval face. Her clothes were expensive and simple, with the kind of simplicity that carries within itself a hint of the extravagant. Huge dark eyes smiled up at the smooth man. Charles knew that he would never get that smile out of his mind again.

She sat down on the other side of the fireplace while the smooth man went over to the bar for their drinks. Charles realized that he must swivel his eyes away from her face. To continue staring at her would be sheer impertinence. He tried to drag his gaze away, but the muscles would not move. He was paralysed into stillness with his eyes staring fixedly.

She must have felt it, for she slowly turned her dark head, looked at him coolly for an instant, and then, without hurry but with utter finality, turned away again. Charles felt sick. He hated himself for his mawkish behaviour, but could do nothing to alter it. He lowered his eyes to his glass, still half full of that good sherry which, a moment before, had been giving him so much pleasure. He drank it quickly. It tasted like urine. His expensive cigarette smouldered between the fingers of his other hand. He threw it savagely into the fireplace.

The smooth man brought two glasses over and set them down. In agony, Charles got to his feet and started for the door. He knew he ought to get out of the hotel altogether, to breathe the cold night air and feel the hard pavement under his feet. But the obstinate demon that had forced him to keep his eyes trained on that oval face, forced him now to stumble along to the dining-room. As long as he stayed in the hotel, there was a chance that he might see her again.

He rationalized it as pride. He had come here for dinner, and he would *have* dinner. Still, he had the sense not to keep up any imbecile pretence of actually enjoying it. His pride, hoping to conceal the still more unpalatable truth, told him to see the thing in terms of a face-saving ordeal. Mechanically he ordered random dishes from the menu; the wine-waiter placed the list before him, and he forced himself to look through it and choose a sound claret. Ritual gestures, to clutch at the rags of his self-respect! All the time he felt certain that he would never again see any experience as meaningful unless it were connected in some way with the girl in the Oak Lounge. He recalled, wryly, the callow scorn he had once poured on the irrational and 'romantic' obsessions—the death-wish, the dream-world, love at first sight, and the rest—for, like all the immature, he had looked down on romanticism for its immaturity.

How many more of his failures in comprehension was he doomed to expiate? Did this happen to everyone, that their errors swung back upon them and crushed them? He lifted his eyes questioningly, as if some answer to his problems might be written in code on the wall, but they met only the expressionless eyes of the waiter who was coming over to serve him with a dish of ice cream and plums, though he had ordered cheese and biscuits.

The ice cream tasted of soap. The plums were sour. Charles pushed the dish aside with a despairing gesture; despairing because he knew that even if the food had been delicious he would have been unable to swallow it. His throat muscles had been tightening and tightening until, by now, he would have felt unequal to swallowing a sip of water. His mouth was dry. His heart hammered. Dragging out one of his expensive cigarettes, he lit it, and took a great draught of the smoke. Feeling a little better as the nicotine muffled the keenness of his nervous anguish, he exhaled and watched the smoke spread out like a fan in front of his face. Through it he saw the door open gently. The smooth man, reflecting the shaded lights in a benign radiance from his glasses, padded in. He held the door open again. Again the girl walked through. Again she looked up at him with big dark eyes, and again she smiled. But this time she spoke.

'Thank you, Uncle'—he heard her clearly.

As she passed his table Charles saw that there was no ring on any of her fingers.

Somehow he must have paid his bill and got out, because, although he remembered nothing about it, he was back in the loft later that evening. His companions did not seem to notice anything unusual about him. Froulish asked him if he felt better for having broken the monotony.

'"Rector Denies Assault Charge",' Ern read out from the crumpled newspaper. '"Choir Outing Allegations." Give 'em summat to sing about.' He paused, then looked up. 'You 'aven't been yourself lately, Charley. Anything on your mind?'

'Oh, just what it says in the advertisements,' Charles jerked out with a feeble attempt at lightness. 'A traffic jam somewhere in those twenty-eight feet of digestive tract. I'm going to get myself a guinea's worth of pills.'

He could see that Ern, though forbearing to pursue the topic, was not convinced, and for a moment regretted that he had rejected the invitation to confide in the older man, in whose look and voice there had been a new hint of gentleness and concern. But the regret passed; nothing must shatter the sacred rule of silence between them on personal topics. And in any case, what was there to confide that would not make him look absurd? 'I saw a girl having dinner with her uncle in the Grand ten days ago, and I can't forget about her.' He might as easily have explained to

Mrs. Smythe, that morning in the lodging-house, why it was that he had no job.

It was not that he had succumbed without putting up a fight. On the very first morning after the fatal vision, he had set out briskly in the frosty air, determined to immerse himself in the simple realities that had already saved him from so much folly. When lunch-time came and he realized with a shock that he had not succeeded for five minutes together in banishing the image of that small dark head, he had put it down to a temporary derangement. But that evening it was just as bad. And the next morning, and the next evening, and every morning and evening till he felt, in despair, that his carefree life was being poisoned. All its pleasures had become savourless. As he went about his work, or sat smoking in the loft of an evening, or reeled back from the weekly drinking-bout with Froulish, a voice inside his head would nag, 'Yes, but this isn't bringing you any nearer to HER'. And what else had any meaning?

And yet, how empty was any aspiration, however faint, in her direction! He did not even know who she was or where she lived. And it would profit him nothing to find out. Whoever she was, she clearly moved in circles that demanded money as a condition of entry—money, good clothes, social position. Men he despised, men like Robert Tharkles and Hutchins, would stand more chance than he did. Any crawling vermin who happened to have his pockets well lined could leave him standing in the race. He began to think increasingly about money. The poison was doing its work.

Still he fought back, and there were even moments when he felt, fleetingly, the old symptoms of vitality and spiritual health. He threw himself into his practical concerns, toiling hugely at the job, and perpetually carrying out improvements in the heating and lighting of the loft, till in the end it was almost comfortable. When the thick, smelly heat of the oil-stove, and the mellow glow of the well-trimmed lamps, made the loft friendly on a stormy winter night, and he could stretch out his legs and allow his mind to sink into vacancy, while Betty sat patching up some garment and Froulish dozed in his corner or bent over his stack of typescript, Charles almost felt secure.

Almost, but never quite, even at his best moments. And his worst were unspeakable. Sometimes the sense of desolation would flow over him so deeply that his being would cry out, not for relief, not for the achievement of his desire, but merely for the choice of some other kind of suffering. How he would have welcomed a chance to exchange his mental torment for some painful physical ailment!

At last, on the evening of the day of Ern's question, he capitulated. He put his best clothes on again and went off to the Grand Hotel to see if he could find anyone to give him information about her.

It proved surprisingly easy. The barman in the Oak Lounge readily accepted a couple of gins and, in return, came out with the facts.

That was Mr. Roderick and his niece. They were often in here. Mr. Roderick was managing director of a local factory; he had only recently moved into the district, after having travelled extensively on behalf of the firm and managed their affairs in America and on the Continent. The niece was an orphan, whom Mr. Roderick, as befitted a rich, benevolent bachelor, had brought up, and now that her education was over, she lived in his house. Charles left the hotel saddened, and yet strangely elated. The hopelessness of his position was underlined still further; he could never gain access to Mr. Roderick's social sphere, and certainly not to his house; besides, the barman had indicated that the Rodericks spent much of their time in London and Paris, Switzerland and Capri. Whence, then, the curious elation? Partly because the very futility of his task stimulated a curious beating rhythm in the depths of his mind, hammering out faintly but persistently, 'Stranger things *have* happened. Stranger things *have* happened.'

Snow fell, froze, thawed, and fell again. The aching darkness within him matched that without, as the dormant seed of intoxicating joy in his spirit paralleled the motionless hidden forces of the spring, waiting their turn. Experimenting with various anodynes—drink, the cinema, detective stories—Charles found that the only solace with any power to assuage the fever that gripped him was to lose his identity in lonely contemplation of nature.

So the old sentimental rubbish was true after all! Once again he found a grim amusement in the ironic lessons that life was teaching him. The intolerable prosings of Wordsworth, and the namby-pamby dribblings of Shelley and the others, contained a truth that stood out as vital and important now that he was really in trouble, when the 'advanced' writings he had once admired faded and dissolved from his mind.

He had acquired a rust-eaten bicycle, and increasingly took to pedalling into the countryside to dull his pain with the monotonous grind at the worn-out pedals and the peacefully bitter silence of the fields and woods. Heedless of route or destination, he would turn his handlebars at random; when night fell he lit his lamps and mournfully pushed on. It was a powerful drug, and he turned eagerly to it whenever his daily toil allowed.

So it was that he came to be cycling doggedly, one Saturday afternoon, on a country road slightly too big to be called a lane, about ten miles from home. The image of the dark head and oval face had been particularly obsessive and cruel for some days past, and he had almost reached the stage of deciding on some course of action, however desperate. He was revolving a few ideas as the bicycle creaked and cranked its way between the sodden hedges. Apply to Mr. Roderick for a job—work fantastically hard—become managing director with the social *entrée* into the Roderick household—carry off the niece in legitimate courtship? The furrowed lines of his brow relaxed into a gentle sneer as the foolish notion unrolled itself. Even apart from his temperamental inability to rise to the top in an industrial concern, or even to get himself employed in one, there was the impossibility, even at this stage of his agony and despair, of swallowing the last hard kernel of his pride, and admitting that the life of a Tharkles was preferable; besides, he could hardly have become an important figure in the firm in less than ten years, by which time the girl would be safely matched, leaving him with the alternatives of walking out of the job or staying to witness the hateful complacency of the successful suitor. As he squirmed with disgust at the prospect, his machine wandered towards the middle of the road, and at once a motor horn sounded its hectoring note behind him. Some blasted plutocrat! Some hog with enough money to get at the Roderick girl and have a chance to impress her! He, who had vowed independence of money and social position, turned angrily to scowl at the man behind the wheel as the car drew out to pass him, trying to convey how much he hated him for being able to afford a car instead of a scrap-iron bicycle.

He turned, but instead of scowling he gaped in utter bewilderment as the two faces were carried past him. They did not look at him; the man was keeping his eyes on the road, and moving his mouth in a way that indicated that he was talking; the girl by his side was looking attentively into his face.

The girl was Betty. The man was Robert Tharkles.

Charles stopped pedalling. The bicycle came to a standstill. He got off and leaned it carefully against a tree. He needed to stand still, at once, and think. He leaned over a gate. Two cows stared at him suspiciously.

This was Betty's 'day'; the weekly occasion when she visited her aged and eccentric relative to draw her 'allowance'. Of course, now he looked at it, the story was ludicrously implausible. Why had he swallowed it? The answer came at once. It was because she had returned with the cash. It never crossed his mind that, if she were to deceive Froulish, her unfaithfulness would take the form of simple *quid pro quo* prostitution. And yet he could see it all so clearly! Betty had a simple, literal mind; or, to be more exact, the system of reflexes and elementary perceptions that served her instead of a mind was simple and literal. She and Froulish had to live, to be fed, sheltered, and warmed. She had in some way run across Robert Tharkles and decided, as many a young woman has decided every day throughout human history, that here was a source of material advantage. He, on his side, no doubt found the sour-faced shrew in his lawful bed too monotonous and noxious a diet. The only difference between this affair and all the countless similar ones going on all over the earth, lay in Betty's simplicity and directness. The average girl of her type would have recoiled from the hand-to-hand passage of Treasury notes, but seen nothing amiss in accepting payment in forms only slightly less direct—the rent, meals, clothes, expensive gifts—and no doubt Tharkles would have made an attempt to start her off in this direction; probably the fool had been scandalized when she insisted on a straight cash arrangement, and told him—as she was sure to have done—that she needed it to support the shambling eccentric for whom she really cared. But she had carried the day, and the trio in the loft had benefited.

It was this last thought that struck Charles so immediate and so disabling a blow. It never entered his head to be seriously shocked or disapproving at Betty's action; the amiable slut had never pretended to be anything else, and her life was on the same moral level as those of thousands of women who would have called her an unseemly name. What shook him, what caused the sweat to bead his forehead in the cold air of the winter afternoon was the realization that his own attempt to break out of the net had failed utterly. He had turned his back resolutely on the world represented by Robert Tharkles; he had declared that he wanted none of it, that he would manage without its aid or approval; he had abruptly ended his courtship of a girl whose memory, even now, could at times signal to him a clear and potent message, because she was a part of the Tharkles world—and the first thing he had done was to enter his name on the Tharkles payroll. Unbeknown to either party, doubtless, but he had entered it. He had become a parasite on the world he detested.

Perhaps it was not true. He seized his bicycle and pedalled madly down the road. He must follow them and check up on the situation. Of course it was not true. He was just giving her a lift, out to where her old aunt lived. Perhaps he had an old aunt himself, in the same village.

All the time he knew that it *was* true. He had seen the complacent pride of possession written across Tharkles's face. It was that knowledge that was driving him mad; for, of course, it is madness pure and simple to race wildly on a bicycle down a country road, chasing a motor-car.

Like a good many insane actions, it paid off. In another mile the road broadened into a self-consciously picturesque village street; like all such village streets it was dominated by several hotels of various degrees of vulgarity. Some of them made a point of being horsey, and had names like 'The Fox and Hounds' and 'The Post Horn'. The largest, however, was determinedly and phonily antique. It was called 'Ye Olde Oake Tree'.

Robert's car was outside the 'Ye Olde Oake Tree'. It was empty.

Head down, looking straight in front of him, Charles cycled past. He did not want to be recognized if either of them happened to be looking out. He stopped a few yards farther up the street and leaned his bicycle against the sham black-and-white front of another hotel. A man in a green apron came out and showed him a notice forbidding people to lean bicycles against the wall. Charles moved away until the man went back, then returned and leaned his bicycle against exactly the same spot. Then he went down a narrow alley in the fading light, and came out at the back door of the 'Ye Olde Oake Tree'.

He went in. It was the public bar entrance, although, as it was not yet opening time, the actual door of the bar was locked. In the passage where he stood there was no one about. By looking through a serving hatch he could see across the space behind the bar; at the other end of that space was another serving hatch, opening on to the expensive part of the hotel. He stood still and waited.

'Well, send a telegram,' came the voice of Robert Tharkles. Charles's heart gave a great bound. Could it be that everything was above board? That Betty had some genuine reason for being out here, and was worrying about how to let Froulish know? He froze, and strained his ears for her answer. It made his heart sink.

'All right, but I still don't like it. I never told him I was going to be away for the night. You go and spring it on me just because your wife happens—'

'SHHHHHH!' came the agonized sound. Obviously the sentence was going to end 'happens to be away for the week-end', or in some similar way. It was characteristic of Betty that she could not make even the most perfunctory pretence of being married to Tharkles when they were in public. In this, after all, she showed as usual a certain sense of the realities, for no one could possibly have taken her as such.

A slatternly girl in an overall came down the passage towards Charles.

'That door's not s'posed to be open,' she said in a nagging voice. She meant to convey that he had no right to come in by the back way. Then she looked at him more closely and added, 'Did you want summink?' Meaning to convey that she could not make out, from his appearance, whether he was a potential customer, wanting food or a room, or a workman who had come to do some repair or other.

'I've brought the catgut,' said Charles coldly and distinctly.

'Brought the what?'

'The catgut. The landlord ordered it by telephone.' He stared viciously into her eyes.

'I'll go an' ask Mr. Rogers,' she said uncertainly, and disappeared. Charles left the hotel as he had entered it.

Pedalling back along the arterial road it suddenly came to him. He must ask Ern what to do. Ern was the only person he could possibly turn to. He must go to him and say, quite baldly, that he had suddenly discovered a terrible fact about the way of life on which he had prided himself; namely, that it was made possible by the immoral earnings of a woman. Of that there was no doubt, after the snatch of conversation he had overheard. Evidently they had a regular weekly arrangement, and this week Tharkles, released from supervision by Edith's absence on a week-end trip, had suggested that they, too, should make a week-end of it.

Only Ern could help. There was nothing to be done about the rest of it. Nothing, that is, except leave the loft, quietly and at once, wheeling his few belongings in the cart; Froulish, left at home alone, would be too wrapped up in his endless task to notice what was happening, and, since the cold weather had set in, they had allowed their earlier custom of a weekly pub-crawl to lapse. He could easily get away, and beyond that he found it impossible to think straight about the situation at all; found, indeed, that the effort of trying to think straight about it was intolerably painful. What would Froulish feel if he knew? Anything or nothing: he was as morally null as the wench herself, and might perfectly well shrug his shoulders and say that he had always known that Art flowered from a soil that could not be described as clean or fragrant. Perhaps—more numbing still—he knew all the time, and the two of them had had just sufficient delicacy to keep Charles with them by faking the story of the old relative and the allowance. No: he rejected this idea, partly as too horrible, and partly because he felt sure that the keeping of any such secret, from one who saw him every day, would have been a task quite beyond the powers of the twitching buffoon.

It was suddenly dark and terribly cold. His lamp threw a faint ring of yellow on the wet road. Shivering, he thought of the warmth and light of the hotel where Robert Tharkles had taken Betty. The wages of sin. He thought of soft carpets, imitation log fires looking warm, efficient central heating being warm. By a sudden unexplained twist he found himself picturing the Oak Lounge at the Grand, and the smooth man padding over to set down the two tiny glasses. Can't get a short drink under two bob. Money. The network everywhere: no, a web, sticky and cunningly arranged. You were either a spider, sitting comfortably in the middle or waiting with malicious joy in hiding, or you were a fly, struggling amid the clinging threads. He and Froulish were flies, but Froulish did not mind. His contempt for the spider remained genuine and sustaining even while his wings were being pulled off, even while he was being eaten. But the classification did not work. Which was Betty, a spider or a fly? And which, oh which, was the girl in the Oak Lounge? Could a spider have such delicate bones? Could it make a fly feel that nothing else in the world had any meaning?

He remembered reading about spiders. Sometimes the web caught a wasp by mistake. Then the spider had to dismantle the web. The wasp had to be let go, because it was dangerous.

It seemed as if the wasps had the right idea.

Froulish was going through one of his bad spells. When Charles arrived he was on his knees beside the oil stove, tearing sheet after sheet of paper into long strips with a slow, deliberate bitterness. When he had accumulated about fifty strips he set fire to them, one at a time, and burnt them down until the flame almost touched his stubby fingers. The loft was filled with dense acrid smoke.

'You're at that game again, are you?' Charles could not help saying roughly as he passed him to go into his own compartment. 'How many times have I got to warn you against setting the place on fire?'

'And how many times,' retorted the novelist sullenly, 'have I got to explain that when I come to a standstill, I have to go back and find the obstruction that blocks the flow of inspiration, and that when I find that obstruction, the smoke from its funeral pyre provides the only possible stimulus to enable me to replace the dead matter?'

The flame caressed his fingers, and with a curse he flung a blazing scrap of paper into the middle of the floor. Charles stepped over and trod it out. He felt almost guilty at leaving the idiot to his own devices. No one to cook him a meal or force him to go to bed; no one even to preserve him from the ever-present threat of his pyromania. As he rolled his tiny stock of spare clothing in a sheet of newspaper, something like a lump rose in Charles's throat at the thought that Froulish was, after all, about his nearest approach to an old friend, and that their parting must come at once, and come in a manner so brutal and silent. He looked up almost affectionately at the moody figure crouching at the centre of a blue cloud.

'Shan't be long,' he said, hating himself, as he clambered down the ladder with the newspaper bundle beneath one arm. 'I've just got to go round to Ern's.'

Froulish nodded sulkily. It was, at any rate, a relief that he was so insufferable at the moment. Had he been in one of his more endearing moods Charles might have been led by an onrush of sentiment into attempting impossible explanations. It was better simply to fade out.

Lock, stock, and barrel; he hitched the cart behind his bicycle and pedalled away from the home that had become unbearably sullied, that had been revealed as a mere cess-pit on the Tharkles estate. That episode was over.

Why did he seek out Ern? Was there any hope that Ern could, in any important way, get him out of this mess? Obviously, no; but Charles's pride was beaten down to the point at which he found it impossible to stand alone. Irrational as it was, he felt a vague flutter of hope that Ern would drive the weight of his Manchester common sense into the heart of the problem, as he had driven the weight of his chunky body into the oncoming bulk of the man with the bald head.

The streets were dark and quiet. He cycled quickly, and once the near-side wheel of the cart dragged protestingly along the kerb-stone as he rounded a corner too narrowly. As he approached the quiet, dingy street where Ern lodged, he felt like the one living thing left on earth. The cold wind seemed to have driven everyone and everything into shelter. It was beginning to freeze, and the sparsely planted lamp-posts were islands of yellow silence in the sea of darkness.

Except outside Ern's house. There was quite a lot of activity going on there. A highly-polished black car was drawn up outside the door, with a man in a dark uniform waiting beside it on the pavement. The light was on in the front room on to which the front door opened. Charles stopped his bicycle in time to see, framed in the lighted doorway, three figures. Two of them were dressed in the same dark uniform as the man on the pavement, so that Ern, who was in his ordinary working clothes, seemed quite conspicuous.

He would have been conspicuous in any case, for he walked with the clumsy, rather swaying gait of a man whose wrists are handcuffed together.

The bicycle clattered to the ground as Charles went forward. Idiotically, his voice uttered three syllables.

'What's up, Ern?'

The toothless face turned in his direction. The policemen halted for a minute while one of them opened the car door.

'Go into the 'ouse, Charley,' said Ern. 'The landlord's got summat for you.'

'But can't I—I mean surely there must be—'

One of the policemen turned to him with a kind of sad menace.

'Come on, out of it,' he said in a voice which conveyed the same blend of threat and melancholy. 'Else I shall have to teach you better than to try to hold a conversation with a man under arrest.'

'This is a free—' Charles began weakly.

'I'd pull you in under suspicion,' groaned the policeman gently, as he followed Ern into the car, 'only we know all about you already and we've checked that you're not in this.'

'Not in WHAT?' Charles shouted in exasperation, but the polished car droned away smoothly, with Ern's cloth-capped head just visible through the back window.

He stood, utterly paralysed, in front of the still open door. His bicycle lay on its side a few yards away. Froulish and Betty gone. Ern gone. Policemen in cars. Where was his life? How could he even begin to piece together its fragments, when he was not even certain that he could remember what shape it used to be?

Then he remembered that at least Ern had left him with one concrete instruction. Go into the house, the landlord's got something for you. He turned to go in at the door at the precise instant that an enormously fat man in his shirt-sleeves began to close it.

'You'd be the partner?' said the fat man.

Charles nodded, and entered without speaking. The fat man led the way down the greasy passage to what had been Ern's room. Inside, he waited for Charles to get well into the room, then closed the door with heavy deliberation.

'Now mind,' he said breathily, for he was one of those fat men who are always slightly out of breath, 'I know nothing, not one thing, about that man's business. I've 'ad enough questions from the police, and I don't want any more from you. All I want is to be rid of the 'ole affair. Understood?'

'Understood,' said Charles, faintly.

'Now all I 'ave to do, to *be* rid of it, is to 'and over what 'e left for you, and then wish you a *very* good night.'

He looked at Charles sternly.

'A *very* good night,' he repeated. He put a cheap brown envelope in Charles's hand. Inside it were two florins and a ten shilling note. A scribbled note in Ern's writing said: 'we did not have time to share out this evening, you keep mine, i shant need it where im going.'

'Where *is* he going?' he asked the landlord, too dazed to reflect that he had read the note silently, so that the man could not see the connection.

'It's where *you're* going that interests me,' came the answering wheeze. 'Outside. I wish you a *very*—'

'All right, all right,' said Charles. He went down the passage and opened the door. Then he turned and looked at the fat greasy figure who stood staring at him inimically.

'Thanks at least for giving me what he left for me,' he said.

'I've told you, I want to be rid of the 'ole affair,' answered the landlord. He did not even want to claim credit for his honesty. It seemed that caution was the one virtue he recognized.

Charles picked up his bicycle and, too dispirited to mount, wheeled it aimlessly away.

The Warden of the Y.M.C.A. hostel received Charles back without comment or question, and the old routine picked up as smoothly as if it had never stopped. It was all unbelievably depressing, but Charles had decided that before leaving the district he must wait to find out what had happened to Ern. It was only partly a matter of personal loyalty; he had not known Ern long enough to become attached to him, though, since the episode of the bald-headed man, he had trusted him implicitly; his motive was really the desperate need for more light on the situation. His foundations had been knocked from under him, and he felt that at least he must try to build up as clear a picture as possible before making any fresh move.

The only possible course, therefore, was to watch the local paper until it gave details of Ern's trial. As Stotwell was the county town, the trial would be held at the local assizes. No one seemed to know when this was due to come off, but Charles pinned his faith in the *Stotwell Advertiser* to tell him what happened.

It did better than that. Some ten days after his return to the hostel—ten days spent in fitful pursuit of his usual duties, so long as they did not take him near the quarter of the town frequented by Froulish and Betty—it announced the cases that were to come up at the assizes the following day. Once again Charles's best clothes came out of storage, and the next morning he waited outside the building for an hour, to make sure of a seat in the court's public gallery.

Ern's case was, mercifully, one of the first to be tried. It was over with incredible swiftness; no defence was offered, no legal wrangling was necessary, nothing was to be done but state the facts, hear Ern's plea of Guilty, and sentence him. After the speed of the proceedings, its next most striking feature was the casual atmosphere. It was evidently seen as a business transaction.

Ern had placed such-and-such an amount of illegal conduct on one balance of the scales; the law would place a corresponding weight of punishment on the other, and equilibrium would be restored. Charles had never seen lawyers in action before, but in their rapid, detached handling of the business, their evident lack of personal concern with what to others were matters of supreme importance, they reminded him of clergymen scampering with professional rapidity through a service. No one seemed to be shocked, or to care much, about Ern's crime. It seemed that he had been employed by a firm called the Export Express Bureau, which supplied drivers to motor manufacturers who wanted their newly-finished vehicles driven from the factory to the docks. It was news to Charles, as (evidently) it was to the Judge, that such firms existed. Ern's job had been simply to report at one or other of the large Midland motor firms, pick up the car or lorry that awaited him, and drive it to some major sea-port, usually Liverpool or Southampton. In the course of the Judge's questions (it was, patently, the only part of the proceedings that engaged his interest) it emerged not only that such a job existed, but that it was particularly subject to bribery. The demand for cars was such that theft had become profitable and highly systematized. Gangs would approach an Export Express driver, and make it substantially worth his while to leave his car unattended in a moment of carelessness; it was quite enough to pull up at a wayside café, and on emerging, go round to the lavatory behind the building and stay there for two or three minutes. When the driver returned, the brand-new car had already been driven down the road and into a waiting van, where, even as it drove along, it was resprayed in a different colour and fake licence plates screwed on. A day or two later the driver would receive his bribe. It seemed that he always did receive it; the gangs wanted to stay on good terms with the drivers, and found it worth while to do business genuinely.

Nevertheless, it appeared, rogues sometimes fell out. Ern had succumbed to the offer of a hundred pounds to leave a powerful saloon car unattended for a few minutes at a pre-arranged spot; but before he could receive the money, someone had managed to reach him with a warning not to keep the appointment. The police were in action. That evening he had melted away, and Stotwell had gained a new citizen. All this had happened a mere four months previously, so that Ern's statement to Charles that he had been in Stotwell 'a year or two' was simply a piece of caution; Charles had not the heart to think of it as a lie, for, after all, what was it to him how long Ern had been there?

Impersonally, casually, the case was assessed. A first offence; on the other hand the prisoner had made an unusually determined effort to evade the law. Eighteen months' imprisonment.

That was that. Suddenly Charles felt that his feeling for Ern had evaporated, leaving yet another vacuum inside him. He watched the stocky toothless figure led away, out of the court and out of his life, without emotion. Their association had been, after all, simply a convenience to both of them; a place to hide, for each was a fugitive. It was this shared predicament that had led to the quick formation of the intuitive bond between them, and, now that for one of them the game was up, that bond parted easily and at once. He rose, and, pushing his way to the end of the row, left the courtroom.

Feet clattered down the stone stairs after him. Evidently someone else was leaving too. On emerging into the street, Charles paused for a moment with a hint of the old irresolution, and the other was beside him.

Not only that, but he had halted. Charles glanced sideways and saw a tall, gangling young man dressed in expensive outdoor clothes; a heavy tweed jacket with slits up the back, twill trousers, brogues. He had a flashing wrist-watch and a tie of good material but poor design. He looked like someone who earned more money than he found it advisable to declare for Income Tax, and consequently spent it. His eyes were on Charles's face, and, when Charles looked at him, he spoke at once.

'Interesting, that last case,' he said. His voice was light and rapid, with something of a county accent which shared the faintly uneasy quality of his clothing.

Something made Charles reply, 'Very. Especially to me, I know the man. Knew him, I suppose I ought to say.'

'What?' cried the tall young man. 'You know Ernie Ollershaw?'

It was characteristic that he made 'Ern' into 'Ernie', a name that Ern would never have answered to. (All the same, it was nice to reflect that Ern had not given him a false name; probably he had used one for his dealings with the thieves, and kept his real one for genuine relationships.)

'Not in the game yourself by any chance?' the young man went on in a light casual tone.

'Game?'

'Don't get me wrong. I don't mean what he was pinched for. I mean the straight side of it. Export delivery driving.'

Charles shook his head. The other waited for him to say how, in that case, he had met Ern, but he said nothing. It was not the fellow's business.

The tall man took the hint.

'Well, must be getting on. I just came over to see the trial because I used to know Ernie on the job, and I knew the lads would be interested to hear how he got on. We liked him.'

He nodded and began to stride away. Charles suddenly realized that a door was swinging to. In another second it would slam, and one possible way out would be barred. Whoever this man was, he was making money. If he chose he could, doubtless, move in circles not far below those inhabited by the Rodericks. He would probably never have condescended to start a conversation if Charles had been wearing his working clothes and pushing his cart.

'I say!' he heard himself croak.

The gangling frame halted, and turned.

'I'm—well, interested, in what you were saying,' Charles brought out. 'About the job, I mean. I mean, I often wondered what Ern—you know—'

'It doesn't do to wonder too much, old boy,' came the answer in a light pattering tone. Charles writhed, conscious of a deep shame that his plight forced him to associate with people who called other people 'old boy'. 'But if you're interested in the job, I don't say we couldn't talk turkey over a pot.'

'All right,' said Charles. 'At least we can go and have'—he was going to say 'a drink', but remembered in time to call it 'a pot'. It would help to win the fellow's confidence if he showed that he could talk the same vile jargon.

'Lead me to it, old boy,' said the gangling man.
'This way, old boy,' said Charles.

V

The big car edged uncomfortably close to the ditch as Charles eased it round; he was well on the wrong side of the road, and the camber was dragging the wheels sideways. Never mind! His first run was nearly over, and he had kept up with the convoy. Not that it had been easy; altogether a job for the new Charles, though the old one had learnt to drive sufficiently well to take his mother shopping in the family ten-horsepower saloon. Just a question of being able to climb into the driving seat of his first 'job', and drive it away without too much clashing of the gears—and then the grim struggle to keep the rest of the convoy in sight, to prove that he could do what they could do. If Scrodd could see him now!

They would soon be in Liverpool; the road was lined with houses, and suddenly the five cars ahead stopped. A pedestrian crossing with a crocodile of school children on it. He brought the car to a halt and waited, keeping the clutch out; it was hard, the pedal was new and stiff. As he sat quietly waiting, his mind strove to grasp the swirl of recent events. What a time it had been! How little he had understood of what had gone on! He had felt like Alice in Wonderland. From the moment when, over their drinks (ironically, in the Oak Lounge), the gangling man had introduced himself as Teddy Bunder and announced his intention of 'squeezing you into the racket, old boy—you're the type', he had felt like a spark whirled up from a fire in a current of hot air. At first he had suspected that Bunder was a crook, and that the gang of cronies to whom Bunder had introduced him when they arrived at the Export Express staff canteen and bar were crooks too. They all seemed keen on recruiting the profession from among those who were 'the type'; presumably Ern had been the type, and Ern was now engaged in being the type behind bars for eighteen months. And yet, once Bunder had levered him adroitly into the firm, taking him straight in to the manager with the claim that he had found the ideal man to fill a vacancy that had recently occurred, and inventing on the spot a long record of experience for him, Charles found himself left fairly well alone. No one tried to interest him in dubious schemes; Bunder and his set, though approachable enough, made no effort to sweep him in as one of themselves; for his first job he had been assigned not to a solo trip but to one of the less responsible convoy runs.

The cars ahead moved. Charles dragged heavily on the tapering gear-lever and somehow jerked the motor up through three changes into top. He hoped, for the sake of the people to whom these cars were to be delivered as brand-new, that practice would soon make him a smoother driver.

At the docks came another ordeal he had, fortunately, not had the foresight to worry about in advance; the cars had to be drawn up close together in a dead straight line to facilitate loading on to the ship. With eyes shut he jerked his vehicle violently forward for the last ten yards, swinging on the steering wheel, and stamped on the brake. 'All right, mate! No need ter show yer bloody skill!' came a hoarse shout: opening his eyes he saw that he had drawn up dead level with the car next to him, and left barely one inch of clearance.

Perhaps it was an omen, indicating that, in this new sphere, chance would decide to favour him. Certainly if his luck had followed its old habitual course, he could have driven into the dock and been drowned.

Before catching the train back there were pints of beer in a dockside pub. At first Charles sat rather uncomfortably apart from the others, who all knew each other well, but after a few minutes a serious-looking middle-aged man in a grey cloth cap, whom he knew as Simons, edged towards him along the bench and gave a friendly nod as a signal that he was about to open a conversation.

'Well: get on all right?'

'Yes, thanks; it didn't seem a very difficult job this time,' Charles answered.

'No, not this time, it wasn't,' Simons admitted rather reluctantly, as if implying that it was usually much worse; he was not a pessimist, but he had the habit of mind of the responsible mature artisan, always prepared for huge burdens to drop on his shoulders. Then he looked at Charles rather curiously.

'Friend of Bunder's?'

It was obvious what he really wanted to know; are you with us, or with them? Bunder's set were markedly different in appearance and habits from the rest of the Export Express staff. Charles was about to answer that he was scarcely on nodding terms with the Bunder clique, when it struck him that he might learn more if he kept the issue in suspense a little longer.

'Can't make him out, quite,' he said slowly, hoping to convey the impression that he had been encouraged to throw in his lot with Bunder, and was hesitating. Simons evidently took this as he was meant to.

'Well,' he said with deliberation, 'you'll find as it pays to make him out, even if it takes time, before you—' Leaving the sentence unfinished, he drained his Guinness and set the glass down with a rap on the table.

'He's not difficult to make out,' he said, 'not if you've met his type before.'

Charles maintained silence. It was a policy that was proving its value. As Simons seemed to be waiting for him to say something, he took the simplest way out by pointing to the empty glass and saying, 'Another?'

'Have one with me,' said Simons, thus revealing his hand a little farther. It showed that he was willing to take a little trouble to influence Charles.

When he returned with the drinks he said, 'The long and short of it is this. Bunder and them pals of his aren't bad at the job. They could do all right if they were content to stick to it and do one job at a time, like. But they aren't. The job's not good enough for them.'

He lit his pipe. The match flame flared, inches high, in between guttering almost out.

'So what do they do?' he went on.

Charles did not know what they did. To answer might spoil everything. He buried his face in his glass.

The other drivers were standing up. 'Come on, Jack,' one of them called to Simons. 'Time to be getting on to the station.'

Simons took out his watch and looked at it. 'That's right,' he said. He got up, and Charles followed him out into the street, and fell into step as they trudged along, hoping that Simons would go on with the vitally important part of the story. But some of the others were talking and Simons was listening to them. He seemed to have forgotten that he had been interrupted.

In the train going back they played cards. Charles did not get a chance to speak to Simons again.

Several weeks passed. Life was, on the whole, uneventful; his energies were absorbed in mastering the new job, and he had as little energy to spare for private worries as during his first weeks as a window-cleaner. He had taken lodgings near the Export Express offices; both Bunder and Simons had given him addresses that they recommended, but to accept either would have meant the end of his policy of strict neutrality, and he was determined to preserve it until he saw how the land lay; so he found a place for himself. It was drab, but he did hardly more than sleep there, and the bed was comfortable. He had hoped that removal from Stotwell, combined with the change in his way of life, would rid him of the obsession that had seized him that evening in the Oak Lounge; but his hope was streaked with despair, and even, at the deepest layer of all, ousted by a desire to stay in the struggle. Had he not found himself a job that carried good pay? Not riches, but certainly more than he had earned before, and enough to make it something more than an occasional fling when he ate a meal at a good hotel. And had not his motive, only half unconsciously, been just that—to put himself in a better position for taking stock of his chances *vis-à-vis* the Rodericks?

He tried to shrug the notion away, but one tell-tale symptom prevailed. When his route to the docks lay southward, it took him through Stotwell, which lay about twenty miles away; and, whenever possible, he called at the Grand Hotel and looked into the Oak Lounge for a moment. It was useless to resolve, as he always did resolve, that he would drive straight through the town; doubly useless to maintain to himself, as he always did maintain, a foolish pose of I-can-have-a-drink-if-I-like indifference. A hundred-fold useless to point out to himself the idiocy of imagining that because he had once seen her in the Oak Lounge, he had only to hang around there for long enough and he would see her again. Probably she did not go into the Oak Lounge once in three years. True, the barman had said something about the Rodericks being frequent customers there, but the barman was probably lying, in a charitable attempt to pay for his drink with some good news. Wearily admitting all this, he nevertheless parked his car, whenever possible, and padded up the broad staircase to meet the accustomed disappointment. She was never there, and in any case he would have had no idea what to do about it if she had been.

February passed; Charles started innumerable engines, stamped on pedals, gripped wheels, stared through windscreens, wore out pairs of gloves. One day, muffled up in furs and goggles, he took the road perched above the gigantic chassis of a twelve-wheeler; the next, elegantly flicking cigarette ash through the window, he floated in an expensive limousine. The arterial roads were usually quick to be cleared of snow, and on the whole the weather favoured his novitiate; his solitary mishap—when a van he was driving skidded helplessly, revolved three times, and ran backwards up a bank of earth—served, if anything, to reassure him by the speed at which his ruffled nerves recovered. At least, thank Heaven, he was on top of the job; circumstances had forced him to master one more skill, and he acknowledged, even in his aching emptiness, the tonic effect of that mastery.

It was queer to look out of the carriage window and still be able to see distances and colours at seven o'clock at night; it was well into March, but the longer evenings still seemed a novelty. Charles waited impatiently for the train to start: after a long and tedious journey from Southampton, they had almost reached Stotwell, but evidently the signals were against them, and they had halted outside the station. Well, he had only himself to blame; he could have caught an express, but had discovered that if he travelled by a slower train, he could change trains at Stotwell, and break his journey for long enough to visit the Oak Lounge. Pitiless, humiliating obsession! The train waited and waited. Fretting, he snatched at the leather strap, dropped the window with a crash, and thrust his head out. He was staring angrily up the line, and was on the point of wrenching the door open and leaping out on to the metals, though it would have meant a walk of two or three miles to the town centre, when a rich, husky voice from inside the compartment summoned him back.

'Have a heart, partner! I'm refrigerated to the marrow as it is!'

Charles brought his head and shoulders back inside and looked round. So intensely preoccupied with his gnawing emotions, he had not even looked at the compartment's only other occupant; yet the man was not easy to overlook. Huge and squarely built, with the superfluous flesh that middle-age brings to the powerful physique. A broad face, broadly grinning. Loud, cheerful clothes, worn loudly and cheerfully.

'Sorry,' said Charles, drawing up the window. 'It is a bit chilly, isn't it?'

'Very nicely understated, partner,' came the reply. 'Let's light a bonfire, shall we?' He produced a huge silver case containing what looked at first sight like small, cheap cigars. Charles accepted one and, examining it in the fading light, discovered it to be a cheroot. Obviously! No other kind of smoke would fit in so well with the fat man's raffish good humour.

'Not as good as a night-watchman's brazier,' the fat man apologized, holding out a match. 'But enough to melt an inch or two off the icicles.'

What was that accent? It had a hint of America, a hint of the Antipodes, and a fair slice each of Cockney and Birmingham. Some words even sounded faintly Scottish. Obviously half a century of roaming the world. Could it be show business of some kind? The train had started; they would reach Stotwell in five minutes, and, no doubt, separate and never see each other again. Why not ask straight out? It was months since he had burst out of the strait-jacket of his upbringing—here was a chance to benefit by that escape, if only in a small matter.

'I know it's a bit thick to rob you of a cheroot and then grill you with personal questions into the bargain,' he began. The fat man's face creased into a vast grin, and he interrupted with a bellow of laughter.

'Easy to see you're not used to being free-and-easy with strangers,' he husked powerfully. 'You can't make me out, and you want to know what I make me living at, that's right, isn't it?' Charles nodded, his incipient embarrassment puffed away in the gale of bonhomie.

'All right, but I make one condition. I like a bargain, always did. You tell me about yourself first.'

'I'm an export delivery driver. I take cars from the factories to the docks.'

The fat man assumed an expression of bewilderment theatrically overdone.

'Dear, dear, oh dear, the world's moving too fast for poor old Arthur. Here was I trying to size you up, and failing because you didn't fit into any type I knew, and now it turns out you've got a job I'd never even heard of. And what kind of a job might that be? One of these new kind of jobs, I dare say, where you couldn't rightly say whether a fella was a workman or an office stool percher or a manager. It's all upside-down these days.'

'Well, at least you do know it's upside-down,' said Charles reassuringly. 'Most people of your generation—er—if you don't mind me making you sound very old, I didn't really mean to—anyway, most of them haven't cottoned on to these changes.'

'Ah, but I'm in a job that's changing all the time,' said the fat man, sitting back proudly with one powerful square hand on each knee. 'In my job, when you stop being one jump ahead of the changes, you get it straight where the bottle got the stopper.' Holding his cheroot in his mouth, he devoted all ten fingers to searching his waistcoat pockets and finally producing a card which he handed across.

It said, 'ARTHUR BLEARNEY ENTERTAINMENTS'.

'I don't quite get the whole story from this,' Charles ventured. 'I suppose you promote shows and—act as an agent of some sort.'

Mr. Blearney chuckled richly. 'I promote shows, yes, I act as an agent, yes. As for not quite getting the whole story, well, partner, you weren't altogether meant to get it. That's another lesson of my lifetime—the day anybody gets the *whole* story, you get it where the chicken got the chopper.'

The train drew in to Stotwell station and halted. They stood up. 'No,' said Mr. Blearney, still chuckling, 'I didn't say anything about the *whole* story, partner, now did I?'

Charles looked at him, unable to decide whether to dislike him or relax and join in his amusement, sharing that genuine good humour and unconsciousness of offence. He had still not decided when they had clambered down and emerged, still side by side, through the ticket barrier.

'Busy?' Mr. Blearney asked. 'If not, why don't you come along to my hotel and let's have a drink?'

'What is your hotel?' Charles countered. He must not miss his pilgrimage to the Oak Lounge after taking so much trouble to get here.

'The Grand—only one fit to stay in in this dump,' Mr. Blearney husked, and, when Charles signified assent, he masterfully signalled for a taxi. In a few minutes they were in the hotel foyer, and Mr. Blearney was the centre of a vortex of scurrying employees. The receptionist ran forward with the book; the manager ran out of his office; the page ran towards the lift to take him up to his room; even the porter stumped off with Mr. Blearney's case at twice his usual speed. There was something galvanic about the man as he stood squarely dominating the scene, shouting jovially and keeping up a stream of atrociously unfunny jokes. Charles melted away to the background, content to watch and admire. Mr. Blearney was the first man he had ever met who combined a hearty manner with genuine self-confidence. He contradicted the general rule that heartiness is a sign of self-distrust, thus confirming it.

At last they found themselves comfortably installed in the Oak Lounge. Mr. Blearney insisted on ordering, and paying for, four double whiskies. 'Two each, that's the style, partner,' he said positively. 'Drink the first one down in one swallow, then take the second slowly.' He drained his first, and Charles followed suit.

'Aaaaah,' said Mr. Blearney, sitting back. 'That's the first time I've had the cold out of my marrow-bones for three hours. I'm getting old for this gallivanting, in draughty trains at any rate. I shall have to go everywhere by car, and that'll bankrupt me in six months.'

He lit a cheroot. Charles, refusing the offer of one for himself, took out his cigarettes.

'And no real need to come, either,' Mr. Blearney went on. 'Just keeping my eye on a touring show that's here at the local flea pit.'

'One of your shows?' Charles asked.

'In a manner of speaking, yes. I'm not the backer, but I'm acting for the backer. We've been getting rumours that the zip's gone out of it. Comics need some new gags, chorus could do with a rest—you know the sort of thing.'

Charles tried to look as if he knew the sort of thing. They drank some more of their whisky.

'I shall have to—well, Gawd, look who's here,' said Mr. Blearney suddenly. 'Come on over, Bernard,' he shouted, 'hey, Veronica, come on over, both of you! It's Uncle Arthur.'

Charles looked up, a sudden intuition smashing into the pit of his stomach. Walking over to them, with smiles of recognition directed at Mr. Blearney, were the Rodericks.

Men have been known to commit suicide by standing in front of a train. In such cases there must have been an interval of time—say, between one and three seconds—when the suicide stood between the metals, firmly planted on his feet in the path of the engine, with every nerve and muscle braced for the shocking impact. Such a degree of tension is probably unique, and not to be approached in everyday life. But Charles approached it now. As he jerked to his feet, every muscle went rigid in the violent attempt to stop himself from trembling or falling down.

'Well, well, you gadabouts!' roared Mr. Blearney, delighted. 'I'd forgotten you'd be back from Monte by now! How's the old Med. looking? Blue for a boy, eh? How's the old Casino, eh, Bernard?'

'We didn't go into the Casino,' purred Mr. Roderick, humorously. 'Roulette isn't one of my diversions, you should know that, Arthur.'

'I should know that! Me?' Mr. Blearney rasped in mock horror, turning to Charles with a ludicrous air of injured innocence. 'What should I know of his diversions! Me that's led such a quiet life! By the way,' he continued, dropping into what, for him, was a normal tone, 'I don't suppose you know each other—this is Bernard and Veronica Roderick, old friends of mine—this is, er, I don't believe you gave me your name, anyway, I met this young man in the train just now, and I've taken a big fancy to him already.'

'My name's Charles Lumley.'

Clumsy, oafish performance! When a touch of sparkle, a gay rejoinder to old Blearney's maunderings, a crisp epigram, perhaps (already) a well-turned compliment—when these things were imperiously demanded by the situation, all he could do was to stand stiffly, his arms rigidly held at an unnatural angle from his sides, and mumble out his name.

Easily and naturally, yet with no more warmth than was warranted by the casual introduction of an unimportant stranger, Bernard Roderick held out a plump hand. Charles extended his own. At the contact he had a vivid sensation of the difference between the two hands. His own had become powerful and square; the skin, roughened by incessant exposure to water and air during his window-cleaning days, had since become a little smoother, but remained hard and thick, with a callous at the base of each finger. His nails were short; Roderick's were just long enough to protrude a fraction of an inch beyond his finger-ends, so that Charles distinctly felt them in his palm. Irrationally, a slight tremor of physical revulsion went through him. It was not that Roderick's nails were a little too long, it was not that his general appearance contained in it a slight, indefinable excess of the sleek and the groomed—it was all these together, and something else over and above them, something that Charles could not have indicated even in general terms.

Their eyes met. Charles fought hard to like Mr. Roderick. His muscles, which had relaxed for an instant, drew themselves taut again with the effort of fighting off his revulsion. This man was related to the one being who could bring significance into the random pattern of his life. The effort failed.

'My niece, Veronica,' said Mr. Roderick. His eyes flickered away from Charles's; he was looking at Mr. Blearney.

She put her thin, cool hand in his.

'Whisky!' cried Mr. Blearney.

'Let me get them,' Charles almost shouted in his anxiety. He wanted it to be his turn to pad across the carpet with a tiny glass, and set it down before her. Mr. Blearney subsided in his chair.

'Not for us, we haven't had dinner yet,' protested Mr. Roderick. 'If you're really so kind as to buy a drink for us, I'll have a dry Martini.'

Who cares what he wants? A gentleman would have asked the girl what she wanted first. Turn towards her, look at her enquiringly. Don't trust yourself to speak, something's happened to your throat.

'Thank you, a pink gin, please.' They were her first words to him, for on being introduced she had smiled quickly and easily, but in silence. Her voice was clear, not shrill, but light.

As he hurried over to the bar, Charles was struck by a sudden thought: no family resemblance. The sister, or brother, whose daughter she was, must have been very different from Mr. Roderick himself. Or was he a blood relation at all? Did adoption come in at any stage?

The barman was leering at him sympathetically. He realized how he must appear in the man's eyes; just another crazy lovesick fool.

'A pink gin, two double whiskies and a dry Martini, and don't look now but your glass eye's fallen out,' he said harshly.

When he got back with the drinks, Mr. Blearney had launched into an anecdote that was not so much lengthy as proliferating: it branched out in so many directions, sprouted subsidiary anecdotes by the dozen, and included an enormous amount of what historians of primitive epic describe as 'episodic matter'. His talk was not boring, but even if it had been of unexampled brilliance Charles would not have listened. Under cover of the endless husky roar, he sipped his whisky and kept his eyes on the girl, more discreetly than when he had goggled so idiotically at her on their first encounter. She was sitting opposite him, flanked by the two men, so that Blearney's whisky-laden monologue swirled round her like a heavy sea round a rock. She kept her eyes lowered, for the most part, listening with a quiet but genuine amusement. Once or twice she looked up and caught the eye of one or other of the three, as people do in general conversation, now Blearney's, now her uncle's, now Charles's. It was impossible to decide which of the three she glanced at most frequently. Charles decided that probably, on a total count, Roderick would have been declared the winner. But when she looked at him, Charles, it was in quite a normal and friendly way, without the chill of her first response to his gaping. She was demure, her manner was not forward or even particularly open, but it was not cold.

He suddenly realized that he was drunk again. Was it the three whiskies on an empty stomach, or was it her presence? At any rate, as so often before, he knew that intoxication made it possible for him to act. Only when the higher centres, with their message of restraint and caution, were put out of action—only then could he dare. At lightning speed he revolved a number of possible openings. 'Do you come here often?' No, too silly. And she would just say 'Yes' or 'No', and then what? No, it was better to start from a more general angle. 'I gather you don't spend much time in Stotwell?' Oh, so you gather, do you? Must have been prying into her affairs, asking people questions about her. That must go out. (He did not realize that this admission would have been something like the charming artless compliment he had wished for.) Well, what about leaving out the stuff about 'gathering', and simply saying, 'Do you spend much time in Stotwell?'

He leaned forward. 'Do you spend much time in Stotwell?' he asked.

The words crashed into a silence left by the sudden cessation of Blearney's voice. The effect was like that of a man talking loudly in a Tube train, who barks out the end of his sentence when the train suddenly stops, and the whole carriage hears it. Thus isolated, it seemed crass, thrusting, and impertinent. He felt limp and nauseated. Blearney and Roderick turned and looked at him.

Nevertheless, she answered.

'It depends on how often my uncle has to make business journeys abroad,' she said. 'If he's going to be away for more than a few days, I usually go with him.'

'Need someone to look after you, eh, Bernard?' shouted Blearney, humorously.

Roderick looked at him without expression. 'Yes,' he said. There was a dead silence. Charles felt that he must certainly vomit within the next ninety seconds. The figure, ninety, occurred to him with odd precision.

Roderick got to his feet. 'Well, we'd better go and eat,' he said. 'Are you staying here, Arthur?' He did not ask whether Charles and Mr. Blearney had had their dinner.

'Yes, but I probably shan't be seeing you for the rest of the evening,' replied Mr. Blearney. 'I've got to go round to the flea pit. I shall only see the second half as it is. Tell you what!' he cried excitedly, 'come to my place in town next Sunday night. Got a few of the right sort coming in—you know most of them, Elsa, Stanley, Jimmy, you know the crowd. It's a long time since we saw much of you in W.1.'

'Well—' Roderick began.

'Oh, Gawd, make him come, Veronica,' said Mr. Blearney, impatiently. 'You know you always enjoy my parties, both of you. Look,' he turned and faced the girl, 'you'd like to come, my love, wouldn't you?'

'Yes,' she said simply.

'All right, we'll come,' said Mr. Roderick.

Charles got to his feet. He had to get away. Already the thought of her at a party with Elsa, Stanley, and Jimmy was grinding into him like a blunt drill. You always enjoy my parties! Both of you! What in hell's name was the link between these two worlds? Who spoke of the marriage of Heaven and Hell? At what altar could this rite have taken place?

'Here, don't rush off without saying whether you're coming too, whatsyaname, Charley,' shouted Mr. Blearney. 'You can get up to London in those motor-cars of yours, can't you? 85A Sunflower Court, about eight o'clock, now don't you start saying you can't manage it.'

Charles stood for a moment utterly numbed with bewilderment. Then joy flooded into his being. Wonderful parties Mr. Blearney gave! The most delightful people, Elsa, Freddy, Jimmy, whatever their names were, charming, witty, Jessie, Binkie, Sammy, Socrates, Xenophon, Lao Tse, Stalin, to the hell with it all.

'I can manage it,' he said.

*

The next move was simple. It was late when he got back to the town where Export Express Ltd. had its being, but he went straight round to Teddy Bunder's flat. He rang the bell. His watch showed half-past eleven. It was a long time before Bunder came to the door. He had no tie on, and instead of a shirt he was wearing his pyjama jacket.

'For Christ's sake, old boy,' he said. He meant that Charles ought not to have called so late without saying that he was coming.

'Listen, I must talk to you,' said Charles rapidly. 'I came round because I must talk to you.'

Bunder looked at him for a moment, then turned and led the way into the flat. The living-room was untidy, and there was a big fire burning in the grate. A girl sat on the sofa.

'This is Doris,' said Bunder.

'Can I talk in front of her?' asked Charles openly and rudely.

'She wasn't born yesterday,' said Bunder shortly.

'Well, now, listen,' said Charles in the same rapid voice. He had a tremendous sense of the preciousness of time. 'I'll come straight to the point. I can't be bothered just now to wrap anything up.'

'Neither can I, old boy. Not my style at all. Cough it up, only don't be all night about it. Doris isn't here to see my stamp album.'

'Well, then,' said Charles. 'It seems to be fairly common knowledge that you and your particular pals have got some racket that brings you in pretty big money. No one's said anything, in so many words, and there's no indication that anyone knows a single concrete fact about it, but it's fairly clear that you've found some way of improving on the job from the money point of view, and I'm here to ask you whether you can trust me enough to let me in on it.'

Bunder's eyes narrowed a little, and he took a pull at his cigarette.

'I thought it wouldn't be long before you came round to ask me that,' he said. 'Just tell me one thing. You need to make more money, is that it?'

'That's it,' said Charles.

'I won't ask you what you need it for,' said Bunder. He glanced at Doris, then back at Charles, and smiled. 'It's nearly always the same story.'

'That's right, don't ask me,' said Charles. He stood stiffly, waiting for Bunder to make up his mind.

Bunder crushed out his cigarette. Then he stood up.

'All right, old boy, we'll take you in. I think you're the type.'

'Yes, I'm the type, old boy,' said Charles.

Three days later he found himself posted on a run to the northwestern docks in company with Bunder and five others. He had been given his instructions in private, and so, apparently, had everyone else, for there was no public reference to the job in hand. Nor was there any elaborate parade of casualness. They understood one another.

When they had arrived at the docks, and duly driven the cars to the appointed berth, there remained the two usual formalities. One was to obtain for each car a certificate that it had been delivered in proper fashion—the 'clearance chit'; the other was to unscrew the trade plates which the cars carried in place of the regulation number plates they would have when licensed. Each driver was always responsible for removing these plates, front and rear, from his vehicle and taking them back to Export Express.

Following Bunder's instructions, Charles went, as soon as he was free, to the public lavatory which served that particular berth of the docks. Inside, he found the others already assembled. They had handed over their trade plates to Bunder, who received Charles's from him and vanished, with the complete set, into one of the water-closet compartments. The others stood about, smoking, talking, and either using the urinals or pretending to do so, until, after a few minutes, Bunder reappeared, flushing the cistern noisily for the benefit of any outsiders who happened to be present. None were, and quickly, but without the need for concealment, Bunder handed everyone his trade plates back. Drifting out of the lavatory in ones and twos, they passed out of the dock gates and went off to the station.

Not until he was in the privacy of an empty compartment

in the train did Charles look closely at the two trade plates he was carrying. Each of them had a plastic back, painted to look like metal. A stiff clip held the back in place, but by inserting a half-crown into a slot at one end, it could be levered off fairly easily. He levered one of them off. Snugly fitting into the space between the plate's false back and its real one, a space perhaps three-sixteenths of an inch wide, were five tiny envelopes.

He snapped the back on again, and put the plates up on the luggage rack. He did not need to look inside those envelopes.

A few weeks ago, if asked to make a short list of the lowest human vermin, he would have put drug pedlars fairly near the head of the list—assuming it to be in descending order of loathsomeness—somewhere in the same region as white-slave traders. Now here he was, helping to smuggle heroin, or marijuana, or whatever the vile stuff was, out of the docks and put it in circulation. He had become a member, however insignificant, of the organization that spread these drugs throughout the country; the organization that saw to it that the drugs were brought over in the ships, taken into the pre-arranged lavatories on the docks, concealed inside the cistern or in some other manner, and picked up within a few hours by Bunder and his friends. The whole thing was one vast network; each man was given his particular task and told as little as possible about the rest of the business. For instance, he, Charles, did not even know what steps were to be taken to get these envelopes out of his trade plates. That was someone else's job; all he had to do was to leave them in the usual place when arriving at the Export Express headquarters; they would be got at somehow—perhaps by Bunder, perhaps by someone whom Bunder did not even suspect of being in the organization—and the envelopes removed. Then the filthy stuff would be hawked about and sold, finding its way into the systems of miserable creatures who were half-crazy, lonely, ill, neurotic, or just very young. And he had helped. He stared out of the train window with vacant, heavy eyes, hating himself, hating his failure. And what was he doing it for?

At the thought the vision of Veronica Roderick flashed with blinding intensity upon the screen of his mind, and at once his whole being, down to the smallest reflex and gesture, was drawn into the violent whirlpool of his longing for her. He knew that he would commit any crime, that he would steal, kill, maim, or ruin the lives of people who had never done him harm, for the sake, not of possessing her, but of giving himself even a remote chance of possessing her. He knew that neither his mind nor his body could recognize anything as evil, nor as good, except in direct relation to that desire. And he was helpless, and aghast.

VI

Sunflower Court proved to be a grandiose, ugly block of 'luxury' flats. As Charles walked up the steps he was aware of an unfamiliar sensation, as of something pressing against his right flank. It was his wallet. The reason why it was an unfamiliar sensation was that, for the first time, the wallet was crammed full of notes. For, besides the twenty-five pounds Bunder had handed him for his part in the smuggling trip, he had received his wages that Friday.

The porter told him where Mr. Blearney's flat was, and he took the lift. The flat had a front door like that of a house, complete with leaded window-panes and a letter-box. Even so, a considerable amount of noise filtered through. As Charles waited for Mr. Blearney to come to the door, he thought what a curious thing enjoyment was. The sounds he could hear were made by people who had assembled to have a good time, but they might easily have been cries of anguish. Mr. Blearney's voice, grating on as he told one of his stories, might have been the endless mumbling delirium of a man in great pain. The roars of laughter which punctuated it, reaching him muffled through two closed doors, sounded like the bellowing of a herd of cattle driven towards the slaughter-house. And one woman shrieked at intervals as if she were being disembowelled. He wondered if the Rodericks were there already.

It was not Mr. Blearney but a man in a white coat who opened the door. Charles guessed that this was Mr. Blearney's valet, dressed in a white coat to indicate for the occasion that he was in charge of the drinks. He relieved Charles of his overcoat and showed him into the room where the party was going on.

Mr. Blearney, having just finished his story, had turned to the sideboard for some refreshment, and so had his back to the door, so that he did not notice the arrival of Charles. The guests, who had finished laughing at the *dénouement* of the story, had not yet begun to talk about anything else, and were, for the most part, standing looking at one another as people do at parties before they break up into small groups. They turned and looked at Charles, who at once felt embarrassment surging over him. The valet did not announce him—it was not that kind of occasion and he was not that kind of valet—and the situation was, temporarily, a complete deadlock. Charles took a step or two forward, and tried to take in the scene with a single glance.

He succeeded only to the extent of noticing that there were about nine people in the room besides Mr. Blearney. Most of them were standing together in the middle, holding glasses in their hands. Their appearance, in general, gave the impression of what is usually known as Bohemianism, but without its redeeming features; they looked studiedly theatrical instead of harmlessly eccentric, and gave no impression, *en masse*, of intelligence or sensitivity. Charles's mind flew back to Froulish and Betty, but there was the world of difference between these people and the couple in the loft; they were harder, more brutal, less absorbed in pursuits outside themselves. The group seemed to be dominated, in the temporary absence of Mr. Blearney, by a thick-set, middle-aged man in a loud check suit, who had the biggest face Charles had ever seen. Its total area was big, and all its features were big. Huge eyebrows arched over protruding eyes. His mouth seemed immense even when, as now, he happened to have it closed for the moment. His nose was both long and fantastically bulbous, with nostrils like volcanic craters, from which black hairs peered. Hairs of about the same length covered the backs of his hands. Standing beside him was a young man in grey suède shoes; Charles caught sight of those shoes and decided that he now knew all he wished to know about one guest at least. He avoided glancing in his direction again.

Bernard Roderick was standing in the fireplace leaning his shoulders against the chimney-piece. Veronica Roderick was sitting by herself on a Windsor chair, a little apart from the others.

'Ha, Partner!' cried Mr. Blearney, turning round and seeing Charles. 'Just in time! Now we can really begin the fun—the party's complete! Folks, this is Harry Lumpy, a young motor engineer from the Midlands. This is Jimmy, Stanley, Elsa, Judy,' the succession of names flooded over his mind like dirty water.

Charles nodded and smiled several times, vaguely. He was wondering how soon he could get this part of it over and get across to Veronica. For a few minutes he stood on the fringe of the main group, while Mr. Blearney launched into another of his stories. The valet in the white coat came round with a tray of drinks. Charles took one and drained it. Immediately the valet was at his elbow, offering him another. Mr. Blearney had evidently trained him to encourage his own principle—the first one at a gulp, the second more slowly. He tried to keep his attention on the story, or rather cluster of related stories, into which Mr. Blearney was now fairly launched, but it was useless. He glanced across at Veronica Roderick. She was quite apart from the rest of the gathering. The valet had just handed her another drink, but she had not touched it. She was holding a cigarette in one hand. The slim white tube seemed thicker and clumsier than the fingers which held it. The spiral of smoke seemed less delicate and mysterious than her small, tense form.

She looked up and saw him looking at her. Without embarrassment she gave him a quick smile.

Charles began to edge away from his fellow-guests. If he could get across to her before Mr. Blearney finished his saga, they might have quite a few minutes together without interruption. As he began to steal away he felt a hand laid on his arm. It was the young man in grey suède shoes.

'Oh, *don't* go away,' he breathed in a beautifully modulated undertone, his hand closing round Charles's wrist. '*Do* come over and talk to me. I felt straight away when you came in, what an *interesting* face, I must talk to that young man.'

'Later, later,' muttered Charles impatiently, trying to push past him. But the man in grey suède shoes revealed an unexpected physical strength in the grip he now exerted on Charles's arm.

'Oh, yes, we'll have a nice *long* talk later,' he said. 'We'll go back to my place and we'll be able to talk all night if we want to. And I feel quite *sure* we *shall* want to. But do tell me something about yourself now. You're an engineer—how perfectly *unexpected*. I'd *never* have guessed.'

Charles stopped dead. It was no use trying to slip gracefully away from this kind of thing. It had to be faced and ended abruptly. It was one more of the obstacles that stood between him and Veronica Roderick.

With a considerable effort, he brought himself to look the suède shoe man straight in the eyes. 'Yes,' he said soothingly, 'we'll go to your place and have a nice long talk, and we'll be such good friends, and exchange photographs, and tell each other what we dream in the night, and when you go away for your holidays I'll have a key and call in every day and feed your canary, but for the next ten minutes I want to talk to somebody else, so just take your God-damned dirty hand off my wrist if you want to keep your front teeth.'

The man in grey suède shoes let go his wrist and said, 'At least give me your telephone number.'

Without hesitation Charles gave him a number. It was the number of the laundry to which he sent his clothes. The suède shoe man wrote it down in a small book, giving it a page to itself.

That left nothing except the smoke-filled air between him and the girl. All at once he had drawn a chair up next to hers and they were talking. And there was no stuttering shyness, no inhibition, now. It seemed, at last, so natural and right.

'Hello,' he said.

She replied, 'Hello.'

'Will this number find you during the day, or only in the evenings?' asked the man in grey suède shoes, who had followed him over.

Charles rose to his feet, and turned to Veronica with a courteous half-bow.

'Will you excuse me while I take this gentleman outside and throw him down the lift shaft?'

'Yes,' she said gravely.

'I'll ring you one week-end,' said the man in grey suède shoes, and left them. Charles sat down again.

Then they were talking once more, and again, in spite of the interruption, it seemed all so easy, so natural. Time was terribly limited—it could only be a matter of minutes before Mr. Blearney finished his story and came across to jolly them along—and there seemed so little point in beating about the bush. He had done with evasion.

'I have done with evasion,' he said out loud.

'And what does that mean exactly?'

'Just this.' He looked at her. 'Sooner or later I'd have to confess this, so I'll confess it now. When we met the other night in the Grand at Stotwell, that wasn't a coincidence. I'd been hanging about, in that very room, ever since I saw you in there for the first time. I wasn't sure what good it would do me if you did come in, but I—well, I just hung about.'

She had lowered her head, and remained silent for a moment, then said, 'Why would you have had to confess that sooner or later?'

'Because I love you,' he said.

'Are you all right, Veronica? You seem rather quiet; can I get you anything to drink?' asked Bernard Roderick, coming over to them. Mr. Blearney had finished his recital, and the central group was beginning to break up.

'No thanks, Uncle. Mr. Lumley is looking after me very nicely.' She smiled up at him, quite tense but quite composed. Only the hand that held the cigarette allowed the spiral of smoke to waver a little.

'Well, I'll just sit quietly and talk to you,' said Mr. Roderick levelly, sinking into a chair on the other side of her. 'This party's beginning to tire me. So many noisy people. I'm sure you two are right to get away from it into,' he smiled tinily, 'a quiet corner.'

Charles wanted to stamp on his stomach.

There was a short silence. Veronica sat absolutely still with the untouched glass at her side. She might have been carved, delicately, lovingly, by some patient old artist from a single block of ivory.

Mr. Blearney approached them, leading the man with the big face. 'Hullo, there,' he shouted. 'All happy, partners? All got plenty to drink? Hey listen, Bernard, Jimmy here wants you to tell Elsa about the time you and Alfie Beaner were in Rio. She's never heard that story. Elsa, love, come on over here! Jimmy's been telling me you've never heard Bernard tell the story about the time he was in Rio with Alfie Beaner. You mustn't miss this! Yes, Alfie Beaner. Hell, I didn't know anyone didn't know that story!'

'Is it a good story?' said Elsa slowly, and without much enthusiasm. She had reached a stage of intoxication which made it difficult for her to follow a connected narrative, and she was wondering whether this one would be worth the effort.

'No, it's not a good story, really,' said Bernard Roderick with a firmness that sounded greater than the occasion warranted. He seemed to be trying rather determinedly to get out of performing. But nothing would have put Mr. Blearney off the scent.

'Not a good story!' he shouted incredulously. 'What's come over you, Bernard? You've made more people laugh at my parties with that story—why, don't you remember the time Peter Philp was here, and I bet him he'd have to laugh, and he held out without laughing until you got to the bit where the old woman comes in and says, well, hell, I mustn't give it away, but you remember you were imitating the old woman, standing there and saying, *will you gentlemen have your coffee in here or out in the street in the rain*, don't you remember, and he laughed so much he got some kind of seizure and couldn't straighten his legs?'

'Yes, it's a good story all right,' said the big-faced man. 'I'd like fine for Elsa to hear that story.'

'What did they want to sit out in the rain for?' asked Elsa, beginning her grim struggle to understand.

'Hell, no, that's just *part* of it,' roared Mr. Blearney. 'They didn't want to, and anyway that's just *part* of it. . . . Bernard, you've got to tell her the whole story, so come on!'

They clustered round Mr. Roderick eagerly, and some of the other guests, those who felt like hearing the story again, came over and added themselves to the audience. Mr. Roderick disappeared in the centre of the expectant circle.

Charles stood up and vacated his chair to let Elsa sit down. She could hardly be expected to cope with the double strain of balancing on her legs and following the story. She sank into the chair so rapidly that she nearly pinned him underneath her, but he managed to slip past. Looking round, he saw that Veronica, too, had detached herself unobtrusively and was on the other side of the room brooding over a plate of olives. He went across to her.

'Do you like this party?' she asked, suddenly half-turning so as to face him.

'I haven't thought about it,' he answered. 'I only came because of you.'

She was silent, and Charles began to feel his earlier sense of ease and resolution leaving him. He fought to keep his self-possession, knowing that if he began to slide downwards he would not stop until he reached the very lowest level of gaping idiocy.

'May I call you Veronica?' he burst out, saying the first thing that came into his head.

Her smile this time had a flavour of genuine amusement in it. Probably this was as near as she ever came to laughing. He could not imagine her shaken by laughter.

'How funny to say you love me and then ask if you can call me Veronica—in that order.'

'It's not funny at all. It happened in that order. I loved you before I knew *either* of your names.'

'You mean any of them,' she said. 'I've got three.'

Again he felt himself slipping. Again he succumbed to the old fatal tendency, to stammer out the first piece of lunacy that entered his head.

'Do you like this party yourself?' he asked.

She shook her head with unexpected violence.

'I hate it. I always hate Mr. Blearney's parties, and so does my uncle. He only keeps up with him because of some business connection.'

Charles tried to think what business connection Mr. Roderick, a respectable industrialist, could have with Mr. Blearney and his Entertainments. He did not know the answer, but some instinct told him that it stank. He jerked his mind back on to the rails again.

'Then why did you come to it?' he heard himself saying, horrified at his own foolishness.

For answer she looked him straight in the eyes, for the third or fourth time since they had met, but this time with an indescribable hesitant appeal, a kind of shy warmth, that told him in an instant more than he could ever have dared to hope for. 'I came to see *you*,' said the eyes. For a second everything hung in the balance. He was within three feet of her, and enormous forces seemed to have closed on him and to be about to fling him one way or the other—forward to take her in his arms, or backwards on to the carpet in a swoon. He gripped the edge of the table.

'Listen, please, please, listen,' his voice broke out harshly and jerkily, 'I said I loved you just now, I didn't mean to come out with it as, well, as baldly as that, but somehow, all this has been so—so funny and—'

He stopped and tried to get a grip on himself.

'You don't know, you see, how odd and unreal this has all been—I was a window-cleaner when I first saw you, and then after setting eyes on you I knew I had to go away and throw it up.'

Worse and worse. The horrible suggestion of vomiting in the words 'go away and throw it up' fell terribly on his ears.

'Look, I'm not making this clear,' he said. 'I was a window-cleaner, do you see?'

'What's this, a joke about a window-cleaner?' cried the man with the big face, coming up behind him and catching the last few words. 'So that's what you take the little lady away into a corner for, is it? You want to tell her stories of that nature!' He laughed delightedly.

'Please, please, for God's sake go away,' said Charles sharply, turning to face him like a cornered animal.

'Oh, no, you must let me in on this,' chuckled the big-faced man, showing all thirty-two of his teeth. 'I like stories about window-cleaners myself.'

Veronica Roderick walked away, showing no sign of anger or impatience. She just walked away. Charles stood motionless, his face dead white.

'Something upset the little lady?' asked the big-faced man in a tone of pained surprise.

'Yes, you've upset her, you block-headed bastard, and you've upset me too,' said Charles in a low voice.

For some reason the big-faced man did not take offence at being called a bastard. Instead he did the worst thing he could have done, from Charles's point of view: he began to defend himself vociferously against the charge of tactlessness.

'Well, I must say I like that!' he spluttered. 'Here I am just behaving in a sociable way, like anyone would at a party, and I happen to hear you telling her a joke about a window-cleaner—'

'Shut up, please, PLEASE!' cried Charles urgently.

'—and being fond of funny stories myself,' brayed the big-faced man, 'naturally I came over and said, let me in on this, just like anyone would at a party—'

The others began to gather round to see what was the matter.

'I didn't know I was interrupting a—interrupting—'

'Interrupting a what?' asked Bernard Roderick smoothly.

'Well, I don't mean *interrupting* exactly,' said the big-faced man. 'I just meant, well, I didn't know it was like that.'

'You didn't know it was like what?' said Bernard Roderick again, smoothly.

'Look,' said Charles desperately. 'This gentleman's just making a natural mistake. I happened to be telling Miss Roderick about some of the jobs I've held, and I was just mentioning that I used to be a window-cleaner when—'

'A window-cleaner, oh, whoopee!' cried Elsa, who needed a little excitement after so much work. 'I bet I know what you did it for! Won't you tell us some of your experiences?'

'I bet that's what he *was* telling her,' husked Mr. Blearney in delight. 'No wonder he didn't like being interrupted!' His words were lost in gales of laughter.

Charles stared about him, almost beside himself. He actually felt tears of rage and humiliation forcing themselves up into his eyes. He had got her into this, he had involved her in this smutty inebriated laughter. To say nothing of annoying her uncle, for Bernard Roderick was obviously very angry. How could she ever, ever tolerate the sight of him again?

'I think it's time for me to go,' he said coldly. He pushed past them and went to the door. In the hall he looked for his overcoat, wishing only to get it and go, and leave the whole terrible mess for ever. His life was over.

He burrowed savagely among the coats in the hall, but none of them was his own. Furiously he flung open the door of the little room adjoining the one where the party was being held. He was looking for the valet to ask for his coat. The valet was not there. But his coat was hung over the back of a chair, and standing beside the chair was Veronica. She must have come through the communicating door from the main room.

'I'm sorry! I'm sorry!' he burst out, but before he could go on she had picked up his coat and handed it to him, saying in a rapid undertone, 'Call for me next Thursday and we'll go out for the evening. My uncle won't be at home.'

He stood clutching the coat, but she had vanished. As he hesitated, Mr. Blearney and several of the guests, including Elsa and the man with the big face, came in search of him.

'Here, partner, don't go,' roared Mr. Blearney. 'Hell, the fun's only just beginning!'

'Sorry,' replied Charles, trying to be as pleasant as possible, 'I hate having to go, but I have to be back at work. I have a job to do to-night.'

'Sounds like a burglar,' commented Elsa seriously.

'No, no, baby, he's just going to clean a few more windows,' said the big-faced man. 'He finds it more profitable to clean them at night. They pay him to go away then.'

There was another surge of laughter. Charles bowed politely and went out, slamming the flat door behind him.

Going down in the lift he tried to remember which part of his overcoat she had touched with her hands, so that he could place his own on the same spot. He could not be sure that he had it right.

Bunder smiled as he handed Charles the twenty-five one pound notes. Somehow it was that smile that touched off the profoundly hostile reaction that swept through his frame. Bunder had a way of making his moustache rise about an inch when he smiled, revealing long white teeth that gave a really horrifying impression of animality. They were like a dog's teeth.

But it was not the teeth but the eyes that suddenly disgusted Charles so much that he felt paralysed and could not stretch out his hand to take the money. They were slightly bloodshot; not through dissipation, because Bunder, like most really dissipated men, never showed any outward sign of it, but through driving an open car on a long run without goggles. And they were rather protruding, reminding Charles of the eyes of June Veeber. Worst of all, they were fixed on his own eyes with a horrible air of complicity. 'We know each other and we're both the same,' they signalled, just as clearly as Veronica's eyes, two evenings before, had spelt out a message of hope for him. The two messages jammed each other out. Bunder—drugs—Veronica—happiness; love, drugs in a water closet, huge dark eyes, dog's teeth, a pink gin, please, drink up partner, steady with that gearbox, someone to look after you, eh, Bernard?

'Feeling queer, old boy?'

He steadied himself. 'Just went a bit dizzy for a moment.' He put out his hand and took the money, forcing himself to grin. 'Feel better now I've got this.'

'It's probably your eyes making you feel dizzy, old boy. Mine sometimes go like that on me after a long run.'

'Yes, it's my eyes.'

'Better get some rest, old boy. Cheerio.'

'Cheerio.'

And I a twister love what I abhor.

They were dancing, then they were sitting at a little table, then they were dancing again.

'I hadn't better stay later than eleven.'

'I can drive you back in forty minutes.'

'You're lucky to have a car of your own.'

'It's hired, but I'm getting one of my own soon. Just a few more runs and I'll be able to buy one.'

'Your work must be well paid.'

'Yes, it's well paid.'

'Is it dangerous or something?'

'Yes, sometimes,' he said. 'It's dangerous sometimes.'

'It's always the dangerous jobs that are well paid, isn't it?'

'So it seems.'

She held him a little more tightly.

'I don't really like that, Charles.'

'Don't really like what?'

'You doing something dangerous.'

'Don't worry about me,' he said.

They went back to their table.

'I love you,' he said. 'That's dangerous, too, isn't it?'

'Why is it dangerous?'

'You'd know if you were in love.'

After one of her swift silences, she lifted her eyes to his face and asked, 'How do you know I'm not in love?'

'You'd say so if you were, wouldn't you?'

'I don't know. I don't say much, you know.'

'No,' he said, 'you don't say much.'

At ten past eleven they were outside. They got into the car. Before starting the engine he turned and faced her. There was a lamp in the car park; it shone through the window, palely, on her cheek, and glinted on her dark head.

'Why is it you don't say much?' he asked.

'I used to, once. But I gave it up, a long time ago.'

'Could I ask what happened to make you give it up?'

'Don't ask me,' she said. She kissed him suddenly and violently.

Trembling, he started the engine. They drove back in forty minutes.

It was not at all as he had imagined it. He had seen himself rising, with the aid of his suddenly improved finances, to a social position which would give him the *cachet* required to penetrate the Roderick circle; introducing himself; giving and receiving hospitality; becoming a known and trusted figure in the daily landscape, and finally—he was not quite sure what he had seen himself doing finally. He supposed he had seen himself making a respectable and solidly based offer of marriage, like any Tharkles anxious to establish a home where he could invite the managing director to dinner. But the fact was that he had never thought about it at all; he had not dared lift his eyes so high.

Instead, he had met with a fantastic combination of good fortune and bewildering obstruction. The good, of course, outweighed the bad; he could never have believed that such a girl as Veronica could feel—again his mind trailed off; could feel whatever it was she felt for him. That she could, at the very least, allow herself to be taken about by him (she usually found him at least one evening a week), and to give the appearance of enjoying these occasions, and looking forward to them with pleasure. But there was more than that, he knew there was more than that. Yet it was here that he ran his head into the brick wall, the blankness that barred his way. For one thing, it was obvious that, so far from ingratiating himself with Bernard Roderick, fairly elaborate precautions had to be taken so that the uncle did not even know of their evenings together: Veronica never actually put this into words, but it was clear from the beginning. He was seldom allowed to bring his car to the house and pick her up, except on occasions when Roderick was obviously away from home. Even then he had only to ring the front door bell and she emerged, ready to set off at once; he was never asked inside. Mostly she met him at some prearranged point, and here again he noticed that she never chose the Oak Lounge, her uncle's haunt.

At times he did not care, realizing the foolishness of giving any thought to the future so long as he had her in the present, and aware also, with a certain mild surprise, that he was perfectly happy to go on with no hint at all of what Froulish would have described as 'funny stuff'. Mild surprise, because he had never thought of himself as being particularly subject to the lover's romantic delusions; he was aware, as aware as any other young man, of the main idea underlying the division of mankind into two sexes. Yet as the weeks went by, and spring followed winter and gave a promise of summer beyond, it was enough to be with her, to listen to her voice and look into her dark eyes.

And yet sometimes the uncertainty of his position came clearly into focus, and then the whole burden of his terrible guilt crashed down upon him. He had thrown his humanity into the gutter, he had betrayed the trust that men place in one another, and with his thirty pieces of silver he had bought . . . what had he bought?

Sitting moodily over a drink one evening in a bar close to the

Export Express office, brooding on these problems, he was startled by a voice barking crisply into his ear, 'I'm not wrong, am I? It is Lumley?'

Even before his muscles had carried out their task of turning his head to meet this new challenge to his tranquillity, Charles's brain had recognized the voice. It had the familiarity that is only acquired by voices we have heard all through our formative years.

'Hullo, Dogson,' he said. 'Ready to start filling those inkwells?'

Harry Dogson laughed. Some ten years ago, when they were at school together under Scrodd, someone had made a joke involving himself and some inkwells—no one remembered what it had been; the original joke had dissolved, but the tradition had lingered on; to get a laugh at Dogson's expense, mention inkwells in his presence. A good-humoured boy, he had revelled in this passport to a genial popularity, always content to allow himself to act as butt.

'I drink out of glasses now,' he grinned. 'What are you having?'

Drinks bought, cigarettes alight, the conversation was free to begin. It turned out that Dogson was a reporter on the local evening paper. It was quite an important journal of its kind, but he was ambitious and hankering for Fleet Street.

'There's only one thing that can put you at the top,' he said, his plump face glistening with the sincerity of his devotion to an idea, 'and that's a real out-and-out scoop. Something that really catches the public's eye. Say an important series of articles on some scandal. Set the whole nation talking.'

There was something almost fine, almost admirable, in the selfless zeal with which Dogson worshipped the glory of the gutter press. He really yearned to identify himself with that cult in its most debased form. Charles looked at him, at his shabby sports coat edged with leather, his bitten finger nails, his stringy tie and dented pork pie hat, and wondered what it could be like to live for an ideal.

'As a matter of fact, I'm on to a series now, if I could just get the dope for it,' Dogson confided. 'I've pestered our news editor into promising that he'll find me space for it if I can make it good enough, and publish it as a signed series—it might be the making of me.'

'What is it?' asked Charles in idle curiosity.

'What is it?' echoed Dogson; always easily excitable, it was evident that his temperature was rising as he thought of his cherished project. 'What is it? It's the Foulest Racket in Britain To-day! The Shadow Falling Across Our Youth! The Vile Scandal of the Underworld!'

Charles looked at him to see whether he was joking; surely such a cascade of headline phraseology must indicate an unsuspected gift for self-parody. But Dogson was in deadly earnest; the corrupting air he breathed had already rotted what little critical acumen Nature had allotted him. His professional future seemed bright indeed.

'It's drugs,' said Dogson, coming down to earth. 'It's the drug racket. Of course it's pretty well covered already, what with the Vice Parade series in the *Clamour* and those three articles in *Sperm* with all those colour plates.'

Human misery and folly were merchandise to these people. But what were they to him? However low Dogson had sunk, he was infinitely lower.

'But the way I see it,' went on Dogson, warming to his subject, 'there's still room for a series with a rather specialized angle. You know—concentrating on one particular aspect.'

Charles felt his mouth and throat unnaturally dry. He took a long pull at his beer. As soon as the beer had splashed over it, his throat was dry again. He lit a fresh cigarette.

'What particular aspect?' he asked.

'Well,' said Dogson, 'I've been going into it, and I think too much attention has been paid to the distribution of the stuff once it's entered the country—you know, the way it's supposed to be hawked round at these jazz clubs and so on. Well, I know that makes a more obviously sensational story—a few photographs of addicts undergoing treatment, a shot of the interior of a typical club, and so on. But I think they've overlooked another aspect, one that's more difficult to ferret out, of course, but it seems to me that's just where the golden opportunity lies.'

'Opportunity to do just what?'

'Why, to dig in and find some facts and reveal them to the country at large,' cried Dogson. 'Anyway, I haven't told you what this aspect is that I have in mind. It's the actual smuggling in of the muck. *That's* the target.'

'But—but surely,' said Charles, speaking with a great effort, 'all that's taken care of by the Customs authorities and the dock police? They must be up to all the dodges. And it's precious little information you'll get out of them.'

'Oh, the customs! the police!' snorted Dogson in contempt. 'A fat lot they know. In any case I shan't go to them. I shall work on my own. I'm bound to turn something up. I shall have to use my own spare time, of course, and that skinflint Richards isn't even allowing me a quid or two for expenses, but I'll make it.'

He paused, then fixed Charles with an attentive eye. Evidently an idea was about to emerge.

'Now look here, Lumley,' he said, 'I've got a notion you could help me a lot here. You say you're an export delivery driver. You must be in and out of every principal dock in the country.'

Charles was silent. He had, indeed, outlined his work to Dogson in the first moments of their conversation, and now he could have bitten off his tongue. But how was he to have known what the maniac would do? He waited, miserably, for some crazy scheme to be outlined. His heart pounded savagely.

'Now, look here,' said Dogson again. 'I haven't got any official backing, you realize that. Left to myself, I couldn't even get access to the docks when the ships were being unloaded. It would be no use saying that as a member of the public I had a right to keep my eye on the smuggling in of injurious drugs.'

'Besides,' Charles put in harshly, 'you're not a member of the public. You're just a news-hound on the trail of a lurid story.'

'That's right, insult me,' said Dogson amiably. 'You always were a sharp-tongued swine, even at school. But look here, you can see what I'm driving at, can't you? It would surely be quite easy for you to get me in on your visits to the docks. You could run me down in one of these cars of yours—'

'Impossible,' Charles broke in with nervous loudness. 'We're strictly forbidden to carry any passengers.'

'Hell, that means train fares out of my own pocket,' Dogson sighed. 'Well, anyway, you just tip me off when you're going to the docks, and what berth you're going to and so on, and then I can meet you at the entrance and you can wave your magic wand and get me a pass in.'

He looked like a terrier as he met Charles's eyes with a frank friendly appeal. Charles crushed out his cigarette and leaned forward.

'Look,' he said slowly. 'I'm very sorry, Harry, but you must get this idea out of your head and keep it out. I can't get you into the docks, I can't give you any inside information, I can't wangle you a ringside seat while the country's drug traffic is being arranged, in fact I can't help you with your articles at all. Get it?'

'No, I damned well don't get it,' cried Dogson. 'For one thing, I don't see why you need be so bloody emphatic about it. Anybody'd think I was asking you to risk your neck for me, instead of just suggesting that you do me a little favour.'

Risk your neck. The words took Charles back to the dark doorway next to Harry's, with the bald-headed man holding the knuckle-duster under his nose. First time, you get this. Second time, you get your bloody neck broke. Then he saw the heavy boot stamping on the brass-ringed hand. Violence, agony, dark bruises. He did not want any more of that: he had been on the fringe of that world, and never wanted to go so close to it again. If Bunder, or any of the myriad others in the organization, thought he was responsible for putting this barking little terrier on the scent, it would certainly mean violence on a scale he had never known before, with himself at the wrong end of it. Oh, damn this innocent fool!

'Now, see here, Harry,' he said, forcing himself to relax and grin. 'Just let's drop the whole thing. It took me a long time to get this job, and I don't want the sack, and I don't want the reputation of bringing casual strangers along to keep an eye on our conditions of work. I don't want anything to do with your schemes for becoming a Fleet Street Tycoon. Just you do your job and I'll do mine.'

'Do my job?' echoed Dogson with some bitterness. 'God! Isn't that just what I'm trying to do? How else do you think a newspaper man works except by personal contacts like this? You're a disappointment to me, Lumley, you really are.'

'The road to Fleet Street,' said Charles with mock solemnity, 'is paved with disappointments. I've taught you a useful lesson.'

Dogson finished his drink and went out. Charles sat staring into his glass. His heart was heavy with a vague sense of menace; something inside him stirred with the gnawing consciousness that the evil consequences of his surrender could not for ever remain hidden from his sight, and that, when the time came for them to break and blaze forth, one more iron door would slam behind him.

The hot sun, that year's first, had drawn birds, insects, and plants into the open to receive its benediction: only human beings, sitting in offices, standing at benches and lathes, and going down coal mines with lamps in their helmets, withdrew themselves from it. In the College, however, all pretence of work had ceased at lunch-time. The undergraduates, who had been chosen from among many applicants on the strength of their intelligence, breeding, and ability to uphold the academic tradition of six centuries, were sitting on the grass in the garden with their shirts off, making clumsy and inexperienced overtures to the giggling maidens who accompanied them. Some had also removed their shoes and socks. The sunlight glinted on their spectacles, and the sound of their voices, delivering volleys of vulgar badinage in a variety of uncouth provincial accents, offered serious competition to the riot of bird-song that went on above their heads. The formal beauty of the groves and flower-beds, set off by the breathtaking perfection of the grey stonework of the College itself, strove to the limit of its power to soften and contain their boorishness, but was defeated by their appalling mental and physical ugliness as they sprawled on the ground or loafed coarsely to and fro, smoking cigarettes and scattering stubs, empty packets, and match-sticks on the velvety turf. Now and again some don, blinded by habit both to the beauty and the sordidness of the scene about him, scurried through the garden with the brisk, proprietary stride of a shop-walker in a big store: none of the wealth on show is his, but somehow it lends him some of its prestige.

Charles and Veronica sat on a wicker seat under a beech tree.

Its lower branches were close above their heads, and the green transparency of the fresh young leaves seemed an exact counterpart to the vivid innocence of their emotion. It had been a good idea to bring her here. When he had first driven up for her in a car of his own, and they had decided on a day's excursion as soon as it could be arranged, he had left the choice of direction to her; and when she had said she wished to see his college, he had felt a flush of discomfort at the thought of revisiting the scene of so much folly and embarrassment; he had been on the point of explaining to her his revulsion against the place, and people, by whose means he had been so painstakingly unfitted for life. But he had suppressed it, and now, all was perfection. The car had run beautifully, the day was superb—one of those freak hot days in late April—and here was the College putting forth all its beauty as if to make amends to him for all it had denied. The garden took her slight form and enthroned it in a splendour that left no detail of perfection to be desired. The sun shone warmly on his utter contentment.

As they sat, silently happy, a tall shambling figure swayed slowly across the lawn in front of them. It was Lockwood, his brows furrowed in what passed for thought. Something stirred in Charles, prompting him to issue a challenge.

'Lockwood,' he said sharply and brutally.

The loose-knit figure swayed to a standstill, the watery eyes looked over the upper rims of horn circles. Slowly the tutor brought his mind to bear on this new disturbance. He opened and shut his mouth several times; it was obvious that he was trying to remember, first, who this was, and secondly, whether he was one of the present generation of undergraduates or had gone down. Then he noticed Veronica, and a hungry look challenged the presiding bewilderment on his features.

'Oh, er,' he said, and paused for a long time. Taking out a brown metal case, he removed his spectacles and put them inside it. Then he replaced the case in his pocket and took out another, similar case. From it he drew out another pair of glasses, this time with shiny metal rims. These he held in his hand. Two small egg-shaped patches of light, reflected from their lenses, swayed gently to and fro on the grass by Veronica's sandalled feet.

Charles had the odd sensation that if one of them should actually rest for an instant on her bare skin it would burn her.

'It's you, Lumley,' said Lockwood. 'Haven't seen you since you went down.'

'I haven't seen you either,' said Charles flatly. There was a pause. Two of the young gentlemen chosen from a large number of applicants came slouching past. As Lockwood was standing about seven feet away from the seat on which Charles and Veronica were sitting, they had room to pass between them, interrupting the conversation. This they did with no sign of hesitation or apology. One of them, who was in the middle of a facetious anecdote, did not moderate his voice. 'And when they put it to her,' he was saying, 'all she said was, "Well, you couldn't expect me to keep it in the living room."'

When they had passed, Charles said, 'Of course, I've been busy earning my living.' He did not offer to introduce Veronica: Lockwood must wait for that privilege.

'Ah, yes, earning your living,' said Lockwood cautiously. 'We all have to come to it,' he added in a half-attempt at geniality. 'And in what, ah, sphere, in what . . . ?'

'Well, I say *earning*,' said Charles with the air of one wishing to be perfectly accurate, 'but of course it's only a nominal salary I'm getting at present: I'm still in training under an apprenticeship scheme.'

'Yes?'

'And of course it'll be some time before I'm admitted to full status.'

'Yes?' said Lockwood again, with a hint of impatience.

'It can't be learnt in a few months, of course.'

'*What* can't?' cried the scholar sharply. The ovals of light jerked, traversed Veronica's ankles, and came to rest on the hem of her skirt. It was the signal to stand up.

'Allow me to introduce you,' Charles said, rising. 'Veronica, this is Mr. Lockwood, whom you remember my having mentioned so often. This is Miss Roderick.'

'How do you do?' said Lockwood bemusedly. He stood swaying in the sunlight, looking from one to the other like a stupefied bull.

She answered him with the appropriate formula. Silence fell, and before any of them could speak again a young man with a prematurely bald head waddled on short legs round the edge of a flower bed.

'About those papers, Lockwood,' he began abruptly, ignoring Charles and Veronica. Evidently this was some colleague from another part of the University. Charles and Veronica moved silently away. The staccato voice of the young don, crassly forcing its way through the sunlit air, followed them as they went.

He had not, at any stage of his preparations for to-day, envisaged the possibility that they would 'go on the river'. It was too much the expected, obvious thing, a *cliché* embodied in action; young love, the murmuring water, the shared isolation of the boat, holding them together within its hard, flat narrowness. He was getting a little too old for such a formula to keep its appeal. But actuality, once again, proved him wrong, showing up the shallow stupidity of his post-adolescent rejection of the 'romantic' paraphernalia, with all its significance and strength still to be drawn out of it. They found themselves walking by the river as it flowed between the moist, level meadows: it invited them: a man handed Charles a pole, wrote a number in a book, and pushed them out into midstream: and the expected, trite setting was immediately mustered, ready once again to produce the expected, trite emotion.

Except that the setting and the emotion were not expected and trite. After so many false starts, so many occasions when the equipment was all in order but the product stale, factitious, mis-shapen, the mixture worked at last. The magic spell, mumbled wearily and with less and less conviction, suddenly rang out sharply and turned the frogs and rats back into men, the fairy came down from the Christmas tree, the straw was spun into valuable gold. Was it just because he was with *her*? Charles wondered; but no, there was, really and genuinely, an element of luck or magic (two names, same thing) which had whisked up the tired ingredients and made everything vital and beautiful. The sunlight on the water knew exactly how to behave; after so many centuries it could produce the precisely needed effect as it flickered in reflection on the dark underneath of the leaves which the trees held out at just the correct height above it. The birds were rehearsed, the flowers and grass knew precisely what to do; the cool grey shapes of revered buildings formed, in the background, a perfectly contrived contrast and balance for the calm, heavy cattle lying down in the fields. So slick, so confident in its much-photographed guide-book-and-calendar charm, the ensemble ought to have been a flop. But in fact, it worked, and Charles had to admit that its method was the only one; like all beautiful old fakes, it had ended by believing in itself, and that conviction could not, ultimately, be resisted.

Actually, he found afterwards that he could remember nothing, in detail, about the two hours they had spent on the water. Nothing except, oddly, Veronica's handbag, which lay on the floor of the boat. It was of a rather distinctive shape, square and chunky, with a clip that looked like a coiled golden serpent. Each time he swayed forward, letting the wet pole slide down between his hands for its hook to bite into the gravel, his eyes focused on the handbag as it lay beside its owner's feet, like a dog, quietly and trustfully, wishing only to hold and carry things for her, and to give up its secrets at the touch of her hands.

The funny thing about what happened afterwards was the naturalness, the ease, the absence of any fuss or strain. He had always, when he allowed himself to think about it, assumed that if ever they became lovers, it would be as a result of some 'significant' and purposely built up scene, a matter of formal declaration and overt discussion, or, at the very least, the outcome of some period of obvious and mutually communicated tension. But this, the actuality, was upon them silently and with no sense at all of anything to be *done*, consciously or sternly, no stepping over a threshold. It was merely as if they had been looking at one another through plate glass, and, being momentarily dazzled, had closed their eyes, and opened them to find that the hard, transparent barrier had dissolved with air.

They knew it before either of them spoke. They knew it as they walked between crumbling stone walls in the straight, golden rays of the sunset; as they sat, with glasses in their hands, at a stained wooden bench, not speaking, but thinking to each other.

At last he said, foolishly:

'Time to be getting back, I suppose.'

She put her glass down, quietly and peacefully, and said, 'You *know*, don't you?'

'Know what?' he said, still foolishly, but calm, not hating himself.

'That we're not going back,' she said.

'No, we're not going back,' he repeated. 'Not to-night. We're here, and we're together, and happy, and we're not going back.'

'Go and arrange it,' she said. 'I'll stay here and wait. Don't be long, Charles.'

He got up to go and arrange it.

'Please don't be long,' she said again.

'Look out of the window,' he said. 'That's me coming back already.'

He went and arranged it.

VII

There were nine cars to go down that morning, and they were driving through light summer rain in a loose convoy, about a hundred yards apart. Charles was last. He sat relaxed behind the wheel; there was not much traffic, and only the surface of his mind was occupied in guiding the car; the rest of his being directed itself, in a glow of tranquil devotion, towards the thought of Veronica. This glorious sense of having *won*, come what may, was entirely new to him. Searching his mind for something that would pin down, by comparison, his state of mind, he thought of an outclassed player at some strenuous game such as tennis, who has managed to stay level with his opponent, and finally, by a superhuman effort, to gain a few points' lead; and is then suddenly told that, although the game is to continue for some time, no more points will be awarded. Whatever happens now, however many mistakes he commits, he is, irreversibly, the winner. His game would probably rise to heights of unforeseen brilliance through sheer carefree confidence; and such, Charles reflected, would be his own life from now on. It had succeeded.

He had attained the one object that he had ever pursued without finding it to be an illusion. There was indisputable evidence, in the lightness of his heart, in the tonic joyfulness of every breath he drew, that he was happy.

Something reached inwards from the fringe of his consciousness. For about fifteen minutes his driving mirror had picked up, now and again, a shape that swayed into its orbit and then swayed out again. Now that shape drew more determinedly into focus, and, although he was travelling fairly fast, Charles drew over, to allow a motor-cyclist to pass. The mirror picked up the front wheel and windscreen of the machine as it came up; it was one of those large and ornate American motor-cycles, painted cream and draped all over with lamps, fenders and horns. The rider was a mere wad of sacking humped over the tank.

Until a second glance disclosed that the wad of sacking had a distinct head. And that the front of the head, as is usual, was occupied by a face. And that the face was turned to look straight into Charles's own, with a ludicrous expression of smugness and triumph.

Viciously, Charles pushed the brake pedal down into the floorboards. The car skidded, dragging itself to a stop in a series of half-turns on the wet road. Rain drummed on the roof as he sat in silence, the engine ticking over. The motor-cyclist, taken by surprise, was already fifty yards ahead. He slowed down more cautiously, turned his machine in a tight circle, and clattered back in low gear. Charles wound his window down and they faced each other.

'Rather handy, this,' said Dogson in a bright, embarrassed way. 'Got it on the never-never, of course.'

'Going anywhere particular?' asked Charles, coming straight to the point.

'Well, yes, actually,' said Dogson. He paused, unwilling to specify. Relentlessly, Charles took him up.

'Can I guess where?'

'Have a shot,' chuckled the other with a constrained *bonhomie.*

'Stop acting like a bloody fool, Harry. You're going down to the docks to make a nuisance of yourself to our lot. Don't spin me any fool yarns. You've been following me for miles, probably ever since we left the works, but I've only just noticed it since we got clear of other traffic.'

'Well, what of it, blast you?' growled the journalist, his over-hearty demeanour turning in an instant to sulkiness. 'You needn't think it's fun, sitting on this damned thing mile after mile, chasing you over wet roads, and all because you wouldn't stretch a point and let me ride with you.' Water trickled from his lank hair.

Charles looked at him in despair. It was obvious that the bland and foolish face masked a determination that, however it might issue only in the form of silly obstinacy, was not to be put off. Dogson, inspired by the potent blend of ambition and devotion to an ideal, would hang on until the end.

Until the end! And what would the end be? Sick at heart, he thrust his head out of the window and spoke savagely.

'I'm telling you here and now to let this rubbishy idea drop. You'll go to insane lengths to get on to the docks while the export drivers are there, and make a blasted nuisance of yourself to everyone concerned, and in the end you'll find nothing and simply add to your reputation as a flaming silly fool.'

Dogson kicked at his machine. The engine started with a great bellow. In open hostility, he faced Charles from the centre of a storm of noise and smoke.

'How do you know I'll find nothing?' he shouted. The words came through the inferno with an oddly eerie effect. He circled and was gone, in pursuit of the cars.

Charles started up and began to follow. His happiness of a few minutes before was strangely dulled. The game must be played on, he suddenly felt, under some new and crushing handicap.

About noon, he arrived at the docks, and joined the others outside the entrance to the appropriate berth. While they waited for the official routine to complete itself, the drivers clustered together by the gate, smoking and talking; Bunder, who seemed in high spirits, was telling a story which the others punctuated, as Charles approached, with bursts of laughter. Jack Simons, his grey cloth cap set straight on the top of his head, leaned against the wall a few yards away from the others. Bunder's particular cronies avoided, rather too carefully, the appearance of forming a group among themselves; they took pains not to stand next to one another or begin any private discussion. They were all, undeniably, glad that there was no 'job' on to-day. Bunder had received no word of a consignment to be picked up, and they were free to come and go like honest men. For himself, Charles reflected, he cared very little. His life had so long ceased to move to the ordinary rhythms at all; his happiness was concentrated absolutely in his dealings with Veronica, and the effect was to blot out the concept of guilt from his mind altogether. With it, surprisingly, went his fear. Although detection and arrest would lead immediately to the only evil he was still able to imagine—separation from Veronica—he had so completely accepted the fact that only his crime made her accessible to him, that his terrors had been laid to sleep as under an anæsthetic. He did not share the terrible nerve-shaking that the others, even Bunder, so manifestly underwent. It was another example of the fantastic narrowing of his mind. One idea possessed it utterly, and his obsession gave him all the strength and obstinacy he needed.

He leaned against the wall. Only one thing troubled him, and that was the possibility—indeed, certainty—that the journalist was about somewhere. He glanced about, irritably, but there was no sign of the fanatic or of his motor-cycle.

Simons broke into his thoughts with some question about the morning's run. Charles answered perfunctorily, and Simons resumed his silence. He seldom spoke to Charles nowadays, being shrewd enough to see, in spite of all the precautions Charles took, that his warning not to associate with Bunder had been disregarded. When their eyes chanced to meet, the older man's had a directly reproachful look in them; however little he wished to show it—for it was obviously his policy to meddle no farther in the matter—his own honesty, brought into contact with this duplicity, sparked into something like accusation. Charles, who in his pre-Oak Lounge days would have been desperately troubled by the disapprobation of such a man, was now totally indifferent to it, when he noticed it at all.

'All right, come on out of it,' said a voice, loudly but with a kind of forbearance in its tone. Everyone turned in surprise.

'I've got a perfect right, I can prove it—a MORAL right—the

people must KNOW—' came a squawk. Charles stiffened into weariness and disgust. Round from behind the row of shining black cars came a policeman leading Dogson by the arm. The scene was so obviously farcical that most of the drivers, and others who were standing about, grinned broadly or laughed outright. The constable, mellowed by the sudden relaxation of tension, condescended to say, as he passed, 'Spotted him climbing into one of your cars. Trying to get access to the dock—hiding in the back as it drove in.'

Suddenly Dogson caught sight of Charles. 'Here, Lumley,' he called as the policeman marched him away, 'you put in a word for me, will you? It might make all the difference.'

'You know this man?' said the policeman, halting. 'If so, I shall have to ask you to come across to the Supervisor's office as soon as you're free and identify him.'

'All right,' Charles muttered. The pair clumped away. At that moment the signal was given that the drivers could carry on with moving their cars on to the docks. They broke up at once, and the next half-hour was devoted to the job in hand.

As soon as it was over, Charles went across to the Supervisor's office and identified a sulking Dogson, giving his testimony that the fellow was harmless. He left by himself, leaving Dogson still being interrogated, but conscious that he had probably made all the difference for him between being fined and being released with a caution.

As he walked from the office to the dock gates, another figure fell into step beside him. It was Bunder. Charles wanted to speak, but he felt suddenly choked and unable to think of an opening remark. Bunder for his part remained absolutely silent. They passed into the street. Bunder held open the door of the first public house they came to, and in a moment they were sitting, with drinks before them, in a secluded corner of the saloon bar. Neither had yet spoken to the other.

Bunder looked across at Charles steadily. They sat motionless, with the untouched drinks on the table between them.

There was no doubt that Bunder was absolutely the master. Just at the moment when it seemed their silence was assuming the form of a contest to see who could hold out longest, he suddenly made a nonchalant gesture which indicated, with complete success, that the game was over and that the prize was awarded to himself; and spoke.

'So you had a visit from a friend.'

'Friend nothing,' said Charles with a weak effort at resistance. 'That fellow just knows who I am, that's all.'

Once the words were out of his mouth he appreciated, horribly, their silly emptiness.

'He knows who you are, that's all,' said Bunder calmly. 'And he knows your name, that's all, and he gets you to go and help him out when he's arrested, and he knew there was a consignment of cars coming down this morning, that's all.'

Charles took a long swallow at his drink. It was like a sinister repetition of his encounter, a lifetime ago, with Mrs. Smythe. I'm a private detective. Go ahead, detect something. Detect something to say to Bunder to save yourself from a cut throat or a knock on the head one dark night.

'Look, let's be reasonable,' he began with a violent effort.

'I'm being reasonable, old boy,' said Bunder gravely. 'It strikes me you're the one who's being unreasonable. Bloody unreasonable.'

'Can I help it if I know a loony?' Charles jerked out.

'No,' the other agreed, 'but you can bloody well help it if you act like a loony. You know what I'm getting at. Publicity isn't much of a help in our line. Then a man turns up one day trying to hide in one of the cars and get access to the dock. He's found out somehow that there's a convoy going down on that day. When he's pulled out of it he appeals to you to go and bail him out or whatever you were doing. So you have to go and stand in the Supervisor's office and get your face properly looked at by a lot of officials and policemen, every one of whom will remember you whenever he sees you. And all because some silly bastard wants to get on to the dock without a permit. And what was he doing it for, anyway?'

It suddenly flashed across Charles's mind that Bunder was, mercifully, ignorant of the true facts. Of course! Dogson to him would appear simply as a bum, a sneak-thief or outright imbecile with a simple felonious motive for being where he should not be. He searched his memory for a long second. Had Dogson blurted out anything about being a newspaper man? No: he had said, amid his incoherent protests, 'The people must know', but that fragment of the shapeless mass of rhetoric he carried inside him would not necessarily mean anything to a casual listener. He must keep Bunder absolutely and permanently in the dark about Dogson and his mission to reveal the secrets of the drug traffic. Otherwise it would be the end for both of them.

'You've heard of—er—Jehovah's Witnesses?' he began jerkily. Behind Bunder's long, evil face hovered a vision of the resentful scowl of Mrs. Smythe. This time the act had to be good.

'What would that have to do with it?' came the silky, menacing tone.

'Well, it's quite simple really.' A little of the old fluency was coming back. 'This man's a member, and he's got some bee in his bonnet about sailors, that they need converting more than any other part of the community. He's tried time and again to hold meetings in the evenings at various seaport towns, and having failed, he's got the idea that his only hope is to get aboard the ships themselves, while they're in dock, and go down to the men's living-quarters with his tracts and things. He's regularly in trouble for trying to worm his way into berths that are closed to the public.'

Bunder drank from his glass. He looked meditative.

'I didn't notice that he was carrying a case or anything to hold his tracts in.'

'He's too clever for that,' said Charles solemnly. 'He thinks it would antagonize the men if he were obviously going to distribute literature. He carries them on him. His pockets are bulging with them.'

'Is that so?'

'Bulging,' Charles repeated with great emphasis. His heart was hammering.

Bunder stubbed out his cigarette, and, looking up, held Charles's eyes firmly with his malicious gaze.

'Do you know what I think about that story?'

'What should you think of it?' Charles managed to croak from a dry throat.

'I think it's phony.'

There was a pause that dragged into an eternity.

'Either he's shooting a phony line or you are. I wouldn't know which. That's the only thing I don't get.'

Charles was helplessly silent.

'That bird isn't a Jehovah's Witness or anything of the sort. He's just some little rat who wanted to be on the wharf at the same time as us. I don't know why, and I don't know whether he's fooled you with this crazy yarn, or whether you know what he's really up to, and daren't talk because you're afraid it's your own fault he's hooked on to us. Because you've opened your mouth too wide.'

Another silence. Centuries went by, geological eras came and went, mountains rose from the sea and subsided again. Whole cycles of evolution developed at their leisure. The hands of the clock, by a laughable illusion, recorded this stretch of aeons as forty-five seconds.

'Well,' Charles got out at last, 'what are you going to do about it?'

'I'm not going to do anything about it,' Bunder purred. 'For one thing it's not my job to do anything about it. If you're really sticking your neck out, it'll have been noticed before now, by those whose job it is to notice these things. They'll take care of you. Because,' he finished on a suddenly harsh tone, 'the rest of us have got to be protected.'

'Protected,' said Charles weakly.

'Protected against anybody who for any reason, *for—any—reason*, might land us in trouble. And the funny thing was that the two float chambers weren't identical in shape.'

'Identical in shape?' Charles murmured in bewilderment.

'No, but they seemed to work all right. Gave a very good mixture. But it surprised me when I first saw them.'

Charles realized that a man in a bowler hat had sat down within earshot of their conversation. One had to admire Bunder for some things. At least he was a perfect specimen of adaptation to a particular end. One could imagine him as a baby leaning out of his perambulator to steal a fruit drop and putting the blame on his little sister.

They walked out of the bar and set off in different directions.

'Look, don't let's dance,' he said. 'Let's sit down.'

'You're looking terribly tired, my poor thing,' she said. 'Are you ill or something?'

'No, not ill. Just a bit tired.'

'I'm sure you're ill. Either that or terribly worried about something. Please, please, dear, why don't you tell me?'

'Tell you what?' he said.

She frowned. 'I shall lose my temper. You'll make me lose my temper. Why do you hide so much from me?'

He was at a loss. She had become, of late, so much a part of him that it was increasingly difficult to hide the slightest corner of his mind from her knowledge. Normally it did not matter, since, when they were together, everything else was banished, and there was nothing he could not fully and frankly reveal to her. But the interview with Bunder had shaken him.

'Oh, my darling,' she said sadly. 'Why do you pretend so hard that you love me, when it's obvious all along that you can't if you don't trust me?'

'I do love you,' he muttered earnestly. 'And I do trust you. It's just that there are some things I don't want to burden you with.'

She looked at him with astonishment.

'How can you say that? Don't you know that when a woman loves a man she wants everything, *everything* about him, including what you call burdens—yes, especially those: can't you see that the only burden to her is to feel that he's keeping something from her?'

'Will you marry me?' he said abruptly.

She drew in her breath sharply, as if to speak with vehemence, but was silent.

'I said, will you marry me?' he said again, flatly and without emphasis. The waiter heard him and moved discreetly away.

'Would you mind not asking me that, not just at present?' she said slowly.

'But Veronica, for God's sake, why not?'

'There are things,' she said, still slowly, and with eyes fixed on the stem of her glass. 'Things you don't know about.'

'Don't you know,' he said bitterly, 'that when a man loves a woman he wants everything, *everything* about her, and that the only burden to him is to feel that she's keeping—'

'Stop!' she cried suddenly. They looked at each other, baffled and inquiring.

'Take me away from here, Charles. Anywhere, I don't care. We'll go to an hotel if you like.'

Moving towards the door, he felt, and knew that she felt, that they were running away, hard, in panic, from something that they had never seen or heard, and about which they knew only that it was terrible.

The evening had that sudden chill dampness that the end of May will sometimes produce; a cold, salty wind blew from the sea. Charles had no overcoat with him, and he shivered continually in his thin jacket as he paced between the bleak, ugly sheds. The cold was, in fact, more present to his mind than the nervous demands of the situation—demands which, but for the immunity accorded him by his demented state, would have been considerable, for that evening there was a 'job' to be done. They were to assemble, with trade-plates at the ready, for an unusually large consignment.

All this was, to him, a surprise in itself. For about three weeks, neither Bunder nor anyone else had mentioned such matters in his hearing. He had not even known, and had been scrupulous in doing nothing to find out, whether there were any 'jobs' going on. It was, for one thing, by no means certain that he would be used any more after the débâcle over Dogson; and in any case, probably, an interval would have to elapse in which he could be watched to see if any of his activities indicated danger or treachery. With complete fatalism he had even faced, at odd moments, the possibility of being murdered: Bunder's 'the rest of us have got to be protected' certainly contained a clear hint of it; but he had taken no steps to safeguard himself. As for leaving his job, it was obviously out of the question. His one chance of safety was to stay where he could be watched until suspicion died away; in any case, what else could he do? Even as it was, he was beginning to find himself short of money after three weeks on his bare wages. And then, without fuss, and with no indication that anything had happened since their last assignment, Bunder had quietly given him his instructions, just before setting out that morning.

A squall of rain sent him back to the shelter of the shed wall. The vehicle he had driven down, a light van, had been taken away for loading at once, and before they could leave the dock for the warmth of some bar or café, there was the usual delay over the official clearance forms. Besides the job: his glance flickered nervously over to the door set in a concrete wall, with 'MEN' painted in dark crude letters beside it.

It was time. The forms were issued, and folding them into their pockets, the drivers trailed away in ones and twos to the gate. Charles stepped behind some crates to be out of sight during the few minutes he must wait before entering the lavatory. Another of the men concerned had already had the same idea, and he silently produced a cigarette. Charles, laying down his trade-plates on the ground, made a lengthy business of bringing out a match and lighting it for him; should anyone chance to pass and see them, they were just sheltering from the wind to keep the match alive. After a moment the other, his eyes deep-set and dark beneath his cap, looked at his watch and jerked his head in the direction they must go. He set off, and Charles followed. He felt sick; his flannel trousers were dark with rain at the front, where he had faced the drizzle-carrying wind.

They were the last to enter. The lavatory was shadowy and damp, with an incessant dripping from pipes and cisterns that matched the weather outside. Come on, get it over. Bunder seemed unnaturally thin and elongated as he collected the trade-plates in a bundle under his arm and turned to one of the cubicles. Suddenly there was a concerted stirring and stiffening of attitudes. Someone else had come in. Charles, who was standing with his back to the scene, using the urinal, felt immediately and desperately certain that something terribly wrong had happened. He shivered violently. There was no sound from behind him. After a long moment he buttoned and turned round. Bunder was there, motionless, with the plates under his arm; the other drivers were gathered into a knot, staring fixedly towards the newcomer. Dogson, rigid as the others, was staring back at them.

He did not look towards Charles. It was impossible to tell whether he was aware of his presence. All that he was aware of, all that any of them were aware of, was that the swift and ultimate crisis had been reached.

It came too suddenly to be anything but a scene from a nightmare. Bunder jerked forward and threw open one of the doors. A short, squat man in a black leather cap reached across and grasped Dogson, pinioning his arms behind him. The mouth in the foolish round face opened, but no sound came out. Bunder used his free arm to seize Dogson's shoulder as the man in the leather cap dragged him in through the door. It slammed. The three of them must have had barely room to stand inside.

'Break! Clear out!' came a voice. Charles could not tell who spoke. But the group broke suddenly into motion. In panic, a panic he knew was shared, he butted his way out of the door into the rain. Outside, some stood indecisively for a second before forcing themselves to walk, not run, in a parody of normal gait, in different directions; others ran madly for a few yards before getting a grip on themselves and slowing to a walk. The horrible silence of the scene emphasized its dream-like flavour.

In an agony, he shambled towards the gate, mechanically fumbling for his pass. On the level of conscious, intentional action, he had no wish at all to go back and help Dogson, though he knew that by acquiescing he was leaving a man to his death. But something caught at his knees and weakened them as he stumbled away. His body, or some mysterious part of the complex of his being, cried out to be back in there, holding Bunder by the throat, shielding Dogson from the silent, vicious onslaught from which, now, it was already too late to save him. Over and above it was a surge, recognizable and clear, of anger. Damn the fool! Damn the blundering fool!

Two of the others who had started out in a different direction and already reached the gate, suddenly appeared running, their faces creased with fear. They rushed heavily past him, and he sprang, with a pure reflex action, behind the same pile of crates that had sheltered him earlier. Peering through a narrow gap he saw a group of purposeful figures in dark uniforms walking past; not running, but walking, like men whose task is not to pursue but merely to move in and clear up an ugly mess.

He shrank back. In a moment they would begin a systematic search, and he would inevitably be taken.

His brain misted over for a moment, then cleared suddenly. It had an old trick of doing that. The new gain in clarity was always startling, and never more so than now. When he had been taken with Dogson to the Supervisor's office three weeks before, he had noted, mechanically, that the sanctum was housed in a block of offices which clustered and leaned on one another in a large ramshackle building, looking from the outside like a warehouse. That building had several entrances. Some of them gave on to the street outside. One of them gave on the wharf where he was now standing.

It was a choice between a fantastic risk on the one hand, and the complete certainty of capture on the other. Keeping out of sight as far as possible, he moved along to within twenty yards of the door he was making for. Dusk was beginning to fall, but he knew that this was no great help to him: within a few minutes, when the police had gathered fresh men and spread the net systematically over the area, a suspect would be picked up even if it were pitch dark. As yet, however, the general alarm had not been given, and the small, blurred drama was acting itself out in a framework of general indifference and orderliness. Workmen were leaning against a shed wall, watching with happy curiosity the knot of officers moving along the wharf; elsewhere the routine was going on in ignorance of any disturbance of its peace.

Amazingly, no one stopped Charles, no one pointed him out and began to run towards him, no one heeded him. There was the lull of a few seconds before the oiled machinery of pursuit came into action, and, by pure coincidence, he had achieved the miracle of timing that enabled him to use those few seconds. He entered the building by a clouded glass door that looked as if it were only occasionally used and then not by anyone of importance. A flight of stairs led upward. Long, dark corridors branched. The office staff had long gone home, but it was not yet time for the caretaker to inspect and lock up. Again he had chanced on the one brief space of time that most favoured him.

He lost his way; and, pausing to look out of a window, found that he was already on the side of the building that overlooked the street. The nearest door on the street side, if they had not already placed a guard over it, would free him, temporarily, at least.

Footsteps clumped up the stairs, and a bowed figure with an oval pail in one hand and a broom in the other came scowling up to him. But the voice that accompanied it was casual, not angry.

'Been workin' late, aincher?'

'I had to see about the catgut. Writing a report on the catgut,' Charles's whirling memory prompted him to stammer.

'Oh,' said the man with complete indifference, not listening. 'Well, you'll find the door open just down the bottom of these stairs. I'd rather you went out that way. If you go over to the main doors, I'll 'ave to come with you because we're supposed to keep the place clear after a certain time. Just you go down these stairs, and then I know you're off the place. An' you're the last.'

His rambling semi-explanation was not clear, but Charles seized on the directions as to the way out. Plunging down the stairs with no attempt to conceal his haste (after all he was a young clerk who had had to stay over time and write a report on catgut, which had made him late for a date with his girl), he found an open door leading to an alley. Emerging on to the street, he turned sharply away from the direction of the main entrance and walked as fast as he dared. The rain had abated, but the wind still blew in chill gusts, and he felt himself shivering, as if in the midst of all this horror, his body was, as it were, jogging at his elbow, asserting its claim to a little consideration, trying to get him to put on an overcoat.

He crossed the street at a point mid-way between two lamp-posts. As he passed a darkened shop doorway a hand reached out and caught his arm.

'Let me go,' he said, then, 'how did you get out?'

'I swam,' said Bunder briefly. He was soaking wet. In some way Charles could not imagine, he had managed to reach the water, and leave it again undetected. 'Don't be a fool. You can't get away from here on your feet. They'll have the whole town alerted already. The only chance is a car—one they're not looking for.'

'Leave me out of it,' Charles breathed fiercely. The wet hand was still clutching his wrist. He tried to drag it away.

'Don't be a fool,' Bunder said again. He seemed desperately avid for someone to share his plight, as if his hunted condition would only be tolerable if shared.

'Where's Dogson?' Charles could not help asking although he knew, terribly, sickeningly knew.

'Dogson?'

'The man who came in.'

'He came in,' Bunder said, 'but he didn't go out. He won't go out. They'll have to take him.' He breathed heavily and his protruding eyes, which Charles had always hated, seemed to glow like a wolf's in the deep dusk. 'They'll have to take him,' he repeated.

For a few seconds they stood motionless. Water dripped heavily from Bunder's clothes. Then, without relaxing his grip on Charles's wrist, he started forward from the shop doorway. Charles jerked his wrist free, but continued to walk beside him. What else was there to do, and what, anyway, did it matter now? He was implicated in a murder, and sooner or later they would pick him up. Only one thing was clear. He would arrange, somehow or other, to be hanged. He would never contemplate a sentence of years during which he was shut away from Veronica.

'It's the first one we come to, or nothing,' said Bunder. 'If we're not out of the city in twenty minutes we might as well stop at the station and give ourselves up.'

They emerged from a side street into a rather more prosperous street lined with quiet office buildings. Three cars stood parked within a few yards. Charles had to admire Bunder's coolness. Without haste he looked into the window of the largest one. Then he calmly took out his key-ring.

'Go round to the other side, will you?' he said to Charles in a casual matter-of-fact tone, exactly as the owner would speak to a business acquaintance to whom he was offering a lift.

Charles went round to the passenger's door. He watched

through the glass as Bunder went through the motion of selecting a key from his ring. But he did not open the door with a key. Instead he leaned suddenly and unobtrusively on the handle and appeared to pivot in some way on his forearm. There was a slight crunching noise, and a jagged hole appeared in the panelling. Bunder opened the door and, stepping into the car, reached across and opened Charles's door for him. As he did so it was obvious that he had a short length of lead pipe up his sleeve: the old car-thief's device for wrenching off a door handle. In a few seconds he had wedged the door with its shattered lock, started the engine, and they were purring down the street.

'We've got one chance in a thousand. Hit that main road and get out into the country. Ditch the car and travel from a country station, or hide in the fields,' said Bunder half to himself. Charles sat hunched in his seat, feeling a heavy numbness stealing over him. Something had happened to the part of him that ought to be feeling fear, pity, remorse, excitement: he felt no trace of any of them. Only a deadness that was indescribably more painful.

Then he saw something as they swung round a corner and began the climb up the hill away from the dock area. A bizarre, lopsided piece of machinery, painted cream and leaning drunkenly against a wall. Two small boys were standing gravely by it with handfuls of mud, which they were plastering over it with serious concentration.

It was Dogson's motor-cycle. It was waiting for him to come and ride it away, but he would never come again.

'Christ! They're on to us!' Bunder suddenly cried. In the driving mirror appeared a black saloon with a small lighted sign on the front—'Police'.

It was odd how little Charles cared. Something about the sight of that pathetic clumsy object, waiting patiently, like a mule, to be led away, brought into delayed action the full complex of emotions roused by Dogson's death. It was like a series of explosions, each setting off another. Whole areas of his mind that had for months been frozen or jammed, freed themselves now with a succession of violent jerks. He felt like a man waking from a drugged sleep. With fantastic vividness, now that it was all over and too late for questions, one question flared before his eyes:

what was he doing here? How could he ever have led himself, by what crazy route and with what blind footsteps, to the position he was in at this moment? Sitting beside a tall, thin crook in a soaking wet lounge suit, being driven in a stolen car, pursued by the police, wanted for dope-smuggling and murder, was this he, Charles Lumley?

'Veronica,' he said aloud. 'You didn't know, you didn't know.'

'You bloody well bet I didn't know,' replied Bunder, who had not caught the first word. 'I suppose they were just patrolling and saw us immediately after getting the wireless message. Blast their guts. We'll cook them yet: we've got five miles an hour more than they have, flat out, and in any case they're not taking me alive.'

They're not taking me alive either, his heart signalled as the image of Veronica danced before it. *They didn't take Harry alive either,* the motor-cycle called faintly from somewhere in his brain. *He came in, but he won't go out.*

By now it was almost completely dark. The horrible white light from concrete lamp-standards illuminated the fish-and-chip shops, the advertisement hoardings, the trolley-buses crawling along in convoy. They were in that long, hideous street, lined by alternate stretches of cheap shops and depressed houses, which inevitably leads out of all English cities, connecting the centre with the outer suburbs. Bunder drove fiercely in the crown of the road, aiming from one trolley-bus to the next, since each one blocked any possibility of seeing the road ahead. As the street became gradually clearer of traffic, he drove faster and more wildly, staking everything on the fact that the police in the following car would have to retain, amid their haste, some consideration for the public safety. Courting death, their own and anyone else's, was the one possible chance of escape.

The ghastly patches of white light, gleaming on the wet road beneath the concrete standards, flicked beneath them rhythmically. A steamy smell began to come from Bunder's wet clothes. The car swayed and surged in its furious pace. Charles sat hunched, staring through the windscreen, his mind echoing to the shouts of his returning sensibilities. Now and again he shook his head, as if to clear it, like a boxer recovering from a knockout. After a time a terrible, strained rigour seized him; his muscles tensed, he sat braced in his seat with jaws clenched and eyeballs fixed. It was as if he were in labour, fighting to be delivered of something that must either be born or kill him in the process. Once before, as he had lain in the ditch and felt his previous life coming away in floods of stale beer, his fate had jerked him violently into a new direction; but the essence of that former time had been relaxation; his rejection had consisted simply of a refusal to strive for a meaningless object. Now all was effort. Something positive was thrashing in violent struggle just below the conscious level of his mind.

They had reached a roundabout, where the road branched in three directions towards the country. Bunder threw the car round it in a long skid; the soft springing, ill-adapted for such methods, allowed the massive steel body to tilt and sway madly, and they were dragged further still off their course. The near-side wheel hit the kerbstone and grated violently along it; for an instant they seemed certain to overturn. Charles was flung against the side of the car with a tremendous jolt. His vision blacked out for a moment, and when he recovered they had regained an even keel and were fleeing madly along a concrete road, on either side of which the houses were growing larger and more sparsely set as they drew further towards the country.

The physical shock snapped his condition of semi-paralysis, and with that moment his agonizing parturition was over. Everything moved back into focus. All this must cease; either prison or execution would be logical, sane and releasing, compared with the hell in which he had lived for months. He acted immediately and calmly. Bunder would never, of course, let himself be talked into stopping so that they could give themselves up. Yet stop they must. He moved forward slightly and grasped the hand-brake.

Bunder also acted immediately and calmly. He reached across in front of Charles, keeping his eyes on the road as it curved slightly ahead of them, and, opening the door, gave a sudden and violent shove. Charles clutched wildly, but his hands closed on emptiness. Photographed on his brain as he fell was the fleeting picture of a dark grass verge, with a flowing ribbon of stone that was the kerb. Then, with a flash of blinding light, all sensation was extinguished.

*

'I don't imagine the portable one will be suitable,' said the man's voice.

'I didn't think so myself,' said the woman's voice. 'I was just carrying out Dr. Bulcastle's instructions.'

He could not hear what the man's voice said in reply. 'Dr. Bulcastle, something something experience of this type of case.' They seemed to have pinned his legs down under a heavy weight. He struggled to move, but the only result was a sharp pain in his left shoulder as the upper part of his body stirred slightly.

'Well, we'll just have to carry on and see what we can do,' said the man's voice.

Charles's head was packed tightly, inside, with cotton wool. When he tried to shut his eyes he found cotton wool instead of eyeballs under the lids. Revolving layers of thick blankets descended on him every few seconds and suffocated him. His bed was slowly rotating. But all these inconveniences, even the shooting pain in his shoulder, troubled him less than the inconsiderateness of these people, whoever they were, in leaving a heavy oak chest, or some similar weight, on his legs. It must have been there for a long time, because his legs were quite numb.

He struggled to speak. At the third attempt his vocal chords vibrated slightly, and a hoarse whisper came out:

'Take that thing off my legs.'

The woman heard him and approached.

'He's awake, Doctor. How do you feel now? Are you getting much pain?'

'Thing—off my . . . legs,' he said.

'He's saying something about his legs,' she said.

'I'm not surprised to hear it,' said the man's voice drily. 'Well, we can't hang about all night. Bring Perkins in and let's have a try with this portable.'

During the few minutes that followed Charles died, was born again, lived whole life-times of pain and fever, contemplated the worm-eaten sides of his coffin for centuries. Complete unconsciousness supervened before they had quite finished.

Coming half-round, he heard: 'The only thing is to get him down to the X-ray room. I didn't want to have to move him, but it's inevitable. Get Perkins in again.'

Then they went away, all of them, and he was alone. The mists cleared a little and he looked about him. Screens by his bed: those green things were screens. Didn't they only put screens by your bed when you were dying? You'd got to be dying before they put screens round your bed. Screens round the bed, dead. Dead round the screens. Screams in the bed. Dreams of the dead.

'Take that weight off my legs, damn you!' He thought he was yelling. Actually a few whimpering sounds emerged.

'You be quiet, then you'll be all right,' said a woman's voice, not the same one. He had a glimpse of starched cuffs moving near his pillow. 'They'll be coming to move you in a minute.'

'What are the screens for?' he asked, suddenly quite coherent.

'The screens?' she said. 'Just to make it comfortable for you. To make it nice and comfortable for you.'

'Careful, now, Perkins,' said a man's voice. 'This is a serious case.'

Voices murmured for a few moments, then suddenly they began to drag him in two. The top half of his body was twisted and dragged off. The revolving blankets fell on his face. Death, decomposition, rebirth, lingering death, the cycle began again. Vaguely beneath it all he felt the sensation of being wheeled along. Then he was flung, suddenly and violently, down a pit shaft. He crashed into the coal dust at the bottom. The sea flooded into the workings, and his head, which had bounded from his shoulders at the impact, showed signs of drowning.

'You're awake this morning, are you?' said the sister with brisk semi-indifference. 'This is Dr. Bulcastle. He's going to see what can be done to put you right again.'

Grey eyes looked at him over half-moon glasses. Then they dropped and looked through the glasses at his legs.

'I want you to tell me if you can feel this,' came the doctor's creamy, rather tired voice. But he did not do anything.

'Feel what?' said Charles. He wished the man would get on with it. He wanted to sleep, because he had a delicious certainty that death awaited him if he could only get properly to sleep.

The idea of death had possessed his mind with its beauty and necessity.

'Can't feel it, eh?' said the creamy voice.

An ant seemed to be crawling over the sole of his left foot.

'My foot,' he said.

'Feel something in the foot, do you?' The creamy voice had taken on a note almost of urgency. 'Which one?'

'That one,' he muttered.

'Good. There's a chance.'

'What's the matter with me?' he asked faintly.

'The matter,' said the voice, tired again. 'Well, apart from abrasions and a broken collar-bone, and considerable concussion—that's wearing off now, of course—the main trouble is that the lamina of your lumbar vertebrae are pressing on the spinal cord. It's induced paralysis of the legs. But the fact that you can feel something when I scratch the soles of your feet, as I've been doing with this pair of scissors, shows that we've a fair chance of operating successfully. Can you tell us what happened to you?'

'Happened,' he said wearily. He closed his eyes. Tell us what happened to you, Veronica, Bunder wouldn't stop. Tell us what happened to Dogson. Finish with the whole thing. Tell us what happened, partner. Bernard. Need somebody to look after you. Yes.

'Not much good trying to talk to him for some time yet,' he heard the voice. 'I know you'll see to everything that's necessary, sister. I'll be ready for him about twelve.'

After that, nothing was clear for a long time, perhaps days. He felt them inject things into him and move him now and then. The blankets folded themselves tightly about his face, and the cotton wool sprouted from his ears and filled his mouth. The screens were always round his bed. Sometimes, when he woke up, there were electric lights burning. That was night. It was day when they were off, because you could see without them. Grotesque fragments of talk mingled with his dreams; reality hung its head defeated.

Then the time came when he woke up properly. He could tell he was awake. Things seemed clear and normal; the lights were not burning; it was day, probably morning. There was a morning feeling in the place. The nurse noticed that he seemed better. 'You seem better,' she told him. He moved his right hand down the bed to his waist and below. Plaster, heavy and stiff. Inside were his legs, lying quietly, waiting to see if they would ever serve him again. Poor legs, he felt sorry for them. Never did any harm. A few tears came into his eyes.

Then the sister and a man he had never seen before were standing by his bed. The question again: can you tell us what happened to you? I'm too clever, he thought. I won't remember. I've forgotten all about it.

'You see,' the sister said, 'you were found lying by the roadside, but your injuries aren't really the type that we associate with people who are knocked down by cars. They seemed to suggest that you had, say, fallen from the pillion of a motor-cycle.'

'I can't remember,' he said.

'Don't you remember anything?' said the man quickly. 'What you were doing there or anything?'

Mustn't overdo it. 'Oh yes,' he said. 'I remember who I am. I remember my name.' He told them his name.

'Yes, we know that,' said the sister. 'We got your name and address from things in your pocket. But don't you remember the accident?'

'Had you been drinking?' the man put in.

'No,' he said obstinately. 'I hadn't been drinking. I don't remember what I was doing. I don't remember the accident. I was sober but I don't remember.'

'Do you remember definitely that you *hadn't* been drinking?' the man asked him.

He shut his eyes. 'I feel tired,' he said.

'I think we'd better not disturb him any more,' said the sister definitely. They went away. He felt an intoxicating sense of Machiavellian triumph. It was all so easy: you just said you were tired and they had to stop. He was going to feel tired every time they asked him anything. Every time they asked him if Bernard Roderick and Veronica had fallen off the pillion of Harry Dogson's motor-cycle, if Mr. Blearney had nose-dived out of the sky on a motor-cycle, if Harry Dogson had run over Froulish on his motor-cycle, leaving him with injuries not usually associated with people who could remember if they had been drinking.

One day when the nurse came to wash him she told him he

was lucky. 'You're lucky,' she said. He asked her what she meant.

'You're being moved to the Private Block, with a room of your own,' she said.

'Using what for money?' he asked.

'A friend of yours is paying,' she said, plying the flannel. 'Haven't you heard anything about it?'

'You must be making a mistake,' he said round the edges of the flannel. 'No friend of mine could possibly pay for me to go into a private ward, and anyway they don't know I'm here.'

'Oh, but they do. There was something in the paper,' she retorted. 'Mr. Perkins cut it out. I'll show it you when I come round this afternoon.'

That afternoon she brought him a tiny cutting from one of the more gossipy evening newspapers. He looked at it and read, 'The Shah declared at a press conference that it was the will of Allah that he should take a tenth wife. Miss Wadder, speaking on the telephone from Los Angeles, said that the wedding was scheduled for the fourteenth.'

'You're looking at the wrong side,' she said.

He turned it over and read: 'HIT AND RUN. Charles Lumley (23) was admitted to hospital last night suffering from severe internal injuries, after being found lying unconscious by the roadside,' the paper was torn and he could not make out a line or two, 'believed to be another case of a motorist failing to stop after knocking down a pedestrian.'

'What's this about internal injuries?' he asked the nurse.

'Oh,' she said, 'that's what they always put when they don't know. The reporter didn't know anything about you except that you were injured, but he thought it would sound as if he knew if he just called it "internal". We often get them doing that.'

'Was there anything about . . .' He stopped just short of the fatal word. He had been about to ask if there had been, in the same issue of the paper, anything about a murder at the docks. But what had all that to do with him? It was a former life, over and done with, something he had forgotten about. Since then he had died and been reborn a score of times.

'About what?' she prompted him.

He looked at her blankly. 'What about what?' he muttered.

She decided that he must be tired. 'You must be tired,' she told him.

'But what about this private ward business?'

'Oh, that's tomorrow,' she said. 'You're being moved tomorrow.'

'Yes, but who's behind it?'

'Some friend of yours,' she said impatiently, as if it were his business to know the names of his friends. 'I don't know the name. They'll tell you tomorrow when they move you.'

They moved him the next morning, out of the ceaseless racket of the public ward with its communal wireless and echoing vastness, over to a tall, narrow room with big windows and only one bed. He looked round bewildered at the trappings of comfort, the neat washbasin, the vase of flowers, the wireless set on the bedside table. Mr. Perkins, who brought him over, could tell him nothing. But just as they had finished getting him into bed, the sister came in.

'I expect you'd like to dictate a letter to your friend, thanking him,' she said.

'I would if I only knew who it was,' he answered.

'Haven't they told you that? Dear me, how silly. I thought you knew. It's a Mr. Roderick. Mr. Bernard Roderick, of Stotwell.'

He lay back in silence.

'You can dictate your letter to me if you like,' she said.

'You're sure they got the name right?' he asked.

'Of course the name's right. We had quite a lot of dealings with him, over the telephone and by letter. He's even arranged all the details, like having the wireless hired by the week and the bills sent to him. Didn't they give you that note he sent?'

'A note to me?' He was still stupefied.

'Who else?' she said in the tone that comes to those who control their impatience, either masking it or releasing it in calculated amounts, for years together. 'Here it is on the dressing-table.' She handed it to him. It was a small, neat envelope with a card in it, such as expensive florists enclose with flowers sent by wire. He took out the card. It said, 'Hoping you will be as comfortable as can be expected. Bernard Roderick.'

'You're lucky to have such a generous friend,' said the sister.

Her inquisitiveness, like her impatience, had never been off the lead, but she was human.

'Lucky,' he said.

'I suppose it's someone you've known for a long time,' she prompted.

'A long time,' he repeated.

'Would you like to dictate your letter now?' she asked.

'I feel tired,' he said.

It worked: she left him alone.

The comfort of his new quarters aided his resolution not to think. Attempts to puzzle out this mystery of Bernard Roderick's generosity simply brought on an acute pain behind the eyes; it was safer to push it into the limbo where he had pushed the Bunder episode and all that led up to it. If ever he came out of this and resumed normal life, so much would have to be forgotten that one or two items on the list did not matter much.

The greatest surprise of all was that he did not find it difficult to avoid thinking of Veronica. In fact it was easier, as well as more comfortable, not to think of her. Once or twice, when he allowed his mind to recall their moments of profoundest happiness, of joy so deep that he had no means of telling whether he was remembering or imagining, the pain became, simply, intolerable: frightened, he lay back and allowed blankness to flood over him. If in his day-dreaming he saw her at all clearly, the agony of lying helpless, not being able to go to her, was not to be borne; if she were merely there as a vague presence, the effect was comforting. Obviously his fierce mental shying away from the thought of her was, in origin, physical; his body, in the struggle to piece itself together, required the co-operation of his mind, and when insanity was threatened, took swift action by means of drowsiness or nausea. And so the impossible happened: he passed long stretches, amounting to hours, without thinking of Veronica.

The wireless with its ceaseless half-heard droning was a great help. On the afternoon of the second day in his new room, he was lying half-asleep, listening to Children's Hour. A bright, sexless female voice had just said, 'And now we're going over to the Birmingham studio for a new story for the under-nines, told by

Jeremy,' when the door opened and the nurse ushered in a visitor. It was Bernard Roderick.

Prone in bed, plaster from waist to knees, Charles felt more than ever at a disadvantage in dealing with this man who had always subtly overpowered him with suave self-assurance and blandness. The whole tangle of his emotions towards Roderick, the ambivalence of his hatred for Veronica's seemingly jealous guardian and his will to feel kindly towards him as her relative and benefactor, had been mirrored in his utter inability to measure up to Roderick, to play, as it were, in his key. But his former difficulty was nothing compared with this; for his physical weakness and imprisonment now had its analogy in the moral handcuffs which Roderick had clicked on and locked by his display of expensive generosity. He wished to feel gratitude, but the whole machinery of his reactions was too complex, and too much out of order, for any such simple and good emotion to be possible. He looked stonily, yet with obvious helplessness, at his captor.

Roderick, for his part, was smoothness itself. He was giving a first-rate performance in the rôle of himself being smooth. He padded towards the bed, mimicking with great skill his own soft-footed manner of progression. His head was inclined slightly forward; he was imitating himself being calmly, gently concerned for another's welfare.

'And how do you find yourself after all these ordeals?'

'Quite easily,' Charles replied with a grotesque attempt at a light laugh. 'I just look inside the plaster and there I am.'

The jarring note had been struck already. Roderick had had his usual effect of throwing him off balance, rendering him absolutely incapable of judging the right tone, reducing him to an imbecile.

'I really must thank you for your great kindness,' he went on primly, veering wildly to the other extreme. It was like a decayed gentlewoman thanking some charitable institution for helping her with the quarter's rent.

Roderick gave a brilliant, rather impressionistic imitation of himself being slightly pained and at the same time touched and pleased. 'Look into my eyes,' his manner said, 'and notice the blend of rather shy pleasure at finding my kindness appreciated and genuine regret that I could not manage to help you anonymously.' When Charles had had a reasonable chance to notice this, the expression was switched off, and replaced by one that indicated the responsible man, aware of his obligations to humanity.

'I simply heard about your unfortunate accident—read about it in the paper as a matter of fact,' he said, 'and as soon as I could get the details about where you were and so on, I naturally did what I could to make you more comfortable.'

'I', not 'we', read about it. All right, you bastard, if you won't mention her first, I won't. We'll go through the whole visit without mentioning her if you like, since you're evidently doing it on purpose.

'A nice change from the public ward. It was noisy down there,' he said.

Roderick nodded agreement. His eye wandered round the room, noting that everything was in order. He kept his responsible man's expression in place a little longer, then allowed it to fade into a sympathetic one. Charles watched fascinated as the performance became richer and richer: compassion tempered with a certain robust cheerfulness, as of one who understood all the suffering, shared it even, but had come as the messenger of hope.

'The sister was telling me downstairs that they've every hope of your complete recovery,' he said impressively. (If they told *me* that, it must be true. I'm not a man who gets lied to.)

'Yes, they might get me walking when this plaster comes off,' said Charles. This mechanical repeating of everything Roderick said, in an attempt to avoid breaking any fresh ground, was terribly boring and fatiguing. He felt listless. How soon would it be permissible for him to say he was tired?

'I don't want to stay too long: I know you mustn't be tired,' said Roderick. He leaned forward slightly in his chair as if on the point of standing up to go, then relapsed. 'Just a few more minutes to think of anything I can send you—I tried to think of everything, but one can't be sure. Or,' he added, 'any messages.'

Charles stiffened. That last word was the first piece of open bullying Roderick had indulged in: obviously he had not been able to resist it. Instinctively he rejected the (in theory) possible explanation that the man really wished to give him a chance to communicate with her, and was thus delicately introducing the subject. No, it was an insult. Messages! When the only message Charles could possibly care about was one that could under no circumstances be entrusted to him.

'No, no messages,' Charles said faintly. At any moment he could say he was tired, and the powerful magic would sweep this ghoul away.

'That's funny,' said Roderick, standing up. 'Because I've got one for you.' He produced an envelope from his pocket. 'I don't know whether you recognize the writing.'

'Charles Lumley, Esq.,' in Veronica's handwriting. His heart, after so long and so illusory a quietness, smashed at his ribs under the pyjama jacket.

As Roderick handed the envelope over he did not give an imitation of himself being anything. His face had become empty, quiescent, utterly without character.

Roughly Charles tore the letter open. A single sheet of paper, with only a few words written carefully.

'It is true what Bernard tells you. There is nothing for it. I am sorry. V.'

He looked up at Roderick. Everything in him was nerved for some terrible blow.

'Well, go on,' he said. 'Tell me what it is she says is true.'

Roderick looked down at him. His face was like a pumpkin on which a child has idly made a slit for a mouth, two dark holes for eyes.

'If you think for a minute, Lumley, can't you guess?'

A great weariness possessed him, turning his bones to jelly and his muscles to water, dirty water.

'Yes,' he said, his voice coming from a long way off. 'I suppose I can guess.'

'And do you really mean to say that you didn't guess all along? That you really thought she was my niece?'

Charles was silent. The knowledge that Veronica was Roderick's mistress had been there all along, in his bones, in his arms and legs, in the blood in his veins. Now it had risen at last to his brain, bursting through the pathetic little barrier of self-hypnotism that had kept it down all these months.

'In every important sense,' he said, 'I've known that since I first met you both. That stuff about her being your niece wouldn't have deceived anyone unless they wanted to be deceived.'

'And you did want to, didn't you?'

'Yes,' he said simply, 'I did want to.'

Roderick moved towards the door. Before reaching it he stopped and turned his pumpkin-face steadily towards Charles.

'We shan't meet again. Veronica has told me that she will never communicate with you any more. I may say, in case you're puzzled, that this little gift of mine,' he waved his hand to indicate the room and its furnishings, 'was made at her request. She agreed with me that you must be told about the real nature of the position, and told, what's more, before you grew strong enough to begin building hopes on what had happened between the two of you, hopes about the time when you came out of here. But she wanted me to see that you were comfortable before breaking the news. She felt you would need that little extra help if you were to stand the shock.'

Charles was silent.

'Well, have you anything to say before I go?' Roderick asked, clearing his face of its pumpkinhood and resuming his imitation of himself being bland—only this time there was a touch of parody in the performance, so that it was a slightly malicious portrait. He stood, waiting. Charles just managed to speak.

'Yes. Get out.'

He went out quietly, shutting the door.

The nurse noticed at six o'clock that his temperature was up. 'Your temperature's up,' she told him.

'It is true. There's nothing for it,' he replied. She looked at him with mild surprise, but made no comment. When she had gone, he lay perfectly still, searching within the huge hollow space in his mind, hoping that in some neglected corner he would find the strength to keep him sane, the will to begin from the beginning. So much had to be altered; he had known it; and now this, too, the foundation on which everything else had rested. Lying there, still and frightened, he knew that the next few hours would bring him, finally, to sanity or madness. Either the loss of Veronica—not merely the loss but the need to reject every thought of her—would kill him, or it would set him free, and give meaning to his decision to sweep the violent and senseless elements from his life. Outside, the summer evening was bright; before darkness finally fell and the birds slept, he would have wrestled with his angel. The full meaning of Roderick's message filtered piecemeal into his mind, crushing, exploding, searing, as its delayed action brought wave after wave of pain. And yet there was, at the core, a hint of release and a new strength. The night-sister, coming on duty, was told that Lumley was behaving strangely and seemed to be talking to himself; she went in to cheer him up, but met only perfunctory, listless answers, and his mutterings began again before she was out of the room: 'the new life', she heard him say. She was not unduly worried, being experienced enough to know that serious cases have minor relapses as a matter of course.

He himself knew only that the new life, if he could reach it without going mad or dying, contained his salvation. The long hours of slowly fading light witnessed the immensity of his struggle: it is true what he tells you, forward, to the new life, there is nothing for it. Now and then he slept, and in his tangled dreams caught glimpses of an unimaginable state of peace. There was nothing for it, time must carry him on, without a pause, forward, to the new life, it is true, it is true, I am sorry.

VIII

Charles was recovering. He could move his legs when they took the plaster off, and soon they gave him a stick with a rubber end to it and he was walking round the room.

He was not transferred to a convalescent home; either there was no such institution available, or it was too full, he did not enquire; but this was the reason why he spent an unusually long time, in a semi-invalid condition, at the same hospital. As soon as he was no longer definitely ill, he persuaded the sister to write to Roderick saying that he had left the hospital and that the payments for the private ward need no longer be kept up; transferred to one of the smaller public wards, he lived a life half-way between that of the patients and the hospital staff, making himself useful in odd ways to fill in the time.

It seemed simple and natural, therefore, that when his cure was finally completed—by this time it was the middle of July—he should solve the problem of employment by taking on a job as orderly in the hospital. He had grown familiar with the place, inured to its curious blend of atmospheres—part factory, part hotel, part battle-ground, part mortuary—and had, in any case, no wish to leave its shelter and begin again the task at which he had already failed twice, the task of adjustment to the world. His physical cure had been successfully completed; his mental cure was taking longer, and the hospital offered facilities here too.

And so he moved no farther than a quiet, dingy lodging-house where he slept at night, spending most of the twenty-four hours inside the vast hospital. His work was not quite so congenial as window-cleaning had been; for one thing, it was irksome, in fine weather, not to be out of doors; still, it was simple, and fulfilled his major needs in being laborious but not quite back-breaking, and in being obviously useful—a badly-needed refreshment for his rudimentary social conscience.

Sweeping, polishing, fetching and carrying, occasionally helping to move a patient, conscious or unconscious, under the sergeant-majorly supervision of Mr. Perkins, his time passed smoothly. With satisfaction he noticed himself becoming accepted and integrated into the community of the hospital, finding his place in a feudal pyramid-shaped society that brooked no vagueness as to questions of status. He found this refreshingly different from the world outside; here, there could be no false pretensions, for rank, prestige and privileges were settled automatically. At the top were the doctors: these had their own hierarchy, but it was too distant to be observed from below, and concerned no one but themselves and the few uppermost nurses—Matrons and Sisters—who shared the same status. Next came the nurses in general, again with an elaborate hierarchy from Staff Nurse to Probationer. At the bottom, the broad base of the triangle, came the cooks, technicians, clerical and domestic workers. There was, of course, a rigid line of demarcation between each trade here. Charles found his place somewhere near the bottom. As an orderly he cut rather little ice, being inexperienced and without knowledge of any technical trade: it was soon discovered that he was little use at emergency patching up of electrical equipment, plumbing, or any other deep mystery. So he was tolerated and kept busy on humble tasks; which suited him perfectly. Anonymity, obscurity, a relief from strain, the situation was exactly what he had prescribed for himself. Finally, he found with gratitude that hospital life, being so grotesquely unlike anything in the world outside, did not admit of any of the usual social classifications. It was not considered strange that he should be working at a manual occupation and still sounding his aitches.

Morning coffee was a great ritual on his block; convention had long since sanctioned a generous mugful for each patient, and for any of the nurses or members of the staff who could arrange to be on hand when it was being distributed. It was Charles's one social half-hour of the day, when, having taken round trays of coffee, collected them, and washed them up, he sat down in a small room between sinks and stoves, and chatted to women with dusters round their heads as they helped themselves from a freshly made pot.

The women themselves were an interesting sociological study, in so far as he could look beyond the rigid world of the hospital to their probable place in the shifting structure outside. Though their work was cleaning and dishing up food, few of them were the ordinary charwoman type; mostly they were obviously welcoming the chance to earn a little extra money by plying the only trade they knew, yet would have starved rather than become even a 'lady help' to another woman, with the personal relationship that it would involve. Hospital meant charing as far as work went, but in its social atmosphere it meant something more interesting, more romantic, and, in the long run, more respectable.

At least one of Charles's coffee-time circle, however, was free of any such preoccupations. Rosa had taken work at the hospital because it was 'more like life—you could meet more people and get to see and hear more,' she confided to Charles as they washed mugs. She was a sturdily built girl of twenty, not pretty, but alive, with a touch of exuberance that proclaimed itself in the big scarlet mouth that she daubed across her already full lips, and the animation of her voice in talk. She found everything interesting, though she was quite without curiosity and never tried to puzzle things out. What was, was, and that was the end of it; but she lived in a perpetual state of deep wonderment, bordering on excitement, that people and things were so various. Charles found her refreshing and slightly comical. She in turn took, he sometimes felt, a degree of interest in him that was a shade deeper, even, than her general interest in human personality. He was unlike any other young man she had ever met, and, without trying to account for his differences, she found him absorbing. He knew that when a lively girl of that age finds a man absorbing, it is sometimes not long before she finds him other things as well. While knowing this, he did not know what to do about it, or even whether he wanted to do anything about it.

One day, as he was wheeling a trolley down a corridor, he nearly ran into a young man in a white coat who said, 'It's Lumley, isn't it?'

It was a man who had been at college with him, a medical student, but by some odd chance Charles had never learnt his name. They had only known one another very distantly. Obviously he had either to ask him his name at once, or to pretend for ever that he knew it.

'Hullo,' he said. It was too much trouble to ask his name: he would simply have to call him You.

'What are you doing here?'

'Wheeling these drums down to the theatre.'

The other flushed slightly at Charles's discourtesy.

'I meant, of course, what are you doing doing this job?' Annoyance had a poor effect on his syntax.

'I've got to live, haven't I?' said Charles in the patient tone of one who is prepared to discuss the matter fully.

This continued coldness ought to have been enough to brush the fellow off, but evidently he had motives for persevering. Perhaps he was lonely and welcomed the sight of a once-familiar face. Or he thought Charles had come down in the world and was anxious to befriend him. The latter was the less likely of the two.

'Well, let's be seeing something of you,' he said. 'Where do you live?'

Charles wondered whether it would be a legitimate continuation of his surly-independence act if he merely replied 'At home', like a character out of W. W. Jacobs, but decided it would be over the borderline into unjustifiable rudeness, so gave his address.

'I'll be having a few people round for a beer one of these evenings,' said the man, writing it down. 'You must come. There are one or two men you know here. We're doing our hospital training.'

'I'm doing my hospital training, too,' said Charles, but the other had hurried on. With a muttered exclamation of annoyance he wheeled the trolley forward again.

That day, in one of the private wards he attended, a new patient appeared: a thin, pallid, bird-like man in advanced middle-age, who spoke in a faint voice and lay back as if he were afraid and wanted to efface himself and make his bed look empty. Charles did his best to make a little cheering conversation as he swept out the room, and the bird-like man seemed grateful and responded at once.

'You'd better put a special bit of elbow-grease on in number three,' Rosa said to him at coffee-time. 'There's a man there it'd pay you to get in his good books.'

'Why, who is he?'

'You know Braceweight's Chocolates? Well, that's Mr. Braceweight. They say he's very rich. A proper millionaire they say he is!' She glowed with suppressed excitement at the thought that a man who makes chocolate on a big scale can become rich, and can then fall ill, and that he should have come to 'their' hospital, and that Charles should be cleaning out the room where he lay in fear and suffering. It all thrilled her genuinely.

Even Charles took, from then on, a fresh interest in the frail, scared figure in that bed. From time to time people have genuinely believed that money 'doesn't matter', 'isn't everything', and so forth, but no one has ever failed, on being told 'Mr. X is a millionaire' to look at him with keen interest, keener than if they had been told 'Mr. X is a veterinary surgeon', or 'Mr. X has an interesting hobby: he carves chessmen'. And yet the result of his observation was, for some time, mere bewilderment; it revealed no extraordinary or compelling qualities in Mr. Braceweight. He seemed to have no personality at all, even allowing for the fact that the obvious outward trappings by which a man advertises his personality—clothes, possessions, pursuits—were not available to him as he lay helpless in bed. He was obviously afraid of his operation: he was having his tonsils out, which is a severe operation for an ageing man; but even his fear did not make itself felt in any marked way. It was restrained, not by courage, but the lack of any equipment for making itself significant or noticeable. Afterwards his relief was the same, obviously and genuinely there, but flavourless and only faintly apparent.

In the end Charles realized the truth, that it was this negativeness, this lack of any real Braceweighthood, that had brought the man to his power and wealth. Having no definite character of his own, he had gladly accepted a lifetime of application to the routine of buying and selling, his protective colouring enabling him to move through that jungle in safety. He was not, Charles gathered, a self-made man; that struggle, which turns those who win it into stunted giants—half maimed, half Herculean figures—had been unnecessary in his case. He had simply inherited a good business, and turned it into a huge one with the aid of his colourless persistence. Charles liked him; he had the faint, but genuine, appeal of the harmless and ordinary character. He, on his part, seemed to find in Charles his one ray of hope. The doctors overawed him, the nurses domineered him, the charwomen were too large and healthy for his peace of mind, and Charles fell into an intermediate category. He asked Charles his name, and addressed him punctiliously as 'Mr.' Lumley, confiding in him at every stage of his circuitous road to recovery. 'Do you think I could ask them not to give me cascara to-night, Mr. Lumley? Or is it a regulation, do you think?' Or: 'Mr. Lumley, is it usual, when the nurse takes a patient's temperature, for her not to tell him what it is? They never tell me what mine is.' Charles was reassuring, calling into play that softness and slight hesitancy of speech that the University had made, once upon a time, his normal utterance. He had long since laid it aside in favour of the curter, more aggressive manner of the normal world, but something about Mr. Braceweight's helplessness, he found, called it out again despite himself, and made him realize afresh that it was a speech-habit common to the disabled.

The man in the white coat, acting from his obscure motives, duly sent his invitation, and Charles found himself walking down a suburban road one evening after duty. He was not looking forward to the gathering, but found himself, nowadays, bored and irritated by making excuses and evasions; it was simpler to go and be done with it. As he walked up the gravel path to the large, semi-detached house ('Stockbroker's Tudor') where the man lived or lodged, he saw the lighted window on the first floor, and heard gruff laughter. Hearties. He had kept clear, during his college days, of the sporadic warfare between athlete and aesthete, but felt, looking back, that if he had disliked each party equally, it had, nevertheless, been for different reasons. He had distrusted the cooing, pink-shirted aesthetes because he perceived inside himself the germs of the same disease, and had been afraid of allowing the tendency any free play. The hearties he had simply disliked as one dislikes a foggy day or a bad smell. And here he was walking into a nest of them.

It was all exactly as he had known it would be. The featureless lounge, with imitation oak furniture and square-cut 'comfy' armchairs and sofa, was full of tall, erect young men and tweedy young women who all somehow echoed the same *ersatz* note as their surroundings. The landlady, a forty-ish blonde aspiring wildly to a chic slightly above her own level, the degree of chic represented by the present company, was acting as hostess: the man whose name he did not know was evidently 'more like a friend than a lodger'. The lady probably kept Cairn terriers, or a Labrador, but fortunately the creatures were out of sight at the moment.

No attempt was, of course, made at an introduction: Charles was launched into the company with a vague intimation that some of them knew him, carrying with it the implication that the others were the lucky ones. Beer was available, and he took a glass in his hand and prepared to wait out in patience the time he must endure before going home. But his calm resignation was suddenly disturbed. His ears picked up a familiar braying noise, and a broad back that had been turned towards him was abruptly reversed, becoming a broad chest. The same immature, arrogant face, the same cold eyes behind glasses. It was Burge, one of the medical set who had been at College with him, and possibly the only one of his contemporaries for whom he had ever felt a really vivid dislike.

For Burge contained within himself all the unpleasant characteristics of Robert Tharkles and Hutchins combined, while blending and applying them in a way that was all his own. Charles disliked him too much to be able to pity him, and yet he, too, was one of the disabled. At first profoundly uneasy at exchanging the seniority and power of his last year at school for the insignificance of his first year at the University, he had quickly remedied this sense of insecurity, partly by making no new friends—he confined himself entirely to the set who had come up from his school and their immediate cronies—and partly by taking advantage of the fact that a University career is very short, only three years for most men, and therefore a medical student, whose course takes much longer, easily becomes a senior figure in the Junior Common Room as he stays on year after year. By the time Charles had come up as a freshman, Burge was already in his fourth year, and had devoted himself with complete success to reproducing the *milieu* in which he had been so happy and successful as a Head Prefect. Charles, inclined to be lazy and tolerant, had welcomed the University largely—almost solely—because it meant the maximum release from the atmosphere of school with its incessant discipline and public spirit, and he had been roused from his lethargy to several open clashes with Burge: who now nodded to him coldly before resuming his conversation. It was, characteristically, on the very topic—the war of the athletes and the aesthetes—about which Charles had been musing as he walked up the path.

'Remember Reilly?' he was saying. 'My God, he was a fool. He was a bloody fool. Remember that bloody monocle he used to wear?'

The others laughed. They were quite good humoured: but Burge was angry. When he thought of this man Reilly, who had worn a monocle, he wanted to seek him out and do him some physical injury. Something inside Charles prompted him to ignore all the dictates of common sense and speak out.

'Perhaps he wore a monocle because he had something wrong with one eye,' he said.

Burge turned to face him. 'Won't wash,' he said curtly. 'If he had something wrong with one eye, why didn't he simply wear a pair of spectacles? He could have had ordinary plain glass in the good eye.' He spoke rapidly and impatiently, as if it were only just worth his trouble to answer such a foolish remark.

Charles, insanely, persisted.

'Why should he look through plain glass with his good eye when he could see all right without looking through anything at all?'

Burge now gave him his full attention. He spoke so that those guests who had been talking to one another stopped and listened.

'I'll tell you why he should look through plain glass,' he said, 'if you really can't think it out for yourself. He should do it so as not to make himself look a bloody fool. By wearing a monocle he just made himself bloody conspicuous. Everybody looking at him wherever he went. And that's what he did it for. You know that as well as we do. He just wanted to draw attention to himself.'

Something had got into Charles. He felt a mad compulsion to bait Burge. He insisted on dragging out the argument. The fourth form boy was defying the Head Prefect, the hospital orderly standing up to the almost-qualified doctor. The other guests began to look uncomfortable.

'Look, Burge,' he said hotly and roughly. 'You talk about this bird Reilly drawing attention to himself. Now you were captain of the College rugger team, weren't you?'

Burge just managed a nod. His face was totally without expression, save for the faint sneer that never left it, even when he was asleep at night.

'When you scored a try,' Charles persisted, 'and the spectators applauded, can you honestly deny that you were glad that there were spectators present, and that you had done something that pleased them so that they applauded? Weren't you glad of their admiration?'

Not even a nod this time. Burge simply stared at him with fixed loathing.

'Didn't you, in other words, believe, or act as if you believed, that there are some forms of drawing attention to oneself, as you call it, that are harmless or even good?'

'Blimey,' said a youth in a yellow pullover, affecting a Cockney accent, 'ain't we 'alf getting Socratic?'

One or two people tittered, in an attempt to break the tension. But Burge had set down his glass on the table and was staring at Charles. His face had gone a dull red.

'You always were liable to say bloody silly things. I must say I thought after I went down I should have heard the last of people saying bloody silly things.'

'Answer my point,' snapped Charles. He was losing his temper: this was getting serious.

'I'll answer your bloody point,' Burge said in the 'dangerously cool' voice he had used to over-awe children of twelve when he was a prefect. ('If he speaks to you quietly it's a beating: if he shouts you're all right', the white-faced urchins had told one another.) He advanced towards Charles, and halted about six feet away, holding himself unnaturally erect.

'If a man does something in a decent game like rugger,' he said coldly and distinctly, 'it's a sign that he's a good bloke. If the people watching start clapping, that's their way of saying to him, "We appreciate that. You're a good bloke." It takes a good bloke to play well at a decent game like rugger. If that's what you call drawing attention to oneself, that's not what I call it. I call it just being a good bloke.'

'At a decent game like rugger,' said Charles in a parody of Burge's manner.

Burge took a step forward. Charles thought he was going to hit him, and almost threw up his fists. But Burge checked himself. There were females present, females of his own species.

'I suppose people like you wouldn't call rugger a decent game,' he said, challenging Charles to say something really outrageous, to brand himself.

'And there's another thing,' he said, raising his voice, when his challenge was received in silence. 'Just what the bloody hell do you think you're playing at, Lumley, eh? They tell me you've taken a job at the hospital as an orderly. Carrying buckets about and emptying bedpans. What the bloody hell's the big idea?'

Charles was roused to a degree he would have believed impossible. His heart was pounding with rage, and he felt the blood surging behind his eyes.

'Do I understand, Burge,' he said, with a hint of a choke in his voice, 'that you are interfering with my right, the absolute right of a citizen, to do just whatever work I may choose?'

Two people moved forward and began to speak in an attempt to stop this before it went any farther: the landlady who was more of a friend, and a tall girl with a bad complexion who was evidently connected with Burge in some way, probably his fiancée. But it was too late. Everyone was listening intently, and Burge was not to be halted.

'Yes, you bloody well do understand it,' he cried. 'That sort of work ought to be done by people who are born to it. You had some sort of education, some sort of upbringing, though I must say you don't bloody well behave like it. You ought to have taken on some decent job, the sort of thing you were brought up and educated to do, and leave this bloody slop-emptying to people who were brought up and educated for slop-emptying.'

There was a murmur among the company that indicated agreement. Burge had expressed one of the prime articles of all their faith.

'You deny, then, that hospital orderly work is a valuable and necessary job?'

'No, I don't. You're bloody well not catching me out with your smart questions. It's necessary, and so is emptying bloody dustbins,' cried the educated man, 'but there are some classes of society that are born and bred to it, and ours isn't. If you take a job like that, you're just—' he fumbled among his small stock of metaphors, and brought out the inevitable, 'letting the side down. And I don't like people who let the side down. None of us here like it. We were discussing you before you turned up, and agreeing it was a bloody disgrace, if you want to know.'

The man whose name he did not know looked a little uncomfortable, and so did most of the guests. Not being as ruthless as Burge, they did not like to have it known that they had been discussing him prior to giving him hospitality; but Burge's girl, he noticed, did not share in the discomfort, and looked at him with cold contempt. It was too late to stop the scene, so she silently threw in her support on the side of Burge.

'No, I don't want to know,' Charles retorted. 'And I don't want your silly Edwardian notions of an upper-class Herrenvolk thrown up at me, either. By "letting the side down" all you mean is that the nigger-driving sahib oughtn't to do anything that reveals that he shares a common humanity with the niggers he drives. That idea's dead everywhere in practice, and it only survives in theory in the minds of people like you.'

'God!' said Burge, in tones of sincere and utter loathing. 'You're talking just like a bloody Socialist. Workers of the world, unite!' he shouted, raising his clenched fist.

'All I'm saying is that work, necessary and good work—'

'Workers of the world, unite!' shrieked Burge again, waving his fist wildly. He seemed possessed. It was no good going on.

'If I were you,' the girl with the bad complexion said to Charles in tones of cold hatred, 'I'd clear out of here before you start any more trouble with your Red notions.'

He had been prepared to go, that minute, but something snapped at the thought of so much unthinking, emotional intolerance.

'Red be damned!' he shouted. 'I've nothing against you men,

in the main—you're going to do useful work and you'll learn what life's all about when you come to do it, but I might as well tell you that, as you are here and now, I despise you.'

They clustered round him in open hostility.

'I despise you on two counts,' he continued rapidly and fiercely. 'First, because my education, which you throw in my face, was an education along humane lines that didn't leave me with any illusions about the division of human beings into cricket teams called Classes, and secondly because while you've been living this inane life of—of good mixing, beer-drinking, and slapping the nurses' bottoms on night duty, I've been out, out in the world learning the truth about things—and what's more—'

He never said what was more, for he had trampled too heavily and they considered themselves hard-driven men. Even as they laid hands on him his reason told him to bear no grudge, nor would he have borne any if the loathsome knuckly hands of Burge had not been prominent among them, grasping his collar. He struck out, aiming to hurt, and the man next to Burge stumbled backwards with an exclamation. He had missed. They frog-marched him to the door and launched him into the air at the top of the stairs. He bumped dizzily down them, but the carpet saved him from hurt: he was on his feet, passionately calling Burge to come out in the garden and put his fists up, but they had closed the door. The outsider was outside, and they were inside.

He walked home, marvelling at the depth, range, and richness of the humiliation he felt; it was so terribly, urgently, out of proportion to the simple, almost good-humoured, insult they had put upon him. In his disturbed sleep the girl with the bad complexion looked coldly, with Burge's eyes, through spectacles. 'One lens is just plain glass, just bloody plain glass,' she kept saying.

Next morning, over their coffee, Rosa told him the plot of a film she had seen the night before. 'Don't you ever do nothing with your spare time?' she asked him when she had finished. He roused himself from his torpid, resentful reverie and looked at her. She met his gaze composedly, but he saw that her usual hint of suppressed excitement was perhaps a little more pronounced than normally. At all events, he understood that this was a definite invitation. She was prepared to 'walk out' with him. He did not know whether girls like Rosa still used the expression 'walking out': he himself had only met it in novels dealing with Victorian or Edwardian village life. But the institution itself survived, of that he was certain. Half a dozen visits to the cinema, then a Sunday afternoon tea at her parental home, and they would be 'going steady'; and afterwards . . . well, why not? Would he be less contented than Burge, coupled with his frozen-faced long-toothed product of Roedean or Cheltenham?

'I don't do much with my spare time,' he said, 'but I might if I had anybody to do it with. Are you very booked up yourself?'

She looked dissatisfied: 'are you booked up' was too indirect a way of putting the vital preliminary question. Hastily, he altered it to 'What about coming out with me one of these evenings?' and her brow cleared.

A buzzer sounded and a light flashed.

'Mr. Braceweight's ringing,' she said, sufficiently feminine not to answer his question immediately.

'I said, what about coming out one evening?' Charles repeated patiently.

'What to do?' she asked.

'Anything you want to do.'

The staff nurse came in. 'Anybody going to answer that bell?' she demanded.

'Yes,' said Rosa, going out. The staff nurse thought this answer intended for her, but Charles knew it meant, yes, she would come out with him. Cheerful and tranquil, he washed up the coffee mugs and went about his work.

'Have you always worked in hospitals, Mr. Lumley?' asked the rich patient, lying back paper-thin and parchment-grey amid his pillows.

'No,' he answered, busy with the broom. 'I was an export delivery driver before this. Drove motor cars for a living.'

Mr. Braceweight appeared to think this over. 'I suppose you left it and came into this work because you had a special interest—er—in this direction?'

'Not particularly. I was a patient here and I took the job because I hadn't any other.'

The manufacturer ought to have been displeased at this display of indifference and lack of initiative by a young man; but the glance he shot at Charles from beneath his straggling white eyebrows was, of all things, a slightly envious one. What could it be like, he seemed to be thinking, to be free? Just to take any job that came along? Was it really, as he had always accepted and believed, the ultimate damnation?

'You were out of work, then?' He enunciated the dread words.

'Well, yes. Not that it really bothered me much. Something reasonable always turns up once you've abandoned the idea that one particular job is the only one you're cut out for.'

He gathered up his dusters and prepared to leave. 'Is there anything you want, Mr. Braceweight?'

'Yes,' said the frail, prostrate figure with sudden energy. 'I want to know what experience you went through that gave you this indifferent attitude to questions like the choice of work. Something must have happened to make you so different from other young fellows. Usually if they talk like that they're just wasters, living by sponging on others, and you're not a waster. But I'm not going to ask you. I haven't any right to ask personal questions. Tell me some time if you feel like it.'

Charles leaned on his broom.

'Tell *me* something first. Why do you feel this personal interest in me? If I'm any judge at all, you're not a man with a big streak of inquisitiveness, or even much ordinary interest, about what other people are like in themselves. But something's given you a wish to know more about the orderly who cleans out your hospital room. Is it something in me or something in you?'

Mr. Braceweight closed his eyes. He looked incredibly feeble; Charles could imagine the blood thinly pulsing along the tiny veins in his eyelids. He was thinking hard, along lines new to him, and it was exhausting.

'Two reasons,' he said at last. 'I've never had a long spell in bed before, with nothing to think about. At first I just thought about *things*—money, organization, that kind of subject. But that was just habit. I'm thinking about people now: and yet when I try to think about people I've known in the past, I find I can't really remember them. I've never really noticed anybody. Not noticed what kind of person he was: just whether he was a good business man, a sound employee, or a serious rival—you know. Women too,' he said more slowly, and paused for a moment.

'And the second reason?'

'The second reason is that you don't want to get anything out of me.'

'Jabber, jabber, jabber, gossip, gossip!' said the staff nurse to Charles, coming in with a tray of surgical instruments and dressings. 'I wish I was like you. Nothing to do but talk all day and lean on that brush.'

Charles went out, but not before his eyes had rested on Mr. Braceweight's face for an instant with an expression of respect. The man may have come late in life to the beginnings of wisdom, but not too late. The heavy cloth that had bound his eyes was beginning to come unwound: he was beginning to see.

He went up the broad stone steps with Rosa. Knots of youths were standing about, on the steps, inside the vestibule, on the pavement outside. Most of them wore blue or brown suits and shoes with pointed toes; but here and there was one with a loud tweed jacket and flannels, with broader shoes, sometimes in suède. The ones in blue or brown suits had their hair swept into shiny quiffs, stiff with grease, above the forehead; the others had theirs brushed smoothly back, with no parting, or cut off entirely except for a thin covering of scrub, some three-eighths of an inch long. They stood with cigarettes cupped in their palms, as if to hide them. When they raised the cigarettes to their lips it looked as if they were biting their finger-nails. Those who had violent-coloured shirts on, to make them look like their own conception of Americans, stood with their jackets unbuttoned and hanging a long way open. There were no corresponding knots of girls.

When Rosa came back from the ladies' cloak-room, Charles took her to the ballroom door. He paid one-and-six each for them to enter, and the evening had begun. The band had just played and was momentarily silent, so that the huge floor was crowded with people walking to and fro, and every one of the chairs ranged round the walls was occupied. Cigarette smoke drifted in clouds towards the great lights in the ceiling. Charles and Rosa stood just inside the door; he said nothing, for he was taking the scene in. Dances like these, in provincial town halls, were the main recreation of millions of his fellow Britons below the age of thirty, and he had never been to one before. Rosa was signalling to acquaintances; she had probably been to a dance in this hall once a week since she was fifteen. How much and how quickly he would have to notice and absorb, if he wanted to speak her language!

The band began to scream and clatter, and immediately the throng broke into movement. Still Charles hung back, making a note of the obviously complex traditions of the place before venturing into the ritual. He noticed, for instance, that the chairs lining the walls did not empty when dancing was resumed; on the contrary, about a third of those present walked off the floor and stood in a thick layer, three or four deep, making a human ring round the shiny floor with its solemnly entranced procession. The procession itself moved in an intricate pattern. There was an inner circle of the slow and comparatively sedate; a main circle of average animation; and, in each corner, under the 'No Jitterbugging' notices, were clustered pairs who did not circulate at all, but faced one another and moved their bodies in such a way as to suggest the extremes of sexual desire. Sometimes these couples entered each other's arms, in the normal fashion of dancers, but usually they allowed themselves no contact beyond, at prearranged intervals, grasping each other by the right hand.

He and Rosa began to dance. Immediately he realized that she was in love with him. He could not quite define how she conveyed it, but it was unmistakably there. They took their place in the outer ring of dancers, between the two extremes, and joined the mass-hypnotic swaying and gliding. Charles was slightly horrified—horror is an extreme emotion but it is, nevertheless, possible to experience it in a slight form—to find that instead of worrying about the fact of Rosa's being in love with him, he was simply accepting it as a rather pleasant sensation, rounding off his evening and completing the satisfactory state of affairs. He was not asking himself what he ought to do, but simply drifting, happily, in the direction the current took him; and the current, at the moment, was Rosa; just as the current, a month ago, had been the hospital, offering him its economic and emotional protection in return for his services with brush and pail. This must be his drifting period; he had finished with his period of intense effort, and his initial phase of revolt was a thing of the distant past. Drift! The band pumped its rhythms into his ears, and vibrated them up through the soles of his feet on the shiny floor, Rosa in his arms ceased to be a person and became something without individuality, but still powerful, drawing and guiding him in the same way as the beat of the music, the heat of the air in the hall, and the deep, deep fatigue and resignation at the core of his being. Drift, he would drift, and if it happened to him to slide over the edge of a waterfall, at least the water at the bottom of a waterfall was no worse than at the top of it, and he could not, any longer, be hurt by the fall.

When the dance finished he took her home, down airless streets of low, brown houses. All the houses were alike, and yet each was unique and lovable to the people who lived in it. The night was warm, so that the faint chill he felt through his sweat-damped shirt was welcome. Rosa held his arm, and was silent. He saw that he, so little involved or stirred, was giving her one of the memorable moments of her life; this evening would remain as a pin-point of light which she would still see when, as an old woman by some fireside, she looked back along the dark corridor of the years. He knew that when they reached the door of her home he must kiss her.

The street lamps were a long way apart in this quarter, and the door at which she halted was in a patch of deep dusk. Without speaking, she took off her hat; a gesture that exactly summed her up, for it was both slightly quaint, and also natural and right, as indicating that she was going in and had finished with her out-door clothes. She glanced at the plain wooden door, innocent of knocker or bell, but made no move to knock or open it.

As he kissed her she trembled slightly, but without losing her wonted blend of strength and repose. Holding her in his arms for a moment, he felt the sturdiness of her body, and how her strong legs stood firmly on the earth. Still calm, still not stirred to any damaging or ennobling depth, he felt a tranquil and comforting sense of being welcome and in his right place. He had come, not home perhaps, but to *a* home, a place where he could be received and left to root himself in peace, until the day when, at last, he belonged.

That was Thursday, and on the Sunday they took the bus into the country. But before it got further than the outskirts of the city, Rosa looked through the window and saw a small fair encamped in a dingy field.

'Oo, do let's go to that fair,' she said excitedly. 'I haven't been on a roundabout since I was, well, not since I was quite a kid.'

'You're quite a kid now,' he told her. She was happy enough to take every remark that was capable of several interpretations as a compliment, and smiled and sparkled at him as they got off the bus at the next stop. The conductor looked sourly at them because they had bought sixpenny tickets and only taken a threepenny ride, thereby upsetting his notions of order.

At the fair Rosa was perfect. If anything had been needed to confirm Charles in his sense of the rightness of this business, he had it now. Her animal vitality, and her capacity for small but whole-hearted enjoyments, showed themselves vividly. Years dropped from him, reducing all three or four lifetimes he had endured to the simple chronological total of his twenty-three years. They bucketed round and round on staring wooden horses, flung a hail of cracked wooden balls at cast-iron coconuts, laughed at each other in paper hats. Rosa's said 'Kiss Me, Sailor' on the front. 'I'm not a sailor,' he said, and kissed her. Some children cheered and laughed, and Rosa pretended to chase them. They watched a man pour sugar into a whirling machine; it came out as cotton wool, and they each had a huge bunch of it on the end of a splintery wooden stick. 'Don't swallow the splinters,' said Rosa seriously. Time passed as time ought to pass, unreflective, leaving no sediment.

They were to go to tea afterwards with her family; this had seemed, when first mooted, an ordeal, but the afternoon had put him into such a rosy frame of mind that he positively welcomed it. Everything, the new happiness with Rosa, the lingering traces of resentment after the Burge evening, even the recent odd little conversation with Mr. Braceweight, conspired to bring him to the test with an eager willingness to pass it and a serene confidence that he would be able to.

It was about five o'clock when Rosa knocked for them to be let in. The door was immediately opened by Rosa twenty-five years older. Sturdy, rather lined about the eyes and mouth, with heavy shoulders and arms—not a pretty sight—but with the same air of eagerness and vivacity. If Rosa were like this in twenty-five years, well, it would suit him. He would be no oil painting himself by that time.

Rosa's mother said she was pleased to see him. He said he was pleased to see her too. She obviously had a Sunday dress on, and the way she was wearing it indicated that this was not just because it was Sunday.

There was no passage, the front door opened straight into the parlour, but of course it was empty and stiff, with photographs in silvered frames cluttering the furniture. Having two downstairs rooms for the whole family, they lived in one and kept the other as a museum: this was England. So Charles did not get his first sight of Rosa's father until they had gone through into the room at the back.

No concessions here. This was Rosa's father's Sunday afternoon, and he had been spending it as he always did, in his armchair by the fire with the *News of the World* on his knee, fast asleep. No doubt his wife had nagged him to put a collar and tie on for once, but if so she had not succeeded. He sat blinking in his armchair, still not quite focusing; the knock on the door, and the entrance of his daughter and Charles, had woken him up, and he was not quite with them yet. But he did his best. His braces tightened as he leaned forward in his chair, his heavy moustache expanded as the mouth behind it widened into a smile, and with a genuine blend of dignity and affability he told Charles to sit down and make himself at home.

'The kettle's just boiling. Where's Stan, dad? We'll start tea when Stan comes in,' Rosa's mother said.

'If you don't know where Stan is,' returned the head of the household, poking the fire, 'don't ask me. I haven't been noticing. I must a nodded off. I sometimes do, on a Sunday, over me paper,' he added to Charles.

Charles made some suitable answer, and at that moment a small girl ran in from the yard.

'Oh, Glad!' cried Rosa, 'you've been playing down the embankment again!'

The child did not answer, but fixed her eyes on Charles's face and stood motionless.

'Did you say the embankment?' called Rosa's mother, coming in with the teapot from the scullery. 'Turn round, Gladys, this minute. Yes, my girl, and how many times do you have to be told,' etc. etc.

Still ignoring them, Gladys stood quite still, staring intently at the visitor.

'Upstairs this minute!' It seemed that everything Gladys did must be done that minute. 'Take her up, Rosa, dear. See that she gets her other things on, buzz, buzz,' something Charles was not meant to hear.

'Tea ready, Mom?' said a youth with a shiny pimply forehead, coming in through the museum. 'Ajadoo,' he said to Charles.

This was Stan. A few minutes of disjointed conversation, while Rosa was seeing to buzz, buzz, upstairs, revealed that Stan had been round to Len's, and that Wilf had been lucky with his permutations that week, and that Jeff and Arn were in danger of getting laid off while the dispute went to arbitration. None of Stan's friends seemed to have monosyllabic names of the older type, like Jack and Bob; they had all been given inconveniently long names by inconsiderate parents at the font, and now mutilated them with savage glee.

Charles liked Rosa's father, but he did not like Stan. This was not so much a disappointment as a confirmation of the whole tendency of his preferences just now, for Stan was making a fairly determined effort to 'better himself' by rising out of the world of strictly manual work—his father was a foreman at some kind of brickyard or quarry, it was not quite clear which—into the circle immediately above it. This circle seemed, by all accounts, a good deal slimier. At sixty, Stan would have neither the massive good humour nor the genuine dignity of his father, and already he was immersed in learning the technique of cheap smartness. He talked a different language, for one thing; it was demotic English of the mid-twentieth century, rapid, slurred, essentially a city dialect and, in origin, essentially American. By contrast it was a pleasure to hear his father, whose speech had been formed, along with all his other habits, before 1914; the last injection of new elements into his vocabulary had been in the trenches, and a slight seasoning of the Army slang of those days gave his talk a touch of colour.

Not that either of them said much. Rosa brought Glad downstairs, the finishing touches were put to the tea, and they sat down. Stan had lit a cheap American-style cigarette just before the meal began, and instead of extinguishing it, he kept it burning while he demolished his ham and pickles. The smoke drifted into Charles's face and made his eyes water. No one seemed to think Stan's behaviour unusual; in fact, Charles soon realized that the essential procedure governing this meal was to do as many things as possible. Tea was poured out, passed round, stirred, and drunk incessantly from the beginning of the meal; and if tea, why not tobacco?

The talk kept itself alive on gossip from Stan. Not that Stan wanted to gossip; but he was a hairdresser, and so heard everything. It appeared that he worked as assistant to a man who did a thriving trade a few streets away, and all the men in the locality left their latest news and opinions with the top inch of their hair, lying about in the shop to be swept up by Stan. Charles could see him in a few years, running his own place, flashy but dingy, with little cards about rubber goods among the hair-cream ads. in the window.

'What's Sam Boulton doin' with them pigeons now, Stan?' his father asked.

'I dunno. But we had Les in yestdy saying they was a ruddy noosance. They come in the bedroom windows.'

'I told him he wants to get some new stock. It'll be all Na Poo with 'em if he keeps breeding from the same ones. I told him that.'

Stan did not answer. They usually talked at cross purposes, since the father's questions only concerned men of his own generation, by whom Stan was bored.

'What about his mother's bad back?' asked Rosa. 'We'll be getting her in the hospital one of these days, with that back.'

'Dunno,' he said, smoking and eating a piece of cake.

'She's still under the doctor,' said Rosa's mother. 'More tea for anybody? Rosa, we want some water, love, out of the kitchen.'

Charles sat silent, with Glad's eyes boring into his face. He was quite peaceful, content not to talk. They accepted him without much curiosity and with complete friendliness. He was Rosa's business, and it was up to her to make something of him.

Finally, stuffed with ham, cake, bread and butter, and pints of dark tea, they moved from the table. Stan went out abruptly and silently, the women disappeared into the scullery to wash up, and Rosa's father lit his pipe and addressed himself to making a little conversation to Charles until Rosa should come and take him away.

Charles kept his end up fairly well. The invaluable *News of the World* provided them with topics; first what Rosa's father thought about the burning issue raised by their football correspondent, then the slightly less burning, but still urgent, controversy on the boxing page. Finally the murders, and how disgracefully easy it was to escape from Broadmoor and these places. Twice during the fifteen minutes, Rosa's father spat into the fire, and the second time he did so, Charles decided to co-operate and spat too. He could not decide whether this had been the right move. The old man appeared not to notice it, but Glad, who was standing in a corner staring at him, giggled softly.

During a lull in the talk, he tried to show an intelligent interest in the family. What school did Glad go to? Did Stan think of starting on his own? and so forth. This, however, was not a success, and he soon dropped it. Rosa's father had evidently fulfilled his duty towards his children by begetting them and providing them with food and clothing during their non-productive years, and he seemed vague about other matters. Out of politeness, he turned and asked Glad how she liked being at school, but she kept her eye on Charles's face and only giggled.

Rosa came in, dressed for going out to the pictures. The initiation was over. They went out, and sat gazing, doped, at the immense screen peopled with futile shadows, in a state of calm and content. Charles felt that his search was over. No demands were to be made on him other than merely being there, merely existing. He thought of Rosa's father, and how well he compared as a human being, with Sheila's father. And there was no Tharkles here. Stan was the family Tharkles, and he was quite harmless. It would do; his demands on life had grown smaller and smaller, until that stuffy, cosy room contained everything that he needed to fulfil them. That, and a bed upstairs with Rosa in it. Burge, Hutchins, Lockwood, Tharkles, Roderick, might be looking for him to torment him again, but in that room, that bed, they would never find him. He would be free and unnoticed.

True to the ingrained decorum and reticence of her race, only once did Rosa ask him the expected question: the question about 'the others'.

'Did you ever have a girl before?' she asked on their way home from the cinema one night. 'I mean, steady?'

He had to translate this. In his former circles, 'to have a girl' would bear its own precise meaning. What she was asking him was whether he had been in love before.

'Once,' he said. Might as well confess it.

'Was she nice? Did you—like her as much as me?'

Again that shying away from the word *love.* And the poor little broken word 'nice', doing so much duty. But her real, urgent meaning shone through.

Perversely, he clung to the word 'like', though he knew it was not what she meant.

'I didn't *like* her at all, really,' he said slowly, trying to be honest. 'I could divide my feelings about her pretty well into three parts. About one third was hatred: another third, the feeling that I wanted to make her keep perfectly still and just look at her, without saying anything, for ever: and the last third, a desire—'

He was about to say, 'a desire to bite her shoulders, arms and legs', but checked himself just in time. That would never do. If he wanted to avoid wounding Rosa, he must break the habit, lingering from his undergraduate days, of casual frankness and honesty in speaking of these things. He ended limply, 'a desire to touch her'.

Rosa was silent. He wondered whether even this was enough to affront her respectability. But she said, 'And is that what you feel about me? Any of those things?'

'No,' he answered, still slowly, still honestly. 'None of them, in quite the same way, I—I like you too much—I don't know whether you see this—I didn't at all *like* her—'

'You only loved her,' she put in unexpectedly. He was surprised into silence.

'If that's how you love people,' she went on, speaking calmly, 'it doesn't sound as if you do love me; if it's all so different.'

He stopped and faced her.

'Why shouldn't there be more than one way of loving someone?' he demanded. 'And why shouldn't one way be better than another? For that matter, why shouldn't one way be hateful and damaging?—and another healing, helpful, wonderful?'

The strength and sincerity of his own emotion surprised him, and she was reassured and made happy by it. Looking back on the conversation, he reflected that something new could be dated from that moment. It was a milestone on the way to somewhere he wanted, deeply and increasingly, to go. Or, rather, a sign-post; for a milestone would have told him how far he had still to travel.

'There's some news in this letter, rather inconvenient news,' said Mr. Braceweight, feebly waving an envelope. He was much better now, sitting up in bed. 'My chauffeur's given notice. He's going to get married.'

'Oh, yes?' said Charles perfunctorily, adding, to make conversation, 'does your chauffeur have to be a bachelor?'

'Well, it's not the job for a married man,' said Mr. Braceweight. 'He has a small room over the garage where he lives. There wouldn't be room for two people.'

Charles dusted the wireless set and moved it to a more convenient position.

'I—you said you were a driver, a delivery driver, wasn't it?'

'Yes,' said Charles, not seeing his drift.

'I suppose the job wouldn't—wouldn't suit you at all, would it?'

He was grateful, rather touched, even, but shook his head.

'I'm sorry, Mr. Braceweight, but as a matter of fact I'm thinking of getting married myself one of these days.'

'Oh,' said Mr. Braceweight faintly. 'Oh, well. That's that, of course.'

'You'll soon get another chauffeur,' said Charles reassuringly, gathering up his broom.

He saw a lot of Rosa in the next week. They went out on Monday, Tuesday, and Thursday evenings. Each time he called for her at the house, and chatted for a time with anyone who happened to be at home. Even Glad began to get used to him, and learnt to take her eyes off his face now and again. It was pleasant, but he was not altogether sorry to get an evening to himself on the Friday, when Rosa was busy doing something or other. Such repeated doses of affection and domesticity, with nothing to balance it, could become a little oppressive. He needed it, like bread, but one can be surfeited with bread.

He tried this metaphor over in his mind as he sat in his digs after tea, trying to analyse his feelings. Yes, surfeit; and yet perhaps it was something more acute than just a mild bout of emotional over-eating. Somewhere, he could not quite localize it, there was a hunger as well. A sensation not properly defined, not possible properly to define, was faintly present under the surface of his contentment. Like the itching of a wound as it finally healed. But where was he wounded? His smashed life, like his smashed body, had become whole again. Itch, itch. Something was the matter.

'A couple of drinks, that's what you need, my man,' he said to himself in the hall mirror as he went out. It was heavy and thundery outside; early August and beginning to get that washed-out feeling of high summer, when the freshness has gone from the leaves. Not that there were any leaves in the streets where he was walking, but outside, in the country, the leaves were drying slowly, and they had whispered their message to be heard in the backyards within the smoke-ring of the city.

He tried a pub near the hospital, but it was dirty and lonely. A few old men sat staring with red-rimmed eyes into their pints, making the beer look like tears they had dripped into their glasses and were saving for some purpose. He went out, leaving half his drink unfinished, and walked for a long way, keeping to the quiet back streets. Every road, every junction and square, was the same as every other. The low brown houses watched him as he walked past. 'One of us is your home,' they muttered to him. 'You'll find Rosa in the kitchen and the bed upstairs in the front room, the photographs talking to each other in the cold parlour, the lavatory down the back yard, for ever and ever, Amen.' Well, what of it? He would be safe and hidden. Nothing ever happened in houses like this, nothing except things people could understand. No problems, no art, no discussions and perplexities, just birth, death, eating, resting, sitting in front of the fire on Sunday afternoons with the *News of the World*. The factory sirens, instead of birds, would wake him in the morning, he would leave off his collar and tie and grow fat round the middle. As the years padded past, a troop of horse on felt, he would grow closer to his Rosa, making her happy and reflecting her happiness like a tarnished mirror, wrong in only a few spots that didn't matter.

This looked like a more cheerful pub. He went in and got a drink and carried it to a seat. He had been wrong. It was a gin-palace when you got inside. He must have wandered somewhere near the middle of the town, and the place seemed to cater for a smarter clientèle, very much the kind of people he wanted to avoid from now on. Besides, by not keeping his eyes open he had come in at the wrong door; the public bar might be all right, but this was the Saloon. He looked round him in disgust. It was the sort of place where you met people like Tharkles.

A tart came and sat next to him. 'Feeling lonely, dear?' she asked. 'I'm waiting for someone,' he replied to drive her away. She had a hideous green coat and skirt on, shrieking at her peroxide hair. Odd how they sometimes seemed to choose the ugliest colours; perhaps it was a trade convention to make them conspicuous, or perhaps that life sapped their aesthetic sense. He had half a mind to ask her what made her choose that colour scheme, but if he did he would never get rid of her; in any case she had gone across the room and transferred her attention to an old gentleman with a white moustache who ought to have been at home, watering his roses.

It had been a mistake to drink beer. He was feeling drowsy and miserable. But if he switched to something short, now, he would get drunk. What a wasted evening! Was this what you had to do to give yourself a change from going out with Rosa? He thought of the little room over Mr. Braceweight's garage; imagination showed it as a quiet retreat, rather like a cottage on a calendar, with roses climbing round a lattice window. What rubbish, it was probably more like a pre-fab in a slum, with the petrol fumes seeping up through the floor. He must get a grip on himself, a real grip.

He went up to the bar and ordered a whisky. Just one ought not to make any difference to him, and in any case it was difference he wanted, in any direction. He had just paid for it and was about to take it back to his seat, when his eye fell on an object lying on the bar at his elbow. It was a bar with tall red stools, repulsively suggesting a milk-bar, and a girl was sitting on the stool next to where he stood. She was with a man he did not bother to look at.

The object lying on the counter was the girl's handbag. It was of a rather distinctive shape, square and chunky, with a clip that looked like a coiled golden serpent.

The whisky could not very well spill out of his glass, for it was only about half an inch at the bottom. But it climbed steeply up the sides and circled there giddily. His hand could not keep still; he put the glass down. The girl, without looking at him, turned to get her handkerchief out of the handbag. Her fingers unfastened the coiled golden serpent. They were the wrong fingers, rather chubby, too many rings, bottle-green on the nails.

It was a mistake, this couldn't happen to him, he was free, free, he had been free for a long time. He didn't care about the handbag and whose handbag it was and who had had one just like that, God, they couldn't be doing this to him. The pain was beyond anything he believed possible. He clung to the bar. Waves of agony radiated from the centre, somewhere about the solar plexus, and splashed down as far as his toes and finger-ends. No one could do this to him, not really, not if they knew what they were doing. All these people in this bar, everyone in the world, if they only knew they would help him, they would find Veronica and bring her to him. They would find her if they could only realize that a man was dying, a man who had not deserved to die and go down to Hell. If they could see inside him, for one second feel what he was feeling, they would seek her out. Messages would flash along wires, brr, brr, is that you, a very urgent call, hold everything, a man here's in Hell. The message would be typewritten, swiftly, on a sheet of paper, someone would knock on the door of the room where she was sitting, or run out to the meadow where she walked by herself. If you were drowning they threw a rope. This was worse than drowning, he was being broken to pieces, humanity would not let this happen to him.

No, no, no one will help you. Take your drink, move away from the bar. But the handbag! There could not be two like that. Had she stolen it? Perhaps this was Veronica's way of coming to him: she might be inside the handbag, shrunk by magic to the size of a white mouse, waiting only till he opened it and took her out. Then put her in water and she would become her real size. Dehydrated. He was going mad, in earnest this time. He drank the whisky.

All at once he felt tired, tired and old. It was the girl's own handbag, they sold them in shops, there must be plenty just like that. Serpent clip and all. Anyone could go into a shop and buy one. He could go and buy one himself, and give it to Rosa.

Rosa! As he sat, empty glass in hand, staring across at the bag on the counter, he knew suddenly and finally that it was over. He would never give anything to Rosa now, not even himself, because he was not his own to give. Another whisky. Thoughts of Veronica ebbed away. That was over too, there must never be any thoughts of her again. He did not, ultimately, want any. If she came in now, into this very bar, he would go out by another door without speaking to her, without letting her see him even. He was broken. The wheels had passed over him. This latest dream, of peace in a smoky brown house, he now recognized for what it was. A stage in his recovery. Recovery meant nothing but coming to terms with your illness, gauging accurately the extent to which you had been maimed. He did not want Rosa, he did not want Veronica, he wanted nothing.

'Snap out of it. Bloody self-pity,' he said, going out into the street.

'That's over, anyhow,' he said, walking into another pub a few yards away.

'Just a freak,' he said into his glass of stout. 'Tricks you play on yourself.'

'Say something, mate?' said a man in a muffler, leaning across.

'No. Just catgut. I've got the catgut,' he said, standing up to go. 'That's all I came in for, to leave the catgut.'

He went out.

'No good fooling yourself,' he said to the lamp-post.

And I a twister love what I abhor. And buy a hoar love twisting what and eye. Oh, shut up, shut up.

'Still by yourself, dear?' asked the tart, coming up to him.

'Yes,' he said. 'And I'm staying like that.'

'No offence, dear,' she said.

'No offence,' he said.

'About that job, Mr. Braceweight,' he said. 'If you haven't filled it yet, I could take it, as things have turned out.'

'You won't be getting married just yet, then?'

'Apparently not.'

'You realize you've accepted the job without asking me anything about pay or hours?' Mr. Braceweight asked, pained; it was obviously very hard for him to get used to anyone like Charles.

'Was that so very improvident of me? Remember I've seen a lot of you during the time you've been here, enough to feel sure that you're not a man who underpays his employees. Sir,' he added, feeling that relations between them would obviously have to become more formal soon, and the sooner the better. He liked Mr. Braceweight, and for a moment, once, they had approached something like confessional intimacy. But instinct warned him to shy away from the complicated relationship that would result from any attempt to mix the employer and the friend. He must fend off any sign of the paternal.

'You're only just in time,' said Mr. Braceweight, switching off the personal note as if he, too, felt the danger. 'I'm being discharged from here tomorrow. I shall go down to my place in Sussex and stay there for the rest of the summer. As soon as you're free to come down, you'll find everything ready for you. But I suppose you'll have to give a week or two's notice here?'

'No,' said Charles with unnecessary emphasis. 'I can leave straight away. I never signed anything to say I'd stay here: I just lose a week's pay if I go without notice, and—' then he remembered that he was talking to his prospective employer and so ought not to sound too carefree about leaving without notice, and added, 'the fact is that things have cropped up that make my position here rather difficult, for myself and others. I can leave when you leave tomorrow.'

'That's lucky, because I was wondering who would drive me down to Sussex.'

'It's definite then, Sir? I'm employed?'

Mr. Braceweight nodded.

'From tomorrow.'

'Look,' he said to Rosa. 'Something's happened. I'm going away.'

'When will you be back?' she asked, not understanding him.

'I shan't,' he said, hating himself. 'Not back, ever.'

She turned to face him. Her vivacity drained away, leaving only pallor and emptiness.

'Tell me why.'

'I can't.'

'Tell me. You must tell me.'

'Rosa, my dear, my dear, I wish, it's all so crazy, I wish I could—'

'Is it something I've done?'

'No.'

'Is it something I haven't done, then? Something you wanted me to?'

'There's nothing either of us has done. It isn't anything either of us could possibly have avoided.'

'You mustn't treat me like this,' she said, deadly calm. 'You can't do this to a girl. Not to a decent girl. I'm not trying to hold you, I only want to know where I went wrong with you.'

'Oh, God, Rosa, I tell you you never went wrong. You were always sweet and right. You were yourself.'

'What was it, then?'

He faced her. His brain was dry and empty. He wanted to explain to her that it was not his fault. He had not meant to injure her, he had only thought, mistakenly, that he was the kind of man who could bring her happiness and help her to profit by her own particular kind of life-giving simplicity. Now she faced him across the dirty dishes on the table, with nothing left in her face and bearing except numbness and pain.

Innocent and tranquil as his dealings with her had been, he had, after all, known a greater degree of happiness, and therefore of intimacy, with her than with any other woman, and so they were able to converse, instantaneously, without the use of words. Helplessly, silently, he tried to explain that it had all been a mistake. Silently, in answer, she condemned him.

'You sinned against me,' her expression and stance told him. 'You injured me in the one way that can never be forgiven. Because, ultimately, you were committing the one great offence against a fellow-creature: you tried to use me. Not to give, not to combine, but to use me.' 'It wasn't so simple,' he tried, with his eyes, to plead, but she cut across his defence. 'I was ready to love you, and all you were doing was taking me as a drug.' Accusation and apology, inadmissable, lame apology, flashed across the table. He felt stricken and soiled.

'What was it?' she repeated, aloud.

Crushed and ashamed, he muttered, 'I can't explain—only—it was just—'

'Tell me what *happened*. Something must have happened, something you could tell me about,' she said in a new voice, flat and without overtone.

'I saw a handbag. It was a handbag,' he burst out, painfully, madly.

'Heavens! Haven't you got these dishes done *yet*?' exclaimed the staff nurse, bustling in. 'It beats me what you people do with your time.' Then she saw that Rosa was crying. She was crying heavily, helplessly, without any attempt at concealment. The staff nurse rounded on Charles, violently partisan, a woman standing up for another woman against the common enemy.

'What have you been doing to her?' she demanded bitterly.

'Oh, please, please,' said Charles, utterly defeated and miserable. 'It isn't anything you could understand. Please don't let's go into it.'

Rosa had turned away. Her shoulders were moving rhythmically as she sobbed without making a sound. The staff nurse was passionately angry and insulted that Charles should have said this was something she could not understand.

'Can't understand, my foot,' she said. 'That's the line all you dirty cads take. I can understand all right. You've been messing about with her, you've been making her unhappy. I know you, damn the lot of you. Don't take on, kiddie,' she said to Rosa. 'You'll be better off without a rotten bastard like him. You're a rotten bastard,' she added to Charles.

'Yes,' he said, and nodded.

'Well, get out of here,' she stormed. 'Get out of here and do some work for your living.'

Dumbly, head bowed, he collected his broom and duster.

'And there's another thing, Mister Don Juan,' she said, her arm round Rosa's shoulders. 'Just let me catch you putting your foot wrong and I'll see you sacked quicker than that.' She snapped the fingers of her free hand.

'I'm going anyway,' he said dully. 'This'll be my last night on duty.'

'Well, go on, get out,' she said, impatient for him to leave her alone with Rosa. 'Get out and do some work, even if it is your last night. And next time you meet a decent girl, leave her alone, will you?'

'Yes,' he said obediently, as if she had given him some order relating to his duties as an orderly. 'I'll do that.'

IX

It was characteristic of Mr. Braceweight not to have a Rolls-Royce. He was rich, but he had refrained from going the whole hog and becoming a millionaire, and he showed the same spirit of restraint in his style of living. Another two thousand a year and Charles might have been dressed in an elaborate uniform, with leather gaiters and buttons to polish, driving a Rolls and sleeping among the cockroaches. As it was, he had only a simple uniform, a brown suit with a peaked cap, found his tiny bed-sitting room perfectly comfortable, and cruised round the country lanes in a Daimler; fluid flywheel, three and a half tons, making him feel like a bus driver, except that he did not have to stop to let people get on.

He had fallen on his feet. For the first week he was wary, expecting some crippling snag to reveal itself, but once over the initial feeling that this was too good to be true, he had lived in a trance of self-congratulation. Peace: an obscurity as great as anything he could have found by marrying Rosa and disguising himself as Stan's brother-in-law. And coupled with it a sense of idyllic, almost pastoral calm, flowing in upon him from the tranquil beauty of the countryside. The house was a modest brick building, probably a seventeenth- or eighteenth-century farmhouse, with a few unobtrusive but thorough-going innovations in the cause of comfort for the inhabitants, but no messing about with the outside. Mr. Braceweight's moderation again, his refusal to be rushed by his own wealth. Through the window of his room Charles could see how the expensively tended garden (cottage style) broadened into the expensively tended countryside that slumbered around it. For this was not what Charles secretly considered the 'real' countryside; it was rural, yes, it produced its crops and milk, yes, and the pubs were full of ruddy broad-shouldered men speaking slowly and loudly in Mummerset, yes, but he had grown up accustomed to the countryside of the middle of England, which earns its own living. Sussex, with its fabulous beauty, its groomed cottages in Hollywood black and white, its glossy cows and immense trees, was to him a stage set, a fake, something supported by the prosperous in search of peace and quiet and food in their week-ends out of town. As he drove slowly through the deep lanes with their nodding green edges, sounding his horn in tiny spotless villages, the blatant self-consciousness of it made him feel as American visitors must feel—glad that a good show has been put on, but somehow wistful at finding the organization so perfect.

Of course, it had taken some luck to produce these ideal conditions for his introduction to the job; he admitted that. For one thing, Mr. Braceweight was taking a holiday after his operation. There was no need to drive him up to London, or to spend long periods at his house there, ready at any time of the day to face the nightmare crawling traffic of the city. It was half-pressure as yet. Then again, the man had had the sense, at some remote period of his life, to choose a wife who was exactly like himself. So entirely without flavour or distinction, for good or ill, was Mrs. Braceweight, that for the first fortnight Charles found himself unable to remember, between one meeting with her and the next, what she looked or sounded like. He carted her like a parcel on her shopping excursions, touched his cap to her in the garden, sat in the car and read his newspaper while she paid calls in the district, and that was all.

Life, in fact, had slowed down to a welcome jog-trot. He had forgotten the taste of peace since those first golden weeks as a window-cleaner, before it had begun to turn sour. Now something of that spirit was returning; his room above the garage, when he climbed to it after his day's work, had about it a pleasantly nostalgic reminder of the Froulish loft. Not even his fellow-servants presented a problem, for there were none. There was only a harassed housekeeper who tried to train a succession of more or less mentally deficient girls from the village. All the intelligent ones had gone into the towns, mostly to serve in milk-bars within striking distance of American airfields. Ten years previously and there would have been a full-scale servants' hall, presided over by a butler looking like an eighteenth-century statesman at Madame Tussaud's, and a rigid hierarchy, smaller and more vigilant than the one at the hospital, into which he would have had to squeeze himself somehow. Now there was nothing; he did not even know the name of the old man who dug the garden, or the youth who helped him on Saturdays. He was a Crusoe with no need to look for footprints in the sand.

He was polishing the headlamps, one slack afternoon, when a high-pitched buzzing, like that of an angry bee, began to cut through the drowsy August air. Approaching, it turned into a series of deep, choking snorts, then renewed itself into a mad bellowing. Charles straightened up and stared down the drive. It was a curving one, which skirted the kitchen garden so as to leave the flower-garden with its cottage atmosphere unsullied, and he saw through the gaps in the bushes that something was taking it, gravel surface and hairpin bend included, at little short of forty miles an hour. Hastily he backed behind the solid bulk of the Daimler.

The motor-cycle swept into the small courtyard in front of the garage with its front forks whipping up and down as the brakes went on. Gravel spurted like the spray from a fast launch. With wheels locked, the abominable machine clawed its way round in a tight circle. One handlebar scored a deep line in the paintwork of the garage door. It stopped, and there was silence.

Before Charles could collect himself to protest, a young man had heaved the bicycle on to its stand and turned to face him.

'Not bad,' he said. 'Sixty-two minutes from town. From Highgate to be precise.'

He was powerfully built, with black brows and a heavy jowl. His face showed no trace of intelligence or sensibility, but it was not unattractive. His general manner was of untroubled, genial capability; obviously there were quite a number of things he could do well, and as for the things he could not do at all, he had simply never heard of them.

'How are you finding the old carriage?' he jerked his thumb at the Daimler. 'Deadly bore, eh? Nought to twenty in five minutes.' He laughed loudly, then suddenly became serious. 'Look!' he said, swiftly moving over and dragging open the bonnet, 'I've been thinking of one or two things we could do to increase performance. It ought to be the simplest thing on earth to get the compression ratio up by about two-thirds. And see the position of that jet? Possibilities there, you know.'

'Before we go into it in more detail,' said Charles, able to speak at last, 'could you just clear up one point for me? Just who the hell are you?'

The young man laughed.

'Of course, I was forgetting. You wouldn't know. I'm—'

'Walter,' said Mr. Braceweight's voice from behind them in a tone Charles had never heard him use before, 'is this thing yours?' He had come round from the garden to investigate the noise made by the motor-cycle.

The young man turned and began talking with a false eagerness, like a salesman making an all-out effort on someone who never buys.

'That's right, Daddy. I didn't think your ban would apply to this, as it was such a soundly constructed—'

'I told you no motor-cycle and I meant no motor-cycle,' said Mr. Braceweight stonily.

'Yes, but you see—'

'I thought I had made myself perfectly plain.'

'Well, yes, of course, but when I had a chance of a good thing like this, solid as a rock—you see there's no danger with a thing like—'

'I don't want the details. This is not what your allowance is given you for.'

'—telescopics, you see here, and—'

'I don't see anything to discuss, Walter.'

'—graphite lubrication—all perfectly—'

Mr. Braceweight had turned and gone into the house.

Walter turned to Charles. The confidence had gone from his bearing, being replaced by half-comical ruefulness. The large circular white patches round his eyes, where his goggles had kept off the dust and oil, enhanced the effect by giving him the look of a Walt Disney animal.

'Drat it. I might have known it was fatal to bring it down here. Ought to have kept it at school, or in the village, rather. No motor-bikes, that was the decree on my sixteenth birthday. Some crazy idea that they're dangerous. Hell, I can't go another six months without any form of motoring at all.'

Charles was still trying to get a grip on the situation.

'Forgive my obtuseness,' he said, 'but I've been used to a quiet life lately. I've let myself get out of touch with the march of events and it's made me so that I can only take in one fact at a time. To get this straight—your name is Walter and I heard you call my employer Daddy, which means you're his son.'

'Yes.'

'And you're sixteen and a half although you look thirty.'

Walter brightened. 'Yes, I do look a bit old for sixteen-six, don't I? Not much chance of being stopped to show my licence. No one would take me for under age, would they?'

'And I'll add another thing I know about you,' Charles went on, still concentrating on keeping his head clear. 'You're a motor enthusiast. History started for you when the sparking-plug was invented.'

A happy smile came over Walter's square-cut, dusty face.

'Well, don't let's say the sparking-plug,' he said in the tone of a connoisseur who dwells lovingly on some abstruse point in his pet subject, 'let's say—let's say the differential.'

Mrs. Braceweight had spent the morning shopping at the neighbouring market town. 'By the way, I nearly forgot, Lumley,' she said as he held the door open for her to get out of the car, 'my husband wants you to meet the 2.45 at the station. I didn't catch the name quite, but it's a young man who's coming to be Mr. Walter's tutor during the summer. There won't be more than one person who looks like a tutor getting off the train.'

He murmured some kind of discreet agreement—he never talked to his employers—and carried her parcels into the house.

After lunch he took the Daimler over. The tiny station was in the midst of its one daily half-hour of alertness, for the next train in was the one which waited patiently for any passengers alighting from the express, and clattered round the neighbourhood dropping them at smaller and smaller stations. It was the only train on which anything, or anyone, from the larger world ever reached them.

Charles sat smoking on the bench outside the waiting-room. His peaked cap lay on the seat beside him. The Daimler stood patiently in the sun outside, its leather giving off a hot smell. The train was signalled, and fussed into the station. Charles kept a look out for someone who looked like tutor to a rich man's son. Two people got off. One was a middle-aged woman carrying a side of bacon. The other was George Hutchins.

In spite of his tranquillity, and the fading of his various grudges against life, Charles had to admit that his character was not really growing more benign as he lived longer. On the contrary, he was less willing to sit down under an insult than he had ever been. And the very existence of Hutchins, within five miles of himself, was an insult. He decided to be offensive.

Hutchins looked round keenly and nervously. He had his pipe at the ready in case it should be necessary to put on his don's act at short notice. Even at first glance Charles could see that the act had grown richer and more professional during his year of close contact with the real thing. There was something in the way he glanced about him—vital, intelligent, and yet with an endearing touch of absent-mindedness—that revealed a fresh mastery of the academic bag of tricks. He sat on the bench appreciatively watching the performance.

'I was to have been met,' he heard Hutchins say to the porter. 'Mr. Braceweight, something, something,' he could not quite catch what came next, 'definitely arranged to have me driven over.'

'Can't say nothin' 'bout that. Doano nothin' 'bout that,' said the porter over his shoulder, going into a shed marked 'Staff only.' He knew, of course, that Mr. Braceweight's car was outside, and Mr. Braceweight's chauffeur was sitting on the bench a few yards away, but he had his own job to do.

Hutchins turned round, irresolute. Charles folded his peaked cap and hid it carefully in his pocket. In his brown suit he had nothing about him to suggest the chauffeur. Just in time: Hutchins had spotted him.

'Well, this is a surprise, Lumley,' he said, coming up the platform.

'I'm astonished,' said Charles.

'What are you doing down here? Did you come down on that train?'

'No,' said Charles, avoiding the larger question, 'I was here when the train came in.'

'I'm doing some tutoring for a family down here,' said Hutchins carelessly. It was wonderful how modest and unassuming he was. He talked about his tutoring as if anybody could have done it. Just as he had said 'we' at the Stotwell Literary Society. Success had not spoilt him. 'Awkward, actually,' he went on, 'because I wanted to get across to America to look at some of the stuff in Princeton. I shall have to do that next year instead.'

'Yes,' said Charles pleasantly, 'and meanwhile, tutoring is useful work.'

'That's what I thought.'

'A man like you can do a lot of good by sharing his knowledge.'

'Just so.'

'And you can't have too many friends and patrons among the rich. It all helps.'

Hutchins flushed dully. 'If you're implying that my motive in tutoring is an unworthy one, of course, I—'

'Not at all. Social climbing isn't unworthy. When a man's got half-way up the ladder by hard work, as you have, it's only human for him to decide that he might as well jump the rest of the rungs by a quicker method.'

The old Hutchins might have been drawn by such elementary gambits. But the new one was too snug. The veneer had been applied very skilfully.

'Just the same as ever, Lumley, I see, living in a muddle of unexamined ideas. What you would call social climbing, I, from perhaps a more impartial standpoint, would describe as,' and so he went on for three or four minutes, until he had talked himself back into poise and self-confidence. 'And now, what about this car they're supposed to be sending for me?'

'Well, there is a Daimler outside,' said Charles. 'Perhaps you ought to go and get into that.'

They went out. Hutchins looked doubtfully at the car.

'It seems the only one, certainly, but I hesitate to get in without anyone here to ask. And yet, damn it,' he went on, irritated, 'how do they expect me to get there without a car?'

'Tell you what,' said Charles. 'You get in and I'll drive the thing myself. That'll get you there, anyway.'

'You'll drive? What on earth do you mean?'

For answer Charles held the door open for him. When Hutchins still did not understand, he took his peaked cap from his pocket and, putting it on, stood grotesquely at the salute.

'You've started a taxi firm, then?' asked Hutchins.

'Keep guessing and you'll get the answer in less than three. Yes, as one parasite to another, I'll confide. I'm the chauffeur.'

Hutchins was startled out of his new urbanity. The old

Black Country expression and manner came back with a rush.

'Well, Lumley, I'm sorry you're down on your luck. I should have thought you could have got a better job than this, though, I must say. Of course, I could see years ago that you hadn't got a real grip on things. But I didn't think you would have come down to this.'

'What do you mean, come down?'

'I could give you a recommendation that would probably get you a job in a prep. school. That would be a start, at least.'

'Listen, George,' Charles said wearily. 'Never mind the missionary zeal. I don't want honest work. I'm like you, I prefer to be a parasite. A louse on the scalp of society.'

'I don't see the comparison, I must say,' said Hutchins stiffly.

'What could be plainer? I drive the great man's car. You try to tinker with the brain-box of his son. The only effective difference between us is that my work is obviously of some practical use, whereas you'll have nothing to show for it. I've met the boy. He's perfectly decent, but ten of you working in relays wouldn't give him any academic intelligence. He's a mechanic.'

'That's as may be. And in any case, Lumley, if you *have* taken a job as chauffeur, and seem to like it so much, I shall have to remind you, when you get too obstreperous, to *behave* like a chauffeur.'

'Of course, you're a believer in acting the part, aren't you? Well, get that pipe out and rehearse some of your better opening moves while I get your suitcase. The old boy's quite sharp-eyed although he seems a nonentity. And don't worry about me. I won't let on that you've ever associated with a man who's working as a chauffeur. And I'll call you "sir" in front of the family, as long as you'll tip me five bob when you leave.'

'I see you're determined to make my position uncomfortable.'

'It'll be uncomfortable without my doing anything about it. Wait till you meet your pupil. You'll be lucky if he doesn't take one look at you and ask you to run away and tell your mother she wants you.'

'Whose mother what?' asked Hutchins, becoming seriously confused.

'Never mind. Get in and I'll fetch your bag. Sir.'

'The main trouble is this,' said Walter. 'I could see when I bought the engine that the valve seats were going to give trouble. It was just what I expected. The valve stem was too long, and what do I have to do but pack up the rocker-shaft standards, to bring up the height of the rocker fulcrums; and now, of course, I've got push-rod trouble.'

'Of course,' said Charles.

Walter sighed, and bent over the grotesque mass of machinery on the bench. It reminded Charles of one of Cecil Beaton's photographs of wrecked tanks in the North African desert. Walter's square, powerful hands, with black-edged nails broader than they were long, moved lovingly about among the entrails of the beast, tapping, levering, adjusting. He was wearing dungarees black and stiff with oil, and wherever his person emerged from their protection it, too, was flecked and streaked with dark grease. A long stripe of it ran up the side of his face.

'Of course,' he said bitterly, 'I'm handicapped all along the line. No money, and having to do the whole job on the quiet. I can't even afford the proper tools. I spend hours checking my piston rings to get the gaps right, and then I have to mess them up just because I haven't got a proper ring expander. Just have to slide the bastards on over the pistons any old how.'

'Why are you having to do it on the sly, anyhow?'

'Well, ask yourself,' said Walter, turning to face him. 'If the Pater knew I was building a special, he knows me well enough to know that when it's finished I shan't just put it in a glass case. I shall use it. I shall enter it in sprints and hill-climbs if I can't race it. And we've had one or two almighty scenes already. It's the only thing we *have* had scenes over, as a matter of fact. Nothing of that sort till I'm twenty-one, if you please.'

He scowled at the spanner in his hand, the grease mark on his face twisting itself into an irritable line.

'And here's me having to put every brass farthing of my allowance into getting a few worn-out old parts off the junk heaps. I was actually offered a double-knocker Norton unit for twenty quid the other day. Think of it! Unique offer! I could have built the best five-hundred that ever raced. But twenty quid, twenty measly quid—not me. So I have to get along without even proper equipment, and work in a damned shack like this.'

The damned shack was Walter's workshop at the bottom of the kitchen garden. It had doubtless been handed over to him when, in more tender years, he first showed an interest in working with his hands. Certainly it was not a suitable place for the building of motor cars. What a paradox the whole thing was!

'Forgive my asking this,' said Charles, 'but don't you sometimes feel it was a stroke of bad luck for you to be born with a well-to-do father who's got ideas about educating you, and so forth, inflicting a tutor on you in the holidays?—when if you were the son of, let's say, a chimney-sweep, you could have been happily employed by now as a garage hand.'

But Walter, surprisingly, shook his head.

'Not much fun in being a garage-hand. They very seldom see anything interesting. Working on stock jobs most of the time.' He paused, then suddenly bellowed with laughter. 'I'd soon get the sack for trying my ideas on the customers' chariots. Imagine a fellow's face if he brought his car in to have the brakes tested, or something, and found when he got away that I'd machined his guides for him and got double valve springs in!'

Charles joined, a trifle uncertainly, in the laughter.

'Or better still,' Walter spluttered, 'fitted him a bigger sump and brought his pressure up—particularly if I'd forgotten to get a pump shroud in for him to stop his oil surge!'

Then his laughter was suddenly cut short by a sobering recollection. He looked at his watch.

'Oh, flaming hell,' he said, 'got another spell with my tutor in ten minutes' time. Latin, Latin, always Latin.'

'How do you get on with him?'

'With who? Oh him? I believe he's all right.'

It was clear that Walter had never really noticed Hutchins. No doubt he stolidly sat through their sessions, living for the time when he could get to his inlet valve springs. Nor was it likely that Hutchins himself would have his mind squarely on the job. Sweetness and light. A liberal education. Wragg is in custody.

*

The summer had been going on for a long time; it had reached its highest point of ripeness and profusion, just before the season when a few menacing hints of frost would come to remind plant, insect, and man that winter must follow. Charles sat looking out of his window at the hot rich night. The garden had worked itself up to an almost intolerable fragrance. An impossibly fat, full moon hung in the sky, provoking manufacturers of similes to fresh jumps into the ludicrous: it contrived to suggest everything from a Dutch cheese to the polished bell of a trombone, without being like anything except itself. Now and again a cow lowed in the distance. Peace, warmth, and glimmering light rested on the self-confident landscape.

Moths swerved in at Charles's window. The smoke from his cigarette streamed out and upwards on the faintest of breezes. He was thinking of Bunder. Why had no one ever questioned him? Could it be that Bunder had escaped? Or had he been arrested and still kept his mouth shut about his accomplices? Obviously he, Charles, could never know the answer to these and a hundred other questions. The men who had scattered and run before the police at the dock, for instance, surely some or all of them had been arrested. How long would it take for enquiries to lead to him wherever he hid himself? On the face of it, he ought to have been afraid; but he could not frighten himself. His deepest instincts told him that the whole business was over, for him at least. For one thing, if Bunder had only been a comparatively minor figure in a large organization, headed by men who never revealed their identity, some way had probably been found of intimidating the captured men into revealing nothing, not even the little that they knew. It was all quite beyond him, and yet he felt secure. When the police patrol car had swept past his unconscious form as he lay by the roadside, the law had brushed its net across him, and it had not picked him up. All he had to do was to stay a long way away from publicity, and especially police-court publicity. Deepest of all, generating a calm that spread through his mind, was the intuitive conviction that Bunder had not, in fact, been captured. 'In any case they're not taking me alive,' he had said, and Charles had absolute confidence that he meant it. The pace, and the manner, of his driving had probably led him into a fatal accident; or he had taken some other way of following his victim out of this life. Somehow, and certainly, he had slipped through the net by the smallest hole of all.

A rustling and whispering from down below. Two figures, one of each gender, were making their way through the bushes. Whoever they were, they had some reason for not wanting to be seen. Walter and the latest kitchen-maid, perhaps. He froze and watched intently.

'I hope you're right when you say this is simple,' came a female voice. It was subdued almost to a whisper, but its clear, bell-like quality was unmistakable. 'I still say you ought to have come to the hotel.'

'I tell you this is much the simpler way,' hissed Hutchins. 'It would be absolutely impossible to avoid being seen down there. I've got to keep my job.'

So the June Veeber game was still going on, after a year! And the harpy had followed him down here.

'Nobody uses this side entrance. We can go straight up the back stairs to my room,' said Hutchins tensely fiddling with a key-ring in the moonlight. 'Ah, here it is. Quick, let's get inside.'

They disappeared. In a moment, light flashed from the window of Hutchins's room. It was dimmed at once, evidently by the drawing of the curtains. About twenty minutes later it was extinguished. Charles sat quietly and sardonically smoking. There was something about the whole sordid little episode that made him feel slightly sorry for Hutchins, sorry in a superior way that flattered his self-esteem. A social climber can ill afford an Achilles' heel, and this particular weakness on Hutchins's part would probably be disastrous to him sooner or later, especially in view of the profession he had chosen. Charles sat on, in the moonlight, smoking, and sinking deeper and deeper into the fatal condition of hubris.

He even felt rather sorry for Hutchins. If the man had his difficulties, it was rather a shame to add to them. And he had been adding to them. While waiting for Mrs. Braceweight in the main street of the local shopping centre, he had been unable to resist slipping into the Post Office and sending him a telegram: ARRIV-

ING FRIDAY LOOK FORWARD TO SEEING YOU MERDE. The thought of Hutchins slitting open the yellow envelope and reading so perplexing a message had amused him richly. The following day, finding that Walter was going for a day's excursion to visit a friend at Winchester, he had enlisted the boy's help, and got him to send another telegram to Hutchins, giving only the telephone number of Mr. Braceweight's house so that the message would be dictated. They had timed it to arrive when the family was at lunch, and no doubt the housekeeper had copied it on to a piece of paper and taken it to Hutchins at the table. THANKS FOR SYMPATHY WILL DISCUSS MATTERS ON FRIDAY MERDE. It was Friday evening now, and he rocked with laughter at the thought that June Veeber had probably arrived that day. He could imagine Hutchins asking her crossly why she had sent him two telegrams and signed herself Merde.

Warm, stagnant and dreamlike, the days went by. Nothing interrupted the calm: even the one major drawback of his job, the lack of personal freedom, was an advantage in his eyes. He could never be far away, but must be ready at need during most of the twenty-four hours. This feature of the job had caused so many of Mr. Braceweight's chauffeurs to become discontented and leave him, that he had been compelled to counter-balance it by the bribe of an unusually high wage. Charles enjoyed the high wage without any hankering for more freedom; he never wanted to go farther than the village pub on his evening out, and he could always leave word with the housekeeper that his employers could find him there.

One evening after closing time, he was sauntering along the lane from the inn, relishing the deep tranquillity of the dusky hedgerow, when voices reached him from a few yards away. He halted; there was a gate a few yards farther on, and just inside the field stood a haystack, its top visible over the tall hedge. Hutchins and June Veeber were in the field. He could picture them sitting with their backs to the warm, rustling wall of hay. He began to cross to the other side of the lane, hoping to walk past quietly without being seen, but June's next words, the first he had heard clearly, arrested his movement. He paused in the deep shadow, and, after a brief inward struggle, listened.

'I don't care what you say, George. I won't have it and that's the end of that.'

'I don't want you to have it, damn it,' came the voice of Hutchins, petulant and flustered. 'All I'm saying is that you can't just come up to me and say, "I'm pregnant. Now it's your move," as coolly as that. These things cost money, and I just haven't enough.'

'You'll get hold of it soon enough if you have to. And you *have* got to, that's all there is to it. There are any number of people who would lend it to you.'

'That's what you think. Who, for instance?'

'I'm not concerned with that. It's up to you to find out who'll lend it to you. But there must be dozens. Even in your own college: what about Lockwood, for a start?'

'Lockwood!' came his voice sardonically; then a short, sour laugh. 'Well, he'll serve as an example if you want one. Where do you think I got the money for our trip to Spain? Did you think that came out of my salary?'

'You mean Lockwood lent it to you?'

'He and two other people. He lent me twenty-five of it. The fact is, darling, I don't want to say this, but—it hasn't been chicken-feed all these months. You've cost me plenty—'

Her clear voice was raised, and had a cutting edge to its anger.

'Go on, put it that way if you like! I suppose every time we've been to bed you've gone back to your rooms and worked out how much per time it's been costing you.'

There was a silence.

'Dearest,' came the voice of Hutchins in a crushed, wheedling tone, 'you must be very angry with me to talk like that. After all we've—'

'Never mind all we've this and all we've that,' she snapped, the fishwife under the skin becoming more audible (and doubtless, more visible too) with every second. 'All I know is you've had your fun, and now I'm going to have a baby, and you aren't man enough to scrape up a miserable seventy-five pounds without all this whining. Well, you'll have to scrape it up. I'm not going to dip into my funds to save you from a scandal.'

'Why to save me? You'd be saving yourself too.'

'It's no good trying that line either—frightening me into paying for it myself because I'm just as anxious to avoid it as you are. You stand to lose everything if there's a real stink—and I warn you I'd stir one up. You'd never hold your job and you'd never get another.'

'They couldn't prove I was the father,' Hutchins blustered, with terrible lack of confidence. She laughed.

'Well, I must say, you're more of a fool than I took you for, George. Do you mean you don't see how I could prove it up to the hilt? Oh, you've been very clever about not writing me any letters, you poor sap, but you needn't think that'll cut any ice. There are all the hotels too. I took good care the maids and the reception clerks got a proper look at us.'

'Taking care of yourself, weren't you?' he sneered weakly.

'Yes, and it looks as if I was right to take care, if you're the kind of louse who'd leave me to it after you've—'

'Oh, please, June, don't!' he burst out. Charles was surprised to hear a note of real emotion, not at all to be accounted for by panic, in his shrill note. 'This really has meant something to me, really, and you know yourself those—things—you say aren't—' he sounded choking. There was a long silence; perhaps she had taken him in her arms.

'Mutter, mutter, mumble,' he heard, evidently some kind of endearment, then 'and you will make it all right, darling, won't you?'

'I'll get it somehow,' Hutchins said in a shaking voice. It was obvious that all this was a terrible ordeal for him. 'You say we've got another three or four weeks. I'll see to it. Just get in touch with the man and tell him it'll be all right about the money.'

'You mean about the rest of the money,' she reminded him, sweetly reasonable. 'Half is payable in advance.'

'You certainly seem to know the details,' said Hutchins with a return to something like his earlier would-be hardness of manner. 'Have you been to him before by any chance?'

Her answer began on an icy tone of calm, and worked up to a raging torrent. Charles only stayed for the first sentence, 'I don't know what it is in you that makes you say something beastly and hateful every time you open your mouth,' then crept away, taking a wide detour through a field. He could not bear to listen to them quarrelling. As it was, the healing peace of the evening was sadly disturbed for him.

Walter came hurrying up as Charles switched off the engine and got out of the car.

'Have they gone?' he asked.

'I saw them off at Northolt,' Charles replied a trifle stiffly. He was not sure that he ought, as a loyal employee, to countenance the boy's obvious glee over the departure of his parents.

'That gives us a week,' said Walter meditatively. 'Not long enough, of course, and it's hell having nothing but this gravel drive, but at least we can see how she picks up in the lower gears.'

Charles, ignoring the 'we', went into the garage. Mr. Braceweight had declared himself well enough to spend a week seeing to some necessary details at his branch in Brussels, and he had taken his wife with him. Walter was under instructions to continue his work under Mr. Hutchins. No doubt he would, but the absence of his father meant that the frightening machine he had been so patiently assembling could be wheeled out of its hiding-place, and allowed to make unlimited noise and smell with no fear of detection.

He wheeled it out now. Charles looked at it critically.

'I thought they only used piano wire for pianos these days,' he said. 'And doesn't that silver paper make it too heavy?'

'No soul,' said Walter, rocking the apparition from side to side on its springs. 'For a chauffeur you're the most soulless bastard I've ever met. Gave me quite a shock when I first realized that you honestly hadn't a clue about engineering.'

'Modern chauffeurs haven't,' Charles admitted cheerfully. 'They leave it all to chaps like you.'

He genuinely admired Walter. Brainless lout as he was, the boy had achieved, with absolutely no effort, what it had taken him, Charles, a shattering mental revolution to accomplish: he had cleared at one stride the artificial barriers of environment and upbringing. Partly, of course, because his environment and upbringing had never worked on him. From the time he grew old enough to lie on his back and look up at the back axle of a motor-car, in the way a lover of Nature looks up at the sky through the branches of a tree, nothing else had counted for him. Mankind was divided into those who did, or did not, share his passion. Charles was ranked fairly low down, but his willingness to listen saved him at least from being pushed right outside the pale.

'Just give me a shove for a few yards,' Walter said. 'We'll get her firing.'

'Once and for all,' Charles protested, 'leave me out of this. You seem to assume that I'm going to aid and abet you in fooling about with this contraption and going against your father's wishes. Well, I'm not losing my job for you or anyone else.'

'Look, you've got it all wrong,' said Walter in a wheedling tone. 'You seem to think you've got to come down definitely on one side or the other. The Pater's or mine. Well, you needn't; you can be neutral. When he's here, you play his game. When he's away, you play mine.'

'What about my own game? When do I play that?'

'Be a pal. Come on, now, don't leave me in the lurch. All I want is a little help now and again. Life's difficult enough as it is.'

'All right, all right. Get behind the wheel and I'll push. Anything for a quiet life.'

He pushed until the engine began to give off intermittent bangs and puffs of black smoke. Walter made one or two efforts to accelerate up to a smooth rate of firing, then silenced the machine and wheeled it moodily away to his workshop. Charles smoked a cigarette, relaxing in the still warmth of the afternoon, and then began to make up arrears of work. He was putting oil in the Daimler when Hutchins came out of the side door and walked across to him, flushing darkly with annoyance.

'Have you been sending me a lot of damn fool telegrams signed Merde?' he demanded.

Charles straightened up and looked at him in stupefaction.

'Have I been doing *what*?'

'You heard. Some damned swine has been sending me telegrams, with idiotic messages, calling themselves Merde.'

'Can I help it if you've got friends with peculiar names?'

Hutchins had his fists clenched and thrust inside his hip pockets. He was really angry.

'Look here, Lumley, blast you, come clean. I don't know anyone else who would send telegrams from this area, all from different places. And if it comes to that, I don't know anyone else who would want to annoy and embarrass me.'

'You must be lucky,' said Charles in a tone that implied that Hutchins was also lucky to have his own front teeth.

'I'll get you sacked, you blasted well see if I don't.'

'You want to think carefully, George. You may be making a terrible mistake. Perhaps you really have a friend called Merde and it's slipped your mind. People can't help their names.'

At that moment the housekeeper came out and handed Hutchins a telegram. He turned white and stood holding it, looking straight in front of him.

'The boy wants to know if there's any answer, sir,' said the housekeeper.

'Tell him there isn't,' Hutchins grated.

Charles was bubbling with happiness behind his impassive front. He knew that he had not sent one of his telegrams that day. Hutchins would either refuse to open it, and thereby miss an important message, or open it too late and find he should have sent an answer.

The housekeeper stumped away. Hutchins, trembling, held out the envelope to Charles.

'Now open it, damn you.'

'I've got greasy hands. Open it yourself. It's for you.'

'You heard what I said. Open it.'

Charles shrugged and broke open the envelope. He took the telegram out. It had been handed in at Birmingham and read: GET READY COMING OVER IN ROLLS MERDE.

Walter had excelled himself. He must have given instructions to some friend in Birmingham. No doubt a rapid volley of telegrams would shower upon them from all parts of the country, and possibly even from abroad, for Walter did nothing by halves.

Silently he handed the telegram to Hutchins, who glanced at it before flinging it violently to the ground in a ball.

'That settles it. I'll get you sacked if it's the last thing I do.'

'You'll have to prove that I was in Birmingham, or that I know anyone in Birmingham, first,' said Charles smoothly.

'Prove nothing. I'll just get you sacked some other way.'

'It's no good, George. There's only one thing you can do about it, and that's grow up. Stop being the kind of person that people play practical jokes on.'

'It's just my misfortune that I know blasted swine like you,' said Hutchins, more calmly than he had yet spoken.

'Yes,' said Charles. 'Like me and Merde.'

He picked up the dipstick and went back to the Daimler's entrails. Hutchins walked away.

The next morning Walter proved at once that he meant to make hay while the sun shone. Charles went across to the kitchen for his breakfast at half-past seven, and already he could see the stocky, overall-clad figure at work on some elaborate piece of makeshift at the other end of the drive. Still hankering for neutrality, he slipped across the yard unperceived; but when he returned, half an hour later, Walter was waiting to collar him. He had laid down a rubber strip at the end of the drive, just where it broadened into the small concrete yard in front of the garage doors.

'Ah, there you are,' he said as soon as Charles emerged. 'You'll be at a loose end for a bit this morning, I expect?'

'Not a second to myself,' Charles asserted solemnly. 'Busy from morn to dewy eve. Never been so busy in my life.'

'Oh, hell, don't make me go through all that again. I thought you said you'd help. I was counting on it. All you've got to do is to stand half-way along the drive and watch the dial.'

The amazing youth had actually constructed an electrical timing device. He explained it to Charles. When the wheels of his juggernaut touched the first strip, just inside the gates of the drive, an electrical impulse started the stop-watch moving; when he ran across the second, another impulse stopped it. He must have been working since the first streak of day. What chance had Hutchins against this?

'Just stand over here and keep the watch lying flat on the board. The thing's fool-proof,' said Walter kindly. 'I shall keep inside the gates, so no one can say I've driven on the public roads without a licence. Everything above board, that's my motto.'

He walked over to his machine.

'Just a minute,' said Charles in alarm. 'Do you mean you're going to rush along the drive in that thing with me timing you?'

Walter nodded.

'But it's absolutely impossible. You'll kill yourself when you run into the yard at full tilt.'

'Not on your life. The braking'll stand it.'

Charles shook his head.

'Walter, I ought to tell you I was in hospital myself once with the kind of injuries you're going to get. It wasn't nice.'

'Oh, God,' said the youth wearily. 'Look, if it'll make any difference to your state of mind, we'll adopt safety measures. You open the garage doors—that'll give me an escape route—and I'll put my hat on.'

'Your hat?'

He answered by taking out of his tool-box a huge red steel helmet, with the word 'Norton' stencilled across the front.

'Oh, I give up, I give up,' Charles groaned. He opened the garage doors, and turned round to see Walter fastening the strap under his chin. The immense steel cup reduced the face below it to a dwarfed mask. Circular metal shells contained the ears.

'Come on, let's get weaving,' said Hutchins's pupil, settling himself in the cockpit. The steering wheel pushed into his abdomen. Charles had visions of horrible injuries.

'You wouldn't care to leave a signed statement that I warned you not to do it?' he asked, with desperation in his voice.

'Oh, rats to all that. Push me off and let's get some practice in. It's nearly half-past eight already, and I've got a spell with my tutor at ten.'

Charles bent and pushed. Silently, except for an occasional sibilant squelching noise from the engine, they crawled down the drive.

'Hell, what's happened now?'

'Just a couple of blood-vessels,' Charles panted, throwing himself down in the long grass.

Walter climbed out and began to burrow in the engine. 'That ought to do it,' he said after a moment. 'Let's try again.'

They tried three times more, and finally, at the cost of as many years of Charles's life, the engine began to bray loudly.

'Up to the middle! The dial!' shouted the helmeted figure from amid a haze of oily vapour.

Charles stumbled away, wiping the sweat from his forehead with the back of one hand. Did everyone get into these farcical situations? Or was there something about him that attracted them? Here he was, pushed into helping his employer's son to kill himself, and all because he lacked the strength of mind to refuse. And yet inwardly he knew that he could not have refused Walter; a really single-minded person is always given what he wants. What a man lives for, he gets; witness Hutchins, Froulish, Mr. Blearney, Roderick, Stan, Burge, and now Walter.

The crackling and bellowing at the far end of the drive suddenly took on a more violent tone. The needle before him jumped, and began to circulate. It was too late to stop the maniac: Charles stood appalled, as he had looked appalled at the rapt face of Harry Dogson, humbled by the mystical power of humanity in pursuit of an ideal. He heard a vicious spluttering as the engine moved into second gear, and then the grotesque junk-heap flew past him round the sharp bend, flinging pebbles into the air. It was a fantastic sight; the engine was placed behind the driver, giving a nightmare impression that the machine was going backwards. The four naked jets that served as exhaust pipes were pouring black smoke, which was whipped behind in a straight line to mingle with the shower of fine dirt. Bouncing wildly, Walter aimed himself like a torpedo towards the second timing strip and, beyond it, the garage doors.

Hutchins must have been nervous about getting June out of the house unobserved; it was, evidently, the absence of Mr. and Mrs. Braceweight that had emboldened him to keep her there dangerously late. So flustered that the ear-splitting racket outside made no impression on him, he jerked open the side door and hurried out, dragging June by the arm, into the path of Walter's flying hell-bat.

Charles lacked the power to cover his eyes. He stood motionless, his hands spread out on the wooden board. The stop-watch, its hurrying finger arrested, gleamed up at him innocently.

There was a loud, non-human scream from Walter's tyres. Hutchins and June Veeber were stone figures, absolutely immobile. He was about five feet away from the protection of the wall; she, lagging behind, had still one foot on the doorstep. It seemed to Charles's tricked eyesight that the machine changed its shape, grotesquely, in a twinkling. It appeared enormously elongated, then squat and contracted. Only the helmed figure in the cockpit remained recognizable as he wrenched the wheel violently from side to side. Smearing its locked wheels horribly across the concrete, the car flitted past the two petrified figures like a giant bat. The garage door was not quite wide enough to admit it on its present trajectory, and the rear end smashed into a corner of the wall. Leaping into the air and spinning round, it vanished into the building. An appalling metallic crash announced the presence of the unsuspecting Daimler. Outside, flung pebbles pattered to the ground in the silence.

Hutchins stood swaying and twisting his chalk-white face from side to side in the sunlight. June Veeber leaned back against the lintel of the door with her eyes closed. Charles pushed himself away from the timing apparatus and began to walk towards the garage.

Before he could reach it, Walter came out. At first it seemed that he had been injured. His face was terribly mis-shapen, as if it had been violently knocked sideways. Then Charles realized that it was twisted with rage. His creation had been smashed, the sacred object of his highest endeavours was taken away from him in the moment when it had begun to work its magic. Any normal sensation of relief that he had not been smashed with it was absolutely excluded by his violent passion. As well might one imagine Napoleon feeling warmed and comforted by the thought that he, at least, had not been killed in the Russian campaign. He advanced on Hutchins to murder him. Charles stood helplessly, paralyzed by his recent shock as well as by his instinctive reluctance to do anything to protect Hutchins. Walter tramped across the yard, his contorted face capped by the dented steel toadstool that had saved his life, his powerful arms swinging loosely by his sides. June Veeber had not yet opened her eyes.

Then Walter sprang his great surprise. The decision he took, at whatever level of consciousness it was reached, stood out for ever in Charles's mind as having provided the most purely astonishing moment he would ever live through. Halting before Hutchins, who was still too rattled to grasp fully that he was about to be set upon, he gazed at him squarely for a moment, and then spoke in a calm and unwavering voice.

'I see you've got her with you.'

'Got who with me?' Hutchins quavered.

'Murd,' said Walter, and went into the house.

For a moment the boy's pronunciation had them baffled. Then, simultaneously, Charles and Hutchins began to laugh hysterically, not amused, hating each other, wanting to stop. June opened her eyes and burst into tears. Standing in the yard, with the four black smears across the concrete between them and the smell of high octane fuel still in their nostrils, they shrieked and bellowed and sobbed. The housekeeper came out and stared at them, then turned and went back.

That had finished it, of course. There was not even any point in waiting for Mr. Braceweight to come back and give him the sack. The Daimler had stood massively on its wheels and allowed Walter's projectile to be smashed into a heap of smoking, twisted metal against its side, but the fact remained that one wing was crumpled beyond any hope of repair, a rear mudgard half torn off, and a window smashed. In addition, hot oil had splashed liberally over the whole car and ruined its glossy finish. No chauffeur could let that happen to a Daimler and keep his job.

He would, of course, take any blame that was going. He had skidded into a stone wall while driving back from Northolt: any story would do that did not involve another vehicle, whose owner might have to be identified. Walter should be—what was that word they always used in school stories?—'shielded'. Yes, it was only fair that he should be shielded. After so devastating a disappointment it was unthinkable that he should be handed over to the attentions of a disciplinarian father on top of everything else.

Sitting moodily in his room above the garage he wrote on a sheet of cheap letter-paper:

Dear Mr. Braceweight,

When you return I am afraid you will already be annoyed at

not having been met at the airport. You will notice, on getting here, that your car has gone, and so have I. It is being repaired: I will arrange for them to pick it up before I go. My negligence was responsible for its being damaged, and, in deciding that I am not a good enough chauffeur for you, I am merely anticipating the judgment you will inevitably form for yourself. I will mention to an agency that you need a new one, and they will no doubt be sending you some applicants. As regards the cost of the repairs, you have, in the first place, a fortnight's wages of mine that I shall not be claiming; if this does not meet the bill, and you feel I should pay the rest, please communicate with me c/o Charing Cross Road Post Office, London.

It may be, of course, that you will take steps to have me arrested in order to make sure of reimbursement. In that case it is only fair to warn you that I shall make a very determined effort to evade the police. But I do not think you will.

In any case, in saying Goodbye and hoping we shall never meet again, I should like to thank you for your kindness. I regard it as one of the ironies of my life that the only man who has treated me with unalloyed decency should be one who is exposed to the greatest of all temptations to bully and oppress his fellows: namely, non-inherited wealth.

I remain, Sir,

yours with respect and gratitude,

Charles Lumley.

The effort of composition put him into a serious frame of mind, and he went out for a walk. It was evening, and the still, golden sunlight enfolded the luxury countryside. No, it was not for him, not for him. Even the cows who stood grazing in the fields where he walked, even the trees, even the artfully disposed brooks chattering over cleaned pebbles, unanimously assured him of it. *We knew you wouldn't be staying. You're not the type.* They were right; he was not. This dream of semi-retirement, of dignified parasitism in the service of a good rich man in a Technicolor landscape, was foreign to his nature. Whatever the outcome, he belonged to the world where real actions were undertaken. He belonged with Froulish thumping his typewriter in a derelict loft, with Dogson getting himself murdered in the quest for a story, even with Ern serving a prison sentence or Mr. Blearney getting up dreary leg-shows in the provinces. The people he belonged with were ill, disgusting, unsuccessful, comic, but still alive, still generating some kind of human force. This expensive bucolic setting had offered nothing more than an escape down a blind alley, and it had taken a crack-brained mechanic, a nymphomaniac and a deranged careerist to show him that. As ever, the serious point had emerged through the machinery of the ludicrous. His life was a dialogue, full of deep and tragic truths, expressed in hoarse shouts by red-nosed music-hall comics. Nothing happened straight: in future it had better be enough that things happened at all.

When he got back to his room it was about nine o'clock. It was not yet dark enough for lights to be switched on, except by a person who wanted to sew or read fine print, so there was nothing to warn him that there was someone waiting there. It was June Veeber. She was sitting in the armchair. As the room contained no other chair, except a hard wooden one that he put his clothes over at night, there was nowhere for him to sit except on the divan. He sat down, at the end farthest away from the armchair.

'Did you want something?' he asked.

'I came to do you a good turn,' she said in her clear, distinct, impudent voice.

'Such as what?' he asked.

Instead of answering, she looked slowly round the tiny room, till her eyes came to rest on him.

'You're quite comfortable up here, aren't you? I think it's much nicer than George's room in the house.'

'There's one big advantage, of course,' he said. 'George isn't in this one.'

He wanted her to become angry, or at least to laugh, for the tension she was trying to generate had to be broken quickly. But she merely nodded seriously, as if he had said something true and important.

'It *is* nicer without him, isn't it? And do you live here all the time? I mean, do you use that couch thing for sleeping on?'

'Look,' he said. 'Would you mind leaving me with some of my childish secrets and getting on with this good turn you're going to do me?' 'Unless it's what I think it is', he almost added, but the vestigial power of his upbringing checked him.

'Oh, the good turn, yes,' she said, speaking deliberately. 'It's a warning. I wanted to warn you.'

'What against?' he asked, impatiently, when she did not go on. He wanted her out of his room. It was small, it was over a garage, it did not belong to him, but he liked it and did not want it contaminated.

'Against George,' she said, still in the half-hypnotized voice that dragged across his nerves. 'He doesn't like you. In fact he hates you. It seems that you've been playing some kind of joke on him, he won't say what, and he takes these things terribly badly.'

'I know he does,' said Charles to fill up another silence.

'Terribly badly,' she repeated. 'He hasn't told me anything, but I know he wants to injure you. He'd like to get you sacked. And he'll try to do it, one way or another.'

'He needn't worry. After what happened this morning, I'm going anyway. D'you think I could stay here after letting the car get smashed about like that?'

'But that wasn't your fault,' she said slowly and seriously.

'Well, whose fault was it? The kid's fault for building himself that lunatic machine and racing it along the drive? Yours and Hutchins's for coming out of the house at the wrong moment? Mine for not putting my foot down? It's no good arguing it out. When a thing like that happens, the chauffeur goes. Particularly when the alternative is to expose a couple of things that everybody would rather have hushed up.'

'Oh, so you're being noble,' she said coolly, with a note of something resembling scorn.

'Noble and obliging. Clearing out five seconds ahead of the boot.'

There was a pause. The discussion seemed to have reached its logical ending. But she did not move.

'Was there anything else?' he asked gently, in a parody of chauffeurly deference.

'Don't be in such a hurry to get rid of me.' She looked at

him steadily. 'I'm doing nothing in particular between now and tomorrow morning.'

He stood up.

'Well, I am. I'm packing and then sleeping and then clearing out. There must be other places where you can do nothing in particular.'

'Not the kind of nothing in particular I'm thinking about,' she said slowly and precisely.

He felt defiled, as if warm treacle were pouring on to the crown of his head from a tap in the ceiling, and then spreading down his face and running down his back, over his chest, into his armpits. He must get her out. If he had felt anything so clear and unambiguous as ordinary disgust or resentment, it would have been easy to prolong the sparring until she tired of it; but he was aware of other feelings that he did not care to examine.

'I've had enough of this,' he said roughly. 'If I didn't happen to know you were pregnant I'd manhandle you out of here without any more discussion. But as things are, I'll give you one more verbal warning to get out of here before I turn the fire-extinguisher on you.'

'Oh, you know that, do you?' she said. She looked at him fixedly; he supposed her condition amounted to a kind of hypnotism. She came over and sat on the divan, drawing up her legs. 'I'm comfortable here,' she said.

'I told you to get out.' He looked at her with hatred.

'Listen,' she said more urgently. 'If that bit of information is what's worrying you, don't let it. In the early stages it doesn't make any difference.'

'Why are you trying to make me throw you down those stairs?' he asked.

'I tell you it doesn't make any difference at all.'

He took a step towards her, to grasp her arm and jerk her upright. Then their eyes met, and suddenly the tension faded, leaving merely two people not liking each other, recognizing and confirming each other's hostility.

'You're deranged, I suppose,' she said carefully, speaking to hurt. 'Probably suffering from some psychosomatic form of impotence, and afraid of revealing it.'

'I'd certainly be afraid of revealing it when you were about,' he said.

'You're ill. It's too long since you had a woman. I can see it.'

'Thanks for the solicitude,' he said, 'but I'll wait till it comes under the National Health Scheme.'

She went out. He lay on his bed and brushed the sweat from his temples and upper lip. Outside, the week-end landscape slumbered in illusory calm, illusory contentment.

X

It was cold on the bench. For the first hour or two he was grateful that, at least, it wasn't raining, but after about one o'clock the cold became so intense that it could certainly not have been worse even if he had been soaking wet. There must be some knack of sleeping on these things; one more lesson that he had still to learn. You mustn't lie down, he knew that, or a policeman could pull you in. You must keep sitting up and looking more or less as if you were awake. He tried drawing his knees up and hunching his body into a tight ball, then clasping his hands round his knees, leaning his head forward, and relaxing as far as possible with his fingers interlaced. But somehow it seemed to cramp the muscles of his back, and after about ten minutes he abandoned it. That was about every position he could think of: all no good. The clear chimes of some City clock came through the cold air. One-fifteen. A night or two without sleep didn't necessarily harm you, if you were fit. Walk about a bit. He dragged himself along by the side of the quietly lapping, malevolent river. A litter box made of wire netting attracted his attention by gleaming whitely: it was full of sheets of newspaper. A piece of luck. One of the easiest ways of keeping warm. He stuffed loosely-rolled pads of it into the bottoms of his trousers, up to the knees, and inside his jacket. One or two of the sheets were rather greasy, as if they had been used for wrapping fish and chips. He should worry. The cold had affected the membranes of his nostrils so that he couldn't smell anything. If he stank to high heaven of fish, he wouldn't offend himself, only other people, and when you were a tramp you didn't mind offending other people. It was what was expected of you. Always do what they expect of you, and you'll be a success. How to make friends and influence people. How to influence friends and make people. How to people your friends' influences. Stop that. Make your influences your friends, stop that, get a grip on yourself. I'll get you sacked, Merde, see if I won't. How to influence Merde.

What was it the tramp had told him? A sure way to make a few bob. Piccadilly Circus at six o'clock in the morning, always full of people dying for a smoke. Many's the time if I'd had a packet of cigarettes on me I could have made enough to eat for two or three days. Give you sixpence, a shilling, for a cigarette some of them. More if you had the heart to ask for it. That was why he had saved his cigarettes, an intact packet of ten. He got them out and looked at them hungrily in the seedy moonlight. A smoke now would do him the world of good. Help pass the time. Just one: sell the rest. Sixpence each for nine, that was four and six. No. Keep the lot. Then get enough for a day's food and another packet of ten. Keep alive till a decent job came up. Came up where? Daren't go to the Labour Exchange. Steer clear of anything that involved officialdom, registration, all that stuff. Somewhere, it was someone's business to find him, to pull him in for the drug business. He would have to wait and let something good happen to him. I'm sorry you've come down to this, Lumley. Don't worry about me. I can make friends and influence people. And I'm big. I let them influence me in return. Just watch this dial, time the speed in the lower gears. Just clean these windows. A perfectly honest profession. Harry Dogson. Do you know this man? He's harmless. Not like me. Let me be your father. I'm cold, Rosa, Veronica, come closer. Sticky newspaper. You're a good bloke, we like you. We were just talking about you when you came in. A good bloke, partner, Mr. Froulish will read to us from his novel, Mr. Froulish will make friends with us and influence us, have you been sending me a lot of damn fool telegrams? No, I'm too cold for that, I'm a good bloke, it's time you told me what you did for a living, it's time, it's time.

Somehow it was five, then half-past, then six. Daylight. He walked through the windy streets to Piccadilly Circus. Men in overcoats loafing about. Not many girls: the girls were all off the streets by now. The men had nowhere to go. The drink inside them had worn off, leaving only a sour feeling in the stomach. He knew how they felt. The lowest ebb. Mouth like an Arab's armpit. What's wrong with Arabs anyway? They were doing better than he was, they were sitting under date palms in the warm sun. But then it was probably night where they lived, and cold, too. He felt sorry for the Arabs. They must have something pretty badly wrong with them if their armpits felt like his mouth.

Make a start somewhere. There was one man standing by himself under the arches. Looking very forlorn, but well dressed; he ought to have a few shillings left even if he had had a night on the tiles. Charles sauntered up to him, trying to stop shivering, and halted a couple of yards off. Now get into conversation.

'Not much doing at this time in the morning,' he said.

The face that turned towards him was solid, carved with deep lines of responsibility, pouchy eyes staring through rimless glasses. Some provincial business man, doing well, with a comfortable wife and children in a suburban house. Just the type who lined the pockets of the vice racketeers on his business trips to the metropolis.

'Eh, yer never spoke a truer word. But what can a chap do when 'e finds himself spent up at four in the morning and too late to go to bed anyway?'

'What indeed?' Charles murmured.

'All I can do,' the other continued positively, 'is to 'ang about till nine o'clock. There's a fast train then, and I'll thank them to get me back 'ome as quick as they like. This is no place to be in.' He dropped his voice confidentially. 'There's a sight too many folks after a man's munny in this town.'

'And what's more, they get it,' said Charles sympathetically.

'Get it!' echoed the pillar of society angrily. 'I tell you it really 'urts to think of the amount they got out of me since ten o'clock last night. I'll give yer a piece of advice, yung man. Don't you take any notice of these fellers as stand on the pavement an' invite yer into these clubs. Affable as yer please. In town for the night, sir? What about steppin' into the club? 'Ave a drink. Enjoy yerself. Some nice girls, 'e says. Nice!' his voice rang out angrily under the windy arches.

'It's all experience, I suppose,' said Charles, feeling this particular line had better be dropped. If the man worked himself into a rage over having been fleeced, he would be less likely to pay handsomely for a smoke when the time came to try it on.

'Experience!' said the heavy, bitter voice. 'I'll give yer another piece of advice while I'm at it. There's—some experience,' he went on emphatically, 'as just—isn't—worth—'aving. Not if yer got it for nowt.'

Charles looked at him in pitying contempt. This type, armoured heavily in the smugness of business success, simply could not leave off showering advice on others. The present specimen, dead beat, robbed of his loose cash in the pursuit of disgusting pleasures, loitering with an empty stomach in a ghastly dawn, twitched into sententiousness by a reflex action. It was Tharkles all over again.

Anyway, he could try it on. Carelessly producing his cigarettes, he took one out and lit it with elaborate slowness. Inhaling deeply, he leaned back against the wall. His companion looked at him anxiously, waiting for him to proffer the packet. For a few seconds he fought a one-sided battle with his pride, then spoke.

'You don't 'appen to have one of those to spare?'

Charles looked at him, as if the question were surprising.

'I got through the last o' mine about midnight,' the man went on, talking fast and eagerly. Obviously he wanted a smoke very badly. 'You 'and 'em round in those places, when yer get with a crowd. The bloody cheatin' swine,' he added violently.

'Well,' said Charles carefully, 'I suppose you know cigarettes are at a bit of a premium in the West End at this time of day. Supply and demand. As a business man you'll appreciate that.'

Their eyes met. Hatred and suspicion glowed behind the rimless lenses.

'The price of an article is what you can get for it in the competitive market,' said Charles, trembling with cold and anxiety. 'Free enterprise. Made this country what it is.'

The approach must have been wrong. After all, the man probably spent half his life prating about the necessity of a free economy: but that would be quite consistent with his bitter resentment when the weapon was used against him in turn. And from his own account it had been used quite successfully the night before.

Instead of answering he leaned across and snatched at the packet Charles held in his hand. Charles saw red. His livelihood was in danger, and after so much fatigue his nerves were raw. He clenched his other hand and hit Mr. Free Enterprise in the face.

The man bounced off the wall and came back with his hands grabbing for Charles's throat. This was the last straw; these lousy London types were going to see that they couldn't go on indefinitely putting it across an honest man from the North. Charles hit him again, hard, over the heart. A policeman across on the other side of the Circus began to walk smartly over, drawing out his whistle in case it should be needed. No hurry. Just a couple of morning-afters. They never had much fight in them at this time in the day.

Charles saw him begin to move, broke away, and ran. The pillar of society, brought up short by the punch to the heart, blinked round, saw the policeman, and shambled rapidly away in another direction. He had a good reason for not wanting police-court publicity, but Charles had a better. Like a hunted hare he fled down one shabby turning after another, afraid to look back to see whether he was being followed. He had dropped his cigarettes; he had struck an older man after trying to swindle him; this was rock-bottom again. His breath began to come painfully, he must stop running, get off the streets somehow. A doorway. He swung himself into it at full speed, with the stitch tearing at his side and his lungs close to bursting point. Smack into Mr. Blearney.

Who said reprovingly, 'You want to take it easy, partner. Why don't you put shorts on and go into the country if you want to run before breakfast?'

He had been putting his overcoat on, and his right arm was pinioned behind his back as Charles rammed him against the wall. He got free, straightened himself, and shook the coat on.

'Good thing I wasn't smoking,' he went on. 'You might have put your eye out on my cheroot if I had been.'

'Take—me upstairs,' Charles gasped. 'Got to stay off the streets—a bit—some unpleasantness—just sit down—get my breath back.'

'Well, the club's just closing,' said Mr. Blearney doubtfully. 'And it's downstairs, anyway, not up. Well, just for a few minutes then.'

They pattered down the grimy steps. A door said, 'Golden Peach Club'. 'The golden peaches have all gone home,' said Mr. Blearney.

The room stank, stale tobacco and drink. Sweat and advanced halitosis fought it out with the dominant odours. Charles breathed deeply, but there was not much that his lungs could use for the benefit of his bloodstream.

'This is Ada. Manageress,' said Mr. Blearney briefly.

A fat woman with a shock of henna-stained hair looked at him across a tray of dirty glasses.

'One of your friends, Arthur? Bit late to come to the club. Better get him out of here so I can lock up. My hours are supposed to be eleven till six.'

'Take it easy, Ada,' he implored. 'I'll take him round to my place for some breakfast.'

'Eleven till six,' she said, 'and don't you forget it.'

'Drink this, partner, and we'll go home.'

It was bad whisky. Charles drank it and they went home.

Mr. Blearney's 'man' was not wearing his white coat this time. His off-white shirt sleeves flickered dully to and fro as he fetched toast, eggs, and coffee. Charles found himself reviving at remarkable speed; in the closing stages of the meal he launched into a rather selective account of his immediate past and present situation. Mr. Blearney, who was obviously shrewd enough to see that a good deal was being missed out, was also old and cautious enough to stifle any feelings of curiosity about the omissions. He had heard enough secrets to last him his lifetime. Looking across at the pouchy, bulbous comedian's face, Charles wondered why this man bothered to be kind to him. Perhaps there was really no explanation other than the obvious one, that geniality had been the driving force of his life for so long that it had consumed everything else: unless there was someone at hand to be genial to, he would die. Besides, there was the undeclared war between people of Mr. Blearney's type and people of the ordinary, conventional type; the smaller group, the active minority, sought each other out for mutual support against the heavy, unleavened mass on which they looked with alternate suspicion, patronizing affection, and contempt. When the mass did the right thing, they were 'the public' ('the public, bless them, took me to their hearts right from the first'); when they did not react satisfactorily, they were simply 'them' ('just can't get them moving to-night', 'if this doesn't knock them in the aisles, well, blast 'em'); and in times of lowered circumstances, you simply preyed on the less reputable impulses to which the mass was subject, when its members became plain suckers ('one born every minute, you needn't starve'). This secret society, unconsciously sworn to the task of providing the vibrations that caused wear and tear in the structure of normal living, consciously pledged to working themselves to a standstill at anything that did not look like normal work, this invisible Trade Union, had been waiting for Charles ever since he first failed to take root in the cliff-side of a shattered bourgeoisie. He had tried manual work, he had tried crime, he had tried being a servant, and now he was sitting opposite Mr. Blearney, director of (among other things) the Golden Peach Club, accepting his hospitality, waiting for him to suggest some way out of his difficulties. With uncanny vividness, derived partly from fatigue, his consciousness freed itself from his body, sitting there at the table, and watched the scene, cleverly picking out the allegorical elements. The young man (Hopeless) breaks out of the prison of Social and Economic Maladjustment; he carries on his back a hundredweight of granite known as Education. After a skirmish with the dragon Sex, in which he is aided by a false friend, Giant Crime, he comes to the illusory citadel called Renunciation of Ambition. And so on. What an allegory it would make! Of course he would have to think up some more catchy names for these abstractions, but that would be easy enough.

'Well, what d'you say?' Mr. Blearney was asking.

'What do I say to what?' stammered Charles, then, realizing that his host had been talking continuously for about five minutes, during which he had not heard a word, he roused himself and apologized profusely, blaming his fatigue and the confusing effect of his adventures.

'All right, I'll cut it short this time,' said Mr. Blearney with surprising patience. 'Just a couple of sentences, so you can follow before it gets too tiring. I was saying that it just happens we need a chucker-out at the Golden Peach. Not that it's a rough place. We've never had a bouncer there before, but Ada's been complaining lately that there's nobody to back her up if anybody gets nasty; there's a couple of waiters, but they're paid to do waiting, and you can't blame them if they look the other way when anyone starts acting rowdy. A man doesn't want a thick ear as well as having to carry things about on a tray.'

Charles did not speak. A chucker-out in a dive like that. Well, who was he to be fussy?

'And as Ada says,' Mr. Blearney went on, 'she's only a woman. I have to take her word for that, mind you. There's what you'd call reasonable doubt.'

'Any pay?' asked Charles. It was with an effort that he stopped himself from speaking out of the side of his mouth. The whole thing was getting too like a film. He lit a cigarette in the manner of Alan Ladd.

'Pay, of course, partner! And what's better, pay in kind, a lot of it. Nothing for the tax inspector to take off you. A square meal every night, a bed in one of the private rooms when they're not all being used,' he spoke rather quickly, as if to hurry over that part of his statement, 'and five bob an hour while you're on duty. Thirty-five bob a night. Why, that's nearly as much as Ada gets!'

'Any compensation for injury?'

'Well,' said Mr. Blearney meditatively, pushing his coffee cup into the exact centre of the table, 'we can keep quiet about you being a professional. Then if anybody hurts you badly, we'll provide witnesses to prove they picked a quarrel with you as another guest at the club, and you can sue them. I believe you get quite a lot,' he said cheerfully, 'for anything that shows, like, well, the loss of an eye.'

'I wouldn't be exorbitant, of course,' said Charles.

'Well, that's settled, partner, eh? Eleven o'clock at the club.

And meanwhile you can stay here. I'd advise you to take your shoes off and stretch out on the sofa there. You might as well get used to doing most of your sleeping in the daytime now.'

'Good idea,' said Charles. 'And by the way, thanks for everything.'

'Don't thank me, partner. It's a pleasure.'

And when the young man that was called Hopeless came to the castle of giant Racket, he lifted up his hand and bravely beat upon the gate. And the giant heard him from within (for indeed he had caused him to be shown the way to that place by Malice and Confusion his servants), and up and welcomed him, calling to him Don't thank me, partner. And the young man that was called Hopeless entered and lay down to sleep in that place.

Twenty-four hours later he was going off duty after his first night's work. He was elated and slightly puzzled: Ada did not look like a person subject to nervous fears, but he could not imagine on what other grounds she had asked for a chucker-out to be engaged. He had had visions of hulking brutes, members of race-gangs with razors at the ready, or, at best, sailors on shore, full of high spirits and liquor. Nothing of the kind! The patrons of the Golden Peach Club were as meek and docile a tribe as the inhabitants of any third-class compartment on a suburban electric train. The two types, indeed, seemed to overlap a good deal, with a solid core of unwary provincial visitors such as Mr. Free Enterprise of the day before, and a sprinkling of genuine night-prowlers, drug-addicts, dipsomaniacs and mental cripples of various kinds, all of whom were far too undermined physically to cause him any anxiety even if their behaviour had threatened trouble.

As to the attractions which drew the club's customers, Charles found it easy to keep his eyes averted from the more sordid of them. There was no need to rush things; he would, inevitably, develop a hard shell to cover what remained of his moral and aesthetic sensibilities, or even shed these sensibilities altogether, but, until that time came, he was paid to watch out for any rough behaviour, and not to poke his nose under the surface. As a matter of fact, he could hardly help noticing, after the first two or three hours, that it was very much the policy of the club to create the illusion of concealing more under the surface than was actually there. Apart from a tiny bar, the preserve of a few regulars and *cognoscenti* who had the privilege of ordering their drinks straight from the barmaid instead of having them brought over by a waiter for three times the price, there was only one room, a large one; it was styled 'the ball-room', and actually did contain a three-piece band who huddled in a corner zinging and tooting in front of a pocket-handkerchief of cleared parquet flooring, but no one danced; the revellers sat morosely at the tiny tables that occupied most of the room, or on the plush-covered bench that lined three of the walls. Two waiters, both of whom would have been entitled to the Old Age pension if they had cared to reveal their identities by applying for it, shambled to and fro with poisonous drinks at lethal prices, Ada sat behind the bar and chatted with the *cognoscenti*, who seemed to be mostly relatives of hers, and Charles perched quietly and watchfully in a corner, still feeling like Alan Ladd.

In this setting it was easy enough to create the impression that the machinery of high-powered vice was roaring away off-stage, but it was soon obvious that the roaring was of the same order of artificiality as a man shaking a thin sheet of metal to simulate a thunderstorm. The 'hostesses', of whom there were half a dozen, were very much in evidence, and now and again one of them would withdraw, hand in hand with some chosen mate, to one of the 'private rooms'—causing Charles early to make up his mind that he would decline the offer of one of these rooms for his daytime repose—but it was clear that, for every one of the chosen mates who succeeded in realizing his ambition, there were ten who were simply overcharged for a succession of nauseous drinks and finally turned out bankrupt and feeling ill. A depressing spectacle, the sight of people failing to enjoy themselves even at this level! Frustration, weariness, and self-betrayal staring from so many human faces at once!

The only people in the room who seemed to be doing anything positive were the three 'musicians'. After about the fifth hour, Charles was driven by boredom and depression to go and sit in their corner, even at the price of placing himself close to the racket they were making. In between numbers, introductions made themselves; Jimmy on the piano, Albert on clarinet, Frankie on guitar. Once they left their instruments behind, there would, he felt, be no telling them apart, for they were all got up to look like identical marionettes; thin, waxy faces, hair cropped to the length of a matchstick, drape jackets, and Windsor ties. They were nice boys, masking an appealing provincial *naïveté* under a mass-produced sophistication gained from incessant study of the *Melody Maker* and *Down Beat*, and expressed in accents learnt in the cinema.

'No, you don't wanner stay here, boy,' Frankie assured him, taking a new plectrum out of his breast pocket and gazing at it intently. 'Reggler hick joint in the daytime, innit fellers?'

'Yeah, proper lousy,' assented Jimmy, bending backwards on the piano stool. 'You wanner stick around with us, boy. We gotter real nice place we room in. Getchew in there, easy. Take you along, personal recommendation, in straight away. Real classy, innit?'

Albert, appealed to, nodded vigorously. 'Right outer this world,' he said.

'Thanks,' said Charles. He did not feel like making longer speeches until he had mastered their *argot*.

And so the morning found them all four walking home. The three artists exchanged cryptic communications, speaking of Charles as if he were not present, but with perfect friendliness. They were like three schoolboys in their second term who had decided to be nice to a new boy.

On his way to the club one night he went into the Charing Cross Road Post Office to see if there was a letter for him. The clerk handed him an envelope, and he sat down at the table and broke it open. It was a typed letter, obviously dictated to a secretary. He read it slowly and carefully.

Mr. C. Lumley.

I found your letter waiting for me, but I do not know why it contained no mention of the fact that, before leaving, you stole a valuable jade figurine from my wife's writing table. It was clever of you to pick this out, as I am not a man of ostentation, and it is the only valuable ornament in my house; but I suppose you have had experience of thieving before. The evidence points unmistakably to you, so please do not make any attempt to deny the charge. I do not intend to put the matter into the hands of the law, for the monetary loss is of little consequence when compared with the betrayal of my confidence in you, for which I could not be compensated. I have never made a serious error in the judgment of character until now; I have to admit that my previous experience did not embrace any specimens of the ordinary criminal type. I neither expect nor wish to hear from you or of you in the future.

Samuel P. Braceweight.

He read the message three times; twice slowly, but the third time very rapidly; and then stared vacantly ahead of him with eyeballs of hot dry cast-iron. The evidence points unmistakably to you, Hutchins, I'll get you sacked, don't worry, we'll get the money somehow, you've been costing me plenty, the evidence points unmistakably, an ordinary criminal type, he hates your guts, see you on Friday, Merde. Next to him sat a woman with a red face and untidy grey hair, writing a telegram. She looked up at him with fierce resentment, and he realized that his vacant stare must have been resting on the form she was filling in. She spoke to him in the tone of one who is unbearably provoked.

'I really don't see what my telegram has to do with you.'

'Sorry,' he said. 'It's all this catgut. Too much catgut.'

She smiled widely and falsely, looking out of the corners of her eyes for possible assistance.

'Too much catgut,' she said, slowly, and with an encouraging nod.

'Much too much,' he said. He got up to go before she released the scream that was waiting in the depths of her weather-beaten throat. As he went out, he crumbled the letter into a tiny hard ball. It was good quality paper and creased into tiny sharp points that hurt the palm of his hand. He dropped it carefully into a litter box and went out of the door. The street was very cold.

*

He hurried on to the club. It was the usual depressed and depressing scene; the band strummed and whimpered in the corner, the patrons stared gloomily into their glasses. Feeling unutterably soiled, Alan Ladd miscast in the part of a heel, he settled down to another night's desolation and spiritual drought. Might as well get used to it. It looked as if this were to be his permanent niche. Just another ruin, a hulk washed up on a dirty shore within sight of the seagulls drowning with oil-clogged wings.

For three hours he stared blankly in front of him, brusquely refusing his usual free allowance of the nauseating liquor served by the unkempt waiters. About one o'clock, he left the room for a few minutes. On returning, he found an unusual atmosphere of tension; the two waiters were in a huddle with Ada behind the bar, and one of them was pointing, with a plaintive expression, into the main room.

'What's the matter?' he asked wearily. He hoped there was going to be some work for him to do. He would like to have a fight, to smash his knuckles viciously, yet easily and without strain, into someone's mouth.

'There's a chap creating,' said the senior and dirtier of the waiters. 'Says he doesn't like the tipple.'

Ada said nothing. She looked at Charles and jerked her head in the direction he was to go. He walked across, following the waiter. The waiter halted beside a man sitting at a table by himself with his back to Charles.

He stood behind the man's right shoulder, not bothering to go round in front of him.

'They tell me the drink doesn't suit you,' he said.

The patron looked up over his shoulder. Above the expensive shirt and new silk tie, his face was a twitching mask of dough.

'Oh, God, it's you, Lumley,' he said. 'Doesn't the joint provide anything better than this kidney water at five bob a glass?'

'We've got some pretty good kidneys round here,' said Charles, 'but before you do any more grumbling, tell me just what you're doing here. I left you in a loft in dear old Stotwell.' He sat down at the table and listened expectantly.

'Well, I don't come to places like this because I enjoy it,' said the novelist, squirming irritably in his chair. 'It just happens that I'm on duty this week as Dirty Joke man. I have to sit about in places like this to gather in the latest crop.'

'Be less abstruse, my riddling days are past,' said Charles. It was a quotation he remembered from his riddling days.

'Oh, well, God,' said the man of letters, screwing up his tiny eyes until they became as small as the blackheads which tesselated his forehead. His suit, though it looked as if he had slept in it, was a very good one.

'Please bring us two glasses of water, Erasmus,' he said to the waiter. 'I feel thirsty.'

The waiter stared at him without any expression on his face.

'You heard what the gentleman said,' Charles told him. 'Two glasses of water out of the cold tap.'

'Well, now,' said Froulish, when the man had moved away, 'I suppose you've heard of Terence Frush.'

'No,' said Charles.

'God, you're out of touch,' said Froulish in a petulant tone which suggested that Charles had done him a personal injury by not having heard of Terence Frush. 'Don't you ever listen to the wireless?'

'I haven't got one,' said Charles.

'Well, look,' said Froulish. 'It just happens that Terence Frush is the biggest name in the gag-writing business. He writes the scripts for some of the top rank radio shows. Millions of people listen to them.'

'What would that have to do with you?' Charles asked.

'I'm one of his team,' said the novelist, seriously. 'Naturally, a job like that has to be run like a business. At the moment we furnish the scripts regularly for the Flimmer and Punque show, *Deadline on Wednesday.* You've got a half-hour programme which includes two musical interludes of three minutes each. Allowing a minute at each end for signature tune and announcements, that makes twenty-two minutes. Two gags a minute works out at forty-four a week.'

The waiter came back with two glasses of water. The glasses were very dirty. Froulish drank his at a gulp and put the glass in his pocket.

'And how many of the forty-four do you think up?'

'Well, it's all a collaboration, you see,' said Froulish. For some reason he seemed genuinely interested in explaining the details of his employment. 'We get together once a week and hammer it out. There's a rota of jobs that different members of the team have to do each week.'

'And it's your turn to be Dirty Joke man,' said Charles. Froulish reached across for Charles's glass, threw the water on the floor and put the glass in his other pocket. At this rate he would soon ruin the shape of his suit.

'Yes, I'll explain about that. If you'd listened to these things at all, you'd know that it was a recognized part of the technique to introduce, two or three times in each script, submerged references to dirty jokes that are current among the audience. All comics do it. You get a big laugh because the ones who know the joke feel flattered at being told how worldly wise they are, and the rest of them laugh because the others do. The point is that the technique works best with jokes that are up to the minute—makes it more flattering. I suppose you don't know any really recent ones?' he added, taking out a notebook.

Charles told him the most obscene joke he had ever heard. He had remembered it ever since first hearing it at the age of eleven. Throughout his adolescence he had often wondered what it meant.

'We used that last week,' said Froulish. 'I can see you're not going to be much help.'

'Well, why the hell should I be?' said Charles aggressively. After all, he had been sent over to chuck Froulish out, and he was still ready to do it.

'Well, that's just it,' said Froulish, looking at him attentively. 'I've got another assignment this week. I've got to find a Seventh Man.'

'What do you mean, a Seventh Man?'

'Mr. Frush has only got five in his team at present. That makes six, counting him. And, like most creative people, he's got fads and superstitions.'

'You mean, about seven being the golden number?'

'Yes, all that bunk,' said the novelist. 'Seven Sleepers of Ephesus, Seven Types of Ambiguity, all that stuff. We don't really need another man, but he says so, and as far as I can see, anybody would do. *You'd* do,' he added kindly.

'Do I understand that you're suggesting I should change my employment?' Charles asked him with dignity.

'Why, do you mean they pay you here? If you're the washer-up, I don't see any evidence that you've been on duty lately.'

'I'm the chucker-out,' said Charles, 'so watch your step. Take those glasses out of your pockets. And if one of the girls comes up to you, don't forget your manners.'

Froulish took an elastic band out of his breast pocket. Stretching it tightly, he slipped it over his head so that it encircled his forehead just above the eyebrows, and began to pick at it, snapping it against his head with his thumb and forefinger. Charles wondered why he did not find this too painful.

'Well, take it or leave it, for God's sake,' he growled.

Charles caught Ada's eye as she stared out of her sanctum. My previous experience did not embrace any specimens of the ordinary criminal type.

'I'll take it,' he said.

Froulish stood up. The glasses made unsightly bulges in his pockets. One of the 'hostesses' came over to him and asked him why he was leaving so early.

'Look, dear,' he said earnestly, 'I wouldn't do you any good. I'm riddled with it.'

They walked across the floor. Charles halted in front of where Ada sat.

'Don't bother about any pay to-night,' he said. 'Keep it in lieu of notice.'

She looked up at him sourly but without surprise. The naked bulb above her head revealed how carelessly she had applied the henna to her hair. It was a dirty grey at the roots.

'So you're walking out on the job, are you?' she said flatly. 'You're just a louse like the rest of them.'

'Louse?' he said with a light laugh. 'I'm just the ordinary criminal type. Somebody's just told me so in a letter.'

He walked up the steps. Froulish was waiting on the pavement.

*

The next script conference was fixed for the following morning. Ready for anything, and especially anything unwelcome, Charles entered Mr. Frush's conference room at the heels of Froulish. With characteristic unpunctuality, the novelist had got them there ten minutes late, and the others had all assembled and were already sitting round a long mahogany table. Mr. Frush himself, a big man who looked like the head of a steel combine, sat at the top of the table. His four hacks, whose dress and deportment suggested that they were trying, with various degrees of success, to parody the appearance of typical provincial bank clerks, sat in submissive silence. Terence Frush nodded, curtly and with a trace of irritation, at Froulish.

'I've got him, Mr. Frush. The Seventh Man.'

'Good,' said his employer. 'And you've got the current jokes as well, I hope. We mustn't waste any time to-day.' He gave Charles a nod, the replica of the one he had given Froulish.

'I take it my secretary has gone through the usual business details with you,' he said. (Charles had not yet seen any secretary.) 'You start at the bottom of the salary scale: forty quid a week for the first three months. Ten minutes' notice on my side. Two years' on yours. You'll find you can make good if you've got it in you.'

Charles sat down in the seat next to Froulish. He glanced round the room. It was bare and surgical. The mahogany table seemed to be the only object that was made of a natural substance; the rest of the furniture was tubular steel, fake leather, and glass. The walls were white and had a glazed look, suggesting the tiled walls of an operating theatre or public lavatory. They were bare of pictures, but two large notices, each neatly framed in black, confronted each other across the widest part of the room. One read 'The Customer is Always Trite'; the other, 'What He'll Say Next is Nobody's Business—and Remember, You're Nobody'.

'Preliminaries first,' said Mr. Frush briskly. 'Who's been on radio duty this week?'

'I have,' said a fat, unhealthy-looking young man with a ragged moustache.

'Well, let's hear if you got hold of anything.'

'What's radio duty?' Charles whispered to Froulish.

'It's when you have to spend the week listening to all the other shows of the same kind, particularly the American ones,' the novelist muttered. 'You have a stenographer with you to take down the scripts entire, but it's your job to edit it for anything that can be pin—used.'

'Quiet, please,' said Mr. Frush. When the young man with the moustache had finished his report, it was Froulish's turn, and Mr. Frush asked him, 'What about the seamy side of things this week?'

'Well, they seem to have come round to the one about the lace curtains. That's in Central London, of course. We really need another man for the Provinces.'

'No need to worry about that,' said Mr. Frush easily. 'After all, remember that we're the only team who do any research at all in that line. The rest simply rely on what they happen to pick up.'

'Would you believe it,' said the radio duty man earnestly, 'but Hudson's gang are still using the brass monkey. You'd hardly credit it.'

'Some of these people,' said Mr. Frush, shaking his head gravely, 'would take money out of a blind man's tin.'

'And then cut the string of his dog,' said Froulish with a high-pitched laugh: he was very nervous.

'All right, hold it, Edwin,' said Mr. Frush, looking at him sternly. 'We haven't started on the gags yet. And when we do, there's no need to take them out of Noah's ark.'

'It wasn't a gag; I was serious,' said the man of letters earnestly.

'Well, now, to business,' said Mr. Frush. 'The theme of the next show is going to be baby-sitting. I estimate that we shall need gags in the following proportion: six of the old-fashioned vulgar type, about nappies and that sort of thing; then, I should say, about twelve turning on the precocity of the elder child who's also left at home while the parents go out; five husband-and-wife ones before they set out; of the remaining twenty-one, fifteen about his ignorance of how to handle the baby—and remember, they're not to overlap with the six nappy ones: I'm thinking of things about feeding it, not being able to understand what it says, that sort of line—and as for the remaining six, they can be off the main theme. We needn't be too perfectionist.'

'Can we bring in anything about breast-feeding?' one of the team asked.

'Definitely not,' said Mr. Frush weightily. 'Remember, we've got a reputation to keep up.'

'You'll want the usual three highbrow ones, I suppose,' put in a man wearing a velvet jacket and with hair growing down the sides of his face.

'That's our culture man,' Froulish whispered to Charles. 'Eton and Trinity.'

'Now switch that machine on and let's get weaving,' said Mr. Frush. One of the men walked across and switched on the tape recorder. Before resuming his seat he took a bottle of whisky and seven glasses from a cupboard on the wall, and poured everyone present a stiff drink.

'Ready? OFF!' Terence Frush roared with sudden violence.

Immediately a wild bedlam was let loose. Their voices, superimposed upon one another, rose and fell in a series of mounting waves. Whisky was drunk and spilt, cigarette ends crushed out on the mahogany table, wild half-completed sentences shrieked across the room. It was all such a sudden surprise to Charles that for the first ten minutes he remained completely outside the atmosphere, staring dumbly from one contorted face to another. It was a scene worthy of the pencil of Blake. Froulish had rolled the elastic band on to his forehead, and had inserted into it strips of equal length torn from the pink blotting paper in front of him. He resembled some fantastic maenad crowned with a hellish garland.

'I've got it,' he was shouting. 'He can tune in to some non-British station on the wireless just when he's flustered after the first spell of trouble with the baby, and get a sponsored programme. Elder child's comments and quick-fire sales talk mixed, see? Do you foam at the mouth when you clean your teeth? Are you worried about those crow's feet? Keep your shoes on, it's hurting you more than it is me, says the kid, that kind of thing.' In the deafening uproar no one heard him. Livid with rage and frustration, he began barking like a sea-lion. 'Diaper was an eighteenth-century poet,' the culture man was shouting. 'Work that in.' Charles suddenly felt the blood rush to his head. Gripping the sides of his chair, he began firing off inane jokes, in a queer snarling voice that did not sound as if it belonged to him. Foolish quips of the matchbox type rose up unprompted from the disordered filing system of his memory. Sweat broke out profusely all over his body. The noise intensified. Even the magisterial Mr. Frush had taken off his collar and tie and allowed his hair to fall forward over his face. Charles felt that his skull would soon explode. Amid a final prolonged burst of bawling, loud coughing and shrieks of laughter, he flung off his jacket and began beating the culture man about the head and shoulders with a rolled-up newspaper.

'All right! There's enough there!' Mr. Frush suddenly shouted above the din in a parade-ground voice. Silence fell. 'Now let's get on with the editing.'

They took their seats quietly, rolling their sleeves down, getting into their jackets, hooking on their spectacles. Froulish dragged off the elastic band; the pink strips of blotting paper cascaded on to the table, where he began crumbling them to invisibility with a nervous motion of his stubby fingers. At a meaning glance from Mr. Frush he controlled himself and sat still.

The recording machine was switched off by the same man who had switched on. Amid silence and calm, they addressed themselves to their work.

Autumn had passed into winter. The yellowest and most obstinate of the leaves had been torn from their moorings by the October gales, and fluttered down on to the damp pavement, like tears shaken from the wrath-bearing tree. Charles sat in front of the electric fire in the living-room of his flat and looked across the carpet at Mr. Blearney.

'And a very nice place too, partner,' Mr. Blearney was rasping appreciatively. 'Just the very thing. Well, well, your luck changed just in time, didn't it?'

'I fell on my feet all right,' Charles admitted.

'Fell on your feet!' Mr. Blearney echoed, comically shocked. 'Can't you find anything better to say about it all than that?'

Charles had been smoking one of his guest's cheroots, and now crushed out the stub in an ashtray and began meditatively unrolling it.

'Well, I suppose I ought to be overjoyed,' he said, 'and yet I can't quite feel that it's anything but a freak of chance, and one doesn't like owing one's way of life to a freak of chance.'

Mr. Blearney exploded with laughter.

'That's rich. I say that's rich. Here you are, only just in the game, and you start talking like all the rest of them.'

'All the rest of whom?'

'It's typical, you see,' Mr. Blearney explained seriously. 'That's what you are, typical. The entertainment world is full of people who think they only got themselves mixed up in it by accident—what you'd call a freak of chance. Every department of the business, it's the same. Fight promoters who think they're country vicars at heart, conjurors who meant to be dentists. Look at me,' he said, violently wrenching his rubbery features into an expression of self-pity, 'a poor old leg-show organizer whose Dad wanted him to be a market gardener!'

'Why? Was he one himself?'

'You bet your life he was. And in a very good way of business. "No need to get your finger-nails dirty, Arthur," he used to say, "not like I had to. Just the office part of it for you, my lad. A gentleman, that's you." But I couldn't see eye to eye with the old man. I kicked over the traces, and I've lived my life in the entertainment business one way and another.'

Charles unrolled the last fragment of leaf. 'Well, I can't help it if I sound typical,' he said. 'I suppose I did turn down a steady, humdrum life, like you, but it wasn't a question of breaking out or kicking over any traces. I never rebelled against ordinary life: it just never admitted me, that's all. I never even got into it.'

'Same thing,' said Mr. Blearney authoritatively. 'You never wanted to get into it because it hadn't got what you wanted.'

'And what's your idea of what I want?' Charles demanded brusquely. He expected Mr. Blearney to come out with some sentimental irrelevance on the lines of 'You're a vagabond at heart like all of us, you need the colour and variety, grand troupers, kind hearts beneath the motley.' He stared challengingly across the hearth-rug.

'What do you think I want?' he repeated.

'Neutrality,' said Mr. Blearney calmly and without pausing to take thought.

Charles looked at him in silence.

'Go on, partner, tell me it isn't true, if you can,' said Mr. Blearney. 'It's the type who wants neutrality who comes into our racket. Doesn't want to take sides in all the silly pettiness that goes on. Doesn't want to spend his time scratching and being scratched. Wants to live his own life.'

Charles was humbled. The man understood him perfectly. His very choice of a word was absolutely right. So far, he had set himself target after target that had proved out of reach: economically, the quest for self-sufficient poverty; socially, for unmolested obscurity; emotionally, first for a grand passion and then for a limited and defined contentment. And now he valued his niche simply because it gave him the means, through his new wealth, to put himself beyond the struggle, and the leisure to meditate sufficiently to keep him on his guard against his own folly.

'By the way, there was a letter for you downstairs, partner,' said Mr. Blearney, moving easily away from the subject now that he had finished with it, 'so I brought it up.'

Charles opened the envelope. A thick, blue-tinted document and a typewritten letter.

'My dear Lumley,

In sending you this three-year contract, which I hope you will sign, I am happy to say how much I have come to appreciate your work during the months you have been with me. You are a valuable counterweight to the more (shall I say?) volatile elements in my team, and I have come to feel that I definitely need your presence. Perhaps you would be good enough to treat this contract as confidential, as I have so far not felt able to offer similar terms to any of your colleagues.

With my congratulations on your work, and wishes for many years of fruitful collaboration,

Yours sincerely,
Terence Frush'

'The glasses and whisky are in that cupboard, Arthur,' Charles said. 'Would you get them out? I feel a bit queer.'

'Nothing the matter, I hope, partner?' Mr. Blearney asked as he poured out four glasses of whisky.

'The reverse, the reverse,' said Charles faintly. 'I'm permanent. He's sent me a contract to sign.'

'And about time too,' shouted his guest joyfully. 'Well! Well! And a very good excuse for drinking this stuff at five o'clock in the afternoon!'

They drained their first and began slowly on their second, in accordance with Mr. Blearney's principles.

'Well, I must be getting,' he said when they had finished. 'Got to see an early rehearsal. So long, partner! Don't take any jokes off match-boxes—they might go on strike!'

Laughing uproariously, he went out. Charles stood looking through the window at the wet sky. Neutrality; he had found it at last. The running fight between himself and society had ended in a draw; he was no nearer, fundamentally, to any *rapprochement* or understanding with it than when he had been a window-cleaner, a crook, or a servant; it had merely decided that he should be paid, and paid handsomely, to capitalize his anomalous position. To his companions in Mr. Frush's team, this was a job like any other. They did it instead of working in industry or commerce. But to him it was an armistice, obviously leading to a permanent armed truce. There could be no forgiveness, but neither party would, in the foreseeable future, launch an offensive. Tharkles, Scrodd, Hutchins, Lockwood, Burge, Roderick, none of them could either despise or respect him now. All they could do would be to look at him in bewilderment, shake their heads, and envy him his salary. He did not want their envy, but it was less of an embarrassment than either their contempt or their approval.

The telephone buzzed, and the janitor's voice croaked that a lady wished to see him.

'What's her name?' he asked.

After a short pause the frog in the man's throat said, 'Miss Flanders, sir.'

He did not know anyone, male or female, whose name even vaguely sounded like 'Flanders'.

'Show her up, please,' he said. As he replaced the instrument, a slight, quick tremor ran through him, as if the indifferent bakelite had tried to warn him that he had said the wrong thing.

Veronica came in as unconcernedly as if this were the Oak Lounge.

'I wasn't quite sure about giving my right name to the man,' she said, 'so I just gave him the first name that entered my head. Moll Flanders. I've just been reading about her.'

'I never got to the end of that book,' he said. 'Has it got a happy ending?'

'Not really. It doesn't end, it just stops. She turns respectable and repents, but you knew that from the beginning.'

He looked away from her, trying not to feel how beautiful and dangerous she had been to him, and could be again.

'I don't like it when I know from the start how things will turn out, do you?' he asked.

She lifted her dark head and looked at him silently. Inside his skull sledge hammers crashed down on metal plates.

'Do you?' he repeated urgently.

'I don't think I ever have known,' she said slowly. 'You always get surprises.'

'Such as what?' he asked.

'Charles, please don't be so strange and awkward. You know what I came to say. At one time it just looked as if our,' she hesitated, 'our thing hadn't got a chance. It looked as if there was simply no way of going on. But things have altered, altered so strangely.'

Mentally he translated this into: *You're rich now, you're doing as well as Roderick. And you're fifteen years younger.*

'I don't really see how things have altered,' he said obstinately. 'Between you and me, I mean.'

She looked at him quietly and possessively, rebuking him, making him feel ashamed of his foolish temporizing.

He stood up and walked to the centre of the room. If an animal who was tame, or born in captivity, went back to what should have been its natural surroundings, it never survived. If it was a bird, the other birds killed it, but usually it just died. Here was his cage, a fine new one, air conditioned, clean, commanding a good view, mod. cons., main services. And she had snapped the lock and was calling him out into the waving jungle. When he got there, he would die.

That was Con. What was Pro?

Pro was that she was beautiful, and he loved her, and to accept her with death and catastrophe in the same packet would be no trouble at all, thank you, anyone would have done the same, don't mention it. Pro was that he could not bear it that she should sit casually in the armchair, talking to him across half the width of the room, when he knew every contour and texture of her body under its demure clothing. Pro was that I a twister love what I abhor.

It was dusk now. He crossed the room and turned a switch. The light sprang suddenly into every corner, dramatizing each outline, emphasizing the shape of the furniture and the shape of their predicament.

They looked at each other, baffled and inquiring.

THE END

CPSIA information can be obtained
at www.ICGtesting.com
Printed in the USA
LVHW090444100421
684055LV00003B/704